Death
in the
Mopane

by

Hugh Chare

Publication Data
Death in the Mopane © Hugh B. Chare 2016

Book and Cover design by Hugh B. Chare
Cover by Hugh B. Chare based on a photograph by Hans Hillewaert, ©Hans Hillewaert, and used with his kind permission.
ISBN: 978-1-940012-11-7
 Kilihune Books

Marieke Englebrecht mysteries
Death in the Mopane
Revenge after twenty years

The James Martin series
African Encounter
Across the Zambezi
Just off the Great North Road
Well, there you go!
Back to Africa
The Sagitta Mishap
Flight 5 to Johannesburg

Other books
The journal of Jan Englebrecht
British Spy in the Bushveld
Federica

Preface

ET 6490 was the Zambian registration number of my own Land Rover; my apologies to subsequent owners. Purists would note that ET 6490 was too high a number to have been assigned to a vehicle registered in 1969.

Contents

Who is that?

Bridget Martin stood in the shade of some trees by the dirt strip that served their safari camp in Botswana and watched as the two Cessna light aircraft circled prior to landing. She was waiting for the next group of tourists to arrive. All of the last group had left the afternoon before, so the camp had had an evening of quiet with no visitors. Normally, the inbound planes would take the outbound visitors, but not today. It was quite warm, at almost noon, the day had already heated up, and the short trip up from Maun, after the obligatory stop to clear customs and immigration after their three-hour flight from Johannesburg, may have been quite bumpy, so she had water and cold towels ready. The first plane landed and taxied up to the turnaround area they had cleared out of the bush. The pilot waved, opened his door, and then got out to help his passengers deplane.

"*Bridget, hoe gaan dit?*" the pilot said as Bridget braved the sunshine and went out to the plane to greet the guests.

"*Môre Koot, hoe gaan dit met jou?*" Bridget replied.

"*Ag,* can't complain, man, can you give me a hand with luggage?" Koot asked.

"Good flight up?" Bridget asked as she took the bags from Koot and loaded them into her Land Rover.

"Jo'burg to Maun was fine, clear skies, smooth as ever, Maun to here got a little bumpy as we came in to land. No one lost their breakfast, so no cleaning up to do," Koot replied. They both watched as the second plane landed and taxied up to join them. That plane pulled up, and the door opened, and the pilot quickly helped a lady out of the plane who scurried for the bushes at the edge of the strip.

"*Piet, hoe gaan dit?*" Bridget greeted him.

"Made it just in time, man," Piet replied. "The one *tannie* didn't do so well between Jo'burg and Maun, and this last forty minutes up from Maun almost did her in."

"Are you staying or leaving?" Bridget asked.

"We got lucky," Koot said. "We've got a load each from Maun back to Jo'burg this afternoon, so we won't stay any longer than we have to. We'll be back in two weeks to pick up these *ouks.*"

The passengers, by this time, had all got out of the planes and were being plied by Bridget with water and were all using the cold towels she had provided.

"I hope you folks enjoyed the trip with us," Koot said. "We'll be back in two weeks to pick you up and take you back. We'll come in a day early and spend the night, then we can make an early start before it heats up, and we'll be back in Jo'burg by lunchtime."

"Thank you," one of the passengers said. "I enjoyed the flight and the commentary on the way."

"All part of the service," Koot said. "Bridget has all your luggage, so we'll say goodbye and see you soon."

The guests all watched as the two planes taxied off to the end of the strip, then both took off and headed back to Maun.

"Why do I feel we have just been abandoned right in the middle of nowhere?" a lady said.

"You haven't been abandoned, just delivered to a new adventure," Bridget said. "Well, welcome to the Pitse Safari Camp. I'm Bridget Martin; I'll be your hostess for the next two weeks. Can I get you to introduce yourselves?"

The eight guests looked at each other, and finally, the lady who had done the bush trip spoke up, "I'll go first," she said. "I'm Fiona White, and this is my husband George."

"We'll go next," another said. "I'm Bronwyn Harris, and this is my husband, Frank."

"Time for a change of pace," another said. "We're all from the States, I'm Bob, this is Cindy, that's Jim, and this is Roberta, we're all from the Salt Lake area."

"Ah, good," Bridget said. "Well, welcome again, just give me a minute or two to finish loading your bags into the *bakkie* and we'll be off."

"What's a *bakkie*?" Cindy Smith asked.

"The Land Rover," Bridget explained.

"How far is it to the camp?" Roberta asked.

"Only about an hour," Bridget said. "I'll take you there, give you a chance to wash your faces, then we'll have lunch, and later you'll take a drive and see what you can spot. You'll all be going together on the drive with my husband, Will. Did you all know each other before this trip?"

"We met all the others for the first time at the airport in Johannesburg," Fiona said.

"We've been friends for years," Cindy said. "So we decided to take this trip together. It's our first trip to Africa."

"And you?" Bridget asked of the Harrises and the Whites.

"First time for us too," they both replied.

"Okay, shall we go?" Bridget asked. On the drive north towards the camp, she pointed out animals, birds and trees as they went. Sometimes she stopped because there was a particularly good opportunity for pictures. The drive was hot and dusty, and they were all quite happy when they arrived at the campsite. Will was there to greet them and help with the luggage that he delivered to each tent. The tents were set up on the banks overlooking the Linyanti River, pitched so that each guest accommodation had its own private view of the river. Two tents for guests were set up on either side of a central sitting and dining area. The staff had their own accommodations behind the main dining area, giving the guests the maximum level of privacy.

Over lunch, Will and Bridget took some time to find out what their guests expected. The "Big Five" was a high priority for the Americans, while the Brits just wanted to enjoy the bush experience. Will then ran through what they had planned for their guests for the next few days.

"Okay, folks, after lunch, you can take a short siesta, then we'll take a drive and see what we can find," he said. "Tomorrow morning, we'll take another drive in a different direction and see what else we can spot. If you fancy the idea, we can also take you on a walk. The experience will be different; we won't get as close to the animals, but our guides can tell you what there is to see and who has been there before us. To help us this afternoon, we'll have Jackson, who will do the spotting for us and explain what we see."

"How long have you been doing this?" Jim Stewart asked.

"A couple of years," Will replied. "We thought this would be a better life than Johannesburg. We took over the concession from Piet and Anna, who had run it since 1968. I think in the end, they just wanted a change. They had had quite a few run-ins with poachers coming across the river from Namibia over the years, but all in all, had done well here. They picked the spot for the camp, and we just made our own changes."

"What can we see here?" Cindy asked.

"Well, this part of Botswana is well known for elephant," Will began. "We should see lion and buffalo and possibly leopard, plus there will be no end of different antelope and other smaller species."

"No rhino?" Bob asked.

"I doubt that we'll see any," Will said. "There are a few left, and occasionally one makes the long trek over from Wankie in Zim, but poaching is already taking its toll, and there are probably only a handful left."

"Why do the poachers shoot them?" Cindy asked.

"Mainly to make a living," Will explained. "A middleman will pay what is, to most Botswanans, good money for rhino horns. The middle man then sells them on at a much higher price."

"Is there nothing else those people can do?" Bob asked.

"Botswana is mainly a subsistence economy," Will explained. "We have a beef industry, with most of the beef going to Europe, we have the diamond mines, we have a copper mine, and now we have the start of a growing tourism business. But, we do not have much in the way of manufacturing or anything that employs large numbers of people, so any opportunity to make some money is welcome."

"Well, when are we going to leave this afternoon?" Cindy asked.

"We'll leave here about 2:30," Will said. "We'll take a drive west and see what we can find."

"What do we need to bring?" Bronwyn asked.

"Just yourselves, cameras, binoculars and perhaps a light jacket, it will cool off a little when the sun goes down," Will suggested. "We'll take a sundowner with us, plus water and some coffee, we'll find a nice spot to take a break and watch the sun go down."

"All set?" Will asked when the group assembled later. He and Jackson watched until they were all settled in the Land Rover, then drove west from the camp along one of the dirt tracks.

"What's that?" Cindy asked. Will stopped the car and pointed towards some impala.

4

"There we have impala," he replied. "If you look a little to the left, you'll see some giraffe headed away from us, and to the right, there are three kudu hiding in the brush."

"I see the impala and the giraffe," Bronwyn said. "But I don't see the kudu."

"Look at that tall tree and then a little to the right and lower," Will instructed.

"Oh, I see them," Jim said. "Boy, they're hard to see."

"They are experts at crypsis," Will explained. "It's a defence technique, they stand perfectly still, most predators, including man, tend to see motion better than still prey, so if they stay quite still, their chances of not being spotted and therefore of survival are higher."

"I see them now," Bronwyn said. "I see one has horns, but the others don't. Does that mean one male and two females?"

"In this case, yes, there is one male and two females, typically the females don't have horns, but some sources have reported females with small horns," Will replied.

"They're big," Bob commented.

"They're the second largest antelope," Will explained. "Second to the eland."

"What are those birds over there?" Frank asked.

"Those are grey loeries," Will said. "They're why all the animals are skittish. They don't like us here and are shouting at us, which causes all the animals to be on alert."

"Aren't those what the hunters used to call go-away-birds?" George asked.

"They are indeed," Will confirmed. "If we were hunting now, we would probably be well advised to give up here at least and walk away and try and lose the loeries."

"Shall we move on then?" Cindy asked. Will took the hint and set off again down the track. He stopped when Jackson held up his hand and pointed to the ground, "*Tshukudu*," he said.

"Sure?" Will asked.

"Sure sure," Jackson said, quite emphatically. He and Will both got out of the Land Rover and examined the tracks that Jackson had seen. The others were curious and wanted to know what they were looking at.

"These are tracks of a black rhino," Will explained. "He joined the track here and is walking ahead of us a little way, less than ten minutes. Man, that is only unusual, he must have got seriously lost."

"How do you know it was that recent?" Bronwyn asked.

"If you look at the track and focus on the dirt ridges, they haven't been blown off by the wind yet; the ants here have only just started to walk over the track again after they were interrupted by the rhino. There are no leaves or other debris at all; there are no other tracks on top of the rhino tracks. Here you can see where the rhino has walked over some older elephant tracks, and here some impala, and there some kudu," Will explained. "He went by here now, now. We'll follow the tracks and see if we can spot him."

They set off again with Jackson trotting in front of the Land Rover. At a junction with another track, the rhino went off the track for a while, but Jackson picked up the trail just a few yards down the road. He stopped and held up his hand, and pointed. Just a little way in front of them, they could see the rhino walking down the road. Will watched as the ears swivelled back, and he knew that the rhino knew that they were there. Now the trick was to get close enough for the visitors to get pictures without spooking the rhino and provoking a charge, or a mad dash off into the bush and away from them. Will watched as the rhino left the road and went off into the bush towards a *dambo*.

"Time for some *bundu* bashing," he said to his passengers. He turned off the road, pausing long enough for Jackson to clamber on board, and then weaved around the trees and bushes until they could see the *dambo* quite clearly and also had a wonderful view of the rhino.

"I thought you said there weren't many rhino here?" Bob joked. "Here we are, we've barely left the camp, and what do we see, a rhino as large as life."

"You should get as many pictures as you can," Will said. "This *ouk* may be the only one we see, in fact, the way poaching is going, he may be dead in a month, maybe even sooner if anyone gets to hear that he is here."

"*Bwana, ena kona lo munya bantu,*" Jackson said. Will looked to where he was pointing and saw another Land Rover in the distance on the other side of the *dambo*. The Land Rover was not the safari type he had, with no roof, but a normal station wagon. He surmised that they were

6

just visiting from somewhere in Botswana, and parked where they were by the *dambo*, probably bird watchers, whoever they were, he needed to come back again and check them out. He wanted to know who was in his concession. When the noise of the camera shutters finally subsided, he asked if everyone had got the picture they wanted.

"That was great," Frank said. "What other surprises do you have in store for us?"

"Who knows," Will laughed. "We'll just back out to the track and go on and see what else there is. Judging by the noise, get ready to see some elephants."

"What do you mean the noise?" Bronwyn asked.

"You can hear them breaking off tree branches," Will explained. "I would guess about a quarter of a mile that way."

Will was as good as his word, and there were elephants, about ten of them, slowly making their way through the bush, eating as they went.

"That's two," Bob said.

"Two what?" Fiona asked.

"Two of the big five," Bob explained. "We came here wanting to see the big five, rhino, elephant, buffalo, lion and leopard. Well, we've already seen two, and it's only our first day here."

"You were extraordinarily lucky," Will said. "We have very few rhino in this area, and to see one is really lucky and very unusual."

After the elephants, it was time to return to camp for a sundowner before dinner. On the way back, they spotted more kudu, then some warthogs, more impala, some waterbuck and just before reaching the camp, a fairly large group of buffalo that held them up for a few minutes, before they all decided to trot off into the bush towards the river and water.

"Three," announced Bob as the buffalo left. "What's the chance that we'll see all of the big five on the first day we're here?"

"Not likely," Will said. "Yesterday we saw lions about an hour's drive north, and I don't think they were moving, they were finishing off a buffalo they'd killed, with leopards, you may be more fortunate, there is one that has us in his territory and we'll occasionally see him at dusk crossing the road. We'll stop over there overlooking that waterhole, we should get a good view of the sunset, and maybe we'll see some game

7

come down to the waterhole to drink, maybe even a leopard, I know there's one around here who likes this waterhole."

They did not see the leopard that evening, which disappointed Bob, but which left the others with the anticipation of what might come. Over dinner, Bridget asked their guests to tell a little about themselves. Fiona and George White hailed from Bristol, where George worked for British Aerospace as an engineer and Fiona had a small art gallery. Bronwyn and Frank Harris came from Cardiff, where Bronwyn taught in a primary school and Frank taught in a grammar school. Cindy and Bob Wheeler ran an estate agency in Bountiful, a northern suburb of Salt Lake City in Utah, and to finish out the litany, Roberta and Jim Stewart had a dealership for Subaru cars, also in Bountiful. Those from Utah were devout practising Mormons, so Bridget had to instruct the kitchen staff to make sure that they had enough to drink on hand that was non-alcoholic. The Brits had no such constraints, and Lion Lager was drunk with appreciation, as was wine with dinner. The guests then turned the tables and asked about Will and Bridget. They got the story about careers with ICI and the desire to do something a little different, which was the safari business. Cindy then asked about children.

"We have two daughters," Bridget replied. "Fifteen and twelve."

"Where are they now?" Cindy asked.

"They go to school in Italy and will be arriving home the day after tomorrow," Bridget explained.

"You mean they go to boarding school?" Cindy asked.

"No," Bridget said. "They stay with my sister-in-law and her husband and go to school with their children."

"So your sister-in-law lives in Italy?" Cindy asked.

"She does, she married an Italian, so they live there," Bridget explained.

"It will be interesting to meet them when they get here," Bob said. "Where will they sleep?"

"We have staff quarters for us and we have a pilot's tent for those times when a pilot has to stay overnight," Bridget explained.

"How will they get here?" Frank asked.

"They fly to Jo'burg, then we have a friend who flies them out to Maun and then on up to here," Bridget said. "They will be coming with my niece and nephew from Italy, who are coming here for a holiday."

"Isn't it dangerous for kids out here in the jungle?" Roberta asked.

"Not at all," Bridget said. "They're probably safer here than in any big city, and the staff know them well; my niece is a very good shot with a rifle and can drive, as can Francesca, our older daughter, so they can be self-sufficient."

"How old is your niece?" Roberta asked.

"She's fifteen and my nephew is twelve," Bridget replied.

"She's only fifteen and she can already drive and shoot?" Roberta asked.

"Out here, we have to pick up those skills quickly," Bridget said. "All the children can drive and shoot; it's just that Valeria is the best shot."

"What do you do when it's not the season?" Bob asked.

"Repairs, maintenance, planning, marketing, all the things that may or may not get done when we are busy," Will replied.

"But, you must live somewhere else then," Roberta commented.

"We have a house in Gaborone," Will explained. "It has a large garage and storage building, so we get busy fixing things to be ready for the next season."

"What do your children want to do later in life?" Frank asked.

"We're not really sure," Bridget laughed. "It seems to depend on the month, or what is the latest trend, we will see. They have time enough before making any serious commitments."

"You said that this is a concession," Bob asked. "Does that mean you have hunting here as well?"

"We do," Will confirmed. "The Botswana Government leases us the concession at a reasonable rate, but they are also banking on the fees for hunting licences, which for non-residents are pretty steep. So, it's a source of income that they don't want to lose. Our camera safari trips are good, but they can't yet fully match what we might otherwise lose in fees for hunting."

"Oh," Bronwyn said. "What do you do with the meat from animals that are hunted?"

"We, and you, eat it," Will explained. "We also provide a lot to some of the villages that you flew over on the way up here."

"Do you do the hunting?" Bronwyn asked.

9

"No, we have a PH come in with the clients," Will explained.

"I'm sorry, a PH?" Fiona asked.

"A professional hunter," Will said.

"Maybe I should come back on a hunt," Bob said.

"Do you hunt?" Will asked.

"In Utah, yes," Bob said. "I usually get a deer or two each season, and I've also had an elk."

"Why do you hunt in the States?" Fiona asked.

"Mainly to keep the herbivore population in check," Bob said. "We've messed up the balance between predator and prey and also provided food for the deer with agriculture, so much so that the population does need thinning at times."

"Oh," was all Fiona could think of at the time.

The conversation then turned to the events of the day and what they might expect tomorrow. Will suggested that they drive north to look for the lions that he had seen the day before. The suggestion met with approval from all, and a plan was made.

Early the next day, Bridget had packed breakfasts and lunches ready for them so that they could get an early start. The drive north took longer than an hour, because there were things to see along the way, and it turned out that Frank was an avid bird watcher, a Twitcher in Brit terms, who was keen to see how many species of birds he could see on this trip. Will began to be concerned that Frank's frequent requests for stops were beginning to annoy the others when they came across the lions. They were actually all walking along the track towards them. Will stopped, and Jackson clambered back from his perch on the front to the seat next to him.

"What do we do?" Cindy asked.

"Just stay in the Land Rover, no hands, arms or feet outside," Will instructed. "They've eaten already, so they're not hungry; they might be curious, but if we have to, we'll dissuade them in their curiosity." He removed his rifle from the rack in front and worked the bolt to chamber a round. They all watched as the lions came down the track, then split up and passed on both sides of the Land Rover, not within touching distance, but close enough for National Geographic quality pictures.

After the lions had passed and gone a little way down the track, Will turned the Land Rover around and they followed the lions at a safe distance. Finally, the lions turned off the track and headed off into some thick bush, so Will and the others wished them goodbye and went on to see what else they might chance upon.

The big event of the day, after the lions, was spotting eland, quite a large herd of them. Will managed to work around them and get downwind, then approach them so they could get a good view. The eland were joined by giraffe, which made Bronwyn and Fiona very happy. Will suggested that they find a spot for lunch and took them to a water hole that he knew. This was heaven for Frank because the water hole edges were teeming with different birds. Will was able to identify them all for him, and Frank happily added to his lists, his trip list, his life list, his year list, and, for all Will knew, his daily list. For the rest, there were waterbuck, duikers, kudu, zebra, giraffe, baboons and impala to photograph. After lunch, they spent the balance of the day wandering apparently aimlessly around the bush, but always in the general direction of the camp, so that when the light began to fade, they came to the camp in time for a sundowner.

"Well, that was a lovely day," Bronwyn said when they were served with their sundowners.
"All we need to see now is a leopard," Bob announced. "And this trip will have been worth every last dollar."
"Well, did any of you notice the fairly new tracks in the road as we came back this evening?" Will asked.
"No, what tracks?" Bob asked.
"Leopard," Will said. "It looked as if he was headed towards the *dambo* where we saw the rhino yesterday. I think tomorrow morning early, we'll take a drive out that way and see if we can spot him."
"Why can't we go now?" Bob asked.
"I think we would have a better chance of seeing him early in the morning," Will suggested. "Jackson told me that the leopard has been

hanging around that *dambo* for a while. He says that the best time to catch him would be soon after sunrise."

"Great, what time do we go?" Bob asked.

"We'll leave here at about 5:45, if that's fine with everyone?" Will asked.

"That's fine," was the general chorus.

"So, what's for dinner tonight?' Frank asked.

"Warthog," Bridget said as she joined the group. "It's been cooking for a while, and my last tasting was really good, so I think you'll enjoy it."

"Warthog, what did we have last night?" Cindy asked.

"Impala," Bridget replied. "As Will explained before, hunting on our concession keeps us supplied."

"How do you cook warthog?" Bronwyn asked.

"I marinade mine in a yoghurt pawpaw mixture for a day, then I cook it with olive oil and oxtail fat and mixed vegetables, for about four hours," Bridget replied. "I don't think you'll be disappointed."

"Pawpaws, those are papayas, right?" Cindy asked.

"They are," Bridget confirmed.

"When do we eat?" Frank asked.

"We're about ready, so any time you feel like it," Bridget said.

"Let's eat," Bob said.

"It's cold," Cindy complained the next morning as they assembled by the Land Rover.

"Well, it is the middle of winter," Will commented. "It will warm up soon enough when the sun comes up. Are we all ready?"

They drove off, headed towards the *dambo* that they had been to before, now looking specifically for the leopard. Jackson pointed to tracks and called out the species as they occurred, which Will then translated for the guests: *ngurungu, nare, tlou, phala* and *nkwe*, or bushbuck, buffalo, elephant, impala and leopard. The latter got everyone excited, more so when Will told them that the tracks were recent, within the last hour, and he was definitely headed towards the *dambo*. They came to the spot where they had left the road before, and Will took the same path, as Jackson pointed out that the leopard had followed their trail. Then, quite suddenly, there he was, standing on a termite mound and looking down on them. There was time for four or five photographs, and he was gone, into the dense bush beyond.

"Did everyone get a picture?" Will asked.

"I did," Bob said. "And, I think everyone else did too. Wow, that was amazing."

"Well, while we're here. Let's see what else we can find," Will suggested.

"We won't try and follow that leopard?" Jim asked.

"No, the bush where he went is too thick for simple *bundu* bashing and following him on foot with such a large group is risky," Will said. "We could see him again, or Jackson tells me that he heard another one to the south of our camp, probably near the waterhole that is there."

"*Bwana, lo munya bantu yena kona lapa futi,*" Jackson said. Will looked across the *dambo* and saw that the Land Rover they had seen before was still there, in exactly the same place. Will got his binoculars and studied the Land Rover and the surrounding area.

"Who is that? There's something wrong over there," he told the others. "Please wait in the Land Rover while Jackson and I take a look."

He and Jackson walked through the bush, skirting the *dambo* edges and working their way around the other side where the Land Rover was. As they got closer, Will was surprised by the fact that there was no number plate. Then he saw that there was no tax disc. As they got to the Land Rover, they could both see that it was empty; there were no people, no boxes of food, no coolers with beer, no camping gear, nothing. Will peered inside and saw a stone sitting next to the accelerator pedal and a stick with a string attached lying on the floor. He and Jackson looked around but saw no tracks of people, either coming or going. It looked as if the Land Rover had driven itself there. They looked back along the track left by the Land Rover, and Will wondered how far it led and to where. He wrapped his hand in a handkerchief and reached in and turned off the ignition, then decided that they should leave it for the day. He could hardly keep his guests sitting around waiting, so he decided that he would call the find into the Botswana Police and let them investigate. Back in the Land Rover, the others asked what they had found, and he told them of the empty Land Rover, just sitting in the bush, but apparently stripped of any means to identify it.

13

At the camp, Will told Bridget what they had found and used his short-wave radio to call it in to the Maun police station. He told them that a plane was passing through Maun later that morning, and if they wanted to send someone ahead, there was a spare seat. Further, they had a run to Maun planned for the next day, so could take whoever came back. Now all they could do was wait. Over a late breakfast, speculation was rife about who, why, when and what. Theories ranged from vehicle theft, ivory poaching, to murder. It was not often that vacationing tourists were caught up in situations like the one they had, something that both Will and Bridget were very thankful for. At about eleven thirty, Will excused himself and drove to the airstrip to meet the plane. He drove south to the strip, parked under the large trees that were at the edge of the cleared area and settled down to wait.

Marieke arrives

Assistant Superintendent Marieke Englebrecht was introducing herself to the staff at the Maun Police Station when the radio call came in. She had recently transferred from Tsabong to Gaborone and was visiting Maun to review a mysterious death that had turned out not to be quite so mysterious. Murder had turned out to be not murder at all, but stupidity and alcohol. But a Land Rover stripped of all identification was at least interesting. She decided to take up the offer of the plane ride and drove to the airport. She watched the Cessna Skymaster land, then walked over to the Customs and Immigration shed where formalities were being observed. Clearly, the staff there knew the pilot, a dark, tall, rangy Afrikaner by the name of Koos Strijdom. The passengers were all European, three girls and a boy; she put their ages at about fifteen and twelve. She approached the pilot and introduced herself.

"*Dumela Rra*," she said. "I understand that you are flying up to the Pitse Safari Camp?"

"*Dumela Mma*," he replied. "Indeed, I am."

"Mr Martin called in some suspicious circumstances and offered a ride if you have room to take me," she explained. "Let me introduce myself, I am Assistant Superintendent Englebrecht from Gaborone."

"Of course," Koos said. Koos looked at her, intrigued. She was probably about five feet six, slim and obviously of mixed racial heritage. Marieke got the sense that she was being appraised and evaluated, so she did likewise.

"Who are your passengers?" she asked.

"Will and Bridget's two, and their niece and nephew from Italy," he replied, all business. "So what's the story at Will's place?"

"I don't know yet," she admitted. "But he says they had come across a Land Rover in the bush, undamaged, but with no number plates or tax discs."

"Sounds suspicious," he agreed. "Hey, let me introduce you to the *lighties*, okay, you *ouks*, you need to be on your best behaviour now, this is Assistant Superintendent Englebrecht of the Botswana Police. This is

15

Francesca, Alessandra, Valeria and Vittorio. Francesca and Alessandra are from here, the other two are from Italy."

"*Dumela*," she said and was pleasantly surprised when Francesca and Alessandra both replied in Setswana and asked her if she was well and all the usual formal greetings. They then switched back to English for the benefit of their cousins, and Francesca became the spokesman.

"Are you coming with us, *Mma*?" she asked.

"I am," Marieke confirmed. "Your father was kind enough to offer me the ride."

"Okay, folks," Koos said. "If we can load up, we'll go. Superintendent, if you'll give me your bag, I'll see if I can fit it into the luggage pod underneath. Valeria, sorry, but would you mind giving up your front seat to the Superintendent?"

"Of course, Koos," Valeria replied. "Please, Superintendent, follow me." They all got settled, and Marieke heard a lot of whispering behind her. "Is something wrong?" she asked.

"Alessandra says that you look a bit like our Auntie Katrina," Francesca said.

"Who is your Auntie Katrina?" Marieke asked.

"She's married to my Dad's brother, they live in the States in Utah," Francesca explained. "They met in Zambia, where she lived. She was also an Englebrecht."

"Were her mom and dad Sussana and Koot?" Marieke said.

"Yes, how did you know?" Valeria asked.

"My dad was Koos, the wayward brother no one talked about," Marieke explained.

"Why?" Vittorio asked with childish innocence.

"Because my mom is Motswana and my dad is an Afrikaner," Marieke explained.

"So?" Vittorio asked.

"Well, the laws in South Africa directly forbade someone white from marrying someone black," Marieke said. "So, the rest of the family kept very quiet about my folks, especially those in South Africa. I've never actually met Katrina."

"But, Auntie Katrina told us that her great-great-great-grandmother was San, so why is that different?" Vittorio asked.

16

"I think that was a different time before attitudes changed," Marieke replied.

"So, you're Auntie Katrina's cousin?" Francesca asked.

"I am," Marieke confirmed. "How is it that you're flying in today?"

"We're coming from school," Francesca explained. "Alessandra and I go to school in Italy with Valeria and Vittorio, we live with them while we're at school, but now it is summer holidays in Italy and we get to come home."

"Do you like school there?" Marieke asked.

"It's fine," Francesca said. "We all go to the same school now, which makes it easy for Auntie Alex and Uncle Vincenzo."

"Okay," Koos interrupted. "I've done my pre-flight, I have your bags stowed, Superintendent, let me give the quick safety briefing. You *ouks* have heard it before, but it won't hurt to hear it again." He handed Marieke a headset so that she could hear the radio traffic and also talk to him. After his short briefing, he talked briefly on the radio to the people at Maun, and then they taxied out and took off.

As they flew north, Marieke looked at the ground below. Once they were away from the river, it was sparse bush with the occasional village, made obvious by thorn bush fencing around the houses and the pathways and tracks that led to the village. The general colour was brown, with darker dots of the trees and the occasional green patch that signalled water. The flight was short, only forty minutes and soon enough she saw the green of the Linyanti swamps and the river and Koos descended and did a flyover of the airstrip to make sure there was nothing on it, and then he made a high banking hourglass turn at the end and came back in to land.

Marieke waited until Koos had come to a stop and opened the door, then she exited and was met by a man she assumed was Will Martin.

"*Dumela Mma,*" he said. "I'm Will Martin."

"*Dumela Rra,*" she replied. "Assistant Superintendent Englebrecht."

"Thanks for coming on such short notice," he said. "I hope the kids didn't bother you too much."

"They were fine," she assured him.

"*Koos, howzit?*" Will asked.

"*Goed dankie*," Koos replied.

"Good flight?" Will asked.

"The best, we landed in one piece," Koos laughed. "Valeria flew us from Jo'burg to Maun. She showed me her pilot's licence and I let her take the stick. She knows what she's doing. But, for the hop up from Maun, I thought it best if I fly and put the Superintendent in the other front seat."

"Hey, Dad," Francesca interrupted. "Superintendent Englebrecht is Auntie Katrina's cousin."

"Really?" Will said, looking to Assistant Superintendent Englebrecht for confirmation. "I thought she had family in Namibia, but didn't know of anyone in Botswana, other than the San connection."

"We lived in Namibia," Marieke confirmed. "My Dad was the brother they never talked about. He ran cattle in South West and the western part of Botswana and used to sell to the abattoir in Lobatse. Somehow, he met my mother, who is Motswana, and he paid the *lobola,* and they got married. When I got out of university, I moved to Botswana and joined the police as part of the second intake of women into the force in 1972. I've recently transferred from Tsabong to Gaborone."

"Tsabong, that's out there. Okay, have you all got your luggage?" Will asked the rest. "Koos, are you staying?"

"No man, sorry, I have a charter from Maun to Cape Town, so got paid for the dead head, so the trip from Jo'burg is on me," Koos said. "I'll be back six weeks from today to collect the *lighties.* Nice to meet you, Superintendent. I hope to see you again. I do fly into Gaborone on occasion. Here's my card with my Jo'burg numbers on it. If you're ever there and need a ride somewhere, call me."

"I will be sure to look out for you," Marieke said.

On the drive to the camp, Will was peppered with questions about the mysterious Land Rover. Valeria, in particular, wanted details, none of which Will had. He was rescued by Jackson when they arrived, who met the children and asked them all about their trip. For Valeria and Vittorio, that meant some translation through Francesca or Alessandra, as they spoke very little Setswana. Superintendent Englebrecht introduced herself to Bridget and was then shown where she could stay, at least until the next day. If she chose to stay longer because there was a serious problem, then Bridget told her that they would make arrangements for her and her team. Bridget then served coffee, and Marieke asked about them.

"Well, we first came to Africa in the early 70s," Will said. "We both worked for ICI, me at the paint factory and Bridget at Modderfontein at the explosives factory. Eventually, we got tired of the Jo'burg life, the locks, the security guards, all the trappings of big city life, so we looked for something different. Katrina and James knew the folks who had this concession before us, Piet and Anna Englebrecht. Piet apparently is a distant cousin of Katrina's and, therefore, I suppose, yours as well. We bought a place in Gabs and moved to Botswana. We've been running this camp for three years now." Marieke digested this information, surprised that Bridget had worked at the explosives factory and wondered what she did there; she might ask later, but, for now, there was the mystery to investigate.

"How did you come to find the Land Rover?" Marieke asked.

"We followed a rhino to a *dambo* two days ago," Will said. "That was really unusual because we almost never see rhino out here. When we were at the *dambo,* we saw this Land Rover on the other side. I thought it might be bird watchers and was going to check back with them because this is our concession, and I like to know who's here. Then this morning we followed a leopard out to the same *dambo,* and the Land Rover is still there, hasn't moved an inch. Well, Jackson and I took a look and found it with no number plates, no tax disc, a large rock on the driver's side floor and no footprints either leading to it or away from it. So we thought we'd better call it in."

"Perhaps we could go there and take a look?" she suggested. She had been watching Will carefully as he told his story and felt that it was a spontaneous recounting of events, not rehearsed as it might have been if had concocted the story to cover his own tracks.

"Of course," Will said. "Francesca, would you take the guests south to that waterhole with the four big sausage trees and see if you can spot the leopard that's been hanging around there?"

"Okay, Dad, I'll take Rice with me," Francesca replied.

"Uncle Will, can I come with you?" Valeria asked.

"You'd better ask the Superintendent," he replied.

"*Mma?*" Valeria asked.

"You may," Marieke agreed. "But, if I tell you to stay somewhere, you must do so and if it may be unpleasant, if we discover any bodies."

"I've seen dead bodies before," Valeria said. "I spent some time at our local hospital observing post-mortem examinations."

"Excuse the question, but why?" Marieke asked.

"I want to be a police officer when I get out of university," Valeria explained.

"You're so young, are you sure? There may be many other opportunities that arise in the future," Marieke asked.

"No, I'm sure, Dad's in the police and he's been trying to dissuade me. But, it's what I want to do," Valeria said.

"Fine, then let me just change clothes and get my bag, and we can go," Marieke said.

Will drove west to the *dambo* and took the path he had taken before and stopped in the same place. They could all see the Land Rover just sitting in the bush. Marieke looked over the scene, then had a discussion with Jackson in Setswana, partly to sound him out and see if he had any knowledge of the Land Rover before he and Will came across it, and partly to give him some instructions. She asked Will and Valeria to stay where they were, and then she and Jackson took opposite paths and began to walk in a fairly wide circle around the Land Rover. They were both looking for tracks, tracks of anyone who might have been up to the Land Rover, or who had left it. When they met on the other side, she called out to Will and Valeria to approach the Land Rover. She asked Will to hand over his rifle to Jackson and asked Jackson to make sure that nothing disturbed them.

"So," she said. "No tracks of any people either leading to the *bakkie* or away from it, other than those of you and Jackson. The *bakkie* came from that direction and finally stopped here, by the look of it, because it got mired in the soft ground and just spun itself in until it stalled. What do you think?"

"I would agree," Will concurred. "What occurs to me is that the Land Rover was pointed into the bush by someone and left to find its own path. The stone inside was probably wedged on the accelerator pedal until vibration caused it to drop free. I am guessing that the stick and string were to pop the clutch from the outside, and that string on the steering wheel limits motion, keeping it more or less in a straight line."

"That sounds reasonable," she agreed. "Is there anything of note on the outside of this Land Rover?"

"No number plates and no tax disc," Will noted.

"So I see," Marieke said. "Valeria, did you bring paper and pencil?"

"Yes, Superintendent," Valeria confirmed.

"Take notes if you would, then," Marieke instructed. "The vehicle came from the North, it appears as if it stalled in the mud, there are no number plates, either front or back, there is no tax disc. What else?"

"Based on a quick walk around, a peek inside, headlight style and placement and radiator grill type, this is a Series IIA Land Rover, 109" long wheelbase station wagon in the twelve-seat configuration, colour Limestone, right-hand drive," Will said. "That dates it to between 1969 and 1971, and for those countries that drive on the left. There is a non-standard light high on the driver's side at the back, probably installed by the owner for reversing. There is a really old-style AA badge on the radiator grill. It has brush guards on the front lights, which may or may not have been factory-installed. They only came out in about August of 1970, so if they were factory-installed, it was after then; if they were owner-installed, the *bakkie* may predate August 1970. It has new Michelin tyres, except for the flat spare that is on the back door, which is an old Goodrich, which is odd because I would have thought that most people would know not to mix radial and cross-ply. My guess is that it was swapped from another *bakkie* because the rim is blue, which doesn't match the other rims. It does not have freewheeling hubs. It does have the dished bonnet for a spare, with a locking post, which is a factory option. There is a drum winch, factory-installed, not after the fact. There are locking hasps on the bonnet and the petrol tank, both, I would guess, factory-installed; there are padlocks on both the bonnet hasp and the petrol tank. It has red reflective tape applied on the back and white reflective tape strips on the front bumper. That would have been applied here in Africa; it's definitely not a factory install. It has wing mirrors on both sides; again, we don't know if that was a factory-installed option or done at a later date. A new standard model from the showroom would only have the driver's side wing mirror. There is a standard towing hitch installed with a ball added. There is little in the way of exterior body damage, no repairs evident, it has been well cared for. It has a roof rack that was not a factory install, clipped onto the roof rack is a high lift jack, a shovel and an axe. As to the mud cast up under the wings, most of it looks like the mud thrown up by churning in the soft ground here. It is possible that there may be different soils beneath that mud, but superficially, all the mud is from here. The grasses, leaves and twigs caught up in the grill, on the front bumper, in the steering arms, and on the front axle are consistent with the vegetation surrounding the *dambo*. Again, there may be clues given by other vegetation, but it will take a closer examination to see them."

"That's all?" Marieke laughed. "Did you get all that, Valeria?"

"I did," Valeria replied. "If there are no number plates and no tax disc, how do we find out who it belongs to?"

"The next step, now that we've done our exterior look over, is to open up and see what is inside," Marieke said. "I brought some gloves, so Will, if you wouldn't mind, try the passenger door, see if the chassis number plate is still there in the middle by the gear sticks. I'll take a look through the driver's side."

"Chassis number plate is not there," Will reported."

"The chassis plate would have been our next means of identification," Marieke explained to Valeria. "The fact that it's gone along with the number plates and tax disc further suggests that someone wanted to conceal who this Land Rover belonged to."

"Shall we look under the bonnet?" Will asked.

"We have no key for the padlock," Marieke said.

"No problem," Will assured her. "Valeria?" he asked.

"Of course," she said, and with a bent piece of wire that she had brought with her, proceeded to pick the lock.

"You came prepared," Marieke remarked dryly.

"You never know," Valeria said, grinning.

"So, what do we have?" Will said as he opened the bonnet and peered inside at the engine. "2.6-litre six-cylinder petrol engine, number filed off."

"So, someone went to great pains to hide the identity of this *bakkie*," Marieke said. "Well, there is one more thing we can try. Will, if you don't mind, would you crawl under on the right-hand side at the front

22

and look at the chassis member by the spring hanger, see if you can read the numbers that should be there."

"Okay," Will agreed. He crawled underneath and called out, "There are some numbers here, let me tell you what I can read." He then sang out a series of numbers, beginning with 350-0082, then said that it would take a wire brush and some cleaning to make the rest legible.

"Good," Marieke noted, also noting that there was no disappointment or alarm in Will's voice as he read out the numbers, where there might have been if he had been the one to not file off those numbers. "That was a mistake by our person, to miss the stamped-on chassis number. With that partial number and your notes, we may have enough to go back to Rover and get the whole number. I wonder how many 12-seat long wheelbases in Limestone with a drum winch were made and shipped to Africa in that time frame? Do you see anything of note inside the *bakkie*?"

"Not that I see," Will said. "You may not have much luck with Rover asking about Land Rovers shipped to Africa. This is a 12-seat configuration, which was an artifice that Rover created to get around UK purchase tax laws. This Land Rover could have been purchased for domestic use and then exported, but possibly it was purchased for export, but not in the ten-seat configuration, as that would have incurred purchase tax if it was brought back into the UK within a certain time. I think if you check the chassis numbers, the prefix will tell you if it was for export or not. I don't remember how the sequence went, but I know it's the first three numbers that tell you. Other things I noted, the key is in the ignition, I turned it off this morning, the hand brake is off, it's in first, low range, and there is a stone by the accelerator pedal which fits the theory that it was set off on its own, as I said before. I'm guessing that the stick and string were used to pop the clutch from outside. The mileage indicator reads 95,657, and there is no separate trip readout. The fuel gauge reads about half a tank, which supports the theory that it stalled and did not just run out of petrol. There is no luggage, or camping gear, no food or anything else, it's remarkably clean inside. The starting handle is in its clip. Let's take a look at the storage bin that's under the passenger side inward inward-facing back seat. Aha, someone failed to clean this out. We have a jack, four D-links, a tow rope, a Schrader spark plug air pump, some old receipts that are really faded, but which may provide some clues, but not much else."

"Let me quickly dust and see if there are any fingerprints on the wheel of the gear levers," Marieke said. "Not one, it's been wiped down, same for the door handles."

"Someone really went to some trouble here," Will commented.

"Let's see how far it travelled on its own," Marieke suggested. They all set off following the tracks that the Land Rover had made through the bush until they finally came to a clearing in the mopane forest that was unusual in that it was so clean. "So, it went about a mile into the bush before it stalled in the *dambo*. I'm amazed it got that far," Marieke commented.

"If you look around this clearing," Will said. "That is the way in, and that is the only direction where the bush is light enough that the *bakkie* would *bundu* bash on its own; in all other directions, there are large enough trees close enough together that it would have stalled out much sooner. It had to have been set off from here because the track is at right angles to the direction the *bakkie* took. It wouldn't do that on its own."

"I agree," Marieke said. "Well, we don't want to be tramping around this clearing messing up possible clues, let's just sit and see what we can see."

"I know this clearing," Will said. "The track we were on swings north a little to avoid a waterhole and then comes back to the West; there is a junction down that way a bit that essentially doubles back to this side of the waterhole. This is a good spot for bird watching, just past those larger trees, there is a good view of the waterhole. If this place was picked, then whoever picked it has been before, which seems likely to me as it is so out of the way and not the kind of place one would stumble across."

"Possibly," Marieke agreed. "I see tracks of birds, kudu, civet and jackal, are there any hyæna packs that live in the area?"

"There is one family that usually can be found about ten miles to the North," Will replied. "There is another about five miles to the South. On occasion, we have seen some here, but that is usually after a big kill of some kind. There is a lion pride whose territory includes this area."

"Why was the Land Rover not fired? That would have destroyed most of the vehicular evidence," Marieke pondered.

"Perhaps whoever stripped it of identification was afraid that the smoke from a fire would attract too much attention. Later in the year, when we get bushfires, we might not investigate, but this time of the year, if we saw a fire, we would check it out," Will replied.

They sat a while longer watching and listening, and then Marieke saw something that attracted her attention. She looked to the others and saw that Jackson had also noticed what she had seen, but so far Will and Valeria had not. There were blow flies landing on a patch of ground near the northern edge of the clearing. She watched them for a while, then turned to Will and asked, "Do you have a shovel in your *bakkie*?"

"I do," he confirmed. "I presume that you've seen something, ah, those blowflies. I'll get the shovel." Marieke watched him go, a little surprised that he didn't do what most Europeans would have done and tell Jackson to go and get it. While she waited for Will to return, she watched the flies, and they seemed to be concentrating on one specific place. When Will came back, he looked to her for instructions, "Over there, I think," she said. "Dig carefully, I'm not sure what you might find."

Will first spread out a tarpaulin he had also brought and started digging in the place Marieke indicated. He dug a hole about three feet square and started going slowly deeper, placing the dirt he dug from the hole onto the tarpaulin. Finally, he stopped and said, "I've got some plastic here."

"Is there anything else?" Marieke asked. Will dug a little more and then put the shovel down and bent down to examine the plastic.

"I've got four feet," he said. "No boots or shoes, just feet, and it looks like they're attached to legs. Looking at the feet, some decomposition, but I would guess that they're normally shod, no barefoot people here."

"Let me take a look," Marieke said. She waited until Will was out of the hole and climbed in herself. "The soil's been well compacted above the feet and legs," she commented. "I'm always surprised at how the blow flies manage to detect decomposition. I'm presuming that there are torsos, arms and the rest here. Can you dig a little more?"

"Sure," Will agreed. He took up the shovel again, and when Marieke had climbed out of the hole, he started digging again. Soon, he had the full length of the bodies uncovered. "No clothes and no heads," he commented. "Just two *muzungus*, minus *skops*.

"Let's leave them in the hole until I get a team up here," Marieke said.

"Okay, I'll fill the hole back in," Will said. "It was nice and cool down there, and damp enough that I would say that whatever feeds that waterhole also influences this area."

"This water hole doesn't dry up, then?" she asked.

"It changes a bit, but there's always water there, my guess is looking at the trees that there was an ancient river here, and it still seeps below the surface," he thought.

"Would Jackson mind staying to make sure that hyæna don't dig up the bodies?" she asked.

There followed a brief conversation between Will and Jackson and then Marieke and Jackson, the upshot of which was that Jackson would stay until Will sent two of the others up to relieve him.

"We should get back to your camp, I think, and call this in," Marieke said. Will gave Jackson the rifle, and then he left with the others to walk back to their own Land Rover.

At the camp, the others were agog to learn what they had discovered. Will deferred to Assistant Superintendent Englebrecht, who told them the basics, that there were two people, both dead and that she was going to call in specialists. She spent some time talking via the radio to the police station in Maun, then came back with the news. "I have some forensics people flying up from Gaborone to the Selinda strip first thing in the morning and some help driving up from the Maun station, again tomorrow morning, so the plane should be here mid-morning and the people from Maun around lunchtime."

Will detailed off two of their staff to go and relieve Jackson, he asked Valeria to drive them there and bring Jackson back. Bridget loaded them up with rifles, food and drink, lanterns and all the other items they would need for a night in the bush.

Over dinner, Will had a flash of memory.

"Superintendent," he said. "I believe it's possible that the Land Rover we found today used to belong to my brother James. I remember him installing a light for reversing and the old man giving him an ancient AA badge."

"Can you be sure?" she asked.

"No, but perhaps there's something else unique that he could tell us," Will suggested. "If we radio to Maun, could they call him in the US and ask?"

"We could certainly try," she agreed. "The girls were telling me that he lived in Zambia, if it was his *bakkie*, then I'll get on to the Zambia Police and see if they can dig up who he sold it to and if and when it was moved to Botswana. If it was moved to Botswana, then we'll have a record of the number change; if not, it had to enter through a border crossing, and there'll be a record of it entering the country."

Will dug out James's telephone number, and Marieke went off briefly and radioed in to Maun and issued some orders. "We'll have to wait for an answer," she said when she returned. "There's an eight-hour time difference to Utah at this time of the year. If it were his Land Rover, would you remember the Zambian number plate?"

"I'm afraid not," Will said. "We might have some pictures somewhere, but they'll be in Gaborone."

"When was your brother in Zambia?" Marieke asked.

"Let's see," Will thought. "He first went to Kitwe in 1969, and did three years there. Then they had an overseas leave, and when they went back, he was sent to another mine in the Mkushi area, which they would have been at until early 1975 or so, when they left to go to the US."

"Thank you," Marieke said. She then turned her attention to the visitors who had been listening to the conversation, but who really had nothing to add. "So, did you people see your leopard?"

"We did," Bob confirmed. "I admit at first I was put out that Will had lumbered us with his daughter, but after the trip to the waterhole, I am amazed by what she knows. She and Rice chattered away about stuff, and they pointed out all kinds of things that we would have certainly missed. The leopard was right where she said it would be. It posed for us nicely for about five minutes before running off into the thicker bush."

27

"Well, I'm glad that worked out for you," Will said. "I'll be back with you tomorrow; I've told Superintendent Englebrecht all I can; now we'll leave it to her and the rest of her team."

Dinner was over, and they were having coffee when there was a radio message for Marieke. She went off and came back shortly with news. "We managed to get hold of your sister-in-law," she told Will. "She remembers that they kept a spare key, spare rotor arm and 100 Kwacha in a plastic bag stuffed inside the driver's side of the front bumper. I suppose there is a chance that it's still there. If it is, then it definitely was your brother's Land Rover."

"Well, good luck tomorrow," he said. "Is there anything else you might need?"

"I don't think so," she said. "You saw the *bakkie* at the *dambo* the day before yesterday, and you hadn't seen it before then?"

"No," Will confirmed. "We hadn't been to that *dambo* in about a month; we only went this time because we followed a rhino there."

"I'll check with the Game Rangers at Chobe and the people at Khwai and see what traffic has been around lately, this is a long way out, and someone surely saw something," she thought. "We called them before, but they had little for us to use. Maybe after we interview them, someone may remember some detail that would help us. For the sake of completeness, we'll formally interview everyone tomorrow, but from what we have seen today, I don't expect to learn anything new. Could you give me details of your movements over the past month?"

"Of course," Will said. "Let me just get the map and the log." He left and came back with a large map mounted on a board, which had pins and notations on it, and a logbook. "I keep track of what we see where," he explained. "It makes it easier if we get a client who wants to see something specific. We can plot the patterns of movement of the various animals and estimate where we have the best chance of finding something."

"I see," she said. "You keep this log for the whole season?"

"I do," Will said. "I have the logs for last year and the first year that we ran the concession."

"So, theoretically, we could get dates when you visited that waterhole?" she asked.

"We can," he agreed. "If you want, I'll get the girls to pore through them tomorrow and pick out the dates for you. With those dates, we can also go back and look at the client lists and see who was here when we went there."

"Thank you," she said. "I know it's only one line of enquiry, but it may be useful."

"Francesca, Alessandra, can you do that tomorrow?" he asked.

"*Certo Pappi*," Francesca replied. "I shouldn't take too long."

How did they get here?

Marieke took the opportunity of the mid-morning coffee break to take statements from the visitors and then spent the rest of the morning pondering the question of who and how the bodies had got where they were. She asked Bridget if they had a map that showed all the tracks in the area. Bridget did and showed her the main track they used to come up from the Selinda airstrip.

"What I'm really interested in are tracks that would bypass you and let someone get to that *dambo* without being seen," Marieke said.

"Well, you have this one and this one," Bridget replied, pointing to two tracks marked on the map. "Beyond that, it's *bundu* bashing, which would leave a lot of evidence of passage; better to stick to the tracks."

"The fact that whoever buried the bodies went to that clearing suggests that they have been here," Marieke said. "Do you have back records of bookings?"

"For this year, I have them here," Bridget replied. "For last year and the year before, we have them in Gabs, and Patience has them in Maun. She has all the records for bookings, even in the early days when Piet and Anna ran the concession."

"Who is Patience?" Marieke asked.

"Patience Botha," Bridget replied. "They have a garage in Maun and she's done the bookings for Pitse since Piet set it up."

"Don't tell me the Bothas are more relatives," Marieke laughed.

"No, I gather just friends of Katrina's family and quite by chance also friends of Piet and Anna," Bridget explained.

"I'll talk to Patience at some time," Marieke said. "Is that my people on the radio?" They both listened, then Bridget replied and confirmed the landing and that someone would be there with transportation.

"Shall we go?" she asked Marieke. On the drive to the airstrip, Bridget quizzed Marieke about her days before Botswana.

"I grew up in South West," Marieke explained. "Went to school there, and then Mom and Dad sent me to university in Lyon to study law. While I was there, I met some of the Interpol people from the main office in Lyon and decided to become a police officer. At the time,

South West was not really an option, so because Mom is Motswana, I moved here."

"So, you speak French then as well as English, and I presume Setswana and Afrikaans?" Bridget asked.

"I do," Marieke laughed. "Add to that, San, I grew up with San kids on the farm, so speak some San, but not as fluently as Setswana."

"And all I speak is English, a smattering of Afrikaans, Italian and am struggling to master Setswana," Bridget complained.

"Why did you learn Italian?" Marieke asked.

"I learned it when the children went to school in Italy," Bridget replied. "I wanted to be able to understand them if they talked to each other."

"And your sister-in-law is married to an Italian, I understand," Marieke said.

"Alex married Vincenzo some time ago," Bridget confirmed. "He's in the Italian Secret Service. Here we are, I'll park over there by those trees, but we won't have to wait long, I can hear the plane."

Marieke watched as the Shorts Skyvan of the Botswana Defence Force circled the strip and then came in to land. She went out to greet the plane and was happy to see Thabo Mosiwa; he was one of the doctors assigned to the police unit at the Princess Marina Hospital in Gaborone and did post-mortem examinations and other forensic work. With him, he had Neo Mogotsi. Neo was one of the forensic technicians, and the brief exposure Marieke had had to his work on some cases in Tsabong suggested that he was very thorough.

"*Dumela* Marieke," Thabo said. "I hate those Skyvans, they're noisy and we might as well have been in a delivery van."

"*Dumela Rra*," Marieke said, quietly amused, she had discovered when she worked out in Tsabong that Thabo liked his creature comforts. She had had to call him out for a few deaths and had had to listen to his complaints about car travel over dusty roads, and air travel in less than luxury. "I think that is the idea of the Skyvan, it is a van, it just delivers from the air instead of on the ground."

"So, what do we have?" Thabo asked, bringing himself back to the job at hand.

"Two bodies, or at least torsos and limbs, no heads," Marieke replied.

"No heads, or no heads that you've found yet?" he asked.

"Good question," she agreed. "We've left the final unearthing for Neo, so perhaps he'll find them. Thabo, this is Bridget Martin. She and her husband run this concession, and it was her husband and one of their people who first called us in."

"*Dumela Mma*," Thabo said.

"*Dumela Rra*," Bridget replied. "I have some water here if you would like, it will take us about an hour to drive to our camp and then perhaps another quarter of an hour to where the bodies are buried. Superintendent, are the pilots going to wait for you?"

"Let me find out," Marieke said. She went and had a conversation with the pilots and came back with the news that they were planning on waiting. Their options were to go to Maun, get fuel and then come back for the police party, or wait for everyone and make a fuel stop on the way back to Gaborone. They had had a brief discussion and agreed upon the latter choice.

"Would they like to come and wait at the camp? We can give them lunch and a place to rest," Bridget suggested. That suggestion went down well, and the pilots closed up their aircraft and joined the others in the Land Rover. On the drive north to the camp, the conversation was generalities about the trip up and complaints from Thabo about the lack of creature comforts in the Skyvan, much to the amusement of the pilots. At the camp, they were greeted by Francesca, who had lunch ready, and they had just started when the police Land Rover from Maun appeared. Inspector Moroka, Sergeant Mochage and Constable Dube had made good time from Maun. They admitted that they had started out really early, long before it was light, hoping to meet the plane at Selinda.

After lunch, Francesca and Valeria led them to the place where Will had first seen the Land Rover. Marieke pointed out the place to the rest of the party, and then Francesca told her that she had worked out how to get close to the place where the bodies were without disturbing any evidence. That saved a walk, so they were all happy with that. When they came close, the people whom Will had sent to guard the place came to see who it was and were very happy to hand over duties to the police.

"I'll be back before sundown to pick you up," she told Marieke. "I have water here for you and tools for digging. We'll also have that list of visits and people when you're done here."

"Thank you," Marieke said. "Inspector, if you follow those tracks, you will come to the Land Rover we just saw. Would you and Sergeant Mochage go and retrieve it. There may be enough life in the battery to start it; if not, I saw the starting handle there. If you cannot get it running, let us know, and we'll tow it out with your Land Rover after we're done here. Have a look inside the front bumper on the driver's side and see if there is anything there, also please take samples of the mud that is under the wings and samples of the grasses and twigs caught in the radiator grill and the steering arms."

"Very good, Superintendent," the inspector replied. Then he and the sergeant left to get the Land Rover.

"Now, Thabo, let's see what we have, shall we?" Marieke suggested.

"Neo, uncover what we have," Thabo said. "Hmm, two bodies, as you said, no clothes, no heads, let's get them out of the hole and see if the heads are buried close by." They watched as Neo and the constable lifted the plastic wrapping out of the hole and then poked and prodded the dirt around the hole. "That soil doesn't look as if it's been disturbed," Thabo said. "My suspicion is that the heads are not here. There is not enough blood, and what better way to confuse the situation. Look here, the fingers have had their ends singed to destroy fingerprints, done post-mortem. Neo take some temperature readings in the undisturbed soil and then take a look around and see what else you can find."

"Someone has gone to pains to delay identification," Marieke said. "I wonder where they were actually killed. Are there any obvious marks on the torsos to indicate cause of death?"

"Not that I can see, but even with only a slight decomposition, I'll have to wait until after I do a full PM to give you a better answer," Thabo said.

"Okay, we'll wrap them in the bags we brought and you can take them back with you to Gabs," Marieke suggested. "I'll come with you as far as Maun, then check on a couple of things and see you back in Gabs."

"This area has been quite thoroughly swept clean," Neo remarked when he returned. "I see no remnants of anything. I am wondering what happened to their clothes; they must have been taken away, because there is no evidence of a fire where they might have been burned. I followed the track that way and found where the tyre tracks were no longer brushed out. There was another vehicle here apart from the Land Rover, you said was that way. It turned around down there, but I didn't find any footprints; it looks as if they had been brushed out, even down there. The other vehicle has a wheelbase and track that is consistent with another Land Rover, and I have casts of the tyre tracks of both."

"So, we are looking for two people, probably," Marieke said. "If we accept the premise that the victims were killed elsewhere and the bodies brought here to be buried." Her further thoughts were interrupted by the sound of a Land Rover coming their way. Inspector Moroka had succeeded in getting it started, and between him and Sergeant Mochage had extracted it from the mud and driven it out.

"We are in luck," the inspector said. "Look what we found in the front bumper."

"Let me guess," Marieke said. "A key, a rotor arm and 100 Zambian Kwacha."

"How did you know?" the inspector asked.

"The first owner of this Land Rover told me that they might be there," Marieke explained. "That at least gives us a place to start. I'll have our Traffic people check back records against the number that the original owner provided us, and I'll also contact the Zambians to see who was the last owner, at least in Zambia."

"So, when were those young ladies coming back for us?" Thabo asked.

"About now," Marieke said. "Inspector, would you bring your Land Rover from where we parked it on the track to here, so that we may load the bodies, then I think we can leave?"

"Of course, Superintendent," Inspector Moroka said. "Sergeant, bring the Land Rover and let's get this done so that we can go back to Maun."

At the Pitse Safari Camp, Marieke briefly told Will and Bridget what they had found and confirmed that the unmarked Land Rover had at one time belonged to James. She then begged a little petrol to be sure that it would reach Maun, then she took her leave of everyone, gathered up the pilots and bid farewell to the camp. At the airstrip, they loaded the bodies onto the plane, and then Marieke instructed the Inspector to take the found Land Rover to Maun. She was going to fly as far as Maun, then pick up her car and go and see Patience Botha for lists of past guests. Before she left, Francesca gave her the list of dates spanning the three-year period that Will and Bridget had run the concession and a list for each date of who the guests were. There had been twenty visits over the period. For the current year, there were 40 names, and for the previous year, there were an additional 62 names, and for the preceding year, there were only dates.

In Maun, Marieke asked the airport staff where she could find the garage of Kobus and Patience Botha and got directions. She drove there and introduced herself.

"Ah, yes, Superintendent," Patience said. "Bridget called us on the radio and said you were coming. Please come in, may I offer you some tea, a Coke, or something else?"

"Tea would be fine, thank you," Marieke replied. "How are you?"

"Well, thank you, and you?" Patience said. "How may I help you?"

"I was wondering if you could tell me who was at the Pits camp on these dates?" she asked, handing Patience a list.

"I have records of past reservations and guests," Patience said. She put the list aside while she made the tea, then came back to it. "Do you want to go back further than that?"

"That's the problem," Marieke admitted. "I'm not certain that this line of enquiry will lead anywhere. Perhaps we might start with the people for those dates and then a general list for five years?"

"Of course," Patience said. "Let me call up the records on my computer and print them out. I'll give you ten years of information."

"You have them all on a computer?" Marieke asked.

"I do," Patience confirmed. "We decided to load all the back records of guests to approach them again for repeat business."

"Has it worked?" Marieke asked.

"It has," Patience confirmed. "The numbers show that in the last two seasons, we have had about a third of our guests who are coming back again."

"They must like what they see," Marieke commented.

"I think it's the experience they get," Patience said. "Piet and Anna were very good at making guests feel comfortable and meeting their requests, and Will and Bridget have continued that level of service."

"Where are the guests typically from?" Marieke asked.

"About half from the UK," Patience thought. "Then the rest split between the US and different countries in Europe."

"Do you have contact details for all the guests?" Marieke asked.

"We do," Patience confirmed. "We make an effort to try and contact all past guests each year and have tried to keep addresses and such up to date. There will always be a few that we just lose track of, but so far, not very many. We did have in the past some block bookings from conferences, and it sometimes took a little work to get the lists of names from them straight. There, printing done, that should keep you busy for a day or two. What are you actually looking for?"

"I suspect that someone knew of a *dambo* in the concession that is Pitse and used that knowledge to bury some bodies," Marieke explained. "It was only a chance sighting of a rhino who had apparently got really lost that took Will to the *dambo* the first time, and then a leopard the second time. Otherwise, it might have been quite some time before the Land Rover was discovered, and it was only by chance that I discovered the burial site. I'm sure that the next time you see Will and Bridget, they'll tell you all about it."

"Ah, I see," Patience said. "I doubt that it was by chance you must have seen something that aroused your interest. So, I presume that what you are looking for is someone who is either from here, or who was a guest before and has since moved to Botswana and who has been to the site before, hence the list of specific dates?"

"That was my thinking," Marieke confirmed. "My supposition is that the Land Rover we found is not from Maun, so it's likely that it passed through here and got petrol, either from you or one of the other stations in town."

"What kind of Land Rover are we talking about?" Patience asked.

"Long wheelbase station wagon, limestone, apparently it belonged to Will's brother once upon a time," Marieke replied.

"I remember it," Patience said. "It is not from Maun. It had a roof rack that we installed. Is that still on it?"

"Yes," Marieke said. "Is it of your design and building too?"

"Yes, Kobus would make them up and install them for customers. I would have remembered that Land Rover if they had stopped here for petrol, perhaps you should try the other stations in town," Patience suggested. "Before you go, are you planning to drive back to Gabs tonight?"

"No, I thought I would stay another night in Maun and get an early start in the morning," Marieke replied.

"You are welcome to stay here," Patience offered.

"Thank you," Marieke said. "I'll be back after I have interviewed the other garages. Oh, by the way, where do Piet and Anna Englebrecht live now?"

"They moved to Calitzdorp," Patience said. "Piet bought a vineyard and they are growing the Hanepoot grape and making wine, with some success, I believe."

Marieke tried the other petrol stations in town with no luck. Either the people in the ill-fated Land Rover did not buy petrol in Maun or they were not memorable. She was puzzled; to get to where the Land Rover was found and still have half a tank of petrol meant that it had to be filled at some point. Her conjecture was that whoever moved it must have filled it from jerry cans and still have enough to get back, at least to Maun in their own vehicle. The logistics of this operation suggested planning, so this was not a chance encounter. Someone knew of the plans of the victims and planned their operation around them. But, the first order of the day was to identify the Land Rover's owner, and she could go from there. That would best be done in Gaborone. She drove back to the house of Patience and there met Kobus, who had come in from retrieving a broken-down car from the road to Ghanzi.

Over dinner, Marieke got background information on Will and Bridget, she had to eliminate them as suspects. After all, they could be part of an elaborate plot to remove unwanted guests and throw off suspicion by drawing attention to the bodies as the discoverers. Added to her earlier observations, the more she heard, the more she was inclined to eliminate Will and Bridget as suspects. It would all be just too unlikely. Also, if they had been part of anything, she would have heard from Jackson or some of the other camp workers, even if not directly, there would have been some conversation or veiled allusions to anything untoward. She also got background information on Patience and Kobus. Apparently, they met when Kobus shot a cow that belonged to Patience's father. During the ensuing negotiations over payment for the cow, he had met and fallen in love with Patience. The negotiations for the cow turned into negotiations for the *lobola* that would secure Patience's hand in marriage. They had then set up shop in Maun and had tried several ventures before settling on the garage. They had one son, Phineas, who was away at the moment collecting a new breakdown lorry from Gaborone. Kobus and Koot, Katrina's father, had grown up together and had stayed friends, even after the marriage, which made Marieke wonder if her own father had misjudged his brother and the reception he and her mother would have received. Kobus and Patience had met Piet and Anna, who had had the Pitse Concession before Will and Bridget, when Piet came into the garage one day for petrol. He had got talking to Kobus and Patience, and the upshot of that was that Patience took on the job of doing the bookings for them. Marieke was intrigued by the fact that Patience had entered all the data into a computer and now did all the booking through her computer set-up. She estimated that Patience must be at least in her mid-sixties, and that did not fit her views and ideas of who used computers; she had thought it was the twenty-to-thirty age group.

The next day, Marieke took her leave of the Bothas and set off to drive back to Gaborone. She called in at the police station first and confirmed that Inspector Moroka and his people had returned. They had made it back and had the Land Rover in a shed covered up. Marieke said that she would send a forensics technician to Maun shortly to go over the

Land Rover with a fine-toothed comb to see if she and Will had missed anything of significance. Then she set off for the nine-hour drive back to Gaborone. She wished that the department budget ran to getting car phones. They were coming out in the US and Europe, and it would make communications easier, especially on the long drives in Botswana. Perhaps one day, meanwhile, she had music and her thoughts. For music, she was torn between opera, Sarah Brightman and Enya. Enya won for the moment, but that would only be for the first hour; after that, she would have to make another choice. The drive back was uneventful as far as Orapa; then she got a puncture on the way to Serowe and had to take the time to change the tyre. Fortunately, her spare was in good condition and properly inflated and was not one of the new compact or doughnut spares, but a real wheel with a full-sized tyre. The department had eschewed the use of the compact spares as they tended to impose restrictions on speed and handling that the police did not want. Marieke finally arrived in Gaborone just after five in the afternoon and went straight to her office. She had only just opened the door when Assistant Commissioner Mochage appeared as if he had been hovering in the wings, waiting for her. Marieke had, in her short time in Gaborone, noticed this about the Commissioner: he either had very good sources of intelligence or he had a sixth sense about who was about and when.

"So, Matshwane," he said. "You are back."

"Yes, Sir," she replied. She did wonder how the name Matshwane, which means ratel in Setswana, had followed her from Tsabong. Perhaps it was his subtle way of letting her know that he had a good back channel to the Tsabong station.

"And what did you find out there that called for Thabo to request a BDF plane to fly him and Neo into the wilds of Linyanti?" he asked.

"Two headless corpses," she explained. "Our preliminary view is two Europeans, beheaded perhaps a week or so ago, Thabo is doing the post-mortems to see what he can discover."

"No heads?" he asked.

"No heads, Sir," she confirmed. "There was not enough evidence of blood at the scene to support beheading there, so our presumption is that they were killed and beheaded elsewhere."

"I bring you in from Tsabong and send you to Maun on a minor case just to get your feet wet, as it were, and you bring back a mystery," he said. "Do you have anything that may help identify these two people?"

"We were lucky," she replied. "Although the Land Rover we found had been stripped of number plates and the chassis plate, the man who found it recognised it as once belonging to his brother in Zambia."

"And, what is your next course of action?" the commissioner asked.

"I was going to call the Zambians in the morning and see if they could tell me the last owner they have on record and if that person brought the Land Rover into Botswana," she said. "I was also going to talk to our motor vehicle people and see if they have any record of a change from the Zambian numbers to our numbers. I also have a list of past visitors to the safari camp, the site where we found the bodies is remote enough that it is possible that whoever buried them had been there before."

"When you call the Zambians, ask to speak to Chief Superintendent Phiri in Lusaka," the commissioner suggested. "He and I have worked together many times and are old friends. I understand that you have a relationship with the Martins, who run the Pitse Safari Camp?"

"So it would seem," she confirmed, wondering how much Thabo had told him. "Will Martin has a brother who now lives in Utah, but who once lived in Zambia. In Zambia, he met and married one Katrina Englebrecht, who is my cousin, whom I have never actually met. My father was considered persona non grata by the rest of the family, who disapproved of a Motswana wife."

"This long-lost family relationship will not influence your objectivity?" he asked.

"No, Sir," she assured him. "I seriously doubt if the Martins had any part in this affair, apart from finding the Land Rover, but if it were to transpire that they do, I will turn over the case if I think I cannot stay truly objective."

"Good, good, then I will leave things in your capable hands," he said. "Be sure to inform me of any significant information pertaining to this case. By the way, I met your cousin Katrina Martin some years ago when we arrested some poachers who also had the temerity to shoot at us. She helped us with that case, as I recall, she is a very good shot."

"Really, Sir?" she said. "It's a small world, I'll be sure to keep you informed of developments." After the commissioner had left, Detective Sergeant Maphosa came in from his place of hiding.

"I thought he would never leave," he said. "Why is it that he makes me nervous, he seems to know far too much, too much for our good?"

"I think he just keeps his ears and eyes open," Marieke commented.

"How was your trip to Maun?" Sergeant Maphosa asked.

"Interesting," she replied. "I came back with two headless bodies and a car that I need identified. Could you contact the vehicle licensing people in the morning and find out if we ever gave a Botswana number to a Land Rover with this Zambian number?"

"Do you know when?" he asked.

"I have no idea yet, but do know that it would be after 1975," she admitted. "I will be calling the Zambians in the morning to see if they can help. If we can identify the owner of the Land Rover, we may be able to identify the bodies. Would you also arrange for a forensic tech to go to Maun and go through the Land Rover that's at the police station there? I'm looking for plant life and soil types that might tell me where it had been before we found it."

"I'll do that," he promised. "Do you know where the heads are?"

"At this time, I have no idea," she said. "So, what other cases do we have to work on?"

"There is some stock theft, but I've passed that on to the stock theft people. There has been a rash of car thefts between here and Lobatse in the last few days. I am investigating. I believe I can get to the bottom of that one, based on some intelligence I have just received," he said.

"Anything else?" she asked.

"No, it's quite quiet just now," he assured her. "Is there anything else?"

"No, Isaac, go home to your wife and family," she suggested. After Isaac had gone, she sat back and pondered her current situation. The move from Tsabong had been a promotion and had offered the chance of cases that were not just stock theft and cross-border smuggling and poaching, with the occasional murder, and just her luck, she had walked into a case that could turn out to be hard to solve. Still, that was why she joined the police: to be able to solve puzzles and riddles and bring some hope of justice to people who had been wronged. Now, if she could just find some companionship in life; her parents had both died when they were in the wrong place at the wrong time and had hit a landmine, she had no siblings and no romantic involvement with anyone since Danie who had been killed in a bad traffic accident on the road between Tsabong and Lobatse. She had not formed any lasting attachments since, instead, focusing on work. She had sold the farm after her parents' deaths to a South African and had moved the money to Botswana and to England, against the day when she retired and she could indulge her desire for travel to exotic destinations. It had surprised her a little that the Assistant Commissioner had already heard of the name that she had been given by the police at Tsabong, they had given it, she had been told one day by one of the sergeants, because when she got hold of a case, she never let go until it was solved and completed. His explanation was that she might be small and slight, but like the ratel, she was fearless and persistent. The sergeant had also told her, in a weak moment, that they used to invoke her name to suspects if they thought they were not getting the answers and cooperation they were looking for, apparently just saying, "We'll bring in the Matshwane," would make even the most recalcitrant villain think twice.

At home, Marieke showered and changed clothes. She had been invited to dinner by the bank manager of the branch where she did her banking. The manager intrigued her, although she was clearly a Zulu by the name of Mbali, she went by the name of Mrs Lamprecht. Mbali was tall and willowy and always dressed very elegantly, quite like a fashion model at times. There was obviously a story about how Mbali and Mr Lamprecht had met, which Marieke was interested to hear. Mbali lived on Sebina Road, and it only took Marieke a few minutes to drive there. The house was set among trees and looked very elegant. She parked next to a Land Cruiser and knocked on the door. The man who came to the door was white, and he was clearly expecting her.

"*Dumela Mma*," he said. "You must be Marieke Englebrecht. I'm Jan Lamprecht, please call me Jannie."

"*Dumela Rra*," she replied.

"Please come in," he said. "Mbali has been telling me all about you."

Marieke went into the house, and Mbali came from the kitchen, "*Dumela Mma*," she said. "I hope you're hungry, I seem to have cooked enough for a football team."

"*Dumela Mma*, I have only eaten a little today, so a good meal would be welcome," Marieke replied.

"Can I get you something to drink, beer, wine, soda, cane and Coke?" Jannie asked.

"Some wine would be welcome," Marieke said.

"Red or white?" Jannie asked. "I have Chablis, a Beaujolais or a Graves."

"The Chablis, please," Marieke replied.

"Wines tend to confuse me," Jannie admitted. "But Mbali likes her wine, so we are learning."

"I was fortunate to go to university in Lyon in France," Marieke said. "So, I had the opportunity to learn and to sample."

"Why did you go to uni in France?" Mbali asked.

"It was easier than trying to deal with the South Africans," Marieke said.

"We understand," Mbali said. "When we got married in 1971, it was fine here, but in South Africa, we would have been breaking the law."

"Excuse me for asking," Marieke said. "But, where did you two meet?"

"Swaziland," Mbali said. "I had taken a short trip and met Jannie in a casino, of all places."

"I was in the army and was taking a short leave. I had just won big at the casino and met Mbali, and it just clicked," Jannie added.

"Wasn't it difficult with the laws in South Africa?" Marieke asked.

"We had to be careful," Mbali agreed. "Then I asked for a transfer at the bank to the Gabs branch, and Jannie got out of the army and joined me here. We first bought a little house on Kaunda Road and then moved here about five years ago. Jannie started a business right when we came here in 1971, repairing diesel lorries and buses, and we now have MJ Motors with a large workshop in the industrial area with about 2,000m² under roof and employ about fifty people."

"How did your families take to the news?" Marieke asked.

"Not well," Mbali admitted. "My family has come around a little, but sadly, Jannie's family still won't talk to him, let alone me."

"Perhaps in time they will see that it is not so bad," Marieke said.

"Perhaps," Jannie said. "But, I am not waiting for that day."

43

"When did you become the manager here, Mbali?" Marieke asked.

"Seven years ago," Mbali replied. "I came here as a cashier, then had other jobs, while I got a degree from the university, then I got the job as manager, I kept on with my studies and have an MBA as well now. I would like to try a job for a while in London, Jo'burg will be out until all the intermarriage laws go away, but London would be fine."

"Do you have children?" Marieke asked.

"Two, both girls," Mbali said. "They are sixteen and fourteen and are staying with some friends tonight. They are both still at school and both want to go to university."

"You've kept your figure well," Marieke said. "I would not have said that you had had two children."

"I work at it," Mbali admitted. "I didn't want to buy a whole new wardrobe, so decided after Nandi that that was it and that I was going to go back to my early twenties clothes."

"What do your daughters want to study?" Marieke asked.

"Well, Khanyo, she is the older, wants to study game management and go into the field of protecting our natural resource heritage; she's quite passionate about it," Mbali said. "Nandi has lately given up the idea of being a rock star and decided that she wants to be a pilot and fly for Air Botswana."

"I'm really proud of them," Jannie said. "They are just so bright, they must get it all from Mbali. I led a different childhood, typical Afrikaner upbringing; then I did my time in the army, did some foolish things, then came here and married Mbali and grew up."

"Some foolish things?" Marieke asked.

"I did some poaching when I was younger, must be over eighteen years ago now," Jannie admitted. "I was lucky, I never got caught, but those I was with all had problems. It was Mbali who made me see that that was wrong and helped me straighten out my life, now the irony of it all is that Khanyo wants to go into Game Management and chase poachers. The authorities here kept an eye on me for the first five years or so when we first came here, then I think they decided that I had reformed and intended to live within the law."

Further discussion about Jannie's past was interrupted by a knock at the door. Jannie went to open it and came back with another man.

"Marieke, this is Phineas Botha from Maun, he's here in Gabs picking up a new breakdown lorry," Jannie explained. "It's the one thing we sell, apart from repair services, we don't deal in new or used cars and vans, but we do sell breakdown lorries."

"*Dumela Rra*," Marieke said. "I just met your folks in Maun."

"*Dumela Mma*," he replied. "I heard, what took you out there?"

"I am investigating a mysterious Land Rover that was found on the concession that Will and Anna Martin have," she explained. "Anna directed me to your mom, who does the bookings."

"Oh yes, Mom told me you'd been to see her about bookings," he said. "Mom also said that Will told her that you'd also found two headless corpses."

"You're with the police?" Jannie asked.

"Didn't Mbali tell you?" Marieke asked.

"She missed that bit out," Jannie said. "All she told me was that you were a client who had recently moved to Gabs from Tsabong."

"Did Jannie tell you he knows all about the concession that Will and Bridget now run?" Phineas laughed. "He used to run with some real *skelms*."

"I was just hearing a little when you arrived," Marieke said.

"Well, Mbali sorted him out and he's a genuine *ou* now, wouldn't surprise me if he didn't run for City Council sometime," Phineas said.

"So, what's the story with the headless *ouks*?" Jannie asked.

"I need to identify two whites in their mid-fifties," Marieke explained. "A man and a woman."

"Visitors or residents?" Jannie asked.

"I have no idea," Marieke admitted. "But, I do know a little about the Land Rover. It used to belong to Will's brother, James, and apparently, your folks, Phineas, fitted a roof rack to it."

"I remember that, "Phineas said. "Katrina and James were on their way to Tsau Hill to recover some items that her ancestor *Oom* Jan had buried there."

"Did they find it?" Marieke asked.

"They did," Phineas confirmed. "Imagine this Jannie, this *ou* treks across the Kalahari in the 1850s, loses his ox team to lions and theft, gets rescued by Bushmen, marries one of them and has kids, then loses just about all of the family in a shoot-out with slave traders in Angola, then walks back to the Cape with his son."

"That was my great-great-grandfather," Marieke said.

"Genuine?" Phineas asked.

"Truly," Marieke confirmed. "Katrina is my cousin."

"So you're part San as well as Motswana?" Mbali asked.

"I am," Marieke confirmed.

"I think we should eat, or my dinner will get cold," Mbali said. "We can get the rest of the story from Marieke after dinner.

Back to Pitse

The next day, Marieke got up early and drove to a karate dojo she had found and went through her morning routine before sparring with another student. She typically left her house and drove on a different route to her office, or to the dojo, each day. Death threats in Tsabong had made her leery of routine, so now she threw a dice in the morning and based on the result picked her route from six she had previously scouted out. She also varied the time that she left her house, not by much, but by enough to have no particular time that she could be relied upon to depart. After her practice session at the dojo, she went to her office and placed a telephone call to the Zambia Police offices in Lusaka and was gratified when she was transferred to the office of Chief Superintendent Phiri.

"Assistant Superintendent Englebrecht, good morning, my friend Ian told me that you would be calling, how may I help you?" Phiri asked.

"Good morning, Chief Superintendent, thank you for taking my call," Marieke replied. "The Assistant Commissioner may have told you that we came across a Land Rover in a remote area stripped of its identity, and subsequently, we unearthed two headless corpses. We were lucky in that the safari operator recognised the Land Rover as once belonging to his brother, who had lived in Zambia."

"Ah, I see," Phiri said. "You need to track the ownership of this Land Rover."

"I do, Sir," Marieke said. "It was brought into Zambia in late 1969, and it had the Zambia number plate, ET 6490, until James Martin left the country in 1975."

"ET puts it in the Copperbelt, as I recall, Kitwe, if I am right," Phiri said. "Where did they live?"

"James lived in Kitwe from 1969 until 1972, then in the Mkushi area from 1972 until 1975," she explained.

"I know this James Martin," Phiri said. "He was at the Kasalia Copper Mines operation at Mtuga, and I helped him bring in a large convoy of earth-moving equipment from Malawi. Where are they now?"

"They live in the States, in Utah," she replied.

"Well, good for them," Phiri said. "So, I imagine what you need from us in the ownership change history from 1975 until either it was moved to Botswana, or if it's still registered in Zambia, who the current owner is?"

"That would be most useful, Sir," Marieke agreed. "I have my people checking back our own records to see if we can find when it may have entered the country, but it's been fifteen years since James Martin sold it, and I'm not sure how quickly we can search through all the records from 1975 until now."

"I understand," he said. "I will have someone look into this chop chop and will call you when I have results," Phiri said.

"Thank you, Sir," Marieke said.

"Give my friend Ian my regards and perhaps one day you and I will meet face to face, go well, how is it that you say it, *tsamaya sentlê*," Phiri said.

"Stay well, Sir, or as we would say, *sala sentlê*, goodbye," Marieke said. She had been surprised that her Assistant Commissioner had called first, but it had helped getting her past all the usual hurdles one finds in any organisation. She thought to herself that Ian must have been a popular name once, as it was also the name of the current Commander of the Botswana Defence Force, Ian Khama. She debated going to see Assistant Commissioner Mochage but decided that with nothing further to report, there was little point. So, instead, she decided to make a trip to the hospital and the morgue and consult with Thabo.

"Marieke," Thabo greeted her when she arrived at the morgue.

"*Dumela Rra,*" she replied. "How has your day begun?"

"Busy," he said. "We had a bad traffic accident last night, and they are all over there waiting. But, for you, I have preliminary findings."

"Thank you," she said. "If you will give me a short précis?"

"Of course," he said. "First person, male, Caucasian, age mid-fifties, based on the normal bone characteristics, circumcised, hair dark brown, based on genital area hair, height, probably 178cm, weight I estimate at 76kg, that may vary a little depending on how much blood was lost when the head was removed, no debilitating illnesses of the major organs, x-rays of the lungs indicate shadowing typical of an upbringing in an industrial society, no apparent cause of death in the torso, simple fracture of the right radius, probably more than some years ago, no other bone injuries, no toxins present in the blood, what was left of it, as we noted before, no fingerprints, burned off post mortem, no skin ailments, that was hard to check as some decomposition had set in, but there is an obvious scar of an old injury on the left forearm. I would put the time of death as about a week before you found the corpses. There were no personal effects on or about the person. Based on my observations of the marks on the vertebræ, I surmise that the beheading was done with an axe. I count three blows to fully sever the head, the actual point of separation was between the fifth and sixth cervical vertebræ."

"So, based on the lung shadowing, likely not someone raised here in Botswana?" she asked.

"No," he confirmed. "I have a friend at the Pneumoconiosis Bureau in Zambia and he has done quite of study of lung shadowing. Those raised in an industrial society, like England or Germany, have a greater degree of shadowing than someone raised even in Kitwe, let alone someone from the rural areas. The same logic would apply here. Even we in Gabs with our traffic and other pollutants cannot compare with European pollution and the effect it has on the lungs."

"Thank you," she said. "And the second?"

"Second person, female, also Caucasian, age mid-fifties, hair colour blonde, height about 167cm, weight estimated at 57kg, unless, of course, she had an unusually large head. No jewellery, no rings, earrings or the like, but judging by skin colour, a ring was worn on the left fourth finger, a scar from appendectomy. Again, no major debilitating illnesses obvious in the major organs, similar lung X-ray shadowing, simple fractures of the right tibia and the left ulna, again more than some years ago. No toxins present in the blood, no apparent cause of death in the torso, no skin ailments, again no fingerprints, time of death about a week ago. Evidence of earlier childbearing, and evidence of more recent sexual activity, I would guess consensual, as there is no evidence of bruising or other tearing. With the beheading, same tool as with the first victim, an axe seems the most likely tool, in her case the severing was between the fourth and fifth cervical vertebræ," he replied.

"I see," she said. "So likely cause of death was something to do with the heads, either directly from beheading or blows to the head or gunshots to the head?"

"That is a reasonable working hypothesis," he agreed. "But, based on my supposition that it took three blows to sever each head, I would suggest that the beheading was done post mortem. I cannot imagine anyone sitting idly by while their partner is having their head hacked off, so cause of death is likely to be something more direct. If you want to find out how they died, you will need the heads. Interestingly, whoever buried the corpses buried them too deep. The soil temperature at the bottom of the hole was only 20°, which would slow up the set-in of decomposition compared to near-surface burial. If they had buried them closer to the surface, decomposition would have been more advanced, or the hyæna would have dug them up and polished them off before you got to them."

"Thank you, Thabo," she said. "I have been thinking that I may have to go back to the site of the burial and try and backtrack the vehicles."

"That's a tall order," Thabo said. "Is it possible?"

"The safari operators told me that the track probably used by the people to get the bodies to the burial site is rarely used, so for some miles at least it may be possible to track them," she said. "I'll take one of the San with me and see what we can do between us."

"I heard that you are pretty good yourself," Thabo commented.

"I have some minor skills," she admitted. "But two sets of eyes are better than one."

"Well, good luck," Thabo said.

Marieke went back to her office. At least she had a starting point; she was looking for a white middle-aged couple. That sounded simple enough, except, was she looking for residents or visitors. The obvious place to start was missing persons' reports, so she called Isaac and asked him to check on that. The thing she really wanted to do was find the heads. But, to find two heads in the whole of Botswana sounded on the face of it like a foolish notion. But she reasoned, she could probably narrow down the search area. As the bodies were buried up near the Linyanti River, the place of beheading was likely to be south of there, but probably not as far south as the Central Kalahari. She guessed it would be between Maun and the Linyanti River. To the West lay the Okavango Delta, and if the heads were in there, she would never find them, except by some sheer chance. The Okavango seemed unlikely, because if that is where the people were killed, why not just dump the bodies into the water and let the crocodiles take care of them. Her search area was beginning to narrow. She consulted a map and saw that the tracks that Bridget had pointed out led back to Khwai, south of Khwai, the chances of backtracking anyone were remote, as the traffic volume was high enough to quickly obscure the tyre tracks she would be looking for. Even on the Transit Roads, it might be difficult, be it also might be possible. Inaction was not her style, so she decided that a trip was in order and went to see Assistant Commissioner Mochage.

"*Dumela Mma*," he greeted her.

"*Dumela Rra*," she replied.

"So, Matshwane, what do you have to tell me?" he asked.

"I called Chief Superintendent Phiri, as you suggested, Sir," she replied. "Thank you for clearing the way for me. He said that he will have someone check on the vehicle, chop chop, as he put it."

"Ah, I see, anything else?" he asked.

"I have the preliminary PM results, cause of death would appear to be directly related to the heads, there is no other cause apparent on the torsos, and nothing in the major organs suggests poisons or other agents," she said. "We are looking for two whites who are middle-aged, probably in their mid-fifties."

"That could be any number of residents or visitors," he remarked. "Are there any reported missing?"

"I have Sergeant Maphosa checking just that," she replied. "But, I have to say that I am not expecting any reports."

"Why not?" he asked.

"There was too much thought and planning given to this," she said. "I believe that our villain or villains had knowledge of the plans of the victims and made their arrangements accordingly. So, the victims were probably on a pre-planned trip and would not be expected back immediately, and therefore would not be reported missing, at least for a while."

"So, what is it that you plan to do?" he asked.

"I want to try backtracking the Land Rovers to see if I can find the place where the murders actually happened," she said.

"Do you believe you can do that?" he asked. "It's been over a week since they were killed."

"I believe I can get a long way to the place," she explained. "The track that our villain probably would have used is rarely travelled, and if I take a San tracker with me, I think that between us we can follow the tracks south a long way."

"So, you see yourself as a present-day Napoleon Bonaparte, the one made famous in the novels of Arthur Upfield?" he asked.

"I'm sorry, Sir, who?" she asked.

"Upfield was a Brit who lived in Australia; he wrote novels about a police inspector with the unlikely name of Napoleon Bonaparte, who was very skilled at tracking and reading the bush and was almost always successful in solving crimes, sometimes months after they had been committed," the commissioner explained.

"Oh," she said. "Perhaps I should read some of his novels."

"Perhaps when this puzzle is solved," the commissioner suggested. "So you want to go back to the wilds and do your own tracking?"

"Yes, Sir," she confirmed.

"How long will that take?" he asked.

"Two days to get there and start, and two to three days to get back, unless I find something of note," she thought.

"Well, I suppose I can spare you for a week," he said. "Take a constable with you, preferably from Maun and one of their trackers. Go armed; I am not sure who you might encounter along the way. That area is mostly concessions; do you know who has which concession and where the boundaries are?"

"No, Sir," she said. "I thought I would visit the Game Department this afternoon and see whose concessions I would be driving through."

"Fine, one more thing," he said. "My wife and I are having a small get-together this evening. Could you drag yourself away from the office and your tracking plans long enough to join us?"

"Of course, Sir," she said. "Not to be indelicate, Sir, but how formal is this get-together?"

"Informal," he replied. "But not bush informal, I think skirt and blouse or a dress would make my wife happy."

"Thank you, Sir," she said, wondering what she had in her wardrobe that would fit the bill.

"Good, then we'll see you at seven," he said. Marieke left his office and wondered if his invitation and that of Mbali the day before were both attempts to match her with someone. She was not averse to the idea but had yet to meet the right person. Danie had been the right person, but his death ten years earlier was still hard to take. Phineas seemed nice enough, but he lived in Maun, which was hardly conducive to any kind of lasting relationship.

Marieke went back to her own office, then decided to see if she could get a decent Land Rover to take. Many that they had were ancient and tended to be temperamental, but she knew that they did have a few newer ones. So, if they were not all checked out, then she would take one. She was in luck; she happened to be in the vehicle garage when they brought in a new Land Rover. It had just come from being painted and having a radio installed. The garage supervisor told her that it had yet to be assigned, so she asked if she could use it for a week. He saw no problems but failed to ask the obvious question: what was she going to do, and where would she be going. He did point out that it had been equipped with extra fuel tanks that gave it a range of about 1,000km, which meant that she could drive all the way to Maun without having to stop for petrol. She then drove to the Game people's offices and asked to see the records of who had what concessions in the Linyanti area and south to Khwai. They provided her with a map with the concessions marked and the names of the current lessees listed. They also told her that several of the lessees actually employed resident managers, who were on the property while they stayed elsewhere, usually in Gaborone. Her next stop was the police armoury, where she signed out a rifle and a shotgun with ammunition for both. From the forensics team, she collected shovels, rakes and a set of sieves as well as evidence bags and plastic boxes, suitable for carrying heads, and some tape to restrict access to possible crime scenes. She then got herself some water containers and the other camping gear she would need for the trip. That done, she checked at the office to see if Chief Superintendent Phiri had called back yet. He had not, so apparently the Zambians were

53

still digging out old records. Sergeant Maphosa stopped at her office and told her that there were no reports of missing white people, which was not unexpected news. Her last task was to call Inspector Moroka and tell him she was coming back to Maun, and why, and request one of his constables, preferably female, and a San tracker. He was happy to oblige and told her that he would assign Constable Sephoto to her, the San tracker he would see who was available. Now she had to go home, wash and decide what in her meagre wardrobe would pass as casual in the big city of Gaborone.

Marieke stood in front of the rack where she had her clothes hanging and pondered. She had a blue skirt that went with a blouse and a blazer, but that looked too much like a uniform; she had a green dress, a red dress and a black dress. Black, she felt, might be too formal, so it was going to be green or red. In the end, she opted for the red and then pondered shoes, heels, flats or sandals. Black sandals won the day, they had a slight heel and dainty straps, so could not be said to be too informal, not that she had that wide a selection of shoes, her mainstays were boots, of which she had several pairs, but they really did not set off a tailored suit or a dress very well. Marieke sighed and accepted the fact that, as much as she disliked shopping, shopping had to be done. In Tsabong, casual clothes were the norm, but here in Gaborone, she would need more variety. So, a trip to Woolworths was in order, unless she could find a dressmaker among the many traders of the town. But, even that meant waiting for measurements to be taken, fabrics to be selected, and fittings to be endured. No, better to buy ready-made if it would fit reasonably well, and she had probably better do it sooner rather than later.

Her only other problem was the fact that she had anticipated an early start in the morning, so she had left her car at the station and brought the Land Rover home. Ah, well, it was an event at the home of the assistant commissioner, so some police vehicles would not be unexpected. She drove to the commissioner's house and found a place to park, not too far away. There were quite a few cars already there, in the driveway and on the nearby street, but as of yet, no other police vehicles. As she walked to the door, she heard her name called and turned to see Thabo Mosiwa.

"*Dumela Rra*," she said. "You are also invited to the commissioner's soirée?"

"*Dumela* Marieke, we are indeed," Thabo confirmed. "Marieke, this is my wife, Violet."

"*Dumela Mma*," Marieke said.

"Assistant Superintendent Marieke Englebrecht was recently transferred from Tsabong to Gabs," Thabo explained to Violet. "She is the reason I went flying off to the wilds of the Linyanti area."

"Your husband is not with you?" Violet asked.

"I'm not married," Marieke replied. "I had a romantic involvement some years ago, but it ended when he died in a bad traffic accident."

"I'm so sorry," Violet said. "That was thoughtless of me."

"No, no, it's fine," Marieke assured her. "It's been ten years now."

"I think the commissioner is trying to set her up with someone," Thabo said. "We'll see who he has invited tonight."

"How does Gaborone compare with Tsabong?" Violet asked.

"Obviously, Gabs is a much bigger city," Marieke said. "Tsabong is truly a rural area and one where speaking Afrikaans had its advantages. We had a lot of cross-border traffic. We had some crime, but at least lately we drove around in cars, it wasn't that long ago when I would do patrols on a camel."

"Who's talking about camels?" Assistant Commissioner Mochage asked as he opened the door, having watched their progress up the driveway.

"I was telling Thabo and Violet that I was thankful not to have to ride camels anymore," Marieke explained.

"No, now you have Land Rovers that you go through quickly. I often wondered what you did out there that you went through so many Land Rovers so quickly. Perhaps we should have kept the camels active instead of keeping them penned up with no work," the commissioner joked.

"The environment is hard on any vehicle," Marieke explained to Violet. "It is hot and dusty, and none of our roads were any good. Plus, it is a large area to administer, so we often have to drive many miles just for the simplest things. In some ways, camels are better, because as long as there is browse for them to find, the only supplies we need for a long trek in the bush are food and water for ourselves, and camels don't break down like Land Rovers."

"Why don't we all go inside?" the commissioner suggested. "There really is no need for you to linger on the threshold."

Marieke looked around the home and decided that the commissioner had good taste, at least. The house was quite large, and the main room opened out to a patio at the back and a yard sheltered by mature trees. There, she saw most of the other guests, all enjoying the slightly cooler air of the evening.

"Come," the commissioner said. "Let me introduce you to some people." He led her around and made introductions to bank managers, Mbali included, solicitors, business people, including at least one mining executive and one from the beef industry, and finally several professors from the university. All in all, a cross-section of the more affluent members of society. Her last introduction was to his wife, Lerato, a tall, elegant woman who could have easily been a model in earlier years. He made the introduction, then excused himself to mingle with other guests.

"Welcome to Gabs," she said to Marieke. "How are you settling in?"

"I've been busy," Marieke replied. "I seem to have spent almost as much time away as I have here."

"I hope Ian gives you enough time to at least find your way around town and meet some people," Lerato said.

"I have met Mbali Lamprecht," Marieke said. "She's my bank manager."

"I like her," Lerato said. "I've only met her husband once or twice, but I like him too, such a pity that the South Africans have such peculiar laws that they have to live here."

"Those same laws were the reason my parents hid away in the wilds of South West," Marieke said. "I never knew the rest of the family; in fact, I discovered just recently that the operator of the safari camp I visited this week is the brother-in-law of my cousin."

"Ian said that you'd come across family," Lerato said. "Where does your cousin live?"

"In the States, in Utah," Marieke said. "I'm not sure what she and her husband do there, but I got the impression from his brother that he's some sort of business executive."

"Ian said that you had some personal tragedy a few years ago," Lerato commented.

"Ten years ago, my parents were killed when their car hit a landmine, and not long after that, a close friend of mine died in a bad traffic accident," Marieke explained. "It was a hard and difficult year."

"I'm so sorry," Lerato said.

"I have put all that behind me," Marieke assured her. "My parents gave me a loving home and a good education. They were just unfortunate to be in the wrong place at the wrong time."

"Even so, it is sad to lose one's loved ones," Lerato sympathised. "Who else do you know here?"

"I know Thabo Mosiwa and met his wife tonight, as I said, I know Mbali and have met her husband once, that's it," Marieke said.

"I suppose Ian paraded you around, and you have no memory of all the people he introduced you to?" Lerato laughed. "But, come; let me introduce you to just a few people."

By nine-thirty, Marieke was ready to leave. She wanted to get an early start in the morning, so she found Lerato and made her apologies, then quietly left.

"I hope you will come and see me when you return from your travels," Lerato said.

"I'm not sure whether it will be travels or travails," Marieke laughed. "But, thank you, I would be delighted to see you again."

"Leaving so soon?" Ian asked as he saw her heading towards the door.

"I'm afraid so, Sir," she apologised. "I want to get an early start in the morning to drive to Maun."

"Try not to scratch that nice new Land Rover," he joked. "I think one of the traffic people had his eye on it."

"I'll do my best, Sir," she promised. "I will try and call in, but I will definitely report in when I get back to Maun after I have visited the crime scene again."

"Good luck," he said. "Go well."

"Stay well," she replied and then left to drive home, pack for the trip and put together a lunch to take.

At five the following morning, Marieke was on the road, driving in the early morning darkness before the sun came up. It would be a while before there was even a glimmer in the Eastern sky as the sun came up. There were only a few lorries on the road and an occasional car, so not much to impede her travel. It was early enough that the traffic stops that the Police Traffic Division often set up were not operating yet, so no queues of cars to wait behind. Once out of the town, the speed limit changed, and she was able to go much faster, almost to 120kph, which was quite exhilarating. Driving on roads around Tsabong generally called for much slower speeds. The gravel surfaces were just not as forgiving as the tarmac on the main road from Gaborone to Mahalapye, which she reached about fifteen minutes after sunrise. After Mahalapye, it was only a short drive before she left the main road and took the road to Serowe. Between the two diamond mines of Letlhakane and Orapa, she did encounter a police roadblock but was gratified that they waved her through with a snappy salute. She reached Maun at two in the afternoon and went straight to the police station.

"Good afternoon, Superintendent," Inspector Moroka said.

"Good afternoon, Inspector," she replied. "How are you today?"

"I am well, thank you," he replied. "And you?"

"Tired, but well," she said.

"May we offer you some tea?" he asked.

"That would be most welcome," she said. "May I use your telephone, I need to call my office and see if I have heard from the Zambians yet."

"Of course," he said. "I will be back with the tea."

Marieke called her office, and Sergeant Maphosa told her that Chief Superintendent Phiri had indeed called and had suggested that she call when she had reached Maun, as it was the weekend, he had left his home number. She thanked Maphosa, and as he had nothing else to share, hung up and called Zambia.

"Good afternoon, Miss Englebrecht," Chief Superintendent Phiri said when he answered the telephone.

"Good afternoon, Sir," she replied. "I understand from my sergeant that you have been successful in your search?"

"We have indeed," he confirmed. "Your Land Rover was sold to a Roy Bennett of Luanshya in 1975. He then sold it to a William Morris, also of Luanshya, in 1985, and Morris subsequently moved to Botswana to the Selibi Pikwe mine in May of 1986. I checked with the tax people and the immigration people, and he left Zambia via the Kazungula ferry for Botswana on the fifteenth of May of 1986."

"Thank you, Sir," she said. "That is most helpful. If there is ever anything that you need from the Botswana Police, please do not hesitate to call upon me for assistance."

"Thank you," he replied. "Well, good hunting."

"Thank you, Sir, good afternoon," she said. She then immediately called Sergeant Maphosa back and told him to check on the change of number for the Land Rover in the latter part of May and early June of 1986, and find out if Morris was still at Selibi Pikwe and, if not, had he sold the Land Rover and to whom.

"Is everything well?" Inspector Moroka asked when he brought the tea.

"We have a lead," Marieke explained. "We now know who brought the Land Rover into Botswana; we now have to find out if that same man still owns the Land Rover and if not, who does."

"Excellent," the inspector said. "Assistant Superintendent Englebrecht, this is Constable Constance Sephoto."

"*Dumela Mma*," Marieke said. "Thank you for coming with me on this trip. Do you have your bag packed for a three or four-day trip into the bush?"

"Yes, Madame," Constance said. "We have also arranged for Tushay, one of our trackers, to join us; he is from the area in the Tsodilo Hills."

"My great great great grandfather was named Tgao," Marieke said. "He was San who lived in the 1850s and painted in the Tsodilo Hills."

"I wonder if our Tushay is also a descendant of your Tgao?" Inspector Moroka said.

"That is unlikely," Marieke said. "All the band were killed in Angola by slavers, except for my great grandfather and his father."

"Where does the Englebrecht side come from?" the inspector asked.

"My great great grandfather, Jan Englebrecht, trekked north through what was then Bechuanaland, lost his team and was rescued by the band of Tgao. He married the daughter of Tgao, and they had a son, Koos. After the slaughter in Angola, *Oom* Jan and Koos walked back to Cape Town and started a new life," Marieke explained.

"Quite a saga," the inspector commented.

"It must have been quite difficult for them," Marieke said. "I confess that until I heard the story, I had no idea the San bands roamed so far afield. But, enough of me, how is my forensic technician doing?"

"He has been cooped up with that Land Rover for a while," the inspector said. "We should go and see him and get him to take a break." They walked out of the police station to an adjacent shed and saw the Land Rover there with the technician, Sipho, making some notes.

"*Dumela Rra,*" Marieke greeted him.

"*Dumela Mma,*" he replied. "Thabo said you would be coming today and would want to know what I've found."

"That would be interesting before we leave to try and backtrack this person," Marieke agreed.

"Well, as you expect, the mud is mainly from the *dambo* where you found it," Sipho said. "Beneath the mud is sand, but sand that is found in most of northern Botswana. I found no soil, sand or mud samples that are unique, so cannot direct you to any particular geographic location, based on soils alone."

"And trees?" Marieke asked.

"As you would expect, most of what I found in the radiator grill, and on the steering gear, front axles and springs, is grass and such, but there were also plenty of leaves and seed pods of mopane, *colophospermum mopane,*" Sipho said. "I also found, *acacia hereroensis*, mountain thorn, *acacia senegai*, three-thorned acacia, *ozoroa paniculosa*, common resin tree, *maytenus senegalensis*, confetti tree and *pappea capensis*, known as doppruim, or jacket plum, but next door in Zim as the *indaba* tree, there was also evidence of the leadwood, *combretum imberbe* and the sycamore fig, *ficus sycomorus*. Look for a place where the *indaba* tree, the confetti tree, a leadwood and a sycamore fig are growing close together."

"Thank you," Marieke said. "How much longer do you think you will be?"

"I think by the end of today, I will have this all done," Sipho said. "Then I'll write it up and have it on your desk by the day after tomorrow."

"Thank you, *Rra*," she said. "So, perhaps a place with an *indaba* tree and confetti trees, plus the other two."

They left Sipho to finish up his work, and the inspector asked if she planned to leave that afternoon. She said that she would as soon as she had filled the Land Rover with petrol and had her lunch.

"Constable, perhaps you could take the Superintendent's Land Rover and fill it with petrol," Inspector Moroka said.

"It has long-range tanks, so expect to put a lot in," Marieke said. "May I use your radio to call Pitse, Inspector?"

"Of course," he said.

When Constance returned with the Land Rover, she also had with her Tushay, Marieke introduced herself, then said her farewells to Inspector Moroka and suggested to Constance that she drive. Tushay sat in the back, quiet as the two women talked about what they were seeing on the road. They had about three hours of daylight left, and then it would be another two hours or so in the dark before they reached the Pitse Safari Camp.

"May I ask Madame?" Constance began. "What do we expect to find?"

"I'm going to try and backtrack the Land Rover we were just looking at, plus another one, to see if we can find where our victims were killed," Marieke replied.

"Excuse the directness of this question," Constance continued. "But how did you acquire the name Matshwane?"

Marieke laughed and said, "That's what the station at Tsabong called me, they thought that I was like the ratel, once I got onto something, I wouldn't let it go until we had a solution."

"Do you know the people at Pitse Safari?" Constance asked.

"I met them when I was here a few days ago," Marieke said. "It turns out that William Martin is the brother-in-law of my cousin."

"Excuse me, Madame," Tushay said. "I heard that you are San?"

"Only a small part from many years ago," Marieke replied. "My *Oom* Jan trekked north to Tsodilo and there met Motshaba, daughter of Tgao."

"I know this story," Tushay said. "I met two people in the Central Kalahari who were there to dig up things that this Jan buried."

61

"That would have been my cousin Katrina and her husband James," Marieke explained.

"Who are the people we are looking for?" Tushay asked.

"I don't know," Marieke admitted. "We found two bodies with no heads, and a Land Rover with no number plates. We have identified the Land Rover, but we don't know who owns it now and even if it was the owner that we found. We know we are looking for two people because there were tracks of two Land Rovers close to the place where we found the bodies. What I want to do is try and follow the Land Rovers back as far as we can to try and find where the people were before. The Land Rover we found belonged to the Katrina and James, whom you met in the Central Kalahari."

"Where will we stay tonight?" Constance asked.

"We will stay at the Pitse Safari camp," Marieke said.

"Don't they have guests?" Constance asked.

"They do," Marieke confirmed. "But they have accommodation for others like us. I stayed there when I was here a few days ago."

It was eight in the evening when they finally came to the Pitse Safari camp. They were expected, and Bridget showed them where they would sleep and then invited them all to dinner. Tushay excused himself and went off to talk to Jackson, Rice and the other trackers, leaving Marieke and Constance to answer questions from the guests. The guests were just finishing dinner and were sitting discussing the day over coffee. They had had a good day with a sighting of a wild dog pack that they had watched for some time, then they had come across a lion kill and had wiled away the rest of the day watching that.

"Good evening, Superintendent," Bob said. "We didn't expect you back so soon."

"Good evening," she replied. "We're going to try and backtrack the Land Rovers to see if we can discover where they came from."

"Won't that be really hard?" Bronwyn asked.

"Probably impossible," Marieke laughed. "But, we will try."

"Who is your companion?" Cindy asked.

"I'm so sorry, this is Constable Constance Sephoto from the Maun police station, she will be coming with me on my expedition," Marieke explained.

"How do you like being a police officer?" Roberta asked Constance.

"It is interesting," Constance replied. "But, most of my work so far has been in Maun and the usual policing duties, this is a very different assignment and I'm really looking forward to it. Excuse me for asking, but where are you from?"

"We're from Bountiful in the state of Utah," Roberta replied. "At least four of us are, the others of us are from England and Wales."

"How do you like our country?" Constance asked.

"I love it," Roberta said. "The people we've met have been so nice, the game viewing is unbelievable, we've had such an amazing time."

"Are you from Maun?" George asked.

"No, I am originally from Ghanzi, which is a small town to the West and south of Maun," Constance explained. "I went through the police training school and was assigned to Maun."

"Well, good luck in your hunt tomorrow," Fiona said. "I don't envy you your task."

"Were you able to learn anything about James's Land Rover?" Bridget asked.

"We were," Marieke replied. "We learned that he sold it in 1975 to a man in Luanshya, who sold it to someone else, and that that person brought it to Botswana when he was transferred to the mine at Selibi Pikwe. On another note, our tracker, Tushay, met your brother-in-law and my cousin Katrina when they visited the Central Kalahari Park sometime in the seventies."

"The world is truly a small place," Cindy commented. "Or, perhaps Botswana is, and paths cross and re-cross."

"Excuse me for changing the subject," Bridget said. "What time do you plan to leave in the morning, Superintendent?"

"I think about 6:00 would be fine," Marieke replied. "I would like to get some of the early morning sun on the tracks."

"I will have a packed breakfast and lunches for you when you leave," Bridget promised.

"Thank you," Marieke said. "Now, if you will all excuse me, it has been a long day."

Just before six the next morning, the police left the safari camp and drove to the *dambo* location where the bodies had been buried.

"So, Constance, what do you see?" she asked.

"A small clearing, I can see where you dug the hole, I see vehicle tracks both going that way and coming back from that way and then leaving down this road," Constance said. "The footprints, I presume, were yours and the others from our station and from Gaborone."

"Quite right," Marieke said. "When we first came here, the clearing was swept clean of any footprints, there was no evidence of any fire, there was no evidence of large blood loss, so we concluded that the heads had been removed elsewhere."

"How did you find the bodies?" Constance asked.

"Blowflies," Marieke explained. She noticed Tushay nodding his head in understanding.

"Madame," he said. "Where do we find the tracks of the Land Rovers that have not been run over by police vehicles?"

"This way," she said, and led the way to the junction in the roads where they could see tracks of the police vehicles coming and going from one direction and another set of tracks going away to the South. Tushay went a little down the road and then said, "Two cars came north and then one of those same cars went back south. It should be easy to follow him. They forgot to brush out the tracks of their boots, here and here."

"We should make plaster casts of the boot tracks," Marieke said. "Your testimony in court would be accepted by most, Tushay, but some lawyers will try and argue that we forced you into identifying the tracks. Constance, if you look in the Land Rover, you will find the kits. Tushay, what can you tell me about these people?"

"Two men, Madame," he replied. "One, short and fussy, about 5' 4", he walks with short steps as though he is always in a hurry. He has no limp or other feature to his walk, but he does turn his toes inwards. The boots may be small for a man, but I would definitely say that this is not a woman. The second is a taller man, probably 6' 2". He walks with his feet straight, turning toes neither inward nor outward. He favours his right leg, so may have had an old injury."

"Thank you," Marieke said.

"I'm finished, Madame," Constance said. "What do we do now, follow these people south?"

"That is what I had hoped," Marieke said. "To follow them as far as we could. I suggest we ride until we see something that indicates they either got out of the car or changed directions."

"Very good, Madame," Tushay agreed. "I will sit on the spare tyre on the bonnet if you do not drive too fast."

"Good," Marieke agreed. "Constance, would you drive, not too fast, we don't want to lose Tushay."

On the trail

They drove south, bouncing along the rough track, but not enough that Tushay was in any danger of being thrown from the vehicle. After an hour, he held up his hand and they stopped. Tushay got down from his perch and walked down the track for a short way, then came back and reported. "When they were driving north, the one pulled up next to the other, perhaps for a short conference, then they set out again with the one we have in Maun leading."

"Did anyone get out, or did they just come up next to each other?" Marieke asked.

"The front one pulled off the track, and the second one left the track there and pulled up beside the first one. Then they left in the same order," Tushay explained. "There, the tracks of the other Land Rover going back south cover the northbound tracks."

"Fine," Marieke said. "Shall we continue? We must be getting close to the end of the Martins' concession, next should be Botha. Do you know anything about him?"

"Not much, Madame," Constance replied. "He only got this concession a year ago and has been leading hunting parties throughout the season. I think the Game Department people are suspicious of his activities, but so far have not been able to find anything definite."

"Do they think he's been poaching?" Marieke asked.

"I think exceeding licence limits, which I suppose puts it into the area of poaching," Constance explained.

"Has the Maun police station had any issues with him?" Marieke asked.

"He's an old-time Afrikaner," Constance replied. "He just has a difficult time dealing with anyone black who has authority, but so far, we've had no reports of crimes that lead back to him."

"How does he deal with the Game Department then?" Marieke asked.

"I think he accepts that he has to deal with them and just mutters away to himself in Afrikaans," Constance said. Tushay signalled a stop and got down to examine the ground. Marieke and Constance joined him. There was a track that cut across the road they were following. It had obviously been used recently and frequently.

"These people went after the ones we are following," Tushay said. "They went west, then returned, about five days ago, then they went west this morning. This is not the Land Rover we are following."

"So, I wonder if they saw anything?" Marieke said. "Well, we'll find out soon enough. It looks as if they are returning." They watched as a Land Rover came from the West and stopped just short of the junction. A white man got out and walked towards them. Marieke heard him muttering and caught, *a fucking kaffir, a verdomde goffel and a Bushman, man what a fucking gemors.* "What are you doing here?" he demanded. "This is my concession, and you need my permission to enter."

"And you are?" Marieke asked.

"Pik Botha, this is my concession. Who are you?" he asked.

"It should be obvious from our Land Rover that we are Botswana Police," Marieke said. "I am Assistant Superintendent Englebrecht, and we are exercising our right to pursue suspects, wherever that might lead."

"Suspects?" Botha said. "My papers are in order, my permits are in order, the licences of all my clients are in order."

"Suspects for murder, Mr Botha," Marieke said.

"Murder, man, don't try and hang anything on me, I've murdered no one," Botha protested.

"I did not say that you had," Marieke said. "How often do you use this track?"

"About once or twice a month," Botha said.

"Last week, when you went west and returned, did you see anyone going north?" Marieke asked.

"How do you know that I went west a week ago? Oh, I suppose the Bushman told you that. No, I didn't see anyone a week ago," Botha said. "Don't tell me that the *rooineks* to the North got rid of one of their tree-hugging, nature-loving clients."

"No, Mr Botha," Marieke said. "We are looking for a Land Rover that went north about a week ago, in company with another, and then came back on its own."

"I haven't seen anyone else for months," Botha said. "You're telling me that someone came through my concession a week ago?"

"Yes, they went north and then came back south, there had to be two people, and we are keen to find them and interview them," Marieke said.

"Can't help you," Botha said.

"What day did you go west and then return?" Marieke asked.

"That would have been Monday," Botha said.

"And you saw no other vehicles?" Marieke asked.

"Sorry, can't help," Botha repeated. "Maybe the PH who takes out clients for me can help, I'll ask him next time he's in Botswana."

"Thank you Mr Botha, *tot siens, geniet die dag*," Marieke said. Botha looked up sharply and had the grace to redden slightly, then he grunted a *tot siens* and drove off quickly to the East. They watched him go and then returned to the task at hand. Marieke looked at Constance and shrugged her shoulders, "I suppose people like him will always exist, it must drive him to distraction that he has to defer to black people."

"I suppose so," Constance agreed. "I don't know if he is a citizen of Botswana or is here on a visa."

"Well, as it is not his Land Rover we are following, we'll leave that to the immigration people, we should carry on south," Marieke said.

Tushay climbed back onto his perch, and they continued south until they came to another road that crossed. Tushay signalled a halt and climbed down to have a look at the tracks. "These are really old," he said. "They were here before our people went north, and there has been no one since."

They went on, and Tushay called a halt. He jumped off the front of the Land Rover and walked about looking at things. "The other Land Rover had a puncture, rear right," he said. "Here they changed the wheels, taking one from the Land Rover we have in Maun. Here also is a track that crosses, and another vehicle was here; they stopped, and here you see he got out and went to talk to that one. Then he got back into his own *bakkie* and left."

That explained the odd tyre that was on the back of the Land Rover that they had found. It also meant that the other Land Rover now had one odd Michelin tyre. Marieke noted that and her best estimate of the location on her map. She also noted to herself that it would be useful if they could find the person who stopped; he, and Tushay had said it was a man, would be able to identify the two drivers. A little farther south, and again Tushay signalled another halt. He got down and walked about a bit, then came back and got a shovel and dug in a couple of places. Finally satisfied with what he had found, he reported to Marieke, "Our second Land Rover is a diesel. Here they filled up, that one with petrol, this one with diesel."

"That's useful, onward then," Marieke said, after also noting that and the place on her map. "We must be almost to Khwai."

"I think we are close to the Khwai Safari Lodge, Madame," Constance said. She was right; Tushay signalled another halt and got down from his perch. "They went that way, Madame," he said. "From here we have other traffic, so it may take more time to follow them."

"Very well, Tushay," Marieke said, hoping that the traffic had been light enough that the tracks were not totally obscured. The road took a sharp turn to the East, then meandered around for a while before it came to another junction. "They came from the South, and one went back to the South," Tushay announced. "You can see the tracks there and there." They followed at a much slower pace until they came to a spot where both sets of tracks could be seen joining the road from a small side track. Marieke thought about it and decided to follow the two trails. It might lead them to the scene of the original crime. They were in the Khwai River floodplain area, so the trees were more lush and animals abounded. There were pockets of water here and there, perfect places to camp near. Tushay led them off the side track they had been following to an even less-used track that eventually led to a small clearing by a *dambo*. Marieke and Constance got out of the Land Rover, and they stood at the edge of the clearing looking for clues. The clearing looked very like the one Marieke had seen to the North. It had been swept clean and only had animal tracks, with some digging by small animals in places. One place in particular seemed to have attracted a lot of attention.

"Over there," Marieke said. "The soil colour suggests the remains of a fire; I would have pitched a tent over there. The first Land Rover was parked there; there are faint indentations in the soil, probably next to the tent. A second Land Rover came, look at the indentations in the soil over there, it's been swept, but if you crouch down, you can still see the tracks. What else do we see?"

"Flies, Madame, lots of them over there, where the animals have been digging," Constance pointed.

"Fine, Constance, park the Land Rover over there and we'll begin by going over this clearing carefully. We're looking for clothing items, anything that might tell us what happened," Marieke instructed. "What trees do we have here?"

"I see an *indaba* tree, over there is a confetti tree, we're parked under a fig, and that's a leadwood, but generally it's mopane," Constance replied.

"Good," Marieke said. "We may be in the right place. When you've parked the Land Rover, please bring a rake, a shovel and a sieve."

"Yes, Madame," Constance said. She then quickly moved the Land Rover and brought the items that Marieke had asked for.

"Before we start, let's take a look around the edge of this clearing," Marieke said. "We'll start here and walk in the tree line and see what we can spot." They set off skirting the clearing, staying in the trees, until Tushay stopped and pointed.

"Ah, I see," Marieke said. "Someone vomited here, and another over there. What else?"

"Something buried there," Tushay said, pointing. Marieke looked to Constance, who took the shovel and started to dig carefully. "Tent poles," she said after unearthing them. "Tent poles and a couple of cooking pots."

"They wouldn't burn easily," Marieke thought. "Perhaps we are in the right place. Anything else?"

"No, Madame," Tushay said. "Those people only went to the trees to vomit; otherwise, they stayed in the clearing, but they have tried to cover all their tracks by raking and smoothing with bundles of leaves."

Marieke nodded agreement and then took the rake and walked carefully to the area where they suspected there had been a fire and started raking away the sand. There were a lot of ashes and little pieces of material that may have been fabric or may have been something else.

"Constance, start sieving this pile here and see what you find," Marieke instructed. While Constance was busy sieving, Marieke and Tushay scrabbled around on hands and knees looking for anything they could find. There was little in the way of large-sized objects, just fragments of paper, cloth and even plastic. Then Marieke found a .22LR cartridge case, just one, no more, no matter how much she raked and sifted sand with her fingers. It was hard to judge the age of the cartridge case, but it was still quite shiny, so not that old, perhaps a week, perhaps two weeks. The .22LR cartridge case might or might not have anything to do with their case. If it did, it would not be much use in identifying the weapon it was fired from, as the firing pin marks were not that distinctive, and the ammunition did not preserve lands and grooves of rifling very well. Constance called her over and showed her the small pile of pieces sieved out of the ashes. There were mainly clothing fragments and parts of the soles of boots, some pieces of leather and what looked like melted plastic. Whoever had burned things had done a good job of keeping the fire going to destroy as much as possible. Marieke asked Constance to get a magnet from their kit and check to see what she might find. Constance found iron filings, which Marieke thought might have been from the engine when the number was filed off. Constance also found the remnants of six pop rivets, which Marieke surmised might have been those that held the chassis plate in place. There seemed to be not much else of interest, so now it was time to turn their attention to other parts of the site.

"Let's have a look at what those flies are interested in," Marieke said to Tushay.

"Blood, Madame," Tushay said, scuffing the sand with his foot.

"So I see," Marieke agreed. "Blood, and a lot of it." She raked the sand and uncovered more bloodied soil, but no bones and certainly no heads. It was apparent that, although there was copious evidence of blood, there were no physical body parts. It was, of course, possible that an animal had been butchered there, but then she would have expected to see animal fur and perhaps small pieces of hide. So, it seemed to her more likely that this was where human heads had been separated from the bodies. Although the area immediately around the blood-soaked soil had been swept clean, there were tracks by the water's edge, tracks that had been slightly modified by the rise and fall of the water level in the *dambo*. The tracks were indistinct, but there was something odd about them.

"Tushay," she said. "If you were going to throw something into the water, what would the *spoor* look like?"

He stood by the water's edge and motioned, throwing something, his resulting tracks essentially matched those that they were looking at.

"How much does a head weigh?" Marieke mused. "Say between 4 and 5 kilos; let's see if we can find a stone that weighs about 4 kilos."

Tushay found a stone that they thought might be suitable, and Marieke checked it for weight by using four one-litre bottles of water suspended from a stick, to which she also attached the stone at the other end. Then, holding it up in the middle, she determined that the stone was at least 4 kilos. Marieke thought about things for a minute, then asked Constance to get a small net bag from their evidence collection box. She put the stone in the bag, tied some thin cord to the bag, then asked Tushay to swing the bag and throw it out into the water as far as he could. Her reasoning was that if someone was going to throw a head into the water, they would probably hold it by the hair and throw it out that way, rather than hold the head itself. They watched as Tushay tried a few practice swings until his tracks matched those already there in terms of orientation and depth of indentation, which would give them which direction heads may have been thrown, then he swung the bag and threw it out into the water. Finding it would just be a matter of following the string tied to the bag.

"I think we'll have some lunch before I go wading," Marieke said.

Bridget had done them proud, and lunch was a repast compared to the more normal meals they would grab when they could. After lunch, Marieke looked over the *dambo* carefully, looking for crocodiles and hippo. There were no hippo, but there were one or two crocodiles on the far bank, but they did not look particularly large, perhaps only a metre in length. Then she scanned the water carefully, looking for eyes and the nostrils that often were the only parts of a crocodile one would see above the water. She spotted three, but again estimated their size at only about a metre, large enough to bite, but not large enough to carry her off.

"How's your shooting, Constance?" she asked.

"I have qualified as a marksman," Constance said.

"Good, while I wade out to see what I can find, watch those crocodiles and dissuade them from coming near, and bring me the shotgun and some buckshot rounds and a towel," Marieke instructed.

"Yes, Madame, Tushay, watch for me so I don't miss any of them," Constance said; then she went to their Land Rover and got the rifle. She checked that it was loaded and chambered a round. She also brought the shotgun and handed it to Marieke, who loaded it fully with buckshot and also chambered a round. The shotgun had a sling so she would be able to carry it and keep her hands free. Finally, she stripped off her clothes down to her underwear and piled her clothes on the water's edge with the towel. Then she stepped out into the water, picking up the string as she went and following it out into the centre.

The water was not very deep, and she considered it likely that later in the dry season it would all be gone, but for now, there was quite a bit of it, fed from the Okavango delta and the runoff from Angola. The water was brownish but reasonably clear, so she could make out the bottom. When she reached the bag with the stone, she then called on Tushay to tie the end of the string to a stake, and when he had done that, she moved in an arc, anchored by the string, looking for anything that should not be there. Her first arc produced nothing, so she called to Tushay to let out a metre of string, and she tried again. That arc produced nothing, so she called for another metre and found her first head, almost straight out from where Tushay and Constance stood. While she was transferring the head to a bag, Constance fired at a crocodile that was slipping into the water in the direction of Marieke. The crocodiles might become annoying, so Marieke shouldered the shotgun and started looking around for more crocodiles. There was one headed her way that Constance could not have fired at because she was in the line of fire. She waited until it got fairly close, then shot it in the head. That took care of that one, then she noticed a second angling in for an attack. A second shotgun blast took care of that one. Satisfied that the threat, for now, was minimal, she called on Tushay for another metre of string and began her next arc. It took another metre of string and the next arc before she found the second head. She bagged that and then headed for the shore.

The gunfire had attracted attention, and they now had an audience. Parked behind their Land Rover was a Toyota Land Cruiser, and two men were getting out and walking their way. Constance saw them and went to intercept them and ask them to wait where they were until her boss arrived. They waited while Marieke got to shore and wrapped herself in the towel.

"*Dumela Rra*," she greeted them.

"*Dumela Mma*," one of the men replied. "We heard gunfire and came to investigate."

"Crocodiles," Marieke said. "I am Assistant Superintendent Englebrecht, and you are?"

"Andries Potgieter, I run the Khwai Safari Lodge."

"I am pleased to meet you," she said. "And, Koos, nice to see you again, did you fly clients in today?"

"Nice to see you again as well, Superintendent," Koos replied. "Yes, I had a charter in today and I have a run to Gabs tomorrow, then back to Jo'burg."

"I wonder if you wouldn't mind taking a package for me to Gaborone?" she asked.

"No man, that's fine," he assured her. "What do you want me to take?"

"I'll need to wrap and package them first, but I need to send these to the lab for analysis," she said, indicating the bags she had slung over her shoulder.

"Do they weigh much?" he asked.

"Perhaps 5 kilos each," she said.

"No, that'll be fine," Koos assured her. "I've only two people tomorrow from here to Gabs and I'll pick up two more there."

"What are you investigating?" Andries asked.

"It'll be those two headless *ouks* that Will and Bridget found on their concession," Koos said.

"We are pursuing leads," Marieke agreed. "Tell me, Mr Potgieter, do you remember anyone camping here about a week ago?"

"No," he said. "It's a little away from us and from the routes we use regularly for visitors."

"We believe there were two people who camped here; they would have arrived in a Series II Land Rover, Limestone in colour," she said. "After them, we believe another Land Rover came and they both left together going north."

"Sorry, we've seen about eight Land Rovers in the past week or so, maybe one of them was the one you're looking for, but I didn't take any special notice," Andries said. "We get a fair amount of traffic that passes us all going to the different camps and lodges. I know people do camp at this *dambo*, there is probably someone here every other week or so."

"Perhaps one of your staff saw someone or something?" she suggested. "There would have been a fire that was burning for some time."

"Why don't you come to the camp and ask everyone?" Andries said. "We can put you up for the night."

"Thank you," Marieke said. "Let us just finish what we are doing, and we'll come to your lodge, Constance, do you know the way?"

"Yes, Madame," Constance assured her.

"Okay," Andries said. "We'll see you in a while." As they walked away, Marieke heard Andries say to Koos, "*That's a lekker cherry,*" and Koos replied, "*Ja baie lekker, something about a meisie dressed only in her brookies and carrying a shotgun*". She was amused by the compliment, but then she thought they had watched her wade ashore in her underwear and that perhaps she should get dressed.

"So, Constance, Tushay," she said. "Is there anything else we can learn here?"

"I don't think so, Madame," Constance said. "I bagged all the small pieces of fabric, leather and plastic that I found. I also bagged that .22 cartridge case, the tent poles and samples of the vomit and the blood-soaked soil."

"Good," Marieke approved. "Tushay?"

"No, Madame," he said. "I may be able to follow the Land Rover that we were looking for, but as we come closer to Khwai and then to Maun, it will become more difficult because of the other traffic."

"Fine, bag and box these for me while I get dressed, then," Marieke said, handing the heads to Constance.

The Khwai Safari Lodge was set on a large pool on the Khwai River, which meandered its way along the edge of the Moremi Reserve. It was not quite as plush as the Khwai River Lodge, but certainly luxurious enough. There were guest quarters set on platforms overlooking the water and a common area with the requisite bar and eating area. Andries saw them arrive and came to meet them. As he had at the Pitse camp, Tushay excused himself and went off to the staff quarters to see what he could learn. Marieke asked if he had a radio they could use. Andries took them to his office, where there was a radio; Marieke called the station in Maun and asked if there were messages for her. There was one, the Land Rover belonging to William Morris, had been registered in Botswana and had been resold to an Ian Ross. Marieke asked the Maun station to get contact information for her and also asked them to inform Dr Mosiwa to expect a package the next day, to be delivered at the airport. She gave them the registration number of the plane and Koos's name. That done, she thanked Andries for the use of his radio, and he then took them to one of the platforms and showed them the showers, beds, and other amenities.

"We'll be serving dinner at about 6:30," he said. "If you'd like to join us? What about your tracker?"

"He's probably learning what he can from your staff; he may be more comfortable staying with your staff, if you don't mind," Marieke said. "Constance and I will join you presently after I've washed off this mud. If we could trouble you for some ice to help keep our specimens fresh?"

"I'll have some delivered," he promised. "I gather you've met Koos before?"

"He was kind enough to fly me to the Pitse camp earlier in the week," she explained.

"Ah, I see," he said. "Well, when you're ready, come and meet my wife, Katrina, and the guests."

Marieke was showering when she heard someone call and deliver ice. Constance re-packed the heads in plastic bags, then put the plastic bags in the plastic boxes, with ice to keep them cool. They would change the ice in the morning before Koos left. While Constance showered and changed, Marieke wrote up some notes for herself and thought that the killers had been careless to not better dispose of the heads. Surely they would have known that there was a high risk that their Land Rover could be tracked back to the *dambo*. Still, the heads did not yet provide any clues as to identity. Cause of death was apparent, though, gunshots to the head. The entry wounds were there, but no exit wounds.

When Marieke and Constance went to the dining area, the guests were already there enjoying a sundowner and the sunset. Andries saw them and waved them over to the bar.

"What will you have?" he asked.

"What white wine do you have?" Marieke asked.

"We have a nice Bellingham Chenin Blanc," Andries said.

"That sounds nice," Marieke said. "I'll try some, Constance?"

"Is it permitted, Madame?" Constance asked.

"We're not on duty at this time," Marieke assured her.

"I've never tried any wines," Constance admitted. "In Ghanzi, it was beer mainly. Let me try some."

"I should introduce you to our guests," Andries said. "Folks, this is Assistant Superintendent Englebrecht of the Botswana Police, and this is?"

"This is Police Constable Constance Sephoto from our Maun station," Marieke added.

"What brings you to Khwai?" one of the guests asked.

"We are conducting an investigation," Marieke dissembled. "How long have you been here at Khwai?"

"Three days now for all of us," the guest replied. "It's been amazing, Andries and his people do a bang-up job, and we've seen all kinds of birds and animals."

"Was it you shooting today?" another guest asked.

"I confess it was," Marieke said. "I have this aversion to being bitten by crocodiles, no matter how small."

"Superintendent, this is my wife, Katrina," Andries said.

"*Aangename kennis*," Marieke said.

"*Bly te kenne*," Katrina said. "Do you have everything you need?"

"We do, thank you," Marieke replied. "Thank you for having us here. Our alternative was to camp out in the bush, which I do enjoy, but hot showers after a long day are most welcome."

"Andries tells me that you are looking for a Land Rover that may have passed by here a week or so ago," Katrina said.

"We are," Marieke confirmed.

"We've seen a few," Katrina said. "There was a station wagon ten days ago, another two a week ago, another one five days ago, and, I think, four *bakkies* in that same time period."

"Nothing about any of them stood out?" Marieke asked. "The one we are looking for would be a diesel."

"I'm not sure," Katrina said. "None of them stopped here; they just passed us by. I only know about those because some of the children try and beg sweeties from the drivers. Oh, maybe there was one, the *lighties* told me that there was a blue *bakkie* went north, then came back south two days later. They remembered it because the driver was very unfriendly. They told me it was a *bakkie* with a canvas hood."

"Thank you," Marieke said. Possibly this might be something, or it might not be.

"So, Superintendent, how's things?" Koos asked, joining them at the bar.

"Cleaner and less muddy now," she replied. "We met before with less formality," she explained to Katrina.

"So Andries told me," Katrina said dryly. "Did you find what you were looking for as you waded around the *dambo*?"

"I found some items of interest," Marieke admitted. "We'll have to see if it is what we wanted."

"How is the Chenin Blanc?" Andries asked.

"Very good, it has tones of peach, passion fruit, honey melon, papaya and pineapple with some subtle oak," Marieke replied. "What do you think, Constance?"

"I've never had another, so cannot judge, but I like this one," she replied. "How did you learn about wines, Madame?"

"I went to university in Lyon in France," Marieke explained. "As well as studying law, I made a point of trying the many wines from the area and tried to learn a little about them."

"Dinner is served," one of the staff announced. There was a move to the table, which was long and would accommodate fourteen people.

Joining the guests and others was Moses, the head guide for the lodge, making up the fourteen for those who were superstitious. Dinner was roast impala with vegetables and other trimmings. Koos made sure that he sat next to Marieke, which amused Constance, who was sandwiched between two of the female guests who proceeded to ask about her life, from early childhood on. Koos made light conversation over dinner, not prying too much but eliciting small bits of information, between telling his own life story. He was from Messina, almost to the Limpopo. He had done his military service in the air force, where he had learned to fly. After getting out of the air force, he had got his commercial pilot's licence and bought a plane. Since then, he had been through two other planes until he had settled on the Skymaster that he now had. He offered to take Marieke on a trip one day, to wherever she wanted to go. He also told her that he was going to take a break from charter flying and try for an MBA at the University of Cape Town. He had been talking to South Africa Airways and a couple of the other carriers that flew in and out of South Africa, and he wanted to get into the management of an airline. He reasoned that an MBA would be an asset.

After dinner, Constance remarked to Marieke that Koos seemed to have taken a real liking to her. Marieke laughed at that and agreed that he was certainly trying hard to get to know her.

"Will you take his offer to fly somewhere?" Constance asked.

"I don't know," Marieke admitted. "I'm not ready for any relationships at this time, so if I do accept his offer, it's probably going to have to do with business."

"Yes, but how romantic," Constance said. "To have him offer to take you anywhere."

"Who knows what his motives are," Marieke said dryly. "Sadly, of late, my experiences with men are that they tend to have little on their minds beyond sex. But, what about you, is there anyone in your life?"

"Not yet," Constance admitted. "My father despairs that I will ever find a husband, but there is time yet, and I would like to progress in the police for a while before I think of anything else. Excuse me for asking, but how do you stay so fit and trim?"

"I run a lot," Marieke replied. "And I also practice at a karate dojo. Did you hear the comment from Katrina about the blue *bakkie* with the canvas hood?"

"I did," Constance said. "She didn't say whether it was a short or long wheelbase, how many blue open-back Land Rovers do you think there are in Botswana?"

"I would guess in the hundreds rather than the thousands," Marieke said. "But, I'll ask the traffic people if they have any quick way of sifting through registration records. We'll get onto that when we get back to Maun in the morning."

In the morning, Marieke begged more ice and they changed the ice in the plastic boxes with the heads and handed them over to Koos, who was keen to get started and be off for Gaborone. Tushay came to join them, and he had learned only what they had gleaned from Katrina, that the only Land Rover that caught the attention of anyone was the blue open-back with the canvas tilt, except that he did have one extra piece of information: it had a long wheelbase. Marieke thanked Andries and Katrina, and they then left to drive to Maun. Tushay took up his perch on the spare tyre on the bonnet, but soon he signalled for a stop and told them that there had just been too much traffic and the tracks were obscured. He said that when they got to Maun, he would keep looking for any signs of the tracks and let Constance know if he saw any. The drive back to Maun took only ninety minutes, and at the police station, Marieke called her office and talked to Sergeant Maphosa, who had little else to tell her, other than they had discovered that Ian Ross taught English at the University of Botswana. Marieke told Maphosa that she would go and see the university people as soon as she got back to Gaborone. She then sat down with Inspector Moroka and told him what they had done and what they had found. She praised both Tushay and Constance for their work and said that if she had to come back again for any reason that she would be delighted to work with them again. She did ask the inspector to canvass the petrol stations in town and find out if a blue open-back Land Rover with a canvas tilt had filled up in the past ten days to a week. Inspector Moroka suggested that Constance might do that and report back to him. Marieke thanked him again for his help and left for Gaborone.

A new house

It was five in the afternoon when Marieke got back to her office. Isaac Maphosa was still there, ard he gave her the information that the vehicle registration people had provided. She was digesting this when the commissioner walked in.

"So, Matshwane, you are back," he commented.

"I am Sir," she confirmed. "I found two heads that Thabo should have already received."

"Do those heads belong to the torsos that you found, or are we looking at an even bigger mystery?" he asked.

"I suspect that they will match," she replied. "But, I will need Thabo to confirm that for me."

"Where did you find them?" the commissioner asked.

"In a *dambo* near Khwai," she replied. "We found evidence of four trees other than mopane in the radiator grill and front axle of the Land Rover, Tushay, our San tracker, backtracked the Land Rover that we found to the *dambo*, where we found all four trees, and then we started looking. We found copious amounts of blood and large amounts of ashes with small remnants of clothing and boots. We brought back samples of everything to check on in the lab."

"Any other leads?" he asked.

"We have the name of the current owner of the Land Rover we found," she said. "I plan to try and interview him in the morning."

"Who is he?" the commissioner asked.

"One Ian Ross, a professor of English at the University," she said.

"If you need help at the University, let me know, the Vice Chancellor is my friend," the commissioner offered.

"Thank you, Sir," she said. "I hope it will not need to do that."

"Keep me informed," the commissioner said. "The Vice-Chancellor will want to know if anything has happened to any of the faculty."

"Very good, Sir," she said.

"I might be better, if there is another occasion, if you sent the tracker or the constable to wade around the *dambo,* one might argue that it is beneath the dignity of an assistant superintendent to do such mundane work," he said as he left. That left her wondering where he had got his information, and decided that it had to be via Inspector Moroka, who would have heard the tale from either Constance or Tushay, unless Koos mentioned it to Thabo, who passed it on to the commissioner. Well, it seemed unlikely that she would be wading again soon, except through the mountain of paper that seemed to have grown over the past few days. It took her until eight that evening to at least sort all the papers and divide them into piles, some she handled immediately, some she promised herself to do the next day, and some would take longer to research and fill out.

Six came quickly the next morning, and Marieke got up and made herself a reasonable breakfast, then she threw her dice and went to work via route number four. She had completed most of what she had set for the day in terms of paperwork when Sergeant Isaac Maphosa arrived.

"Please finish these last forms while I go and see Dr Mosiwa," she asked. "After that, I will be going to the university to see what I can find out about Professor Ross."

"Very good, Madame," Isaac said. "How long did the commissioner stay last night?"

"Long enough," she said. "He seems remarkably well informed."

"He does seem to have sources of information everywhere," Isaac agreed. "I try and stay out of his way."

"Well, I'll be back later," she said. "Let me know if he comes back. I'm going first to the garage to turn in the Land Rover I signed out, then I'll go on to see Dr Mosiwa."

"Well, Thabo, did you get the heads I sent you?" Marieke asked at the hospital.

"I did," Thabo confirmed. "And I heard a wondrous tale about wading around in a *dambo déshabillé*. I gather that your pilot conquest was quite enchanted."

"Oh, he was, was he?" she laughed. "He and his friend Andries arrived after the work was done and just stood around staring. But, enough of Mr Koos and his likes, what can you tell me?"

"The heads come from the bodies you found," Thabo said. "The marks on the vertebræ match perfectly. Judging by the type of marks, the tool you should be looking for is an axe. Death was almost certainly caused by bullet wounds to the heads, two for each, one of them, the male, shot from behind, and the other, the female, shot from the front. I have removed the bullets, but they are deformed considerably, and there is little to learn from them, except that weight and composition say that they are .22 long rifle rounds. So, look for a .22 pistol or rifle. The shots were fired from some distance away, not close up, and the grouping of the entry wounds is tight, suggesting that the shooter had some skill and got off two rounds for each head in very quick succession before the bodies started to fall. Most of the soft tissue is gone, probably to creatures living in the water, the eyes are gone, but much of the hair remains, and confirms hair colour that we had established before."

"Were you able to get dental X-rays?" she asked.

"I did," he confirmed. "But, of course, that will be for verification purposes only; we have no means to find people through dental records."

"I also suppose that if they are visitors, then there would be no dental records in Botswana anyway," she commented.

"True," he agreed. "I gather you have other materials for us?"

"I do," she confirmed. "I have evidence bags here, with remnants of clothing, boots and other items from a fire, and a sample of the bloody soil and some vomit we found."

"Vomit?" he asked.

"My conjecture is that the beheading process was a little more gruesome than anticipated and that first the spectator vomited, then the actual beheader," she said.

"That makes sense," he said. "Particularly when you consider that it took two to three blows of the axe to sever each head."

"Anything else?" she asked.

"Tell me about this, Koos," he said.

"He's a pilot that I happened to have run into twice in the past few days," she explained.

"And?" he asked.

"And nothing," she said. "He flies out of Jo'burg, and even if he comes here regularly, there would be nothing to tell."

84

"So you like him then?" Thabo asked.

"I suppose he's nice enough," she admitted. "But, he seems to have no wife or regular girlfriend, which makes me wonder why."

"Well, I trust things will go well for you," Thabo said. "Now, I must look to see what other treasures you have brought me."

Marieke drove to the university, found her way to the offices, and asked for the administration office. There, she presented her credentials and asked to speak to someone about one of the academic staff. She was directed to an assistant vice chancellor, Doctor Chebani, who was curious to learn what had brought an assistant superintendent of police to their hallowed halls.

"I understand you have Professor Ian Ross on the faculty," Marieke said. "Could you tell me where I might find him?"

"We have Professor Ross on the faculty, but finding him may be difficult at the moment," Dr Chebani said. "He is on an extended leave for three months in Scotland."

"I see," Marieke said. "We have found his Land Rover in the Linyanti area, under odd circumstances, and were concerned that something may have happened to him. When did he leave for Scotland?"

"Well, it could not have been Professor Ross, he left for Scotland a month ago," Dr Chebani said, seeming to Marieke to be trying to hide some confusion or concern on his face. "You are certain that it is his Land Rover?"

"We are certain the chassis number checks against the registration for the vehicle, and the latest registered owner is Professor Ross," Marieke explained. "Could he have loaned the vehicle to someone, or recently sold it?"

"I really could not say," Dr Chebani said. "This is all very mysterious; it cannot be simply a question of the vehicle being stolen; that would hardly require the attention of a superintendent."

"We have an ongoing investigation," Marieke said.

"Oh," Dr Chebani said, a little disappointed that Marieke did not share more. "Well, unless Ian did something really strange, as I said, he is in Scotland at the moment."

"Do you have a telephone number in Scotland where I might try and reach him?" Marieke asked.

"I don't, but I'm sure the English Department does," Dr Chebani said. "If you will excuse me for a minute, let me call and find out." He called a number and asked the person at the other end for a contact telephone number for Professor Ross, and wrote down what was read to him.

"I think this may help," he said. "But they tell me that he is hiking in the mountains, so you may or may not be able to contact him."

"I will try," Marieke said. "Tell me, is Professor Ross married?"

"No, he's a bachelor, probably will always be one, if he has a love, it is for language, that is probably what makes him such a good teacher," Dr Chebani said. "Apart from English, he speaks Setswana, and I believe French, German, Mandarin and Gaelic."

"Thank you for your help," Marieke said. "Were there any people that he was particularly friendly with?"

"Quite a number," Dr Chebani said. "Most of the English Department, and quite a few in Economics and Statistics, plus I believe he has a circle of friends outside the university."

"While Professor Ross is away, do you know if he has anyone staying at his house?" Marieke asked.

"Yes, the English Department just told me that one of his postgraduate students, Thabang Kanedi, is staying there," Dr Chebani said. "Do you have the address?"

"If our vehicle registration people have it right," Marieke laughed. "If you wouldn't mind, perhaps I should confirm it with you."

"Here you are," Dr Chebani said, passing over a paper on which he had written the address. Marieke was gratified to see that it did indeed match the one she had, so their records were correct.

"Perhaps I could return at some time, if I think it necessary, and talk to some of his close friends, perhaps they would know who might have been using his Land Rover," Marieke said.

"That would be fine," Dr Chebani said.

"Just to satisfy my constant curiosity, Doctor, where did you study?" Marieke asked.

"I got my bachelor's degree at Leeds University in England, then went on to do my doctorate at LSE, that's the London School of Economics,

I studied political theory there, it was quite fascinating," Dr Chebani replied. "And you?"

"I went to the University of Lyon and studied law," Marieke said. "It was interesting in that French law traditions are quite different to those we adopted from the British. Well, thank you for your time, Doctor," Marieke said. "I will first try and contact Professor Ross. I should not take up any more of your time, go well."

"Stay well, Madame," Dr Chebani said. "I trust that we might meet again sometime."

At her office, Marieke called the number given. The time difference was two hours, so it was still quite early in the morning in Scotland.

"Good morning," a voice with a very strong accent said. "This is the Skye Lodge, Morag Ross speaking."

"Good morning," Marieke said. "I am looking for Professor Ross."

"I'm afraid he's not here," Morag said.

"Do you know when he might be back?" Marieke asked.

"He should be back the day after tomorrow," Morag said.

"Is there any way I would be able to reach him sooner?" Marieke asked.

"No, he's away in the Cuillins," Morag said. "Is it important?"

"I believe so," Marieke said. "I'm so sorry, I have been rude, I should have explained who I was, I am Assistant Superintendent Englebrecht of the Botswana Police."

"Oh dear," Morag said. "Ian's not in trouble, is he?"

"Not at all," Marieke assured her. "We have found his Land Rover in an odd place and would like to know if he lent it to anyone while he was away."

"I wouldn't know about that," Morag said. "I know Ian has a Land Rover; he was showing us pictures of it and his house last night."

"Are you by chance related to Professor Ross?" Marieke asked.

"Aye," Morag confirmed. "I am his sister. Ian comes every three years or so, sometimes for a week and sometimes for a month, for a visit. He likes the mountains and to get away on his own. He'll be leaving us soon for the Islands, to brush up on his Gaelic."

"When he returns, would you be so kind as to ask him to call me?" Marieke asked.

"Wait while I get a pen and paper," Morag said. "Now tell me again your name and the number."

Marieke gave her full name and title, and the telephone number of her office and she also gave her the number at her house and told Morag to let Professor Ross know that he could call at whatever hour best suited him.

"Tell me, Superintendent, is it hot there today?" Morag asked, deciding that trying to pronounce either Marieke or Englebrecht would be too challenging.

"Not too hot," Marieke said. "Only about 25° today."

"Oh dear, what's that in Fahrenheit?" Morag asked.

"About 77," Marieke said, converting in her head.

"Oh, so very pleasant, but are you not in the middle of winter?" Morag asked.

"We are," Marieke agreed. "In the summer, it will get much hotter. You've never been here to visit with your brother?"

"No, it's such a long way," Morag protested. "But I confess that having seen his latest pictures of birds and animals, I am tempted."

"You should come," Marieke told her. "You would enjoy it. Come at about this time of year when it's dry and not too hot."

"The problem I have is that this is also the high season for me with the Lodge," Morag explained. "But, perhaps I could get my friend Kirsty, from Uig, to look after the place for me while I take a holiday."

"Think about it," Marieke urged. "You will like Botswana."

"I will think upon it, but you must be busy, Superintendent, I mustn't hold you back," Morag said.

"Thank you for your help," Marieke said, taking the hint. "Goodbye, Miss Ross, enjoy the rest of your day."

"Goodbye, Superintendent," Morag said.

The call to Scotland yielding nothing for the moment, Marieke turned her attention back to other things. She called in Sergeant Maphosa and asked him to check with the vehicle registration people to see if there was an easy way to cull through the records and pick out blue open-back Land Rovers. She was not hopeful, but it was a possibility. Her next avenue of enquiry would be the graduate student who was staying at Ian Ross's house. Perhaps she might know something. Marieke called the English Department at the university and asked for Thabang Kanedi and learned that she was teaching a class. Marieke gave her name and number and asked that a message be given to Thabang to call her when it was convenient. She was contemplating what to do next when Mbali called and invited her to lunch. Being invited by one's bank manager to lunch might be purely social, or it might be a prelude to something else. Still, Mbali was always fun. Lunch was interesting. Mbali wanted to talk about houses and mortgages, and such. Marieke had been renting since she arrived in Gaborone, but Mbali thought that she had found the perfect place for her. The purchase price was not out of reach for Marieke, and the monthly payments would only be a little more than the rent she was currently paying. The house was just off Tlokweng Road, away from the traffic, but close enough to the centre of town to be convenient.

"How much longer does your lease run?" Mbali asked Marieke.

"Another two months, I only rented for three months when I moved here, I needed some time to find out where things were in the town and where I might want to stay" Marieke replied.

"We can have everything done by then," Mbali said. "If you make an offer on the house, you can tell them that the financing is all set."

"How did you find out about this house?" Marieke asked.

"One of our customers is moving to a new house out on the road to Mahalapye," Mbali said. "They asked me if I knew of someone suitable who might buy their house."

"What if I don't like it?" Marieke asked.

"Then we'll put it in the hands of an estate agent," Mbali replied. "Do you have time now to go and see it?"

"I do," Marieke said. "Do you have time?"

"Of course," Mbali assured her. "The Patels are a good customer; we do their shop banking and their personal banking, so spending some time with them is quite appropriate."

"Are you sure you should be doing this?" Marieke asked.

"The Patels want a quick sale," Mbali assured her. "It is all quite above board. The Patels specifically asked me if I knew of a possible buyer and to help them through the process."

"But, if they meet me and decide that I am not the right person to live in their house, what then?" Marieke asked.

"They will be happy with you," Mbali assured her. "Shall we go?"

The house off Tlokweng Road was delightful; it was small, which was why the current owners were selling. It had two bedrooms and the usual kitchen and living room, and it had a small yard with mature trees, shading the back of the house nicely. The Patels had a store in town that sold ironmongery, and it was very successful, but they also had a growing family and had built a new house farther out with more space and a larger yard. Mr and Mrs Patel offered tea and wanted to know if Marieke was married. When they learned she was not, they then wanted to know if she was employed. When they learned that she was, in fact, an Assistant Superintendent of the Botswana Police, they were impressed and reassured that their house would be in good hands, lack of a husband notwithstanding. They offered to show Marieke the house, so they all set off on a tour of the house and the grounds. Marieke liked what she saw and could imagine herself living there. Thereafter, it was a matter of details. Marieke could meet the price the Patels had set, which Mbali had assured her was reasonable, and was quite within the price range of other properties in the neighbourhood. The Patels suggested that they should all meet at the earliest convenience at a solicitor's office to have the contract of sale and purchase drawn up and executed. Mbali suggested the offices of Motingwa and Maroke, which the Patels knew and which Marieke had heard of. Mbali suggested that she set up the appointment and let all parties know when it would be; she would also take care of the finances. Feeling a little overwhelmed, Marieke excused herself and said that she had to be getting back to her office. Mbali went with her and promised to have everything ready by the end of the week, and she offered the services of Jannie and a lorry to help her move if she wanted.

Assistant Commissioner Mochage saw her arrive and intercepted her on the way to her office, "So, Matshwane," he said, "what news?"

"Little, I'm afraid," Marieke replied. "It seems that the owner of the Land Rover, Professor Ross, is in Scotland at the moment, in fact, has been there for some weeks, he is on a sabbatical from the university."

"I presume that you are looking into his friends and acquaintances?" the commissioner asked.

"I am Sir," she assured him. "He has a house sitter, and I am waiting for her to return my telephone call. Dr Chebani of the university told me that Professor Ross is a bachelor, wedded more to language than people, that he has a wide circle of friends, both with the university and in the general population. His housesitter is a graduate student of his, who was teaching a class when I called. Professor Ross is staying with his sister at the moment on the Island of Skye and was away hiking in the hills when I called. He is expected back in a day or so."

"So, if someone were to borrow his Land Rover, it could be anyone," the commissioner commented.

"It could, Sir," Marieke agreed. "I will see if the graduate student gave the keys to someone, or if that arrangement was made before Ross went away."

"What else have you been up to?" he asked.

"I just bought a house," she replied.

"You did?" he said. "Where?"

"Just off the Tlokweng Road," she said. "The Patels, who have the shop in town that sells ironmongery are selling, are moving farther out of town to a larger house with more space. I can afford the house, and Mbali Lamprecht put me onto it."

"So, you have decided that you will stay with us in Gaborone for a while," he joked.

"Barring the unexpected and unforeseen, yes, Sir," she confirmed.

"Do you need anything for the house purchase or the move?" he asked.

"I don't think so, Sir," she said. "Mbali has set things up with solicitors for the sale and purchase agreement, and the financing, and I have little enough to move into a new house."

"Do you have furniture?' he asked.

"The minimum," she said. "I have a bed to sleep in, a table and chair to eat off and utensils to cook with."

"If you need help to move, let me know," he offered.

"Thank you, Sir," she said. "Mbali has offered me help in the form of her husband and a lorry if I need it."

"Good," the commissioner said. "Now, I need to go, I have meetings to attend. *Tsamaya sentlê.*"

"*Sala sentlê,*" she replied.

After the commissioner had gone, Marieke checked telephone messages and was pleased to see one from Thabang Kanedi. Marieke called the number provided and was pleased that it was answered by Thabang, so no more trading messages.

"*Dumela Mma,*" Marieke said. "I wonder if I might come and see you sometime soon?"

"Of course, *Mma,*" Thabang said. "Professor Ross is not in any trouble, is he?"

"No, not at all," Marieke assured her. "I just have some questions about his friends and acquaintances. May I come to the house of Professor Ross at five?"

"Of course, *Mma,*" Thabang replied. "Come earlier if you like, I have finished here for the day and was just leaving."

"Good, I'll see you in a few minutes then," Marieke said. She saw Sergeant Maphosa and told him where she was going and asked him to check with the garages in town to see if they could begin to list how many blue open-backed Land Rovers there were in town. To her, the crime was not one of opportunity; it bespoke planning, so to her way of thinking, the perpetrator probably came from the same place as the victims, and, as she had no better information, she was assuming that the victims knew Professor Ross and probably came from Gaborone. The drive to Professor Ross's house took only a few minutes; he lived near the university on Leopard Road. The house on Leopard Road was set back from the road a little, among some trees. She saw a young woman arrive just ahead of her and assumed she would be Thabang.

"*Dumela Mma,*" she said. "Are you Thabang Kanedi?"

"*Dumela Mma,* I am," Thabang replied. "You are, I presume, Assistant Superintendent Englebrecht."

"I am," Marieke confirmed. "I hope this does not inconvenience you."

"Not at all," Thabang assured her. "Please come in. Would you like some tea?"

"Yes, please," Marieke replied. "I understand you are a graduate student of Professor Ross?"

"Yes," Thabang replied. "I am working towards a doctorate, studying the impact of colonialism on Setswana."

"Professor Ross teaches English, doesn't he?" Marieke asked.

"He does," Thabang confirmed as she served the tea. "But he also has studied Setswana, to a great extent, so that he has corrected me on my grammar at times."

"How does one do that for a spoken but not historically written language?" Marieke asked. "Who first committed Setswana to paper?"

"There was a Lichtenstein in the early 1800s who wrote about the language, then it was the missionaries, people like Moffat, then others like Archbell, Casalis and even Plaatjie," Thabang explained. "Setswana is also spoken in much of northern South Africa. Ntsime from South Africa is a very prolific author in Setswana, so we have a common linguistic heritage."

"How are your studies going?" Marieke asked.

"Slowly," Thabang laughed. "I discovered that to truly understand the impact of another culture upon Setswana, I had to look at similar impacts on other language groups, which has broadened the scope of my studies, more than a little."

"I can see there being impacts," Marieke said. "I'm sure that the San I learned was coloured by Setswana, Afrikaans and other languages."

"Where did you learn San?" Thabang asked.

"I was brought up on a farm in Namibia," Marieke explained. "We had a band of San that lived close by, and I learned from them."

"Is the San you learned from them different to that spoken here?" Thabang asked.

"It is," Marieke confirmed. "Both in accent and word usage. How much of that was natural development from isolated bands and how much from outside language influence, I cannot say."

"I would like to talk to you about that at some time, and when Professor Ross gets back, I'm sure he would want to talk to you as well," Thabang said. "And talking about Ian, what trouble is he in?"

"He's in no trouble at all," Marieke assured her. "We found his Land Rover in the Linyanti area and were wondering how it got there. Do you know if he lent it to someone while he was away?"

"He didn't tell me, he must have given the keys to someone before he left," Thabang said. "He left it parked at the university. I regret to say that I didn't even notice it was gone until you called today. More tea?"

"Thank you, yes," Marieke said. "Tell me about Professor Ross and his friends and acquaintances."

"I think I would number all the language school as his friends and he had some more in Statistics and Economics, but then he also had a wide circle outside the university, solicitors, doctors, mechanics and others," Thabang enumerated.

"Mechanics?" Marieke asked. "The others I would expect, tell me about the mechanics."

"I think he had problems with the Land Rover soon after he bought it, it was second or third hand after all, and he went to his friend, who is a mechanic, for help," Thabang explained.

"Who was the mechanic?" Marieke asked.

"Lamprecht, who now has MJ Motors, but I understand that they first became friends soon after Lamprecht had started his business, the way Ian tells it is that he just walked in one day and talked him into looking at his first car, since then he's taken all his cars to Lamprecht," Thabang explained.

"I know Jannie Lamprecht," Marieke said. "Rather, I should say I know his wife quite well and have met Jannie."

"I've never met his wife," Thabang said. "Lamprecht usually comes on his own to have coffee with Ian, and they talk about cars and lorries."

"His wife is very nice," Marieke said. "She's a Zulu and works here as a bank manager. Of the other friends at the university, are they all there at the moment or are any on leave or sabbatical?"

"I'm not sure," Thabang said. "Why don't I make a list of the friends that I know, and then mark off who is away?"

"That would be most useful," Marieke said. "Tell me a little more about Ian Ross."

"Ian is a lovely man," Thabang said. "But, he lives for linguistics and little else. He's sociable and friendly, but as far as I know, has only had one romantic affair, and that was years ago, and, although he doesn't talk about it, I think it ended in tragedy. He's not very tall, about 1.67 metres, reddish hair, slim build, but he does walk and hike a lot. He is a student of human nature; he's a demanding thesis supervisor, as I found out, but a fair one. He doesn't believe in using long, academic-sounding words when simpler language will do. I came across that with my Master's thesis, he asked me if I was trying to win a competition for the use of the longest, most obscure words found. I know it is the case amongst most graduate theses to use sophisticated and erudite-sounding words, but he doesn't like that if there is no absolute need for it. I suppose he doesn't like airs and graces and trying to sound erudite just for the sake of it."

"He sounds like a very interesting man," Marieke said. "Perhaps when he returns, I might meet him?"

"I would be happy to arrange that," Thabang said.

"Thank you," Marieke said. "I have taken up too much of your time. Thank you for the help, and if you could create a list of friends that are not here at the moment, that would be most helpful."

"It would be my pleasure," Thabang said. "*Tsamaya sentlê.*"

"*Sala sentlê,*" Marieke replied, then she left and went home to ponder her next task.

On a whim, she interrupted her homeward journey and went to Woolworths. They had quite a selection of women's clothes and Marieke studied, pondered, tried on and eventually purchased a few items that would go a long way to broadening her selection. She even added to her shoe collection, small as it was, with two new pairs of shoes that would go well with the clothes she purchased. Happy that she had done something about her wardrobe, she finished her journey home in time to meet a deliveryman trying to decide whether or not to leave a large box.

"*Dumela Rra,*" she said. "Is that for me?"

"*Dumela Mma,*" he said. "It is if you are Marieke Englebrecht."

"I am. Here is my identification," she replied, proffering her police card.

"That you, *Mma,*" he said. "If you will just sign here?"

Marieke duly signed and accepted delivery of the box. She looked at the shipping label and was delighted to see that it came from her friend

Melisende Garnier from Lyon. It must be wine! She took the box inside and opened it carefully, and unpacked twelve assorted bottles of wine, including some Médoc, Saint-Émilion, Pomerol and Graves. There was a note included that Melisende had sent, congratulating her on her move to Gaborone and the promotion. Melisende had been one of the people she had spent most time with at university; they shared common interests and had both gone into their respective police forces. Melisende was one of those brilliant people who just seemed to be able to drift through life and absorb everything along the way. She was now a Commissaire de Police in the Sûreté. Marieke went to her bookcase and took her copy of Wines of France by Lichine and scoured through the pages looking for the Chateaux that the wines came from and the ratings given each of them. Melisende had spared no expense; they all were rated highly. On the back of the congratulatory note was another note that told her to drink the wines and not store them up against special occasions that might or might not arise, but today was not the day to be opening any of these wines; they must rest a while after their long journey! She satisfied herself with a glass of a South African Pinot Gris.

On her way to her office the next morning, Marieke stopped at MJ Motors and asked for Jannie.

"Superintendent," Jannie said. "So nice to see you again, what brings you to this place, coffee?"

"*Dumela Rra*," Marieke said. "Coffee would be nice, thank you. Tell me, I understand you know Ian Ross, a professor at the university?"

"*Ja*, I know Ian, we met years ago when he first came to Botswana, he came in here one day with a car that needed fixing. I told him we just did diesel trucks and buses, but he was persuasive and I liked him, so I looked at the car and fixed it up for him," Jannie confirmed. "Is he in trouble?"

"No, not at all," Marieke assured him. "I understand that you maintain his Land Rover for him?"

"*Ja*," Jannie confirmed. "Been doing it for a couple of years. When he first bought it from the *ou* at Selibi Pikwe, it had some issues, but we were able to fix them quickly."

"Do you know if he lent it to anyone while he went away on leave?" she asked.

"*Ja*, he asked me to look it over and then they came with it just before they left on a trip, about two weeks ago," Jannie said.

"Who did he lend it to?" she asked.

"Two of the other profs at the uni," Jannie said. "Man and wife, names of David Turner and Julia Turner, why has something happened?"

"We found the Land Rover up in the Linyanti area," Marieke said.

"You're sure it's the right one?" Jannie asked.

"We've checked, and yes, it is the one belonging to Ian Ross," Marieke said.

"*Magtig*," Jannie said. "You said you'd found the Land Rover, what about the Turners?"

"We found them as well," Marieke said. "But they are not in a position to tell us anything."

"*Dood*, hey?" Jannie said. "Accident or something else?"

"Something else," Marieke said.

"Does Ian know?" Jannie asked.

"I've not been able to reach him," Marieke said. "Apparently, he's away in the hills of Scotland hiking. I'm hoping he will call me in a day or so."

"Well, the Turners had it and left on an extended bush trip," Jannie said. "I think they're leaving Botswana soon to go to England for some big job there."

"Thank you, Jannie," Marieke said. "You've been a great help. Say hello to Mbali for me."

"I will," he confirmed. "Mbali tells me you bought a house just off the Tlokweng Road?"

"Shall we say, I'm in the process of buying one," Marieke said. "Mbali tells me that it will all be finalised this week."

"If she says it will be done this week, it will be done this week," Jannie said. "Congratulations, will we get to see it when you move in?"

"I'll send out invitations when I move in," Marieke promised. "But, I need to get on now, I have much to do, as I'm sure you do. *Tsamaya sentlê.*"

"*Sala sentlê*," he replied.

At the office, Marieke stopped by the commissioner's office to report. He was talking on the telephone, but he waved her to a chair while he finished his conversation.

"So, Matswhane, how are you today?" he asked.

"Well, Sir, thank you," she replied. "And you?"

"I would be better if I could tell the commissioner that we are making progress with your mystery bodies case," he said.

"We may have identified the victims," she said. "Apparently, Professor Ross lent his Land Rover to two other professors, David Turner and Julia Turner, according to Jan Lamprecht, who maintains Ian Ross's cars; they stopped by to get the Land Rover checked out before they left on an extended bush trip. Lamprecht said that would have been about two weeks ago."

"So, we need to confirm that they are actually the Turners, as I recall from your last report, the faces were without most of the soft tissue, so simple facial identification will not be easy, if indeed possible," he said.

"The PMs that were done did show evidence of old bone injuries," she said. "Perhaps someone can recall those injuries. Plus, there were one or two identifying marks on the torsos. They may be recorded somewhere, and we did manage to get dental X-rays, so if they've been to the dentist here, we may be able to match them."

"So, what is your next step?" he asked.

"I was going to go back to the university and talk to Dr Chebani again," she said.

"Good, I think I'll come with you," he said. "If these people are these Turners, we need to start building a file on them so that we can try and guess why someone killed them."

Dr Chebani was surprised to see two police officers; he had suspected that Marieke might be back, but this time she had brought her superior. "*Dumela Rra,*" the commissioner said. "You have already met Assistant Superintendent Englebrecht. I am Assistant Commissioner Mochage."

"*Dumela Mma, Rra,*" Dr Chebani said. "How may I help?"

"We have tentatively identified two bodies as those of David Turner and Julia Turner, both we are led to believe are professors here at the university," the commissioner said.

"David and Julia," Dr Chebani said, his face falling, before he could recover his composure. "That can't be possible, they're away on a bush trip now before they leave for England."

"It is in the bush that the two bodies were found," Marieke explained. "They were found north of Maun."

"They had said that they were going to Maun, then to Khwai, and then I think they were planning to go to Chobe," Dr Chebani said.

"The problem we have is one of positive identification," Marieke said. "Unfortunately, the bodies, particularly the faces, suffered the effects of animals, and there is little for us to make an identification from."

"What about fingerprints, as part of the visa process, they would have had to submit fingerprints, so you should be able to match those?" Dr Chebani suggested.

"Sadly, again no," Marieke said. "We do, however, have dental X-rays, and we have X-rays of the skeletal structures of both that show past injuries."

"Let me find out who they saw, excuse me," Dr Chebani said. He left the office briefly and came back in with two cards. "These are the details for David and Julia for doctors and dentists," he said, proffering the cards.

"Do the professors have next of kin in Botswana or elsewhere?" the commissioner asked.

"Let me get the other cards," Dr Chebani said. He left briefly and came back with two more cards. Looking over them quickly he then read out what was noted, "Dr David Turner, date of birth 11th of January, 1935, married to Julia Turner, neé Roberts, daughter Sara, date of birth 6th July, 1960, resident of England, son, David, date of birth, 23rd October, 1962, also resident of England. There are contact addresses for them both. There is similar information on the card of Julia, matching that of David's, the only new salient point being her date of birth, which is the 25th of February, 1935."

"We won't contact them until we are more certain that we are dealing with the professors Turner," the commissioner said. "It would not be kind to inform a son or daughter of a parent's demise, only to learn that it was not them. We need greater certainty before we call them. Marieke, have you noted doctors and dentists?"

"I have, Sir," she confirmed. "Dr Chebani, you said that the Turners would be leaving soon for England. Do you know where they were going?"

"David received a prestigious chair at an Oxford college," Dr Chebani replied. "David is a renowned economist who has published widely on the economies of developing nations, particularly Botswana. We will miss him, but Oxford will gain a good man, or should I say, would have gained a good man? Julia is a professor of statistics and has done much work for our diamond industry. As I understand it, property valuations are done using sophisticated statistical methods. We have had a search going for some time to replace both of them, and their replacements are both here. David and Julia were taking one last holiday in the bush before they went to the grey skies of Oxford. David had been back and forth to Oxford several times this last year as part of the selection process, and on the last trip, Julia went with him, I suspect, to be vetted for acceptability."

"This prestigious chair of economics in Oxford," Marieke said. "Was it much sought after by many?"

"Oh yes," Dr Chebani confirmed. "It is an endowed chair, and whoever has it is pretty much set for life. I believe there were some fifty people who applied, and that the shortlist was ten, all of whom are renowned and respected in the world of economics. It is the kind of post that could lead to a Nobel, so much sought after."

"Of the others that applied, did any of them ever work here?" Marieke asked.

"I don't know the answer to that," Dr Chebani admitted. "David gave me the numbers and rattled off names, some of whom I recognised, but I don't recall anyone who had worked here, but it is possible, economics is not my field, so apart from the interest in David applying for the post, I confess I was more concerned with the potential need for his replacement."

"How does David Turner's leaving affect you here?" Marieke asked.

"Well," Dr Chebani started. "Obviously it means that we have to find his replacement, but that is much easier than it would have been in the past, to have one of our faculty go on to such a prestigious post confers stature upon us as a university, so whereas in the past we may have had ten applicants, we are now sorting through about fifty, many of whom are from well-recognised universities and all of whom have published."

"Have you settled on anyone yet?" the commissioner asked.

"We are still working on that," Dr Chebani explained.

"Well, we've taken up too much of your time," the commissioner said. "We will check with the dentist and see if we are able to confirm the identities of our bodies, if we confirm that they are indeed the Turners we will be back to inform you in person, and at that time we would need access to their papers, place of lodging and such, so if you would be so kind as to quarantine their papers until then, we would be most appreciative."

"Of course," Dr Chebani agreed. "I do have keys to their offices, which are not yet cleared out and to the house in town. I will attend to that now."

"Thank you, Dr Chebani," the commissioner said. "Good day to you, Sir."

Commissioner Mochage asked Marieke to take him back to the office and then suggested that she and Dr Mosiwa go and see the dentist that the Turners used. Marieke found Thabo cleaning up after another post-mortem, this time on a traffic accident victim. Establishing what was the actual cause of death was important to the police and the victim's family, whether the heart attack occurred before or after. In Thabo's opinion, it was before contributing to the accident.

"So, Matshwane, what brings you to our hideaway?" he asked.

"I would like you to come with me to a dentist and bring the X-rays we took of our beheadings," Marieke replied.

"Oh, you have an identification?" he asked.

"Tentative, pending confirmation," she said. "We think they are David and Julia Turner, both profs at the uni. They are, were, on a bush trip in the Maun area in the Land Rover we found."

"Turner, that's the chap that just got that chair at Oxford," Thabo said. "So, he might be headless horseman number one."

"Do you have time to come with me now?" she asked.

"Of course," he said. "Let me get the X-rays, and we can go. How did you get onto them?"

"The grad student staying in Ian Ross's house told me that Ross had a regular mechanic, and that turned out to be Jan Lamprecht of MJ Motors. Jannie told me that he had checked out the *bakkie* a couple of weeks ago for the Turners."

"Gaborone is a small town," Thabo remarked. "Remember that if you ever decide to go *déshabillé* in the reservoir."

"If I ever need anything dragged again for heads or a body, I'm sending you or one of your techs," she laughed. "The commissioner told me that it was beneath my dignity to do such things."

"Where are we going?" Thabo asked.

"To the office of Dr Wilson," she said. "He's on Kaunda Road."

It was only a short drive to Kaunda Road, and Thabo saw the office and pointed it out to Marieke. The receptionist was a little concerned that the police were there, but Marieke assured her that their visit had nothing to do with anything untoward. They only had to wait a few minutes before the doctor had a break between patients and could see them.

"*Dumela*," he greeted them. "How can I help you?"

"*Dumela Rra*," Marieke said. "Thank you for seeing us, I am Assistant Superintendent Englebrecht, and this is Dr Mosiwa of our medico-legal unit. We are trying to confirm the identities of two bodies we have recovered. We have dental X-rays and would like you to compare them to those of Dr David Turner and Dr Julia Turner, both of whom we understand are patients of yours."

"David and Julia are both patients," Dr Wilson confirmed. "They were here recently getting ready for a trip into the bush. Do you have the X-rays?"

"Here is the one for the male," Thabo said.

"Let's see," Dr Miller said, retrieving his own X-rays from a file. "Well, there seems to be little doubt that your X-rays match mine, see here and here, these crowns and this inlay match perfectly."

"This is the one for the female," Thabo said.

"Yes, definitely," Dr Miller said. "This is for Julia, she has this crown and this crown, plus other features. I would state, in court if I have to, that the X-rays you have match those of the records of David and Julia

Turner. The fact that you're here asking for confirmation of identity tells me that they're dead?"

"Sadly, that is true," Marieke confirmed.

"Were the deaths accidental or not?" Dr Wilson asked.

Marieke avoided that question and asked one of her own. "How well did you know the Turners?"

"They were patients," Dr Wilson said. "I knew them as such, we never socialised, our conversations were typically about dental issues they had or might develop and current events."

"Did either of them ever talk about their fields of study?" Marieke asked.

"Not really," Dr Wilson said. "I know David is, was, an economist and that he just got a new appointment in Oxford, and Julia was a statistics expert; she helped me a couple of times when I was trying to tie tooth decay issues with diet and water quality."

"So, they never mentioned friends or acquaintances?" Marieke asked.

"No," Dr Wilson said. "How did they die?"

"We will be releasing information to the press and the public after we have contacted next of kin," Marieke explained. "Until we had positive identification, we could not inform any family members. May we have the films for David and Julia Turner? We would like them in the files we are building."

"Of course," Dr Wilson said. "As they are dead, I will not be seeing them again."

"Thank you for your time," Marieke said. "We wish you a good day, and if necessary, may we call upon you again?"

"Certainly," Dr Wilson said. "I'm glad to have been of help."

"Where to now?" Thabo asked as they left the dentist's office.

"The office, I think," Marieke said. "I need to call the next of kin and let them know about this. Then I'll call the university."

"Who is, are, next of kin?" Thabo asked.

"A daughter and a son," Marieke replied. "I have the contact numbers here."

"That's a task I can never get used to, telling someone that their relative is dead," Thabo said. "No matter how you phrase it, it never sounds quite good enough, or compassionate enough."

"But, it must be done," Marieke said.

Marieke sat at her desk in the office and contemplated the calls that she must now make. It was lunchtime in Gaborone, so mid-morning in England. The addresses and telephone numbers she had been given were both in London, with home and work numbers. She would try the work numbers first and see who she could contact, the daughter, as the older should be first. She dialled the number and listened to the phone ringing at the other end. It was answered fairly promptly.

"Good morning, Bentham Investments, how may I direct your call?" a voice said.

"I would like to speak to Sara Turner, please," Marieke said.

"I'm sorry, Ms Turner is in a meeting at the moment, may I take a name and number and have you call back?" the voice asked.

"I really need to speak to Ms Turner," Marieke said. "Would you be so kind as to interrupt her meeting and take her a message that Assistant Superintendent Englebrecht of the Botswana Police is calling regarding her parents, Drs David and Julia Turner?"

"Has something happened?" the voice asked.

"I am afraid I cannot discuss that until I have talked to Ms Turner," Marieke said, thinking that the voice had to be pretty stupid to ask the question, of course something had happened to the Turners, Botswana Police were not in the habit of calling people in London out of the blue.

"Hold on a minute, I'll get her," the voice said. Marieke waited a few minutes, and then another voice came on the line: "This is Sara Turner. Who did you say you were again?"

"This is Assistant Superintendent Englebrecht of the Botswana Police," Marieke repeated. "I am afraid I have bad news for you."

"You said it was about my Mom and Dad," Sara said.

"Yes," Marieke confirmed. "I'm sorry to have to tell you that we have found them in the bush, both dead, and, again, I'm sorry to say, that they had both been murdered."

"Murdered?" Sara said. "But who would want to kill them?"

"That is what we are now investigating," Marieke explained.

"You're sure it's them?" Sara asked.

"We are sure," Marieke confirmed. "Dental records prove the identities beyond any doubt."

"How were they murdered?' Sara asked.

"They were on a trip into the bush and they were both killed," Marieke replied.

"But, who would do that? Was it robbery, what?" Sara asked.

"We are investigating the circumstances of their deaths and have not ruled anything out," Marieke replied. "We were alerted to the issue by a safari operator who chanced upon the vehicle they had borrowed for the trip. It took us a few days to find and identify them."

"Do you know when they were murdered?" Sara asked.

"Not precisely," Marieke said. "Our best estimates are between a week and ten days ago. Someone went to great pains to hide the bodies and make it difficult for us."

"I will come out there," Sara said. "What do I do, fly to Jo'burg and then on to Botswana?"

"That would be the way," Marieke agreed. "Fly to Jo'burg on SAA or BA, then take an Air Botswana to Gaborone. I should also contact your brother, David, or do you wish to do that?"

"I'll do that," Sara said. "I'll book a flight tonight, do you have a number or Fax number that I can send my flight details to? What do I do in Gaborone?"

"If I have your flight information, I will meet you at the Gaborone airport," Marieke promised. "I will also make a booking for you at a hotel here in Gaborone that is close to the Central Police Station."

"Would you spell your name for me and give me the Fax number?" Sara asked. Marieke did so and listened as Sara gave a blizzard of instructions to the first voice she had heard. "Right, that's in the works," Sara said. "I'll see you sometime tomorrow."

"I will be at the airport," Marieke promised.

"Fine," Sara said. "I'll talk to David and he may come as well, I've a lot to do, so I'll get on, thank you for letting me know. Bye for now."

"Goodbye, Ms Turner," Marieke said.

Who and why?

Marieke went to find the commissioner and saw him just leaving the building. She flagged him down and told him that the identities had been confirmed and that she had informed the next of kin. Her next call would be to the university to let them know. In fact, after she had had some lunch, she was going to go there to start going through the offices of the two Turners to see if there were any clues that might lead to who would want to kill them. The commissioner told her to join him for lunch, and they would go together to the university. He commented dryly that in his experience, academia tended to close ranks when faced with outside scrutiny, so he expected cooperation up to a point, but not a lot of help. Marieke was surprised by this observation; she had always imagined academia as forthright and interested in the truth. The commissioner set her straight on that, his view was that they were interested in their own personal development and standing and that back-biting and stealing of others' work was more common than she might like to imagine.

Dr Chebani was surprised to see them again so quickly. He ushered them into his office and asked if they had news.

"We have confirmed through dental records that the bodies we found are indeed those of Dr David Turner and Dr Julia Turner," Marieke said. "I have informed their next of kin and believe that, at least, the daughter, Sara Turner, will be here tomorrow."

"Oh dear," Dr Chebani said. "I suppose I'll have to contact the people at Oxford and tell them that David isn't coming. Can you tell me the cause of death?"

"We are investigating their deaths as murder," the commissioner said. "We will not release the means of death and other details until our investigations are complete."

"Was it robbery?" Dr Chebani asked.

"We are unable to say at this time," the commissioner replied.

"Well, I suppose you will need to investigate all aspects of their lives to try and find out who and why. Here are the keys to their offices and their house. Unfortunately, we're a little short of secretarial staff today, they are all off at a computer class, learning the latest systems for word processing. I'll have one of our security people take you to the offices of David and Julia," Dr Chebani said.

"Thank you," the commissioner said. "We won't bother you any more for the moment, but we may be back if we need help with anything."

"Of course," Dr Chebani said.

"Whose office do we take first?" Marieke asked the commissioner.

"Let's take David Turner first," he replied, and then he asked their escort if he would take them to the office of David Turner. Once there, he thanked him for his help and opened the door. The office had a window that overlooked Mobutu Avenue, in it was a desk with a computer with a note pasted to it that read, *leave department files, erase only personal files*, there were two file cabinets, a small table with four chairs, a blackboard and a bookcase filled with tomes on economics and one book on birds. "What do you see?" the commissioner asked.

"Organisation," Marieke said. "His desk is ordered, and I suspect the files will be too. This must be the daughter and son," she said, picking up two framed pictures that were on the desk. "I might borrow these so that I can identify them tomorrow at the airport. This looks like a family group. Now, at least we know what the Turners really look like. I have to say that the university pictures in their files were less than flattering. Apart from economics, it looks like he was interested in birds, an amateur ornithologist, what do the Brits call them, Twitchers?"

"I believe they do," the commissioner agreed. "See if his lists are there somewhere, as I understand it, he probably had a life list, an annual list and maybe some special trip lists. I would suppose that his annual list he would have had with him on the trip they had taken."

"There's a book here with notes and dates, this looks like it's what you called the life list," Marieke said. "It starts back about twenty years, and there are notations about species, dates and places. If he is an avid birder, then he probably has his year list and trip lists on him. Let's see what else we can learn about him."

"I'll take the desk if you'll take the file cabinet," the commissioner suggested. They looked through papers, files, and whatever else was in the office for about an hour. "Impressions?" the commissioner asked.

"It looks like most of the personal stuff has already been packed and shipped, but there is a little left, last-minute items to be packed and shipped with them on the plane. I would say that he was looking forward to this Oxford post," she said. "There are several files that deal with the interview process and a shortlist of what I suspect is the competition, there are names and comments, listen to this one, 'George B. wasting his time with Reaganomics', and there's another, 'Paulo should stick to cooking pasta'. There's another list which I think must be the selection committee, same sort of thing, 'John, arrogant prick, but for vote,' another, 'Henry, too smarmy for words, against vote,' and another, "James, on the fence, but I can probably sway him, Susan, yes vote for sure, Nicholas, probably a yes vote, Simon, unknown, keeps his counsel," I suspect they will be more on his computer, is it password protected?"

"To get into the basic screen and files, no," the commissioner said after turning it on and looking at the screen and what came up. "There are some files that call for a password when I click on them. Looking at the names of the files, I suspect that they are to do with economic theory and probably are the basis of his research and the reason he got his chair at Oxford."

"I was wondering," Marieke said, "if any of the people on this list of other candidates also show on the list that Patience Botha gave me of past guests at the Pitse camp."

"You have a nasty suspicious mind," the commissioner laughed. "Do you think it will be that simple?"

"No, but it wouldn't hurt to check," she said. "What you said earlier has made me look at academia a little differently. Maybe someone else wanted the job badly and objected to Turner getting it, so what better way to secure the job than remove the competition?"

"Who's the number two on the list?" the commissioner asked.

"I can't tell," she said. "It's just a list of names in alphabetical order."

"Pity," the commissioner said. "That would have been a great place to start, assuming of course that this isn't to do with love, lust or lucre or the other usual reasons for murder. Shall we take a look at the office of Julia Turner?"

They found a security guard who showed them where the office of Julia Turner was and they spent some time there, poking through files and desk drawers, looking for something that did not fit, or that seemed out of place, as with David's office, much had already been packed and shipped leaving only last-minute personal items to gather up. What they did find was a lot of correspondence with a person by the name of Diana McBride of Broadway and a list of passwords, which seemed to do nothing on her computer, so Marieke collected up the correspondence and they went back to David's office and tried the passwords on his computer. They worked, and they both looked at files full of erudite papers on economic theory. Next was the house. Marieke locked up both offices, and they left to see what the house might hold.

The Turners lived on Oribi, a short cul-de-sac, which meant that their house backed onto the house of Ian Ross. The house was empty, except for a large manila envelope on the kitchen counter. Marieke opened the envelope and took out what was inside. There were several folders, all marked neatly, some smaller envelopes and an artist's sketchbook.
"Tickets and passports," Marieke said, waving two airline tickets and two passports in the air that she had removed from the envelope marked 'Travel'. "Tickets dated a month ago and for flights to leave here in three weeks to go via Jo'burg to London on BA. The passports show a fair amount of travel, and in David's, there are four exits from and entries into Botswana in the past year. The Brits tend not to stamp the passports of their own people, so we can only assume that between the exit dates from Botswana to the entry dates, that's where he was. There's also a set of documents here that deal with moving their household belongings to Oxford, rail to Cape Town and then ocean freight to Southampton, then road to Oxford. It looks like twelve crates were shipped to Cape Town and loaded onto a vessel that sailed three days ago. There's a cover note with the passports and such from an 'L'

that details arrangements made and also sets out a schedule for the last days at the university, including a going away party."

"Hard to tell what kind of lifestyle they had with everything gone" the commissioner said. "Any bank statements or similar items?"

"Yes, here in a folder with the house lease, they weren't short of money," she remarked. "There don't appear to be any unusual payments, rent, doctor, dentist, garage, cash, what you'd expect. Our mutual friend, Mbali Lamprecht, was their bank manager. There're more letters and such from this Diana McBride, it looks like the Turners knew her well, there's a lot of comments and obvious envy about their trip into the bush, but there's nothing to suggest that McBride harboured any animosity to the Turners, in fact it looks like she suggested the route and places to camp, including the spot near Khwai where we found the heads. So, McBride has been to Botswana before. I should see if I can find out anything about her. The sketchbook is interesting, it seems that Julia Turner was quite an accomplished artist, there are sketches of quite a few people, including Dr Chebani and Thabang Kanedi and an older man who I'm assuming is Ian Ross, and these sketches of this quite beautiful young woman are quite remarkable, I wonder who she is?"

"I'm sure we'll find out in time. So, what is it about these people that got them killed, and with such obvious planning?" the commissioner asked.

"Someone clearly didn't like them to chop their heads off," Marieke said. "I need to find out who else knew what their plans were for the bush trip because someone knew where to find them and when. What if McBride passed the information on to someone else?"

"Dr Chebani knew they were going to Maun," the commissioner said. "There may have been others who had more detailed travel plans, people who live here and could make the travel arrangements easily."

"I need to go back to the university and talk to the secretaries for the departments that the two Turners worked in," Marieke said. "Perhaps one of them had a detailed travel plan and that was shared directly or indirectly with our killer."

"That's a good place to start," the commissioner agreed. "If this McBride may know something, take the documents we found and the sketchbook. On another note, I will come with you tomorrow when you go to the airport to meet Sara Turner."

110

"Fine Sir," Marieke said. "I think perhaps we should check at the office to see if there is word from London on flights and I still need to make a booking for them at a hotel. I'll get Sergeant Maphosa to come and go through the house carefully to see if anything has been overlooked or if there are secrets stashed in dark corners."

At the office, there was a fax which detailed the travel plans for both Sara and David Turner. They would be arriving in Gaborone just before 11:00 am the next morning. Marieke then called in Sergeant Maphosa, gave him the key to the Turners' house and instructions to go carefully through the house, in case they had missed something, and bring anything that he found back to the station. Then she turned back to the Fax and was making her plans for the next day when the telephone rang.

"Hello," she said, answering the call.

"Is this Superintendent Englebrecht?" a male voice asked.

"It is," Marieke confirmed. "How may I help you?"

"This is Ian Ross," he said. "My sister said you had called, something to do with my Land Rover?"

"Thank you for returning my call Professor Ross," Marieke said. "We found your Land Rover near the Linyanti area stripped of number plates and tax disc, and we were wondering if you may have lent your Land Rover to anyone while you were away?"

"Please call me Ian; I don't stand on too much formality. I gave the keys to David and Julia Turner, they were going to take one last bush trip before moving to Oxford," Ian explained. "Has something happened to David and Julia?"

"I'm sorry to say that we found two bodies that we concluded were those of the Drs Turner," Marieke confirmed. "We were able to match dental records and satisfy ourselves that we had made the proper identification."

"But, how did they die, accident, or what?" he asked.

"Sadly, they were murdered," she replied. "We are now conducting a murder investigation. Have you any idea who might want to kill them?"

"Not one," he said. "Was it robbery, what?"

"We have ruled nothing out at this time," she said.

"How do you know it was my Land Rover if there were no number plates and no tax disc?" he asked.

"The chassis plate had also been removed, but we were able to read the chassis number from the chassis itself and then make the association," she explained.

"There's a number somewhere?" he asked.

"Yes, the manufacturers physically stamp the chassis number on the metal of the chassis as well as putting a plate inside," she explained.

"I still don't see who would want to kill them," he said. "They were my neighbours in Gabs, lived right behind me; David was excited about taking up a new chair in Oxford, which would have been really good for his career."

"I'm sorry to have to ask this," she said. "But, I have to as part of the investigation, was their marriage stable, were there any extramarital entanglements?"

"I understand that you have to ask that," he said. "But, as far as I could tell, the marriage was good, there was never any hint of someone else, neither of them took much time off without the other, no, I saw no evidence of hanky panky."

"Again, I'm sorry to have to ask this, do you know of, or have you ever heard of gambling debts, money owed, blackmail or anything that may lead to whoever killed the Turners?" she asked.

"Not a whiff," he said. "They really were nice people."

"Were the two Drs Turner respected in their fields?" she asked.

"David more than Julia," he replied. "David was truly in a class of only a few, which is why he got the Oxford chair, Julia was good and well respected as a statistician, but David was sought after."

"Could that have caused jealousies between them?" she asked.

"No, definitely not," he said. "Julia was proud of David's achievements and was really looking forward to Oxford, one to be nearer her children and two so she could indulge her passion for medical statistics without having to worry about paying the bills."

"I am meeting the daughter and son tomorrow," Marieke said. "Have you ever met them?"

"Once," he replied. "They both came out to Botswana about six years ago, about the time that the son, I think he was also a David, finished university."

"Did those relationships seem strained in any way?" she asked.

"I would say not," he replied. "The times I socialised with the whole family, there was laughter and when I met with David and Julia without the children there was no hint of any animosity, and the same when I met the daughter and son away from their parents."

"Do you know a Diana McBride?" Marieke asked.

"I've never met her, but heard Julia talk about her a lot," Ian said. "They were at school together, then they were both up at Cambridge at the same time, then I believe Diana got married to an ornithologist who did a lot of study in Botswana, they never lived in Botswana but would travel extensively each year while Patrick, I think his name is, researched material for his doctorate."

"As far as you know was Julia still on good terms with Diana?" Marieke asked.

"When I saw the Turners before I left, Julia said something about a recent visit the McBrides had made to Botswana and a weekend trip they had taken into the Central Kalahari," Ian said. "I missed meeting them because was on a trip of my own at the time to Cape Town for a seminar."

"I seem to be asking endless questions here," Marieke said. "I'm sure that I'm taking up too much of your time."

"Not at all," he said. "I would like to know who killed David and Julia and why, so any help I can give you I will. If I think of anything may I call you again?"

"Please do, and if I am not here or at my home, then ask to speak to my superior, Assistant Commissioner Mochage," she said.

"Well, I'm sorry I could not be of more help, *tsamaya sentlê*," he said.

"*Sala sentlê*," she replied and hung up. So, this obviously was not going to be easy.

So far, nothing had surfaced that would provide a motive for killing the two. Robbery might be a motive, but they probably were not carrying that much cash that it would warrant the risk of killing, and, the Land Rover was abandoned, not taken, robbery would be more likely if the Land Rover had gone as well, even just as parts it was worth quite a bit, in fact leaving the Land Rover was either extremely careless or an act of sheer bravado. The killers had to know that eventually the Land Rover be found and identified, or perhaps they were unaware of the manufacturer's stamped chassis numbers. There were other possible scenarios, perhaps jealousy over the appointment of David Turner to the chair in Oxford, perhaps some problems with the McBrides, clearly they knew their way around Botswana and William Martin had said that the place where they found the bodies was a favourite for birds and Patrick McBride may well have known it, and, they had been to Botswana recently, perhaps the jaunt in the Kalahari had included more than one kind of bird watching. Well, she might learn something from Diana McBride, so she hunted through the letters she had taken until she found one with the letterhead of the McBride Raptor Centre. There was a telephone number, so it was worth a try.

Marieke called the telephone number and there was an immediate answer, "McBride Raptor Centre, how may I help you?"
"Good afternoon," Marieke said. "I am trying to reach Diana McBride."
"Diana's not here," the voice said.
"Do you know where I might reach her?" Marieke asked.
"May I ask what this is about?" the voice said.
"Of course," Marieke replied. "I am with the Botswana Police and we would like to talk to Mrs McBride."
"You say you're with the Botswana Police," the voice said. "How do I know that that is true?"
"I could give you my telephone number and you could call it," Marieke suggested. "But, then you would still only talk to me and not know if I am genuine or not. Let me give you a little more information, I would like to talk to Mrs McBride about her friend Julia Turner."
"Julia, what's happened to Julia?" the voice asked.
"I'm afraid I cannot discuss that until I have talked to Mrs McBride or perhaps Dr McBride," Marieke replied.
"Wait while I get Patrick," the voice said. Marieke waited and listened to their version of Muzak, which was bird calls, until another voice came on the line. "This is Patrick McBride; I understand you want to talk to my wife about Julia Turner?"

"That is correct Mr McBride," Marieke said. "Let me introduce myself, I am Assistant Superintendent Englebrecht of the Botswana Police and I am investigating the deaths of David and Julia Turner."

"How the hell, sorry, how do you know it's them? David and Julia are dead, how, when, what happened, did their bush trip go bad?" Patrick McBride gabbled out his question.

"I'm sorry to have to tell you, but your friends were murdered," Marieke replied, resisting the urge to say, "You know damn well the bush trip went bad, it went bad when you shot them", to see what kind of reaction she would get, as it was she was intrigued by the first response, he may have been surprised by the fact that they had not only found the bodies, but identified them, which must mean that they had also found the heads.

"Murdered, who would want to murder David and Julia? Have you told Sara and David?" Dr McBride asked.

"They are flying out tonight," Marieke replied. "I will be meeting them at the Gaborone airport tomorrow."

"Let me give you our home number," Dr McBride said. "We only live a short walk from here, give me five minutes then call the home number, Diana will be there."

Marieke gave them fifteen minutes to be sure, then called the telephone number given. Dr McBride answered.

"Good afternoon again, Dr McBride," Marieke said.

"Superintendent, my wife, Diana is on the extension, what happened to David and Julia?" he said.

"We are investigating their deaths," Marieke replied. "I understand you were recently in Botswana?"

"We were," Dr McBride said.

"It was such a lovely time," another voice said, that Marieke assumed must be that of Diana McBride. "How did they die, where do they die, when?"

"We are investigating all those things," Marieke said. "We estimate time of death to be between a week and ten days ago. I'm so sorry I have to ask this question, where were you in the past two weeks?"

"Surely, you can't think we had anything to do with their deaths," Diana exploded. She was interrupted by her husband who pointed out that the Superintendent was just doing her job, and that because they were most definitely not in Botswana over the past two weeks could be removed as possible suspects.

"Can you think of anyone who would wish them harm?" Marieke asked, noting that Dr McBride did not say that he had been in England; merely that he had not been in Botswana.

"Of course not," Diana said. "Julia was my best friend, we've been best friends since school; we went to Cambridge together and have stayed friends. How did they die?"

"Do you know about their move to Oxford?" Marieke asked.

"Oh, yes," Diana confirmed. "It is, I'm sorry was, going to be so much fun having them close. Julia was going to help Patrick with statistical models of raptor distribution; they'd already been building early models to test."

"Where were they murdered?" Dr McBride asked.

"They were on a bush trip," Marieke replied. "I did find some letters where you, Mrs McBride, recommend specific places to visit and camp. Can you tell me about them, so that we may better track their route and perhaps get some clues as to who may have done this?"

"Yes," Diana confirmed. "Patrick and I have been to some really lovely places in Botswana, so we suggested that David and Julia go as well. There was a *dambo* near Khwai that was really nice, and much farther north there was a waterhole near the Linyanti area that Patrick said was excellent for birds. It's funny, the guide that took us there, he was also an Englebrecht, Piet I think his name was. I didn't include that one with my suggestions, because as I recall you had to get permission from a concession holder to go there."

"Where did you find David and Julia?" Patrick asked.

"They were north of Maun, so probably following the route you had suggested," Marieke replied. "Tell me, when you were recently here, where did you go?"

"We went out into the Central Kalahari," Patrick explained. "I was chasing some falcons and we took David and Julia for a weekend trip. David is a keen amateur ornithologist, he has a life list that is at least as good as mine, maybe even a little better if he added any new species on this trip."

"Can you think of any reason at all why anyone would kill the Drs Turner?" Marieke asked again.

"None," Patrick said. "Could it have been robbery?"

"We are not ruling anything out at this time," Marieke temporised. "If you think of anything that they may have said to you in the past that may help us with our investigation, please contact me, if you have a paper and pen to hand I will give you my name and telephone number." She waited until Patrick announced that he was ready, and then she spelt her name for him and gave him the telephone number. That done she wished them good day and repeated how sorry she was that their friends had been killed.

So, perhaps a suspect to begin her list of such. Patrick McBride had not been very forthcoming about his whereabouts in the past few weeks. To say that he had not been in Botswana was not the same as saying he had been in England the whole time. Slipping over the border from Zambia, Namibia or South Africa was simple enough, so she needed to try and find out if he had been in England or had been elsewhere. She would also have preferred to talk to Diana McBride without Patrick there. Her view was that she learned more from separate stories than from a single voice, where one might take the lead and direct or influence the answers. Tomorrow was going to be difficult; it was possible that either Sara or David Turner might wish to actually view their parents. Marieke was not sure how either would react to the condition the bodies were in, apart from the post-mortem incisions, there was the evidence of animal predation on the soft tissue of the faces and the quite obvious bullet holes in the skulls. Well, that was a problem for the morrow. Now it was time to go home, rest and prepare for what was to come.

Her homeward journey was interrupted by Mbali who called just as she was leaving her office. Apparently, there were papers and documents to review and sign. So Marieke made a detour and stopped at the offices of Motingwa and Maroke where she found Mbali waiting for her.

"I thought bankers stopped work at five or even earlier?" Marieke joked to Mbali.

"Sometimes," Mbali agreed. "But, our work does not stop just because we close the bank; there is much to do after hours."

"I suppose this is after hours," Marieke said. "Thank you for helping me with this."

"It won't take long," Mbali assured her. "The mortgage documents are all ready, they just need your signature and the Patels should be here as well, shortly, and then we can sign all the deed transfer documents, in fact here they are now."

The Patels waved, and they all went through the formal greetings before going into the law offices. They were shown to a small conference room where documents and papers had been arranged in some sort of order. To those, Mbali added several cheques, one for the Patels, one for the lawyer's office, and one to the city for transfer taxes and fees. Mr Maroke came in and introduced himself to Marieke; he already knew the Patels and Mbali. Then it was a simple matter of moving around the table and signing one's life away. The whole process took about thirty minutes as both Marieke and Mr Patel read through the documents they were signing, before putting pen to paper. When it was all done, Mr Patel handed the keys to the house to Marieke, and Mr Maroke handed her the deed, and she was now a property owner again. Her first property had been the farm she had inherited from her parents, but that she had sold about a year after their deaths. After handshakes all around, the Patels left to go to their new house, Mr Maroke left to deal with other pressing matters, and Marieke was left looking at Mbali.

"Well?" Mbali said.

"I'm thrilled and scared," Marieke said. "With the farm, there was no debt, but now I feel as if I've indentured my soul to your bank."

"Of course you have," Mbali laughed. "But, you will find us to be very accommodating, except when it comes to payments, and if you miss a payment I know where you live."

"Have I done the right thing Mbali?" Marieke asked.

"Yes," Mbali assured her. "Gaborone is growing, the city will probably double in size in the next few years and your house will appreciate in value."

"I'm sure you're right," Marieke said. "So, I'd better stay employed for the next twenty years."

"That would be advisable," Mbali laughed. "But, Ian tells me that you are destined for great things, so I don't think that that will be an issue."

"That's good to hear," Marieke said.

"I'll take care of getting the telephone transferred to your name, the phone company will give you a new number, I'll let you know what that is tomorrow," Mbali said. "I've also arranged for the transfer of the water and electricity accounts."

"Thank you so much, trying to do all that and investigate my mystery would have been difficult. Do you have time for a glass of wine? My friend Melisende from France just sent me some nice wines and I've been dying to try at least one of them, this seems like a good reason the open a bottle," Marieke asked.

"That would be wonderful," Mbali said. "May I ask Jannie to join us?"

"Of course," Marieke agreed. They packed up their papers and left the lawyers' offices and Mbali followed Marieke to her house, soon to be her old house. She had told the landlord that she was leaving sooner than she had expected, and he had already found another tenant who was keen to move in, so he had terminated the rental agreement, with effect from two days hence, without any charges. Marieke privately thought that if she had not been a police officer he would have probably demanded payment for the full three months, and would have collected from the new tenants as well. She thought that she might have Sergeant Maphosa quietly look at the dealings of the landlord to see how close to the wind he really flew. At home, she showed Mbali the wines that she had received and they settled on a Graves from the Château Belon. Jannie arrived just in time for the opening and Marieke handed around glasses.

"Congratulations," Mbali said. "When would you like to move?"

"I think the day after tomorrow," Marieke said. "I'm going to be busy tomorrow and I'm not sure when I will be finished. But, I will have everything packed and ready to be moved. This Graves is really rather nice, isn't it?"

"Really rather nice?" Mbali said. "It's not really rather nice, it's excellent, your friend has good taste."

"I must write and thank her," Marieke said. "I don't know what I could send her as a gift from Botswana."

"You could always send her a diamond," Jannie joked. "We have plenty of them."

"What does your friend do?" Mbali asked.

"She's with the Sûreté," Marieke explained. "So, she's a policeman like me."

"Is she as good a police officer as you?" Mbali asked.

"Much better," Marieke said. "She was always the first in all our classes and the aggravating thing about her is that never appeared to work, it all seemed to come so easily to her. But, I really like her, so is so much fun to be with."

"Where does she live?" Jannie asked.

"In Lyon," Marieke said. "She's a senior officer there and does work with Interpol as well, and they're based in Lyon."

"Well, thank you for the wine," Mbali said. "We really must go home and see what the girls are up to. Jannie, will you be able to help Marieke move the day after tomorrow?"

"If she gives me a key I can move her at any time," Jannie said. "Is the furniture yours?"

"I'll put notes on what is mine and what came with the house," Marieke said. "I'll put all my own things back in the boxes they came in when I moved from Tsabong."

"Fine, then if you just give me a key, I'll move all your stuff tomorrow, if that's fine with you?" Jannie said. "I'll also check that the phone *ouks* get it working with the new number."

"That would be wonderful, thank you," Marieke said. "Are you sure that it's not too much trouble?"

"No man, it's fine," Jannie assured her. "Tomorrow's better for me, so I'll just get it done. When you finish work tomorrow, go to your new house and it'll be all ready for you."

"Thank you, here's a spare key to this house and here is the key to the new house," Marieke said, giving him the two keys. Mbali and Jannie then left, leaving Marieke with the job of repacking her belongings into the boxes she had so recently taken them from. She also went around the house and labelled all the furniture, hers and that of the landlord. By the time ten came, she was tired and had had enough, but the job was done.

Dressed in her best uniform shirt, blue trousers and polished boots, Marieke went to the station the next day and cleared off the few items that had been dropped on her desk. She pored over the lists of clients that Patience Botha had given her, looking for McBride, and certainly, a Patrick and Diana McBride had been to the Pitse camp twice in the past ten years. The first time eight years ago, the second time the previous year, so quite recently. The probability that there were two Patrick and Diana McBride was unlikely, but that did not make them killers, but they stayed firmly on her suspect list. Quite what his or her motive might be for killing the Turners was not at all evident, but perhaps bird watching and life lists was more cutthroat than she imagined, or perhaps some dalliance had occurred between one or other of the partners and the other had taken exception. The McBrides warranted another look. Marieke called the immigration people and asked them to check dates of entry and exit for her for the years in question. They promised to have the information in a day or so, the last visit would be easier because the records for that year were readily accessible, but for the earlier visit, it would take a little longer to get the information from the archives. At about 10:30 she went to the office of the commissioner and found that he was, in fact, just coming to find her to go to the airport.

"Are we ready for these people?" he asked.

"I think so," she said. "Thabo has the bodies ready in case they want to see them, if they do we'll have to make sure they understand that it won't be pretty."

"Good, shall we go?" he suggested. They drove to the airport in the new Land Rover that Marieke had taken north earlier, the commissioner had had it cleaned and polished and readied for them. At the airport, they picked up an immigration office and drove out onto the tarmac to await the arrival of the Air Botswana plane from Johannesburg. They watched it circle around then come in to land, taxiing up to the hard stand near where they were parked. The first passengers off were business people, some of whom the commissioner recognised then Marieke saw Sara Turner coming down the stairs.

"Good morning, Ms Turner," she said.

"Good morning, are you Superintendent Englebrecht?" Sara asked.

"I am," Marieke confirmed. "This is Assistant Commissioner Mochage of the Botswana Police, and Inspector Dube of our Customs and Immigration Service. Is your brother David with you?"

"He is," Sara confirmed. "He's coming; I think he had problems getting his bag down from the overhead bin. Here he is now. David, this is Superintendent Englebrecht and Commissioner Mochage, Botswana Police, and Inspector Dube from Immigration."

"Good morning, Madame, Sir," Inspector Dube said. "If you would give me your passports please, have you checked luggage?"

"We do," Sara said.

"If you would give me the luggage tags, I will collect the bags for you and meet you at the front of the building," Inspector Dube said. Sara handed her passport and luggage claim ticket to the inspector and waited impatiently while David took out his passport, then proceeded to go through all his pockets until he finally found the luggage ticket. Marieke watching this sensed exasperation on the part of Sara and wondered what the flight from London had been like.

"Welcome to Botswana," the commissioner said to Sara and David. "We are so sorry that this visit is one of such sorrow. If you will come with us will drive to the front of the terminal and collect your bags."

"How did my parents die?" David asked.

"I regret to have to tell you that they were murdered, by whom we do not yet know," the commissioner said.

"That's what Sara told me," David said. "But why were they murdered?"

"That we do not yet know," the commissioner said. "We were hoping that you might be able to help us with that."

"Why would I be able to help you?" David asked.

"Oh, grow up David," Sara said quite shortly. "Don't you watch any Inspector Morse or other shows, more than half of the time the killers are family members, driven by greed or envy. For the record, I was in France, in Bordeaux, for three of the last four weeks, I got back to England about a week ago."

"Thank you, Ms Turner," the commissioner said. "Mr Turner, would you tell us where you were for the last three weeks?"

"You can't think I had anything to do with this?" David asked.

"David, just answer the bloody question," Sara said. "They have to ask; they wouldn't be doing their jobs if they didn't. Really, David, there are times!"

"Fine," he said. "I was in the States, I went there on a business trip, I got back two days ago."

"Thank you, Mr Turner," the commissioner said. "Here is Inspector Dube with your passports and suitcases. Matshwane, will you help the inspector load the bags into the back? Shall we go to the station?"

"I'd like to see my parents," David said.

"Of course," the commissioner said. "But, I have to caution you that what you will see may be disturbing. There has been animal predation of the faces, and many people find that difficult to deal with."

At the morgue, Thabo Mosiwa had arranged the two bodies on tables in anticipation of this request and stood ready to give explanations. The commissioner introduced him to Sara and David Turner and then let him have the floor.

"I am sorry for your loss," Thabo said. "I have here Dr David Turner and here Dr Julia Turner, who would you wish to view first? I must caution you that what you may see may be disturbing; we are not dealing with death by natural causes."

"I understand," Sara said. "I think my mother first."

Thabo pulled back the covering sheet far enough that they could see the skull. The bullet holes were obvious, and so was the general lack of facial flesh. Sara looked at the head for a while, but David took one look and went for the sink. One of the technicians handed him a face cloth, a towel and a glass of water.

"Was the cause of death the bullet wounds?" she asked. "Have you any idea who shot her?"

"The bullet wounds were without doubt the cause of death," Thabo confirmed. "My police colleagues are currently investigating who and why."

"It looks like the head has been severed from the body," Sara said, looking at the neck.

"God, you can be ghoulish," David said. "Why do you insist on this?"

"I want to understand," Sara said. "The fact that the head was severed tells us something about the killer. This was not a random act of robbery; this was something more serious, wouldn't you say, Superintendent?"

"Indeed, Ms Turner," Marieke confirmed. "That caught our attention as well, which is why we need to understand more about your parents and their friends, acquaintances and, if they had any, their enemies."

"Don't be absurd," David said. "They didn't have any enemies."

"Get real, David," Sara said. "Clearly, they had at least one enemy; this whole thing points to that. Can I see my Dad now?"

Thabo covered Julia Turner and pulled back the sheet on David Turner.

"Same thing," Sara said. "Shot, then beheaded?"

"That is correct, Ms Turner," Thabo confirmed. "The only significant difference being the entry points of the bullets."

"Why is that significant?" David asked.

"I would suspect that Dad was shot first and then Mom," Sara said. "What do you think, Superintendent?"

"It's a working hypothesis that we have," Marieke agreed.

"How did you confirm identities?" David asked. "It doesn't seem to me that you could do much from this."

"Your parents had visited a dentist here locally," Thabo said. "We were able to get X-rays of the teeth and compare them to those of the dentist's X-rays. Are there other distinguishing marks?"

"Mom had had her appendix out when she was about twenty," Sara said. "That left a scar. Dad had cut his left forearm quite badly about ten years ago, which also left a scar." Thabo uncovered the left side of David Turner and showed the arm; Sara looked at it and confirmed that it was indeed her father. Thabo then took her back to the other table and carefully arranged the cover so that the PM cuts were not obvious and showed her the appendectomy scar. Sara nodded confirmation.

"Is there anything else?" Thabo asked.

"Dad told me once that he had broken a bone in his arm, I think it was the right one," Sara said. "Mom broke her shin once when she tripped on the stairs and cracked a bone in her left arm trying to save herself from a fall."

"Thank you," Thabo said. "That fits with X-rays we took of the skeletal structures."

124

"Thank you, Ms Turner," the commissioner said. "Is there anything else here that we can show you?"

"There were no rings or other jewellery?" Sara asked.

"I'm afraid there was nothing," the commissioner replied. "Thank you for your time, Dr Mosiwa. When may we release the bodies to Ms Turner and Mr Turner?"

"I'm finished," Thabo said. "I have all the information I need. What would you like done with your parents' remains, Ms Turner?"

"I'll arrange to have them shipped to England," Sara said. "We will bury them in a churchyard in the village where they both grew up."

"There is one more item that you will need," Thabo said. "Here are six copies each of the death certificates; you will need these for such things as insurance policies, banking and the like."

"I see you have causes of death listed as homicide," Sara said.

"That is correct," Thabo confirmed. "We are satisfied, given the nature of the wounds and the impacts they would have upon the body, that the gunshots inflicted would have caused sufficient damage to the brains as to cause death."

"Will the insurance companies be satisfied with that?" David asked. "They won't want to know the actual means of the homicides?"

"In our experience, they will be satisfied with that," Thabo confirmed. "If the deaths were of natural causes, they might want the actual cause, such as heart failure, in case there are insurance clauses that deal with pre-existing conditions, but that is not an issue here."

"Thank you, Doctor," Sara said.

"Shall we go to the station then?" the commissioner suggested.

At the Central Police Station, Marieke ushered Sara into one room, and the commissioner took David to another. Sergeant Maphosa joined Marieke to take notes, and an Inspector Bangwata joined the commissioner. The two interviewers went through the usual litany of questions about the Drs Turner, trying to build a picture of who they were dealing with and who might have reason to dislike them. They broke for lunch at one and took their respective charges to different restaurants in town to the amusement of Sara and the disquiet of David, who obviously had been planning to rely on his sister to supply all the answers. Marieke had sensed frustration on the part of Sara with David and got the story over lunch. He had not wanted to come on this trip, but had wanted to go off with some of his friends, pheasant shooting in the Chiltern Hills. Sara had laid the law down, and he had come along unwillingly, complaining and griping the whole way, to the extent that on the flight to Gaborone from Johannesburg, she had changed her seat to one well away from him. The interviews continued after lunch, and then Marieke asked Sara if she would like to see the house where her parents had lived. Sara saw no point as she assumed that all their personal effects were already on the ocean on their way to England. Marieke took Sara to the offices of both Drs Turner and explained that they had removed certain materials as part of the investigation. Sara asked that when it was all done that they be returned to her, which Marieke agreed to do. After that, Sara asked to go to the hotel. Marieke dropped her off and saw that the commissioner was also dropping off David. Marieke said her goodbyes for the day and told Sara that she would be in touch again the next day.

When the two Turners had been checked into their rooms and bags sent up, Marieke and the commissioner excused themselves and went off to compare notes. The commissioner told his piece first. David worked for a dealer in antiquities, White Horse Antiquities, which raised the antennae of both police officers. To them, dealers in antiquities often sailed close to the wind when it came to provenance, not that there were not scrupulously honest brokers, but their experience had been that the industry was rife with less-than-honest brokers. David had read art at the University of Leeds and had joined the dealer straight from college. Sara had gone to LSE, the London School of Economics, and had subsequently gained an MBA through the Wharton program in the United States and had joined Bentham Investments six years earlier. Judging by her comments, Marieke put her down as a high flyer who was going places with the firm. Sara, rather more than David, knew the McBrides well, and was a fan of Diana's but rather less than a fan of Patrick; she saw him as an opportunistic womaniser, as long as his wife was out of earshot or not present. David, on the other hand, liked Patrick and saw him as rather a rôle model, perhaps because he would like to emulate the conquests with women that Patrick seemed to manage. Marieke and the commissioner scrutinised the copies of the passport pages that Inspector Dube had made for them, and as far as they could tell, their stories held water. David was the easiest to check, as the United States was diligent in stamping entry and exit dates. Sara was not so easy; the British rarely stamped the passports of their own citizens, and the French were haphazard. Still, a call to Melisende would probably confirm Sara's story fairly quickly. The commissioner finally said that he had had enough for the day and suggested that Marieke go home.

Marieke drove to her new house and found Mbali and Jannie waiting for her. All her furniture had been moved and even put into the rooms she had thought of, the boxes of effects had been divided up and were placed in the rooms that matched the labels she had put on them. So, kitchen was in the kitchen, and so on.

"Marieke, how was your day?' Mbali asked.

"Difficult and long," Marieke replied. "This investigation is going to be long and difficult."

"Well, have a shower, change your clothes, we're taking you to dinner," Mbali announced. "Jannie just got a new large contract for truck repair that might even call for an expansion of the shop."

"That's wonderful," Marieke said. "Are you happy with the business, Jannie?"

"No man, it's a good deal," Jannie said. "We'll do well out of it. Oh, and here is your new phone number."

"You should go and shower and change, Marieke," Mbali said.

Dinner was at a popular place in town, and Marieke saw Sara and David Turner there. She asked Jannie to get a table while she and Mbali went to see the Turners.

"Good evening, Ms Turner, Mr Turner," Marieke said. "This is Mbali Lamprecht, she is the bank manager of the branch your parents did business with, you might wish to make an appointment with her to discuss monetary matters."

"Good evening," Sara said. "That sounds like a good idea, what time would be convenient for you, Ms Lamprecht?"

"Would ten be fine with you?" Mbali asked. "Here's my card, get a taxi to the bank, and we'll take care of things."

"Are there large account balances?" David asked.

"Large enough," Mbali said. "We can arrange details for transfer to you both tomorrow. Please bring your passports as a means of identification."

"Thank you," Sara said. "We'll be there a ten."

"What's she like?" Mbali asked as they walked to the table that Jannie had been given.

"She seems very capable," Marieke said. "She certainly seems to know a lot about police procedures. She's a member of an investment firm in London, so expect her business dealings with money transfers to be very professional. The brother, less so, he works for an antiquities dealer, and I think does not have the business acumen that she does."

"Well, I'll let you know what I think tomorrow," Mbali promised.

"All done?" Jannie asked as they sat down.

"All done," Mbali said. "Shall we eat?"

Impressions

Marieke got up to a strange house and remembered that she had moved into what was now her own house. It would take a little while to get used to the idea, but it was gratifying to now be a property owner again. She made breakfast and contemplated the day. There was much to mull over; her board that she had started to pin things up on needed updating, and there were notes to type up. Now that she had moved, she also needed to pick new routes to go to work. This was the first day from the new house, so today she would pick a route and designate it as route one, she would leave the house and turn right and right again at Tlokweng Road, right on Hippopotamus, right on Maratadiba and then work her way to Pula and Botswana until she reached the Central Police Station. It might be circuitous, but one day it might be useful. At her office, she looked at her sparse board. It had pictures of the victims, the crime scenes and now a few other faces, the daughter and son, the McBrides, as placeholders only, Dr Chebani, Ian Ross, as a placeholder and the graduate student, Thabang Kanedi. So far, nothing had arisen that even began to point to a possible motive, unless someone really wanted the chair at Oxford and was bound and determined to get it by hook or by crook. She decided to start eliminating people; the son, David, had been in the United States, or so his passport indicated, so he was unlikely. The daughter said she had been in France, and there were no other stamps in her passport to indicate otherwise, but it would not hurt to check. Marieke called Melisende and was lucky enough to get straight through to her.

"*Bonjour Melisende, ça va?*" she asked.

"Marieke, it is so good to hear from you. Did you get the wine?" Melisende asked.

"I did," Marieke confirmed. "Thank you, I cannot believe that you did that, it was so thoughtful, I hope you did not spend too much money."

"It is of no matter," Melisende said. "How is the new job?"

"Interesting," Marieke said. "The first case I have is two people, both murdered, then beheaded and the heads and bodies buried in different places."

"*Sacrebleu*," Melisende said. "Do you know who they are?"

"I do now," Marieke said. "We were lucky to find the bodies, then we worked backwards to search for the heads. They are Dr David Turner and Dr Julia Turner, both professors here at our university, but were to be leaving soon as David Turner just was awarded a prestigious chair in economics at one of the Oxford colleges."

"What is next in your investigation?" Melisende asked.

"I need to eliminate unlikely suspects," Marieke said. "I have a favour to ask of you?"

"Please, how may I help?' Melisende asked.

"The daughter of the victims said that she was in France at about the time of the murders," Marieke explained. "I need to confirm her story."

"Who is she?" Melisende asked.

"Her name is Sara Turner, date of birth, 6th of July, 1960. I will fax the front page of her passport to you," Marieke said. "She says she was in France for a few weeks, only returning to England about four days ago."

"That should not be too difficult," Melisende said. "I will investigate and tell you what I learn."

"When will you come and visit me in Botswana?" Marieke asked.

"Perhaps at the end of this year," Melisende said. "I have some leave coming, and they are pressuring me to take it. Would that be convenient for you?"

"You are welcome at any time," Marieke said. "When you come, I will show you some of Botswana. *À bientôt.*"

"*À bientôt,*" Melisende promised. "*Au revoir, chérie.*"

Marieke was delighted that Melisende might be coming to visit later in the year; she promised herself a few days' leave and thought about where she might take her friend. She made a few notes of places, then recalled that she had promised to fax the front page of Sara Turner's passport. That only took a minute, and then Marieke went back to her musings.

Marieke sat looking distractedly at her board full of photographs and notes, then sat up bolt upright. She remembered the Land Rover that they had brought in and the roof rack. Clipped to the roof rack were a high lift jack, a shovel and an axe; they were the standard tools one would expect to find, which is perhaps why she had not really noticed them in the context of the crime scene. Could it be that the axe and the shovel had both been used in the crime. Berating herself for not thinking of this sooner, she called the Maun station and talked to Inspector Moroka and asked him to bag up the two items and send them to Gaborone at the earliest possible convenience. How she could have missed something so obvious. She knew that she needed to find an axe, and there was one in plain sight, attached to the victims' Land Rover. It was always possible that the killer had used his or her own axe, but here was one very conveniently placed for the killer to use. What next, Marieke thought. She decided that she should interview the secretaries at the university and find out who knew what the itinerary of the Turners' was going to be. She drove to the university and asked Dr Chebani to direct her to the relevant departments. She started with economics and was introduced to Lillian Mafa, whom Marieke recognised as the beautiful young woman from the sketchbook.

"*Dumela Mma*," Marieke said. "As I am sure you are now aware, Dr David Turner was found dead in the bush, and I am investigating the circumstances of his death. I am sorry if this causes you distress, but I have to ask questions if I am to discover how they both died. I understand that you were privy to the arrangements that Dr Turner made for his trip into the bush?"

"*Dumela Mma*," Lillian said. "Thank you for your concern. I don't think I could have talked about this yesterday, but now I am mostly cross, cross that they are dead and that someone did this, I just want to find out who and why. As for their itinerary, I think most of us knew the schedule. David made no secret of his plans. They were to leave here on the 4th and drive to Maun. They were going to camp near Maun and then drive to Khwai on the 5th, they had planned to stop at a waterhole they knew of near the Khwai Safari Lodge until the 11th and then they were going to drive to Chobe and camp at the Savute campsite, then they were going to drive on up to Kasane via the Ghoha Gate on the 27th, stay overnight at the Chobe Game Lodge, then come back here on the main road through Francistown."

"Did you inform anyone of his plans?" Marieke asked.

"Oh yes," Lillian confirmed. "I let Julia's friend Diana McBride know all the details, and I promised to keep her apprised of any changes to the route or the dates. I also gave the itinerary to Dr Adams from Oxford. He was most anxious to keep tabs on them as he was getting ready to welcome them to Oxford and David's new post. Let's see, David was informed of his appointment six months ago, he started planning the trip to Maun about four months ago, and I let everyone know at least three months ago, we even posted it on the bulletin board with a map of their route, campsites and dates and everything."

"How many people, would you guess, knew of the itinerary?" Marieke asked.

"I don't know," Lillian admitted. "I know I probably told fifteen people, and I am sure they told others. It was the topic of discussion here for a few months."

"You were on good terms with Dr Turner?" Marieke asked.

"Oh yes," Lillian confirmed. "I helped him with all his arrangements and proofread all his papers."

"And with Dr Julia Turner?" Marieke asked.

"Julia is a dear," Lillian said. "She had her own interests and passions. She is a very talented artist. I posed for her a couple of times. She also played tennis a lot and was in really good physical shape, rather like you, Superintendent. She and I spent many evenings together while David was away in England for his interviews."

"You seem very close to both the Doctors Turner?" Marieke asked.

"I am, or should I say, was," Lillian confirmed. "David was even talking about getting me a visa to go and work for him in Oxford."

"Really?" Marieke asked. "Isn't that a little unusual?"

"I suppose it is," Lillian agreed. "But, I think he really liked the way I arranged his papers and did background research for him, and he was especially appreciative of the proofing I did for him. He was talking about getting me a post as a research assistant in the new department he was going to head."

"Aren't his papers a little technical?" Marieke asked.

"They are," Lillian confirmed. "But, I got a degree in economics here at the University after I took a degree in English. I couldn't find a job that I really liked until David interviewed me for a job here, and he hired me on the spot. The salary is perhaps less than I could be earning in another job, but I have had an amazing education in economics since proofing David's papers, and I have had several offers since he got the chair at Oxford."

"Will you stay on to work for the new professor, when he or she is retained?" Marieke asked.

"I don't think so," Lillian said. "I think it's time to move on. I think I'll take a job with the Government in the Treasury Department. I have been talking to them about a post that looks at economic development and how that relates to future tax revenues. Perhaps I'll look at the police department; obviously, women can progress with them."

"Policing tends to be hours of tedium," Marieke laughed. "We get a few hours of excitement, but most of the time it is humdrum."

"I'm sure that cannot be true," Lillian said. "This investigation must be interesting. How did David and Julia die?"

"That is something that we are investigating," Marieke dissembled. "Tell me, did you meet the McBrides ever?"

"I did," Lillian confirmed. "I must say that I was drawn to her, but that he, Mr McBride, made me uncomfortable, I think he has an eye for women and is less than faithful to his wife."

"How would you describe the relationship between the McBrides and the Turners?" Marieke asked.

"Between Julian and Diana, it was very close, I think in the past it had been really close if you see my meaning, but then I understand that many women in British universities experiment with their sexuality, of course, here that would be illegal, so it officially never happens," Lillian expounded.

"And between David Turner and Patrick McBride?" Marieke asked.

"I think their common enthusiasm for birds got the better of them; it even made David look the other way when Patrick McBride made eyes at Julia," Lillian replied. "But, for all that, I don't think Julia ever fell for his advances; he was just not her type, even more so, I think, because she leaned the other way. I do know that when the McBrides were here, they slept in separate rooms."

"Did Mr McBride seem put out by the relationship between his wife and Julia Turner?" Marieke asked.

"I cannot really say," Lillian admitted. "But, I doubt it; he was too self-centred to notice other people's feelings, even those of his wife."

"Is there anyone you can think of who would wish harm to either of the Doctors Turner?" Marieke asked.

"Honestly, no," Lillian said. "They both had their quirks, but were both very sweet. I suppose there were professional jealousies, particularly with David, but he is a brilliant man and must have ruffled feathers in his life. He did tend to be quite critical of work that he did not think was adequate and could be harsh at times with the criticism, but I'm sure the criticisms were justified."

"Did you ever meet the children, Sara and David?" Marieke asked.

"Sadly, no," Lillian said. "I would have liked to, but it was not to be."

"Thank you for your time," Marieke said. "If you think of anything that you believe may help lead us to solving this issue, please call me at the Central Police Station."

Marieke left that office with much to think about. Clearly, Lillian had ambitions and those ambitions were tied to David Turner, but that made it unlikely that she was an obvious suspect. But if she had had any romantic involvement, then that person might object to the closeness that Lillian seemed to have with the Turners. The next interviewee was Nnunu Sejeso, who was the secretary for the Statistics Department. Marieke found her sitting at a desk, talking on the telephone. Marieke estimated that she was probably in her mid-fifties and looked as if she would be prim, proper and organised. She had also featured in the sketchbook of Julia Turner. Nnunu hung up when Marieke came in, looked up and smiled.

"*Dumela Mma*," she said. "How may I help you?"

"*Dumela Mma*, I am Assistant Superintendent Englebrecht," Marieke replied. "I am investigating the deaths of Dr David and Dr Julia Turner."

"That was such a shock," Nnunu said. "And at such a time too, Dr Julia told me how much Dr David was looking forward to his new chair."

"How long have you worked in this department?" Marieke asked.

"Ten years," Nnunu replied. "I started with the university when it was first founded as a lowly typist and have been here ever since."

"Can you think of anyone who might wish either of the Doctors Turner any harm?" Marieke asked.

"Apart from the unsuccessful candidates for the chair at Oxford, no, not really," Nnunu replied. "I know that Dr David was sometimes very critical of others and their work, but then he is, was, a truly brilliant man, and I think that at times he could be insensitive."

"What was your relationship like with Dr Julia Turner?" Marieke asked.

"We managed very well," Nnunu said.

"Did you know of the travel plans of the Turners?" Marieke asked.

"Oh yes," Nnunu said. "We have a map on the wall there, with the dates marked when they planned to be at the various campsites. You can see here, their first night in Maun, then here at the *dambo* near the Khwai Safari Lodge, here at the Savute Camp Site, then the Chobe Lodge, it was all well planned out, almost to the minute."

"Did anyone specifically ask about their travel plans?" Marieke asked.

"Almost everyone who knew them," Nnunu explained. "I would just refer them to the map, and they could see for themselves."

"Ms Lillian Mafa told me that she had informed a Dr Adams of Oxford of the travel plans. Did anyone from outside Botswana ask you about the plans?" Marieke asked.

"Ms Mafa, that one," Nnunu said. "No, I do not recall anyone not from here asking me about them."

"I imagine that Ms Mafa will be looking for a new post now," Marieke said. "She seems to have been very involved with the papers that Dr David Turner published, rather than being the general secretary for the Economics Department."

"Ms Mafa will find another star to hitch her ambitions to," Nnunu said. "If she cannot find one, then she will find an influential woman and attach herself to her."

"How would you describe the relationship she had with the Turners?" Marieke asked.

"Unhealthy," Nnunu said. "I think it a shame that Dr David was so caught up in his work that he did not see the goings on between Dr Julia and Ms Mafa, not that I have any definite idea, it's just that they seemed very close."

"I gather that Dr Julia was an artist?" Marieke asked.

"She was very accomplished," Nnunu agreed. "That painting there of a waterhole is hers, and that one of a young woman is hers, I think either is of a quality that they would be hung in a major art museum."

"Looking at them, I would agree," Marieke said. "How did you get on with Dr Julia?"

"We have a mutual respect for one another's capabilities," Nnunu said. "I know that she is an excellent statistician and she relied on me to type up her work, proofread her papers and collect and collate data for her. Our relationship was very professional, never personal, unlike that of Mafa."

"Did you ever meet Diana McBride?" Marieke asked.

"Once," Nnunu said. "She and her husband, Patrick, came to visit a while ago. Apparently, Mr Patrick wanted to go to the Central Kalahari chasing some hawks, I think it was. Dr David wanted to go as well, but I think that Dr Julia and Mrs McBride were less than keen. But in the end, they did go. I think that Dr Julia and Mrs McBride had been very close at university, very close, in fact I think that apart from the two times that they must have interacted to have the two children, that Julia preferred the company of women, which is probably why she and the Mafa got on so well. But, I have said too much, I should not be saying such things of the dead, particularly as one may draw an inference of illegal behaviour."

"All of this is interesting," Marieke said. "But, nothing that I have heard from anyone suggests any motive for the deaths of the Doctors Turner."

"It is a puzzle, isn't it?" Nnunu agreed. "The only possibility I can come up with is a dissatisfied candidate for the chair that Dr David won. I gather that it is of such prestige that it was much sought after and that the competition for the post was fierce. Dr Julia told me that there was much politicking in the background and I presume much back-biting and unpleasantness in the rounds of interviews."

"If you do think of anything that might be helpful, please call me at the Central Police Station," Marieke said. "Stay well, Ms Sejeso."

Marieke went back to the office of Lillian Mafa and found her there talking to a man. Marieke waited until he had gone, then asked her question. "Please excuse me for returning," she said. "But, I wonder do you have a list of the selection committee for the chair at Oxford and the shortlist of other candidates?"

"The committee I have," Lillian said. "The shortlist of other candidates we pieced together from things we heard, but we were never officially told. Here is the list of committee members, and this is our best guess for the shortlist."

"Thank you, *Mma*," Marieke said. "Again, if you think of anything, no matter how trivial it may seem, that you can recall about the trip of the Turners, their dealings with Oxford, or anything else that may help us solve this mystery, please call me."

"I will," Lillian promised. "I hope we meet again, Superintendent. I am sure we may have much in common. Go well."

"Stay well," Marieke replied and left.

At the police station, Marieke went to see the commissioner and reported on her conversations with the department secretaries.

"So, impressions?" he asked.

"What at first blush appeared to be a nice, normal, happy relationship is becoming murky," she replied. "I have two lines of enquiry that I am thinking of, the first being marital issues stemming from the relationship between Julia Turner and Diana McBride and perhaps Patrick McBride finally deciding that enough is enough and taking action, albeit a little on the drastic side and second, one of the other candidates for the chair who decided that they really wanted the job."

"Do you know who the other candidates were?' he asked.

"We have a best guess put together by David Turner," she replied. "It's probably fairly accurate as I'm assuming he knew the others in his field who would likely apply for the post."

"What about the selection committee?" he asked.

"Well, let's see, we have a Dr Nicholas Adams, listed as the Master of the college, then we have a Dr John Entwhistle, Economics, Professor Henry Wilson, Mathematics, Dr Susan Bullock, Economics, Dr James Webb, Physics, and Mr Simon Bentham," Marieke enumerated.

"Bentham, would that be of Bentham Investments, I wonder?" the commissioner remarked.

"Well, it is an endowed chair, so there has to be someone who has given the money as an endowment. Why not Bentham Investments, I looked at them, and they do a lot of investing in developing nations, so it would make sense for them," Marieke said.

"I wonder why Sara Turner didn't mention that?" he asked. "Are they still here?"

"They had an appointment with Mbali Lamprecht at ten this morning to arrange for the transfer of funds from the accounts the Turners had to England," Marieke said. "I will check to see if that meeting is done and if they went back to their hotel."

Marieke left and went back to her own office. Sergeant Maphosa was there with a box. He had been to the house of the Turners and had gone through all the rooms, including the attic storage space and another storage space he had found under the floor and another in the garage. He had a treasure trove of items, including some 10,000 Pula and 5,000 Rand that he had retrieved from under the floor. The banknotes were old, and he thought it likely that they had been there for some time, probably even before the Turners rented the house. He had also found documents that had been stuffed into the wall. He had noticed a difference in the wall finish behind what had been the hanging spot of a painting and had lightly probed it with a needle to discover a cavity in the concrete block wall and thence the documents. Looking at them, Marieke decided that it was more likely that they related to the cash than to the Turners, as they dealt with stock sales to the abattoir at Lobatse. It looked as if they dealt with stock thefts and the subsequent sale to the abattoir. She decided that they would forward them to the department that dealt with stock thefts and let them investigate. Lastly, Sergeant Maphosa had also found a collection of sketches, probably done by Julia Turner, some of Lillian Mafa, some of animals, some of Botswana scenes, some of birds and several of a woman that Marieke wondered might be Diana McBride. The Mafa and McBride sketches were all nudes, and Sergeant Maphosa was quite embarrassed by them. Marieke decided to keep them until the case was solved, in case they had relevance to the investigation. When it was over, she would send them to Sara Turner as next of kin, but for the moment, they needed to be away from view. That done, she called Mbali and learned that the Turners had left only a few minutes earlier and were on their way back to their hotel. Marieke told Sergeant Maphosa to drive her to the hotel and come back in an hour to pick her up. At the hotel, she called the room of Sara Turner. She came down to meet her in the lobby, and Marieke suggested tea on the terrace while they talked.

"So, have you learned anything new since yesterday?' Sara asked.

"*Dumela Mma*," Marieke said. "I trust things went well at the bank this morning."

"Oh, that," Sara said. "No problems at all, Mbali Lamprecht is all business and sorted things out brilliantly. So, what did you want to see me about?"

"Were you aware that one of the selection committee members for the chair that your father won was Simon Bentham?" Marieke asked.

"Of course I knew that," Sara said. "Simon told us that he was going to endow the chair, and he knew that Dad was a likely candidate."

"Did Mr Bentham ever discuss the interviews with you?" Marieke asked.

"No, Simon was straight and above board; he kept me out of that loop because he knew that someone might misconstrue the relationship and presume that I had traded favours for the appointment," Sara said.

"I see you have thought about this," Marieke said. "Why did you not tell us this yesterday?"

"It never occurred to me that it might be relevant," Sara said.

"Thank you," Marieke said. "What can you tell me about Diana McBride and the relationship with your mother?"

"I didn't want to say too much yesterday, particularly in front of David, because he idolises Patrick McBride who I think is a womaniser and a generally unpleasant arse," Sara started. "But Mom and Diana had an affair in college, which actually continued covertly through the years. I don't think they ever got over each other. Dad was oblivious, as was David, but I could see the signs. Dad was in his own world of economics, and Mom was often left holding the bag and wondering if he ever came down to earth. Diana was always there, but I think lately that Patrick had begun to finally wake up and suspect that the relationship was still active. I didn't say too much yesterday because I know you've got laws here that are not favourable to lesbians or gays, I trust that you will use this information about Mom and Diana with discretion?"

"Of course, it is one of the reasons I came alone, my sergeant would be embarrassed by such things, as he is by the sketches your mother made of Lillian Mafa, your father's secretary. You did not disapprove of your mother's relationship with Diana McBride?" Marieke asked.

"Not at all," Sara replied. "I understand it only too well, but I trust you will keep that to yourself, not even David needs to know that."

"Why does Diana McBride stay with Patrick McBride?" Marieke asked.

"I've asked myself that same question many times," Sara said. "Maybe she's afraid of him, maybe she sees him as financial security, I don't know. I presume you've talked to them?"

"I talked to them on the telephone, yes," Marieke confirmed.

"And, I presume that Patrick organised things so he was in on the act, never letting Diana answer without his coaching or say so?" Sara said.

"That was my impression," Marieke confirmed.

"Check on the whereabouts of Patrick for your dates and see where he actually was," Sara suggested. "I'll bet he was cagey about where he had been over the past month or so."

"All he would say was that he had not been to Botswana in the past month," Marieke said.

"That sounds like Patrick," Sara said. "What that meant was that he was out of the country, and he wasn't going to tell you where. It strikes me that the borders between Botswana, Zambia, South Africa, Namibia and Zimbabwe would be hard to patrol and slipping over the border would not be hard if one were determined."

"The thought had occurred to me," Marieke confirmed.

"You said that Mom had been sketching a Lillian Mafa?" Sara asked. "Can I have those sketches?"

"As soon as this investigation is over, I will send them to you," Marieke promised. "I will share with you that the sketches she drew are most impressive and that Lillian Mafa is an exceptionally beautiful young woman."

"Maybe Mom found someone to be with while she was here," Sara mused. "Dad would have been so focused on this chair that I doubt that he would have noticed them having sex of the floor in front of him."

140

"Surely not?" Marieke protested.

"No, you're right, he would have seen that, but Mom would never have embarrassed him in such a way; she would have been much more discreet," Sara said.

"When do you return to London?" Marieke asked.

"Tomorrow," Sara replied. "I have an appointment with an undertaker this afternoon who has dealt with shipping remains overseas, and then I have to get back to work. If there is anything else you might need from me, then please call my office, I'll let the people there know your name and tell them that if you call to get me immediately. I want to find out who killed Mom and Dad."

"What are we all talking about?" another voice said, and they both looked up to see David Turner walking towards them.

"We were discussing shipping the bodies back to England and why I did not mention that Simon Bentham was on the selection committee for Dad's chair in Oxford," Sara said.

"Oh, right," David said. "Caught you out, did she? Well, that's a first."

"Tell me, Mr Turner, is there anything else you would like to tell me?" Marieke asked.

"Not a thing," he said. "I just want to get out of here and go back for some shooting before all the pheasants are gone."

"Will you come back to Botswana?" Marieke asked.

"I doubt it," he said. "Nothing here for me, the crumblies are dead, it's too bloody hot and dusty, and I've got business coming up in the States that'll keep me busy for a while."

"Well, if you do think of anything that might be in the slightest bit germane to the investigation, please call me," Marieke said. "I've taken too much of your time, thank you for clearing that issue up for me, Ms Turner, Mr Turner, go well."

Marieke went out to the street and waited in the shade for Sergeant Maphosa to come back and collect her. She fell to remembering her own relationship with Melisende while she was at university and wished that her government would relax the laws that banned such behaviour. It was part of her past that she kept a tight lid on; there were plenty of male officers in the hierarchy of the police force who would be happy to see her embarrassed and gone, as she would be if word reached the commissioner of any such current relationship. If and when Melisende did come out for Christmas, she would have to be very careful. She saw Sergeant Maphosa turn the corner by the hotel and walked out of the shade to meet him.

"Where to, Madame?" he asked.

"The morgue, I think, Isaac," she said. At the morgue, she confessed to Thabo her oversight on the axe and shovel and asked him to get them both carefully checked when they arrived. Thabo promised that he would, then excused himself and went off to find Sipho to ask why he had not taken the axe and shovel. He thought he knew the answer; they were both part of what one would expect to find on a Land Rover on a trip into the bush, so much part of what one would expect that you would look right past them. He needed to remind Sipho to gather all evidence, not just that mentioned in a request by the police officer in charge. Marieke had the sergeant drive them back to the station, where she sat down in front of her board and thought. Her musings were interrupted by the commissioner, who came bustling in.

"Matshwane," he said. "I gather you have been out and about."

"Yes, Sir," she confirmed. "I asked Sara Turner why she had omitted to tell us that her boss, Simon Bentham, was on the selection committee."

"What did she say to that?" he asked.

"She was apologetic," Marieke said.

"That's all?" he asked.

"She did say that she had not thought it relevant, and then she did provide me with further insights as to the relationship between Julia Turner and Diana McBride," Marieke explained. "All of which makes me look closer at Patrick McBride. I was thinking of calling your friend in the Zambia Police to see if McBride has visited Zambia lately."

"I will do that," the commissioner promised. "I need to talk to Joseph Phiri about some cross-border traffic."

"Very good, Sir," she said. "I think I'll finish for the day and go and see if my new house is still there. Oh, by the way, a thorough search of the Turner house turned up some interesting documents and cash that seem to be connected with stock theft from some years ago."

"What was it, 10,000 Pula and 5,000 Rand?" the commissioner asked.

"It was Sir," Marieke confirmed. "We're going to turn over the papers to the stock theft department and let them handle it."

"And the sketchbooks?" he asked.

"I'm keeping those under lock and key for a while," she said. "I don't need people spending their time ogling nude sketches."

"Good," he agreed. "When we're finished with this, you can send them off to Sara Turner. Now go home and visit your new house!"

"Yes, Sir, stay well," she said.

"Go well, Matshwane," he said.

At her house, Marieke threw off her clothes and turned on the shower full blast to wash away the day, but unfortunately, water seemed to be in short supply, and she got a trickle, not a blast. Well, it was better than nothing; she would address the water supply in the morning. Perhaps she could get Jannie Lamprecht to take a look for her; she imagined that he would be able to at least diagnose the problem for her, either an issue with her pipes or an inadequate supply from the city. Dinner was next, she had rice, she had chicken and some vegetables, so a stir fry in a wok seemed appropriate. She liked cooking with a wok, one pan did it all and clean up was simple, rice was another matter, she needed another pot for that, and her experience was that she, as often as not, managed to catch and scorch the rice, not knowing that certain Japanese groups liked scorched rice. While she ate her chicken and rice and sipped her Chablis, Marieke thought about the day and what she knew and did not know. The latter was a much more pressing issue. She really did not know yet who and why. She knew when, approximately and how, but who and why still eluded her. Patrick McBride made a nice, convenient suspect, but life was rarely that simple. Still, it might be in this case, so she would not drop him from the list. She really needed more details on who had been to the waterhole in the Linyanti and when. It all hinged around that. The spot had been picked for the burial, of that she was certain, and it was not an easy spot to find, so whoever buried the bodies knew how to get there. The next best thing to do was to track down Piet and Anna Englebrecht and ask them if they remembered going there, when and with whom.

The following morning, Marieke got up early and went through her usual exercise routine before going to the hotel where the Turners were staying. She saw them checking out and went to greet them.

"Superintendent, have you come to check on us again?" David asked.

"*Dumela Rra, dumela Mma*," she said in greeting. "Actually, I've come to ask if you need a ride to the airport?"

"That would be lovely," Sara said. "David, bring the bags, would you?"

"I'm sorry this trip to Botswana was filled with such unhappiness," Marieke said. "Perhaps if you come again, you will enjoy our country better."

"I would like that," Sara said. "If you're ever in London, here's my card, please call on me."

"Thank you," Marieke said. "Tell me, did either of you ever meet Dr Adams, the Master of the College?"

"Not me," David said.

"Nor I," Sara echoed. "Is he a suspect?"

"No," Marieke laughed. "I just wondered what is going to do now."

"I think pick the number two off the list," David said. "Easy, just get your runner up and crown him the new head."

"Here we are at the airport," Marieke said. "Let me help you through the formalities."

Marieke watched as the Air Botswana plane took off for Johannesburg and glanced at the card that Sara had given her, with a hand squeeze that suggested an invitation. Well, that was twice in as many days that she felt that she had been propositioned. But, enough of that, she had to ask the commissioner for permission to go to South Africa and visit with Piet Englebrecht. First, she would call Englebrecht and see what he remembered, and if she had to, she would visit him and jog his memory. At the office, she called the South African information service and got the number for Piet Englebrecht in Calitzdorp. Then she tried the number.

"*Goeiemôre*," a female voice said.

"*Goeiemôre*," Marieke replied. "*Mag ek asseblief met Piet Englebrecht praat?* Is he home today?"

"This is his wife Anna, who's calling, please?" was the reply.

"This is Assistant Superintendent Englebrecht of the Botswana Police," Marieke said.

"Genuine?" Anna asked. "This isn't a joke?"

"No, Mrs Englebrecht, I believe you have met my cousin Katrina and her brother-in-law William Martin, who bought the Pitse Concession from you, and I have also been talking to Patience Botha in Maun," Marieke explained.

"Man, hold on while I get Piet," Anna said. She was gone a little while, and then she came back on the phone with the message that Piet was just coming.

"*Ja*, this is Piet," he said.

"This is Assistant Superintendent Englebrecht of the Botswana Police," Marieke said again. "I believe you know my cousin, Katrina Martin and Patience Botha of Maun. Patience told me where to find you."

"You're Katrina's cousin, genuine man?" he asked.

"Genuine," she confirmed. "My dad was the one they never talked about who lived in South West."

"*Magtig*, what can I do for you?" he asked.

"We are investigating two bodies that were found in the Linyanti area and wondered if you might remember taking any visitors to a particular waterhole?" Marieke explained.

"Man, I took so many visitors to so many places, you'd have to be more specific," he said.

"If I were to come and see you with a map, would that help?" she asked.

"*Ja*," he agreed. "I could try. It's been a couple of years. How are Will and Bridget doing?"

"I would say very well," Marieke reported. "Look, if I were to fly into Oudtshoorn, could you pick me up there?"

"How will you get to Oudtshoorn?" Piet asked.

"A pilot offered to give me a ride," Marieke explained. "I'm going to see if his offer still holds."

"No man, that would be fine," Piet said. "Just call back and let me or Anna know what day and time, and one of us will be there."

"Thank you," Marieke said. "I will call as soon as I know my plans."

Next, Marieke decided that she had better talk to the commissioner before she went any further. She needed his permission to fly to Johannesburg and then south to Oudtshoorn. That would have to wait until Monday morning. Even police assistant commissioners took some time off, and although there was not much left of Saturday, he would probably not relish the idea of work over the weekend. So, she went home, changed into shorts and a shirt and made a tour of her new yard. It was not too large, with a few patches of grass, clinging to life. There would be no exotic lawn of grass without irrigation, and Marieke saw no point in throwing water away on something as trivial as a lawn. She could live with the brown dirt, but she did think that, in time, she might pave the backyard with blocks, so that she did not track too much dust and dirt into the house. The water pressure seemed good, so perhaps her problem before had been the city water supply. She decided to call Mbali and Jannie to see if they would like to come to visit with her.

"May we bring the girls?" Mbali asked when Marieke proposed lunch.

"That would be nice," Marieke said. "I would like to meet them."

"We'll be there at about eleven," Mbali promised. "What should we bring?"

"I think chairs for the outside," Marieke suggested. "I have some chairs and a table, but not enough yet for five people."

Soon after eleven, the Lamprechts arrived and carried chairs, food, drink and all kinds of other things into the house, through the house and into the backyard. Mbali made the introductions, and Marieke found herself relating her life story to the two girls while Mbali and Jannie took care of lunch. After lunch, Khanyo suggested that on Sunday, they take Marieke to the Gaborone Yacht Club for the day; she even offered to teach her to sail. Marieke thought that sounded like a nice day out, a day away from investigations and police work. It was agreed to by all, and arrangements made for them to pick Marieke up and drive out to the club. Access to the club was now by ferry since the dam wall had been raised and the water level had risen, but that made the adventure even better.

After a wonderful day out at the Yacht Club, Marieke was energised and ready to pursue her investigation with new vigour. She bearded the assistant commissioner in his office as soon as she arrived at the police station and presented her request for travel authority. He listened to her reasons and explanation and agreed that their next best course of action was to try and discover who had been to the waterhole and when. They had the data from the recent past from Will and Bridget, but Marieke felt that they should go a little further back.

"I presume your passport is still in order?" he asked.

"It is, Sir," she confirmed. "I would only be gone a day or two."

"I think we should plan for three days," he said. "One day to get to the wilds of South Africa, one day for interviews and one day back. Am I not correct that Calitzdorp is the home of Hanepoot?"

"It is, Sir," she confirmed. "I will try and bring you back a bottle."

"Well, book your flights and let me know when you will be going," he said. "The department will pay for tourist fares on intra-Africa flights."

"Very good, Sir," she said. She left the office and called the number Koos had given her. She got an answering service, so she left a message for him to call her. Before she could make any more calls, she received a call, and it was from Melisende.

"*Bonjour, chérie,*" she said. "*Ça va?*"

"*Bien merci,*" Marieke replied. "*Et vous?*"

"*Toujours bien.* I have checked on your Sara Turner," Melisende said. "She was indeed in France for the dates you gave me. She landed in Paris on May 29th and then rented a car and drove to Bordeaux, where she stayed at the Stars Bordeaux Gare Hotel, a new place that just opened this year. She drove back to Paris and left France on the 17th of June. I'm sorry I could not be of more help, but that is what our records show."

"No, that is fine, thank you, *chérie,*" Marieke said. "I just wanted to be sure that I could take her from the list of suspects."

"Have you made any progress with your investigation?" Melisende asked.

"Not really," Marieke admitted. "I have a suspect, but there could be others, so I keep searching."

147

"Well, I heard that they call you the honey badger," Melisende laughed. "I understand that he is small and fierce and will not let go of whatever he bites into."

"How did you hear that?" Marieke asked.

"One hears these things," Melisende said. "I'm sorry, *chérie,* I must go, I have a meeting that I must be at, I am in charge, so should not be late for my own meeting, *au revoir.*"

"*Au revoir,*" Marieke said.

It was lunchtime before Koos called back, "*Middag,* Superintendent, so nice to hear from you, what can I do for you?"

"*Middag,* Koos," she replied. "I was wondering if your offer of a ride somewhere was still on?"

"Sure, sure," he said. "Where do you want to go?"

"If you could manage it, from Jo'burg to Oudtshoorn or Calitzdorp," she said.

"Calitzdorp, why the hell do you want to go there?" he asked. "That's *regte Boer* country."

"I need to see a man about some past visitors," she explained.

"You don't want me to pick you up in Gabs?" he asked. "It would be much quicker than coming here, then flying down south to the Cape."

"I would need to clear immigration," she said. "I doubt I can do that in Oudtshoorn, and I doubt that Calitzdorp even has an airport."

"I can fix that," Koos said. "We'll stop in Kimberley, clear customs and immigration there; then fly on to Oudtshoorn, good opportunity for a break as well; it's about 650 miles from Gabs to Oudtshoorn."

"Are you sure that you want to do this?" Marieke asked. "It seems to me that the fuel alone would cost a fortune."

"I can work something out," he said. "I'm always getting odd charters. When do you want to go?"

"That's rather up to you," she said.

"Well, tomorrow I have a charter to Maun, then a deadhead on Wednesday to the Cape, then a return on Friday with two passengers for Gabs, from Cape Town," he said. "What if I pick you up on Wednesday after I've dropped off my Maun charter, I'll run you down to Oudtshoorn and pick you up on Friday when I bring my other charter up to Gabs?"

"Why would someone charter you to fly from Cape Town to Gabs?" she asked. "Why would they not take a commercial flight?"

"Who knows," he said. "My guess is that they have some issues with the departure times. We are leaving Cape Town at 5:30 in the morning, so we'd be in Oudtshoorn at about 7:00, we'd pick you up and fly north, maybe stopping for a break at Kimberley if anyone needs it."

"I'm sure I can arrange that," Marieke said. "What time would I need to be at the Gaborone airport?"

"Let's say 8:30 in the morning," he suggested. "That'll put us into Kimberley at about 10:30, say half an hour for customs and such, then another two and a half hours to Oudtshoorn, that would get you there at 1:30 in the afternoon, coming back, you'd be in Gabs by about noon, would that suit?"

"That would be fine," Marieke assured him. "Are you sure that this is fine with you? I don't want to inconvenience you."

"No, man, it's fine," he assured her. "Give me someone to talk to on the way down to the Cape."

"Good, then I'll be at the airport here at 8:30 on Wednesday morning," she promised. "What do we do for lunch, shall I bring something?"

"That would be *lekker* man," he said. "I'll see you Wednesday then."

Now that air transport was arranged, the only thing she needed to check on was accommodations. She was sure that there would be a hotel in Oudtshoorn, but was less certain of Calitzdorp. She decided to call Piet Englebrecht and ask him what was there.

"*Goeiemôre*," Anna said when she answered the phone.

"*Goeiemôre*, this is Assistant Superintendent Englebrecht of the Botswana Police again," Marieke said. "Would it be convenient if I came to see you on Wednesday of this week?"

"Of course, when would you be here?" Anna asked.

"I'm flying into Oudtshoorn at about 1:30 in the afternoon, and I leave again on Friday at 7:00 in the morning," Marieke explained. "Is there a hotel in Calitzdorp?"

"No, man, stay with us," Anna said. "You're family, maybe distant, but family. I'll have Piet pick you up at the Oudtshoorn airport the day after tomorrow, and we'll get you back there in time enough to get your flight back. Who's bringing you that you're flying into Oudtshoorn?"

"Koos Strijdom from Jo'burg," Marieke replied. "I met him when he was flying Will and Bridget Martins' children from Jo'burg to the Selinda strip."

"Oh, we know Koos," Anna said. "He used to bring charters in for us as well. It'll be nice to see him again. Will he be staying as well?"

"He said he has a charter from Cape Town really early Friday morning," Marieke said. "But what his plans are for Thursday, I don't know."

"I'll call him," Anna said. "Does he still have the same number?"

"I've no idea," Marieke said. "But this is the number I called." She read off the number and heard Anna writing it down.

"It's a new number," Anna said. "We look forward to seeing you on the day after tomorrow, *tot siens*."

"*Tot siens*," Marieke said and hung up the phone.

The assistant commissioner would be happy; this was going to be a low-budget trip. She had a flight and place to stay with no outlay. Now, to put together the maps and lists and work out what it was that she wanted to ask Piet. At the moment, she was just collecting background information, looking for lists of people who had been to the waterhole; later, she hoped to be able to compare that with visitors to the country, either legitimate visitors or those who may have slipped in across the border. Her theory was that someone who knew the waterhole and who had obtained the travel plans of the Turners, went to a neighbouring country, slipped across the border, committed the murder, then slipped back and went home, never showing up on the Botswana entry slips. She knew that she was looking for two people, as both Land Rovers had been driven north. It might have been possible to use a rigid tow bar to tow the second Land Rover, but they had seen where the two vehicles had pulled up parallel to one another, which bespoke two drivers. While she was thinking about that, the commissioner came to her office.

"It seems you may be on the right track with Patrick McBride," he said. "My friend, Chief Superintendent Phiri, tells me that he was in Zambia from the 30th of May until the 8th of June. He landed in Lusaka, giving his address as the Ridgeway, but he only stayed there two nights, then he disappeared."

"Would you ask your friend Mr Phiri to make discreet enquiries and find out if anyone purchased a .22LR rifle or pistol and if someone answering to McBride's description hired a car in Lusaka in late May or early June?" she asked.

"That may take a little while," the commissioner said.

"It will take as long as it takes," she said.

"What's your theory?" he asked.

"I think someone entered Botswana from either Zambia or Namibia or even South Africa, crossing the border illicitly, after purchasing a gun, they did the deed, then crossed back, dumping the gun along the way," she said. "To me, Zambia seems very convenient, the Zambezi is easy to cross, even at night, and is a great place to dump a gun. I was thinking, we need a picture of Patrick McBride, and we have to work out who else may have been involved."

"You think it's that simple?" the commissioner asked.

"No, Sir," she said. "Even if I'm right and McBride and or another did do the murders, with no gun, only speculation as to how they intercepted the Turners, killed them, buried the bodies and then left, how am I going to prove it, I would need a confession?"

"You don't include Zimbabwe as an entry point?" he asked.

"It's a possibility, but to me, rivers are a better way to slip across the border and a very convenient way to get rid of a gun, we have the Zambezi, the Limpopo and the Linyanti and the Chobe, but between us and the Zims we have a land border, tracks are easier to find along land borders, on the rivers, one can start upstream and drift down, so that finding matching tracks on both sides of the river is more difficult," she explained. "It's possible, but I like the others better."

"To get from the border to Maun, they would need transport," he said.

"We may be looking for a diesel Land Rover vanette, blue with a full canvas tilt," she said. "One was seen in the same vicinity as the victims' Land Rover at about the time we believe they were murdered. My thought is that we ask in Kasane or Kazungula if anyone rented a Land Rover to a *muzungu* around that time."

"We should also ask around here, between Lobatse and Francistown," he said. "Don't let your theory exclude other possibilities."

"No, Sir," she said. "I would also like to know who was on the shortlist of candidates for this chair in Oxford."

"So would I," he agreed. "Chebani at the university has no idea, and the Oxford people won't tell him. You may have to see the Brits at their embassy and see if they can help."

"Very good, Sir," she agreed. "I'll do that first thing next week when I've been to South Africa. Meanwhile, I wonder if any conferences on the economic theories that deal with developing countries have been held either here or somewhere close in the past five to ten years?"

"Check on that," he said. "You may be lucky and get some matches of people. Is there anything else at the moment?"

"Not at the present, Sir," she said.

"Well, let me know when something else comes your way," he said.

"Very good, Sir," she said.

Marieke checked the time and noted that it was just before six, but that meant it was still before five in London, so she called Sara Turner.

"Bentham Investments, Sara Turner speaking," was the reply.

"Good afternoon, Ms Turner," Marieke said. "How was your flight home?"

"Well enough, thank you," Sara said. "I changed my seat to be away from David and had a nice, quiet flight. How may I help?"

"I was wondering if you have or could get photographs of Patrick and Diana McBride for me?" Marieke asked. "Your parents may have had some, but most of their belongings are on the water."

"I'll get them for you," Sara promised. "Does that mean you're looking at Patrick?"

"He is a person of interest to us," Marieke admitted. "But, I am a long way from naming him as a suspect."

"Pity," Sara said. "I would like to see that arrogant bastard behind bars; does Botswana have the death penalty?"

"We do," Marieke confirmed. "It has been used for cases of aggravated murder, and then the convicted are hanged."

"So, if you can prove who killed my parents, would that be aggravated murder?" Sara asked.

"That would depend on the prosecution service," Marieke explained. "We would give them the facts, details and evidence of the case, and they would then decide how to prosecute."

"Well, I wish you success in your quest for the truth," Sara said. "Do you ever come to London?"

"I haven't been for some years," Marieke admitted. "I went twice when I was at university in Lyon. I enjoyed the city and would like to see it again."

"Well, when you come, be sure to call me and I will show you London," Sara promised.

"Thank you," Marieke said. Do you have my card and the address to post the photographs to?"

"I do," Sara confirmed. "Do you want mug shots or portrait shots?"

"Just something that will let me see what he looks like," Marieke said.

"I'll send you a variety," Sara promised.

"Tell me," Marieke started. "What other interests apart from birds does Patrick McBride have?"

"Medieval warfare and history," Sara replied. "His whole house is full of stuff, suits of armour, bows, arrows, swords, you name it."

"Does Diana share the passion?" Marieke asked.

"Not likely," Sara laughed. "But she has done some illustrations for him for some books he's published."

"Thank you," Marieke said. "I should let you go, stay well."

Before she left the office for the day, Marieke left a note for Sergeant Maphosa that she would be making visits to the university and other places the next day and that she would be out of the country from Wednesday until Friday.

Lists

Marieke stood in a hangar with Inspector Dube of the Customs and Immigration Service and watched as the Cessna Skymaster landed and taxied over towards them. Koos was on time, perhaps a little early, as it was not yet 8:00 in the morning. He must have left Maun early to get there before eight. Koos parked the plane in front of the hangar and waved to her. She was excited to be taking this flight; it would be the first time she had flown over much of South Africa at a low altitude. All the flights she had taken before were on large jets to and from Europe. Her experience with small planes was exclusively in Botswana; this would be different, because there were mountains to see to the south, the diamond mine at Kimberley and other sights. Koos talked to the general aviation people about fuel and waited until the bowser came, then he paid for what he needed and watched as they transferred the fuel. While that was going on, Inspector Dube walked out to the plane and took care of formalities, a simple enough process, just an exit stamp in Koos's passport. When the fuelling was done, Marieke walked out to the plane and said her good mornings.

"So, Superintendent, ready for the trip?" Koos asked.

"I am," she confirmed. "I think we can be less formal, please call me Marieke, I have lunch here, where shall I put it?"

"Give it to me, I'll put it on the seats behind, got your bags, I'll shove them in as well?" Koos said. "Let me make a quick pit stop, and we can be off."

While she waited for Koos to return, Marieke thought about what she had learned the day before. She had spent some time with Lillian Mafa and they had scoured through old calendars, publications, professional journals and notes and found a conference held in Cape Town some ten years earlier and another held at Wits, six years earlier and most recently in Lusaka, just two years ago. She had the programs for all three conferences and the lists of attendees and was intrigued to note that the Wits conference included either a 'Safari excursion' to Botswana in the Linyanti area, sponsored by the tourism authority of Botswana, or a road trip through the Kruger National Park. In fact, they all had some form of field trip, the Cape Town trip was to Addo or a wine tour in

154

Stellenbosch and the Lusaka trip included options to the Luangwa National Park or to Vic Falls. The lists of attendees included many names in common, and David Turner had been to all three. She had noted a George Benson on the lists and wondered if he was the George B. that Turner had referred to. There was also a Paulo Schirano on the two earlier lists. Perhaps he was the pasta-cooking Paulo. Some of the names matched those that Will and Bridget had provided. On the lists that Patience had provided that went back before the time of Will and Bridget, were David Turner, George Benson and Paulo Schirano, but that did not make the latter two suspects. Lillian Mafa had been able to go through the attendee lists and identify all of them, with current places of employment. Most were of academia, but there were also people from various governmental development agencies and some think tanks and foundations. It had taken the better part of the day, but Marieke now had a list of probably the best 120 people in the field of economic development in underdeveloped countries. She wondered out of those 120, how many had applied for the chair at Oxford and who might be on the shortlist.

"Penny for your thought?" she heard Koos say. That brought her out of her reverie and back to the present.

"Oh, sorry, I was just thinking about my day yesterday," she said.

"Nothing bad, I hope?" he said.

"No, just a lot of information for me to sort through," she explained.

"Well, shall we go?" he asked. "Did you bring some warm clothes? It could get chilly in Caltizdorp."

"I did," she confirmed. "I think I brought too many clothes, but I wasn't sure what to expect."

"Well, whatever you brought didn't weigh too much," he said. "Let's hope that the *ouks* I'm picking up on Friday read the pamphlet and kept their luggage to a minimum. We should make you official. Here's a company shirt and hat; I've even awarded you two stripes for your epaulettes. Wear it on Friday, then the charters won't complain about another person in the plane."

"What route will we be taking?" Marieke asked when they were in the air and Koos had stopped talking to various ground controllers.

"We'll go south over Mafikeng, then the little *dorpie* of Schweizer-Reneke, then on into Kimberley," he said. "In the old days, we would have followed the railway to Mafikeng, then down over Vryburg and on to Kimberley, but our nav systems are better now, so we can go direct."

"How was your flight down from Maun?" she asked.

"Pretty sunrise," he said. "I like the early mornings. Nice and quiet, not too much traffic. So, I gather you're going to see Piet and Anna today?"

"Yes, did Anna call you?" Marieke replied.

"She did," Koos confirmed. "I'm going to stay the night and go on down to Cape Town tomorrow, I've got plenty of time. Don't worry, I'll stay out of your way when you ask your questions."

"Do you keep records of charters you have taken?" she asked.

"I keep flight records, have to by law, usually I list the number of passengers, but I also keep the manifests that list the actual passenger names," Koos said.

"How far back do your records go?' she asked.

"Typically seven years," he replied. "That's how long the tax people ask for records to be kept, but I've got all my log books since I started flying."

"Do you have any of your earlier manifests?" she asked.

"When are we talking?" he asked.

"Say six years ago," she said. "I was particularly interested if you did a charter for a group of economists to Linyanti from Jo'burg six years ago?"

"I remember that," he said. "We had four plane loads go out, twenty *ouks* in all, they were crowded flights, they stayed four days, then flew back. I only remember it because we had a flight of four, only time I've submitted a flight plan of four. I felt sorry for Kurt, he had two *ouks* who lost their breakfast on the way up from Maun, it took him almost the whole of the next day to get the plane clean."

"Would you have the manifests for that trip?" she asked.

"No, but my booking agent probably will, she keeps everything," he said. "And, I mean everything. I'll ask her when I get back. If she has it, do you want a copy?"

"Yes, please," she said.

"Still trying to work out who buried those *ouks* up on Wills's place?" he asked.

"It is a puzzle," she agreed. "What's that down there?"

"That's the Mafikeng airport," he said. "Nice little airport, one runway as the winds are pretty reliable. Have you ever flown a plane?"

"No," she said.

"Well, there's always a first time," he said. "Put your hands on the yoke and feet on the pedals, okay?"

"Okay," she said with some trepidation. After that, Koos guided her through the essence of flying straight and level, of making slight banking turns, of climbing and descending, until she realised that she was really enjoying herself. That enjoyment turned to mild panic when he announced that they would begin their approach to Kimberley. But he kept his hands lightly on the controls at all times and guided her carefully through the whole process, until they were on the ground, all the while pointing out the highlights of the scenery, including the Big Hole, as the famous diamond mine was called.

"Now, if you ever are in a bad situation and have to land a plane, you know what to do," he said when they taxied up to the general aviation hard stand. An immigration officer came out to meet them and waved to Koos.

"Koos, *ou maat*," he said. "What brings you to Kimberley?"

"Lunch break," Koos said. "Marieke Englebrecht, meet Hansie Botha, one of the best. We were in the Air Force together. We're on our way to Oudtshoorn to see some friends."

"Oudtshoorn, hey," Hansie said. He took the passport that Marieke proffered and flicked through it. "You're Botswanan, Marieke?"

"I am," she confirmed.

"Well, welcome to South Africa, and if this *ou* gives you any problems, let me know and we'll throw him in gaol," Hansie said, stamping the passport and handing it back to her. "What brings you to our part of the world?"

"I'm going to visit Piet and Anna Englebrecht in Calitzdorp. Piet is a cousin of mine," she explained.

"Calitzdorp, hey, bring me some Hanepoot back when you come north," Hansie joked. "You said this is a lunch break, a bit early for lunch, isn't it?"

"I suppose so," Koos admitted. "You wouldn't have any coffee, would you?"

"*Ja*, of course," Hansie said. "*Kom kom*, we'll get some while they put fuel in your plane."

"We should get going," Koos said. "I promised Anna we'd be there about 1:30; don't want to keep her waiting." He and Marieke said their thanks to Hansie for the coffee and then went out to the plane. For this leg, Koos instructed Marieke on takeoff procedures, which Marieke discovered was far easier than landing. She found that she really enjoyed flying and thought that when she got back to Gaborone, she would look into getting a pilot's licence. They flew south-southwest, basically following the railway line from Kimberley to De Aar, then Beaufort West. Just before they reached Beaufort West, Marieke looked out of the window and asked Koos where Renosterkop was.

"Where?" he asked.

"Renosterkop," she repeated. "It's where the Englebrechts come from, it's just east of Beaufort."

"Looking at the map, it must be that little *dorpie*, just this side of Beaufort," Koos said. "Look, down there, that must be it, because out there is Beaufort. Okay, when we come up to Beaufort, make a turn to the left and head due south, it may get a little bumpy as we head over the Groote Swartberge, and better let me take the controls as we cross them and head on down into Oudtshoorn."

Koos was right, flying over the mountains was a little bumpy, but Marieke was thrilled to see snow on top of the mountains, something they just never saw in Botswana and that she had not seen since she left France. Once over the mountains, they descended to the Little Karoo valley and Koos talked to the controllers at George and got his landing clearance for Oudtshoorn. The wind was coming off the coast between south and south-west, so Koos made a high banking turn to get them over Oudtshoorn and then landed towards the South. He taxied up to the general aviation ramp and saw Piet Englebrecht waving to him.

"*Piet, hoe gaan dit man?*" he asked.

"*Goed dankie, en met jou?*" Piet replied.

"*Goed dankie*. Piet, this is Marieke Englebrecht," Koos said by way of introduction.

"*Aangename kennis*," Marieke said.

"Nice to meet you in the flesh," Piet said. "I've got my *bakkie* over there, we can go whenever you're ready."

"Let me just close up my plane," Koos said. "Then we can go. I'll bring the lunch that Marieke brought."

"So, you're Katrina's cousin," Piet said as he drove them to Calitzdorp. "Patience told me about the family rift, but, hey, maybe that's all going to change now, Mandela's out, many of the more stupid apartheid laws have been repealed, it won't be long before we have elections and everyone will get to vote."

"Big changes," Koos agreed. "So, how are the grapes doing?"

"We've had some good harvests," Piet said. "I've learned a lot about making wine, and my Hanepoot is pretty good. I'll give you some to take home when you leave. You're going to Cape Town tomorrow?"

"I am," Koos confirmed. "I have a charter from Ysterplaat to Gabs on Friday, so I picked up a new co-pilot."

"Is he making you fly him around?" Piet asked of Marieke.

"He showed me some of the basics," she said. "It was fun; I might just take up flying when I go home."

"Well, here we are," Piet said. "Come and meet Anna."

The Englebrechts' house was a Cape Dutch-style and set among farm buildings and vineyards. Piet pointed out the wine press building and where the vats were, even the bottling room. Marieke asked for a tour after they had finished with the business at hand. Piet suggested that they do that the following morning, then Koos could also see the place and the process, before heading off to Cape Town. Anna came out to greet them and offered coffee or tea. Coffee was the general choice, so she suggested they go inside as it was quite chilly out.

"Have you had lunch yet?" Anna asked.

"We have what Marieke brought with us," Koos said. "But, we've not eaten it yet. What did you bring, Marieke?"

"Cold chicken, *boerewors*, salads and tomatoes," she replied.

"Bring it in and I'll add to it and we can eat while we talk," Anna said.

"So, what brings you here?" Piet asked after Anna had set food and drink on the kitchen table.

"I am trying to gather information on when you may have visited a certain waterhole on the concession that you used to run," Marieke explained. "Koos, you may as well stay, because you may remember taking people out to Linyanti."

"Is that where Will found the two *ouks* with no heads?" Piet asked.

"It is," she confirmed. "My conjecture is that whoever buried the people there had been before, it is not the easiest place to find."

"Which waterhole was it?" Piet asked. Marieke opened a map on which she had marked the location. "Oh, that one," Piet said. "Good place for birds, usually plenty of antelope and sometimes lions. When are we talking about?"

"I don't know," she admitted. "Will and Bridget now keep logs of each trip they make and what they see, so Will was able to provide me with information on who had been out there and when. But, before that, I have only the guests' lists that Patience gave me; I don't know where you took any of them."

"*Ag man*, that's going to be hard to remember," Piet admitted. "I probably went there once a month at the most, so if we take the season as May to October, that's six trips a year. No more clues?"

"You remember all those *ouks* that came out in the four planes?" Koos asked.

"*Magtig*, I'd almost forgotten about them," Piet said. "A whole load of professors all running around in the bush, worse than ten-year-olds."

"Did you take them there?" Marieke asked.

"We did," Anna interrupted. "We had to take both *bakkies* and they were full full, Piet drove one and I took the other."

"*Ja*, I remember," Piet said. "That had to be six years ago. Have you got the lists that Patience gave you?"

"Here," Marieke said, offering them to him.

"*Ja*, I remember some of these *ouks*," Piet said. "Turner was from Gabs so was the local expert, who wasn't very expert, this Italian, Schirano, was quite funny, Benson, I remember him, he seemed to be mates with Turner, this *ou* Holmes was a pain, knew everything, even tried to tell Jackson that he was wrong about some tracks."

"I see from the list that there were some women as well," Marieke said.

"*Ja*, the one, Barbara Roberts, a Yank, she was a *regte* pain, frightened of her own bloody shadow," Piet laughed.

160

"Did any of them seem to take a specific interest in the place?" Marieke asked.

"Not that I could really tell," Piet said. "I was too busy trying to keep from losing them. Two *ouks* did spend a lot of time walking around the clearing by the waterhole and asked me where the roads went; that would have been Harold Swanson and the Frog, Pierre Garnier. Come to think of it Swanson's wife, this *ou frou* Emily, she was along as well, I got the feeling that they were arguing about something, certainly were cold towards one another, she was an academic as well, so who knows, maybe he'd pinched her work and put his name to it."

"What about other visits there?" Marieke asked.

"Well, as I said, it's hard to remember," Piet said. "But let me think about it for a while, and I'll check my old files and see if I kept any notes of trips."

"What about the day you saw the elephant kill the lion?" Anna said.

"*Ag, man, ja,*" Piet said. "I'd gone out to the waterhole, must be five years ago, in July, and we saw an elephant take out a lion, trampled it to death, then threw the carcass up into a tree. She was really pissed off and the lion was too slow for words. The other eles in the group saw off the rest of the pride. They'd been after a calf and *ouma* got the hell in and *moor'd* the bloody thing"

"Who was along then?" Marieke asked, thinking about what Piet had just said and her father's admonition, *moenie the twee languages op mix nie.*

"The same two *ouks* that I just mentioned as being really interested in the clearing," Piet said. "I probably wouldn't remember them, but for the ele and the lion."

"So, those two came back only a year or so after their other trip?" Marieke asked. "The wife, Emily, did not come?"

"No man, weird *ja?*" he confirmed. "But I thought it was a good sign that the two *ouks* came, because it was repeat business. Do the lists that Patience gave you show any others coming back?"

"There are names that crop up with repeats," Marieke said. "But, unless the name is unusual or I have more information, I cannot presume that it's the same person."

"*Ja,* like trying to say Piet van de Merwe came back three times," Piet laughed. "How many vans are there? This may take me a while to think about it. Why doesn't Anna show you where you're going to sleep? Later, we'll take you over to the Gamka and meet Katrina's folks. It's not far from here, and they said they'd like to meet you."

"That would be fine," Marieke said. She had never met any of the others in her family, so this would be a first and would be interesting.

At about five, Ann called for Marieke and Koos, and they all drove to the farm of Koot and Sussana Englebrecht. It was set by the banks of the Gamka River and also had vineyards, but was not as extensive as that of Piet and Anna. Koot saw them arrive and came out to meet them.

"*Naand*," he said. "I am so pleased that you came to see us, Marieke."

"I confess to being in two minds," Marieke said.

"I understand," Koot said. "When your Pa left and went to South West and we left and went to Northern Rhodesia, none of us spent much time trying to contact the other, and your *ouma* and *oupa* just didn't want to have anything to do with your Pa after he married Patience."

"You know that they both died about ten years ago?" Marieke asked.

"I do," Koot said. "We knew a little about you, but not much. I'm sorry that things were as they were. Piet and I had been close as kids, so it was strange when we didn't talk. I'm sure we both made excuses about the mail and phones, but if I had really tried, we could have stayed in touch."

"How is Katrina?" Marieke asked.

"No man, she's fine," Koot said. "She and James live in Utah, he runs an aerospace company there. If you ever get to the States, I'm sure she would like to meet you. But let's not stand on the *stoop* talking, come on in and meet Sussana. I'm sorry, we haven't met," he said to Koos.

"Koos Strijdom," Koos said. "I'm the pilot; I flew Marieke down from Gabs this morning."

"Where do you go from here?" Koot asked.

"I'm flying to Cape Town tomorrow, then I'll be back on Friday with a charter, pick up Marieke at Oudtshoorn and then fly back up to Gabs," Koos explained.

"Please to meet you," Koot said. "Please come in."

Marieke and Koos followed Koot in and met Sussana, who was effusive and delighted to meet Marieke. She looked at Koos and Marieke and decided that they did not belong together. Over dinner, Koot told tales about the childhood he and Piet had had and the things they got up to. Koot again expressed his sorrow for not keeping in contact with his brother and hoped that Marieke and Katrina might someday meet. He and Piet then got into a discussion about whose Hanepoot was the better. Marieke suggested that she take a bottle of each back with her and hold a taste test with the people in her office. That met with laughing approval, and Koot went off and came back with not a bottle but a case.

"I hope you have friends in Customs," Koos said. "If Piet gives you a case as well, then that probably exceeds the usual limits."

"Dube is okay," Marieke said. "We'll just make sure that we see him when we land."

"What about your charter?" Koot asked.

"*Ag* man, they won't know," Koos assured him. "I'll stow this in the back and put their luggage on top of it, if it doesn't all fit underneath."

"So, what brings you to South Africa, Marieke?" Koot asked.

"Piet didn't tell you?" Marieke asked. "I'm a police officer, and I have a case that I'm investigating at the moment that Piet may be able to help me with."

"What's he done?" Sussana asked.

"No, no," Marieke assured her. "Piet has done nothing. I'm looking into people who may have visited the concession that he ran."

"Will found two headless *ouks* buried on the concession," Piet said. "Now Marieke needs to find out who killed them and buried them way out there."

"It wasn't Will, I presume?" Koot asked.

"I'm certain that it wasn't," Marieke assured him. "I'm not sure of motive yet, but it all seems very personal and very planned."

"I think Marieke has theories and suspicions," Anna said. "But, she's good at diverting questions."

"I have some theories," Marieke agreed. "But proving anything will be very difficult. It all started when Will found an empty Land Rover with no licence plates and no tax disk. Subsequently, we discovered that it

163

had once belonged to your son-in-law James, who had sold it when they left Zambia."

"Well," marvelled Sussana. "Fancy that!" On that note, Marieke said that she was tired and could use a good night's sleep.

The next day, Anna conducted the tour of the vineyards and the winery while Piet rummaged through old files and papers to see what he could find. He had already set aside a case of his Hanepoot, with the note that he was sure it was infinitely better than that of Koot. At the end of the tour, Anna took Koos to Oudtshoorn so that he could fly on to Cape Town, and Marieke sat down with Piet to see what he had discovered in his files and notes.

"This is a listing of my best memories of when we went to the waterhole and who I think was along for the trip," he said. "I've also included notes of all those I think came back for one or more subsequent visits."

"Thank you," Marieke said. "Is there anything that stands out?"

"Weird," Piet said. "Those professors who came, the economists, ten of them, came back either once or twice, I've listed all the dates here."

"Do you have a list of the professors who made the first visit?" Marieke asked.

"*Ja*," he said. "Here, there are six Bits, five Yanks, three Frenchies, two Eyeties, two Dutchies, one Aussie and one Kiwi, of them, five are *tannies* and the rest are *oomies*."

"Are there any that stand out?" she asked.

"*Ja*," he said. "Four came back just before we sold to Will and Bridget."

"Who?" she asked.

"Harold Swanson, Paulo Schirano, Bernard Leclere and Susan James," he said. "Swanson actually made three trips in all, Schirano just the two, Leclere two, and James also came back three times, interestingly at the same times as Swanson."

"What about Patrick McBride and or Diana McBride?" she asked.

"McBride, yes, there was a McBride, came three times in all, he was nothing to do with the professors," Piet said. "He came twice when Swanson was there, are they your *skelms*?"

"I have no reason to think so at this time," Marieke dissembled.

"But, they're in your sights," Piet insisted. "McBride, I remember him, first-class *does*, avid bird watcher, I think supposed to be some kind of expert on raptors, but he didn't know much about our raptors, chased every woman he saw, even tried it on with Anna, who pointed a rifle at him and told him to *voetsek*. I didn't have to do anything, but checked him out a couple of times and made a comment about how far we were from anywhere and how it would be to find him if he went missing, and he got the message. Any of these *ouks* show up on Will and Bridget's lists?"

"Let's see," she said, looking over the lists that Bridget had provided. "Well, that's interesting, last year Swanson came back again with Susan James, but they didn't go to the waterhole, Will shows that he spent most of the time to the West and the South of their camp."

"*Ag ja*, there is a track that comes up from Khwai, that brings you in from the South to the West of the waterhole," Piet said. "Anyway, here are my lists as best I can remember. Hope they're of use to you."

Anna was back in time for a late lunch, then she suggested a drive back into Oudtshoorn to see an ostrich farm and the Cango Caves. Marieke was intrigued by the ostriches and remembered something her father had told her about the farm that her great-grandfather had had in Oudtshoorn before the Boer War. She would have liked to have known where it was, but all she knew was that it was somewhere near the river. The Cango Caves entranced her, and was particularly interested in the tour guide's comments that the San had known of the caves long before they were discovered by others, after the San had been driven north by other groups moving in. Over dinner that night, she asked Piet and Anna about the time when they had first met Katrina, and they told her the story. She was interested in the tale of the trip to the hill in the Central Kalahari and the recovery of the box compass and other items. She had heard bits of the story from her father but did not know the whole story. She was delighted to hear that Katrina had the journal of her great-great-grandfather, Jan, and his adventures in the Kalahari and then beyond with the San. One day, she would like to be able to read the journal, even if it meant going to the States to do so.

165

The next morning, early, Marieke said her goodbyes to Piet and Anna drove her to Oudtshoorn to meet Koos. They both waited until they saw him circle around and land. Marieke had donned the shirt that Koos had given her and even wore the cap. He saw her and waved and taxied over to them.

"*Môre*," he said, as he opened the door, then he turned back to his passengers and asked, "Do you folks want a break for the facilities, *la salle de bains*?"

"*Oui, merci*," the woman said. "Where do we go?"

"Please come with me," Anna said.

"*S'il vous plâit*, wait for me," the man said.

"*Goed*," Koos said after they had gone. "You've got the Hanepoot?"

"Yes," Marieke confirmed. "I made up two cases, six of each. You take one and I'll take one."

"Sure?" he asked. "Let's get it loaded before they come back."

"Of course," she confirmed. "Who are the French people with Anna?"

"Camille Frou and Bernard Leclere," he said, grinning.

"Wait," she said. "Those names were on the list; they were part of the group that went to Pitse six years ago."

"They were," Koos confirmed. "I didn't have them with me; they were with Brad. They were asking me if I knew Brad and telling me all about their trip to Pitse, I'm surprised they didn't recognise Anna."

"Why didn't they take a commercial flight from Cape Town to Jo'burg, then Gabs?" she asked.

"They told me they wanted to see more of South Africa from the air, but closer than in a commercial jet," he explained. "Apparently, they sent luggage ahead on the train."

Anna came back with the two French people and said her goodbyes to Marieke. Koos made sure that the two passengers were seated and belted in, then told Marieke to taxi out while he talked to the ground controllers in George. After getting clearance, he took the yoke, powered up and took off towards the South. Once in the air, they made a wide banking turn and headed off over the mountains towards Beaufort West. He gave the plane over to Marieke to manage for a while and turned his attention to the passengers. He served up coffee from a Thermos and also had some croissants that he had brought with him from Cape Town. Camille was the more talkative of the two and asked Koos about the places they were flying over. He pointed out the sights, such as they were, until they came within range of Kimberley. Then he took over the plane and took them into land.

At the terminal, Koos saw and waved to Hansie, who came over to complete immigration formalities, then, after a short break for the use of the facilities, they were off again, bound for Gaborone, with Marieke at the helm. Marieke had been listening with half an ear to what the two French people were talking about, and had learned that Camille was going to the university to take over the post vacated by David Turner. Bernard was coming along to interview for the post previously held by Julia Turner. That surprised Marieke, but she supposed that statistics could be the basis of much economic theory. Apparently, they were both excited about their new jobs, but they had also been discussing the recent death of David Turner and wondering who Oxford would now select to have the new chair. Their speculations were interesting, both thought that George Benson could be a likely option, after that they were split, Camille thought that it could be Pierre Garnier, Rick White or Valerio Piaggio, whereas Bernard thought it could be John Wilson, Susan James or George Cooper. Their discussions went on until Koos broke in and pointed to the Gaborone airport in the distance. Then he took the yoke and brought them into land. Marieke saw Inspector Dube and waved. He waved back and waited until Koos had unloaded the passengers and their luggage, then he escorted them to the terminal building, found them a taxi and then came back to see Koos and Marieke.

"I see you have a new job," he laughed, pointing to her shirt, complete with epaulettes and the company insignia.

"I was getting some instruction on flying," Marieke explained. "I think I may try for a pilot's licence."

"So, that would be interesting," Dube said. "Did you have a good trip?"

"I learned much," Marieke said. "I have files and lists to go through, but it remains to be seen if it will help me with my investigation."

"Are you staying, Koos?" Dube asked.

"No, I need to get back to Jo'burg," Koos replied. "Marieke, I'll have my booking agent go through old manifests and send you the ones for flights to the Selinda strip."

"Thank you, Koos," she said. "Thank you for the ride and the lessons. I really enjoyed the trip."

"Any time," he said. "When you start taking lessons, let me know, and if I'm in the area, I'll give you some stick time."

At her office, Marieke changed her shirt, then unpacked the case of Hanepoot and took one bottle of each of the two vineyards with her and went to see the commissioner.

"*Dumela Rra,*" she said.

"*Dumela Mma,*" he replied. "Did you have a productive trip?"

"Perhaps," she said. "I have lists and lists, and it seems that several people who would have probably been in the running for the chair that Turner got have been to the area where the bodies were buried."

"Are there any that are of particular interest?" he asked.

"There may be," she said. "But, what I would really like to know is who was on the shortlist for the chair and who will get it now."

"Perhaps you should try the British High Commission and see if they can get any answers from the people at Oxford," he suggested.

"I was planning to do that next week," she agreed. "I did learn that the post of David Turner has been filled by a Camille Frou, she was the charter that my friend flew up from Cape Town."

"I'm surprised that Chebani didn't tell us that," the commissioner said. "He must have known when we were talking to him that the selection had been made and who it was, as I told you, Matshwane, the academic world is strange at times."

"There's more, Sir," Marieke said. "The post of Julia Turner has also been filled by another French person, a man by the name of Bernard Leclere, who is another economist. Of interest to us is that they both visited the Pitse Safari Camp six years ago on a field trip as part of a conference of economists dealing with developing countries."

"That Chebani," the commissioner complained. "He knew all this and led us to believe that they were still looking. That aside, does this mean that your suspect list is growing?"

"Possibly," she said. "I started with 120 people who are all in the field of economics, and then narrowed that to twenty who had all been to Pitse, then narrowed that even more to those who have made multiple visits. Those are my A list, but the rest are still on my B list. Of interest is that Patrick McBride and some of my A-list were at Pitse at the same time."

"I take it, then, that McBride is on your A list?" the commissioner said.

"He is," she agreed. "I had an interesting conversation with Sara Turner, who would be quite happy to see McBride arrested and thrown in gaol, and who even asked me if we have the death penalty."

"I take it that she does not like Mr McBride," the commissioner said.

"I think that would be the case," she laughed. "Oh, yes, the safari operator before the Martins told me that McBride had been making eyes at his wife, she had pointed a gun at him and suggested that he leave her alone, and then Piet Englebrecht had made the comment that it would be hard to find someone out there. Perhaps McBride recalled that comment and thought that he could get away with burying the bodies there."

"That presupposes that he killed them," the commissioner demurred. "But, I agree, it is an interesting thought. Anything else?"

"I think I may take flying lessons," she said. "I got the chance on the way to Oudtshoorn to take the controls, and it was such fun. I even got to land the plane, with a lot of instruction and with the pilot's hands on the yoke at all times."

"Why not?" he asked. "We have a flying school here in Gaborone. Well, what are your plans for the weekend?"

"I don't know yet, Sir," she said. "I have some housework to do; some washing, and I should probably do something about my garden. Plus, I want to start going through all my lists and try to cross-reference the times and places that different people are present."

"Do not spend all your time buried in papers," he cautioned. "There are times when a break is good, as it gives one a fresh perspective."

"Yes, Sir," she said. "Enjoy your weekend, Sir."

Before she left her office for the day, Marieke checked on messages and reports and found one from Thabo. The axe they had retrieved from the roof rack of the Land Rover had been cleaned, but some blood remained, and it was matched to that of Julia Turner. So, probably it was the axe used to behead the victims. It made sense, therefore, that the shovel had been used to dig the hole in which the victims had been buried. The laboratory people had scoured the shovel, but had found no evidence of blood, and the soil types were typical of the whole region from Maun north to the Namibia border. The commissioner had said nothing about sales of guns in Zambia, so apparently he had not yet heard from Chief Superintendent Phiri. She then called the British High Commission and caught them just before closing time, and asked for an appointment to speak to someone on Monday. She was granted an appointment with a Third Secretary who dealt with Consular and Management issues. She had no doubt that when her request was heard, it would be discussed with the High Commissioner, who would pass it on to London, and then there would be discussions between the Foreign and Commonwealth Office and the Home Office to see if and how they might proceed. But, at least she could get the bureaucratic process in motion. Finally, she talked to Sergeant Maphosa about cars hired in and around Kasane or Kazungula in late May or early June. He had talked to local officers in Kasane, Kazungula, Francistown, Lobatse, Maun and Mahalapye and was following leads that they had provided. So far, he had twenty vehicles that had been hired for cash and of those, twelve were Land Rovers. So, he now had another list to add to those that Marieke already had, a list of Land Rovers hired during the probable time frame. What he really needed was some idea of who may have hired the Land Rover and what they looked like.

Satisfied that there was little else she could do that day, Marieke went home, via the post office to collect her mail, and via a grocery store to buy some essentials. At home, she unpacked her groceries and opened windows in the house to air it out. Being gone for several days had left it stale, but a few hours of night breezes should correct that. She sorted out her mail while she made dinner. There were the inevitable bills, but there was a letter from Melisende. That she saved until dinner was ready, and she would have time to read it without distractions. Melisende had been looking into the David Turner case, using her contacts at Interpol as well as her own resources. It seemed that three French people had been on the interview list for the chair at Oxford: Pierre Garnier, Bernard Leclerc and Camille Frou. What Melisende did not know was whether any of them had made it to the shortlist, but she was still checking on that. The fact that the three had been on the first interview list did not surprise Marieke. She was sure that the college had cast its net far and wide to find the best candidates, just as she was sure that politics, personal preferences, personal vendettas and the "old boy" network played a large part in creating the shortlist of final candidates. But, at least they could claim that they had looked at as many qualified candidates as they could find. Melisende had other news. She had been asked to move to the Paris office of the Sûreté. She was probably going to move within the next month and commented on how they were both now in new assignments. Now Marieke really did have to write back to Melisende; this was the second time Melisende had sent something, and, apart from a quick telephone call, Marieke had not really responded, and she felt guilty. She resolved to take some time on Sunday to write and not just to write about her investigations, but about her new house and her new life in Gaborone.

She was washing up her dishes when the telephone rang, and it was Mbali.

"*Dumela Mma*," Mbali said.

"*Dumela Mma*," Marieke replied. "How are you this evening?"

"I am well, and you?" Mbali replied.

"Well, I have just returned from my trip to South Africa. Tell me, do you drink Hanepoot?" Marieke asked.

"I tried it only once in the past," Mbali said. "Did you bring some back with you?"

'A whole case," Marieke replied. "Half from the vineyard of my uncle and half from the vineyard of a distant cousin. Would you like some?"

"That would be delightful," Mbali said. "Jannie has taken the girls to a school week-end camp near Jwaneng, hopefully, they will bring me back a diamond, but I am footloose tonight, may I come and see you?"

171

"Please do," Marieke said. "Company would be nice."

"I'll be there in twenty minutes," Mbali said.

Mbali was as good as her word, and twenty minutes later she was at the door, bag in hand.

"Are you planning to stay the night?" Marieke laughed.

"I am," Mbali confirmed. "The house is lonely without Jannie and the girls. I could use company tonight. So, where is this Hanepoot you spoke of?"

"This is it," Marieke said. "This one is made by my uncle Koot, and this one by my distant cousin Piet."

"Your uncle Koot, this is the father of your cousin Katrina, who lives in the States?" Mbali asked.

"He is," Marieke confirmed. "I had never met him before, but I like him. He told us all kinds of stories about him and my Pa growing up. So which do you like?"

"I think your uncle's," Mbali said. "But, I think I would need another taste to be sure!"

They finished off the two bottles and collapsed into bed after hours of gossip and discussion about everything from Marieke's trip, to fashion, to husbands, or in Marieke's case, lack thereof. After Melisende Marieke had not had a female friend to whom she could open up and share her heart. Mbali was a great listener and knew how to prompt when needed and when to be quiet and just let Marieke talk. Marieke surprised herself by talking about Julia Turner and Diana McBride, and what she suspected was a newer relationship between Julia Turner and Lillian Mafa, and then her own relationship in days gone by with Melisende.

In the morning, Marieke awoke to the smell of coffee and got up to find Mbali in the kitchen rummaging around, looking for pots and pans and the ingredients for breakfast.

"Good morning," Mbali said. "Do you want coffee black or with milk?"

"With milk, thank you," Marieke said. "You don't have to make any breakfast, I can do that."

"It's already organised," Mbali assured her. "Just go and sit out in your yard, and I will bring it shortly."

Breakfast was brought and eaten, while Marieke nursed a slight headache and made promises to herself about drinking Hanepoot in moderation in the future. She did agree with Mbali, *Oom* Koot's variety was slightly better than Piet's variety. She would check with Koos at some time and see what his opinion was. They spent the rest of the morning talking about Mbali's daughters and what they were doing at school and out of school. Then Marieke said that she needed to go into town and buy at least one other set of clothes that she could wear for interviews. She was anticipating a meeting with Dr Adams to talk about the shortlist and wanted something suitable to wear. She and Mbali then went to all the clothes stores in town and finally found a suit that both felt would be comfortable and yet project an image of command. It was a blazer and skirt, matched with a blouse. Marieke even bought shoes and a matching handbag. Satisfied with her purchases, she treated Mbali to lunch and then they wiled away the rest of the day, being lazy in the backyard and drinking tea, until it was dinner time, which Marieke took care of.

The rest of the evening and Sunday, they spent planning improvements in Marieke's yard until it was time for Mbali to go home to greet Jannie and the girls when they arrived home, sadly, as it turned out, with no large diamond. They had enjoyed themselves and had seen firsthand how diamonds were mined from the earth and then how they were sorted and graded for sale. The scale of the operation impressed them all, and Jannie had been particularly struck by the size of the workshops that were used to maintain all the equipment used in the mine. Nandi, the younger daughter, was now thinking of abandoning the idea of flying and becoming a mining engineer, working in one of the diamond mines.

Interviews

On Monday morning, Marieke, dressed in her new suit, presented herself at the British High Commission and was shown to a small room. She only waited for a few minutes before a man came in and introduced himself as the Third Secretary responsible for consular affairs. Marieke explained her problem, the case of the Drs Turner and the fact that she would like to get a copy of the shortlist for the chair, so that she could perhaps interview those and learn more about Dr David Turner and why someone might kill him.

"Surely you do not think one of those on the shortlist would do such a thing?" the Secretary asked.

"No," Marieke dissembled. "But, I have to try and learn as much about the Doctors as I can so that I may formulate some theory as to why someone would kill them."

"It was not simple robbery then?" he asked.

"We don't see it that way," she replied. "There was too much planning and thought put into this for a simple robbery and the amount of money they were carrying was enough for three weeks of petrol and supplies, but not enough to plan an elaborate scheme for."

"We had heard of the murders, most distressing," the secretary said. "We saw the son and daughter briefly when they came out recently. We helped them arrange transport of the remains to England."

"I understood from Sara Turner that that had been arranged," Marieke said.

"What is it that you would like us to do?" he asked.

"We were wondering if you could use your good offices to persuade someone in the Home Office to help us arrange some interviews," she replied.

"Her Majesty's Government, of course, will do everything we can to help to bring the killers of two of our subjects to justice, but I am not sure how the Home Office will see this, they may not see it as within their purview to influence the Oxford college to disclose confidential information," he stated.

"I appreciate that, Sir," Marieke acknowledged. "But, I must try."

"I will pass on your request to the High Commissioner," he promised. "He may then decide to send it on up to the FCO and then they may talk to the Home Office."

"Thank you," Marieke said. "It is a most frustrating case. I have two victims, but I have no obvious motive, I do have a cause of death, but no actual weapon, and I have no suspects. I am casting around for any and all possible sources of information that may, or may not matter how tenuously, lead me to a suspect."

"We will do what we can," the Secretary promised. "We don't like the idea of our subjects being murdered with potentially no one brought to justice. I gather that you have recently moved to Gaborone from the hinterland?"

"The hinterland," Marieke laughed. "Indeed I have, I was at Tsabong before being transferred here."

"I have not had the opportunity to visit that part of the country," he said.

"It is dry and remote," she said. "If you ever go there, let me know and I will see if I can arrange a camel trek for you."

"A camel trek?" he asked.

"Yes," she confirmed. "We used to do patrols on camels, and the police still keep the camels, even though we have changed to Land Rovers and other vehicles."

"Now, that sounds like an adventure," he said. "I will let you know if and when I can go out there."

"Well, again, thank you for your help," Marieke said. "I have taken up too much of your time, I should bid you good day, stay well."

"Go well," the Secretary said.

Well, the interview at the High Commission went about as well as she expected, now it remained to be seen if anything would come of it. At her office, Marieke found in the mail a large envelope from Sara Turner and it contained photographs of both Patrick and Diana McBride. Now Marieke had pictures of McBride to go on her board, along with those of the Drs Turner. She selected a couple of pictures of Patrick McBride and told Sergeant Maphosa to get copies made to distribute to local police offices along the border, particularly Kasane and Kazungula. She also told him to get copies to the Game Department, to see if anyone in the Chobe National Park saw him enter and leave. Her thinking was that if he was involved and did start at Kazungula as she suspected, then he would have to traverse the Chobe Park to get to and from Maun. Finally, she told the sergeant to send copies to the Zambia police. That done, there was not much more she could do at the moment, except check immigration records for her lists of economists to see who had been in the country and when. That, she knew, would take time as the immigration people were always complaining about the antiquated nature of their computer systems, and she suspected that much of the information was probably still on arrival cards, yet to be entered into the system. It would take time, but it was worth doing. She did not see this as a purely local crime; if it had been, there would have been whispers and chatter, and there had been none.

Before Marieke could decide what to do next, she was summoned to the office of the Assistant Commissioner.

"We are expected in the Commissioner's office in twenty minutes for a report on where we are with the Turner investigation," he told her when she arrived. "Are we ready for that?"

"I can be Sir," Marieke said. "I have a summary of our investigation so far and what we know, what we don't know and what we suspect."

"Very good," he said. "Be back in fifteen minutes, and we will walk over there together and make our report."

"Very good, Sir," she said. What else was there to say. She did have her notes and her lists and had all the reports so far, including those of the pathologist and of the forensic team. The Commissioner, Abel Boateng, kept them waiting for five minutes while he finished some items on his desk, then he signalled for them to come into his office.

"Good morning," he said. "I have been receiving questions from the Minister about the Turner case and need to know where we are."

"Assistant Superintendent?" Ian Mochage invited.

"Sir," Marieke began. "On the 12th of June of this year, a William Martin called in a report on a suspicious Land Rover, apparently left on his game concession in the Linyanti area. Upon investigation, I found two headless corpses that we retrieved and brought back here for examination. Subsequently, on the 17th of June, I found two heads near Khwai, which were determined to match the bodies found earlier. The two people were identified, using dental records and other information, as being Doctor David Turner and Doctor Julia Turner, both of whom were employed at the time by the University here in Gaborone. They were taking a last trip in the bush before leaving Botswana for England, where Dr David Turner had recently been awarded a prestigious chair in economics at Oxford. The two Turners had been shot with a .22LR calibre gun and then beheaded, then the heads were cast into a *dambo* near Khwai and the bodies transported for burial to the Linyanti area."

"Do you know who shot them?" the Commissioner asked.

"No, Sir," Marieke said. "We also do not know exactly when they were shot, but our best estimates are between the 4th and 7th of June."

"Were they robbed?" the Commissioner asked.

"There were no clothes, shoes, personal effects or any other items of value found with the bodies," Marieke reported. "We did find evidence that items consistent with clothing and other effects had been burned at the site where we believe the murders took place."

"You have no motives or suspects?" the Commissioner asked.

"At this time, I would say that we have no definitive motive and no real suspects," Marieke confirmed. "But, we are exploring hypotheses built from interviews that sexual jealousy and or envy over the new chair may be possible motives."

"So, you have potential suspects?" the Commissioner asked.

"Unfortunately, quite a long list," Marieke said.

"Could any of them have done it?" the Commissioner asked.

"None of the people on my list were officially in Botswana at the time," Marieke replied.

"You say, officially, how do you mean?" the Commissioner asked.

"One potential suspect was known to be in Zambia at the time, and his whereabouts in Zambia are unclear at best," Marieke explained. "But, there are ways of crossing the border without coming to the attention of our immigration service. We believe we are looking for two suspects. The movement of two Land Rovers over the distance they went and in the time strongly suggests two people."

"What do you need to be able to solve this riddle?" the Commissioner asked.

"I believe I can piece together a likely scenario," Marieke said. "But, to bring it to trial and have a successful prosecution, I would need a confession. I do not have enough evidence beyond circumstantial to satisfy the prosecution service, nor do I think I can get enough."

"I do not envy you the task," the Commissioner sighed. "I will tell the Minister that we are making progress, but do not expect any arrests in the near future as those arrests may involve foreign nationals who are currently not in Botswana, is that how you see it?"

"Yes, Sir," Marieke confirmed.

"Ian tells me that he has every confidence that you will solve this case. I am sorry that your first case since your transfer from Tsabong is one of such difficulty," the Commissioner said. "Do the best you can."

"Yes, Sir," Marieke said.

"Very good, if you will excuse us, Ian and I have some items we need to discuss," the Commissioner said, dismissing her.

Marieke went back to her office and reviewed her reports and files. She decided to rewrite everything, with footnotes, cross references and indexes, so that she had a good basis for the evidence she had collected so far. As more items became available, she would add them. She left out her conjectures and leaps of faith that had taken her wading in the *dambo* near Khwai and the like. She included as an appendix the report from Chief Superintendent Phiri on the whereabouts of Patrick McBride, included as an appendix, so that it could be easily removed if it transpired that he was truly innocent of any part in the affair. She had almost finished typing when the telephone rang, and it was Chief Superintendent Phiri calling from Lusaka.

"Good morning, Miss Englebrecht," he said. "How are you today?"

"Well, Sir, and you?" she replied.

"I am well enough," he said. "I have news for you. Our people have been making discreet enquiries of the fishermen and others in the area near the Kazungula ferry, and we have two odd reports that merit thought. On the night of the 2nd of June, a fisherman noticed that his *mokoro* was missing. He thought that he had perhaps not secured it properly. Then, on the 7th of June, he discovered his *mokoro*, back where it should have been. Someone seems to have borrowed it for a few days. None of the others in the area is admitting to borrowing it, but we do have an eyewitness who saw two white men poling across the Zambezi on the night of the 2nd of June, he saw them in the same area that the *mokoro* was taken from and they went a little way up the Chobe and then pulled the *mokoro* well up onto the bank and into the long grass. I am sending you a sketch of where they left from and where they landed on the Botswana side. Apparently, he was curious and followed them, which is why he knew where they went. Unfortunately, he did not see them when they returned. Further, a close examination of the *mokoro* did reveal some scraps of fabric, stuck on a jagged piece at one end, that are probably from the sleeve of a khaki safari jacket, the fabric is quite distinctive and is not a common fabric found in Zambia, it is a cotton linen blend that is 52% linen and 48% cotton, apparently that is unusual in that the ratios are more normally, 55% and 45% or 50% and 50% or 35% and 65%. This one is odd."

"You are right, Sir," Marieke agreed. "That does merit thought."

"I will send you the reports of the local officers, the statement of the eyewitness and the fabric for your own evaluation," Phiri said.

"Thank you, Sir," Marieke said. "If and when I develop a list of suspects, would it be possible to check that against your immigration records?"

"We anticipated that and have to hand all entries and exits into and out of Zambia from the 26th of May until the 12th of June," Phiri said. "The lists are quite extensive, we have more visitors than I would have thought. But when you have names, we can quickly check them and give you entry and exit dates if they are there."

"Thank you, Sir," Marieke said. "That is most helpful."

"I will keep searching, we have not found any illicit sales of guns yet, but my people believe they may have identified a source, we have identified several car hires that were done on the 30th and 31st of May, but are far as we can tell, none to your Mr McBride, but perhaps he was using an alias, a picture would be most helpful," Phiri said. "I will call again if we make progress on the purchase of the gun."

"I will send you a package of photographs and drawings of people who are involved in this case and will include some that have nothing to do with it, to test the veracity of witnesses," Marieke promised.

"Thank you, go well," Phiri said.

"Stay well," Marieke replied.

Marieke now needed pictures of people who might be suspects, so she went to the university and found Lillian Mafa.

"*Dumela Mma*," she greeted her.

"*Dumela Mma*," Lillian replied. "How are you today?"

"Quite well, and you?' Marieke asked.

"Fine, thank you," Lillian replied. "How may I help you?"

"I was wondering if you could me find photographs of these people?" Marieke asked. She gave Lillian the list she had.

"These are easy," Lillian said, pointing to the first names. "You already have pictures of David and Julia. Also, we have just finished all the paperwork for Camille Frou and Bernard Leclere; they have both just started here, so we have photographs of them. For the rest, I am sure if I scour the professional journals, I could find photographs."

"May I leave it with you then?" Marieke asked.

"Of course," Lillian said. "I'm only too pleased to be able to help. Is there anything else I can do for you?"

"Not at the moment," Marieke said. "But, if I think of something, may I call upon you?"

"You may call upon me at any time," Lillian said. "I will be happy to be of service to you."

"Thank you," Marieke said. "Stay well."

"Go well," Lillian replied.

Sergeant Maphosa was waiting when Marieke returned to her office.

"I may have identified a person in Kazungula who has a blue diesel Land Rover that he hires out," he said.

"That is good news," she said. "Did he hire it out in early June?"

"The officer I just spoke to was not sure, but they are checking with the man for specific dates," he said.

"Perhaps we should go to Kazungula," Marieke said. "We have some leads on a *mokoro*, a landing spot on the Botswana side of the Chobe, not far up from the Zambezi, now a possible car hire man, we should go and check things out."

180

"Very good Madame," he said. "When should we leave?"

"Let me just check with the commissioner," she said. She made a short telephone call, listened for a while, obviously while the commissioner was making another call and then nodded to Sergeant Maphosa. "We'll leave tomorrow morning at five. Check out a Land Rover when we're finished here, make sure it's one of the newer ones and that the tanks are full. Take some evidence bags, plaster of Paris and buckets to mix it in, check out a rifle and a shotgun from the armoury and check out a camera as well. It's a pity that the new Kasane airport isn't finished, or we could fly into there and just borrow a Land Rover from the station there. The commissioner thought that there might have been a BDF plane flying up there tomorrow to land at a nearby bush strip, but sadly it is not to be, so we must drive."

"Very good Madame," he said. "I will attend to all those items. I will see you here at five in the morning."

"Good, pick me up at my house at five tomorrow, go well," she said. After Sergeant Maphosa had left, she called Inspector Moroka in Maun and asked for the loan of Constable Sephoto and the tracker Tushay. She suggested that they meet her at the police post in Kazungula at about three the following day. She also asked that they talk to the Kazungula police and find out who the man was who had the Land Rover for hire and where he might be found. One item in her theory was troubling her; if the Land Rover was hired in Kazungula, that suggested that the hire was pre-arranged. It seemed to her unlikely that someone would come across the river and then cast about on the off chance that they would find a vehicle for hire. That lacked a degree of certainty that a planned operation would require. So, the person in Kazungula who did hire out the Land Rover was probably contacted ahead of time, but by whom? Perhaps when they talked to him, they might learn who the contact had been and how the transaction was set up. Marieke then collected together such photographs as she had and she added to her collection some incidental pictures, just to test the veracity of potential witnesses, finally she also made copies of all the portraits in the sketchbook of Julia Turner, they were all of a quality that would easily match the best of any police identity sketches. Before Marieke left the office, she had a call from Lillian Mafa, who had actually managed to amass pictures of all those on the list that Marieke had given her. That was fast work indeed, or perhaps either Lillian or David Turner had kept a file of others who were likely to compete for the Oxford chair. Marieke said that she would stop at the university and collect them, and Lillian promised to wait.

As she cooked her dinner that night, Marieke reviewed the case. She still had remarkably little. She knew the identities of the two victims, but was not really any closer to understanding who the killers might be. She had her suspicions, but nothing concrete. She was hoping that the man in Kazungula who had hired out the Land Rover might be able to describe the man who had collected it. She was uncomfortable being in the position of such ignorance and really did not like the idea of placing so much reliance on a single lead. The crime had been very cleverly committed. There were no witnesses, the physical evidence was scant, and one could argue that there was no real motive, unless someone really wanted the Oxford chair and was prepared to go to any lengths to get it. Marieke sighed and sat down with her glass of wine and dinner plate, and tried to plan out her activities for the next few days. The transfer from Tsabong had been cast as a promotion and the chance to work on interesting cases, but this one was more than interesting; it was bordering on the unsolvable.

Sergeant Maphosa was waiting outside the house when Marieke looked out just before five. She collected her bag, locked up and greeted him. "*Dumela Rra*, you're early," she said.

"*Dumela Mma*, I am on time, Madame," he said. "I was told to always be sure and be at the appointed place a few minutes before. I have coffee for you."

"Thank you," she said. "If you will take the first two hours, I will take the next two."

"Very good, Madame," he said.

"Is your wife comfortable with you going away for a few days?" Marieke asked.

"Yes, Madame," he confirmed. "She packed my bag, gave us some lunch to take and the coffee. She will manage the children while I am gone, and they will expect something from me when we return."

"We should look in Kazungula and see what we can find," she said. "What do you think they would like?"

"One of those wire cars," he said. "I think one each, so I need to get two."

"There is too much traffic for so early in the morning," she commented. "Perhaps we should use the lights and the siren and move them out of the way!"

"Yes, Madame," he said, and with great delight, he turned on the lights on the roof and the siren and was gratified to see people getting out of their way. Once out of Gaborone and its environs, the traffic thinned out and they were able to turn off their siren and lights and just pass the few cars and lorries that they met along the way.

At a few minutes before three in the afternoon, they pulled into the Kazungula police post and saw Constable Sephoto and the tracker Tushay waiting for them.

"*Dumela Mma, Rra*," Marieke greeted them.

"*Dumela Mma*," Constance said. "How was your drive north?"

"It went well, Constable Constance Sephoto, Police Tracker Tushay, this is Detective Sergeant Isaac Maphosa who works with me in Gaborone," Marieke said, introducing everyone.

"I have learned that the man you seek is a Styrah Bwalya, he is a Zambian who came to Botswana about twenty years ago," Constance said. "We will probably find him at the Rhino bar between six and seven tonight, one of the local officers, Sergeant Mphoeng will be there tonight, and if Bwalya is there, point him out to us."

"Very good," Marieke said. "Before we do that we have some other items to check."

"What do we need to do?" Constance asked.

"About a month ago, some men poled a *mokoro* across the Zambezi and a little up the Chobe and beached it in long grass. I want to try and find that spot and then track where they went from there," Marieke explained.

"Do you know where they landed?" Tushay asked.

"I have here a map that shows where a witness says he saw them pull the *mokoro* out of the water. Looking at the topographic map of the area, I would say that it was about here, and we can get there by this road. If you will leave your Land Rover here and come with us Constance, I want to get started while we still have light," Marieke explained.

"Yes, Madame," Constance said. "Let me quickly get our things."

When they reached the river bank, Marieke estimated that it was a little way downstream from the place that the witness had indicated, so they started slowly upstream, Tushay leading. He stopped four times and looked at places where the canoes had been pulled up out of the water, but at each place, he shook his head. At the fifth spot, he stopped and carefully examined the old tracks that were there.

"Two *wazungu*," he said. "They came and pulled the *mokoro* from the water in bare feet and then sat down over there and put on boots. They are the same people whose tracks we saw in the Linyanti. Over there are their tracks when they came back and here you can see where they pushed the *mokoro* back into the river."

It said a lot for the faith that the others had in his abilities as a tracker that no one questioned this announcement. Marieke told Constance and Isaac to get the plaster of Paris from the Land Rover and make casts of the tracks that Tushay indicated. Then she and Tushay started following the tracks inland, away from the river. They lost them twice where, first elephants and then waterbuck had crossed the trail and obscured the tracks, but each time Tushay picked them up again after a little casting around. Finally, they came to the Kasane road. From there it looked as if they had walked on the tarmac because there were no tracks evident in the dirt on the side of the road. What they did see was the Rhino bar about half a mile down the road. When they started back to where the others were, Tushay pointed to another set of tracks that led back to the water. "They came back this way," he said. "They were in a hurry."

Back at the water's edge, the plaster casts were ready, so Marieke thought that their next visit should be the Rhino bar. By the time they got there, it should be about six, and with luck, Bwalya would be there. When they got to the Rhino bar, Marieke noticed the blue Land Rover parked to the side of the bar, she and Sergeant Maphosa looked it over carefully, noting the odd Limestone coloured wheel in the back and the jerry cans, about half of which were empty, but had had diesel in them, and oddly for a diesel Land Rover one that had petrol in it and another that smelled as if it had had petrol. They looked around the bar and noted the back door as well as the front door. She sent Constance to the back door with the riot shotgun and told her to let no one out. She told Isaac to stay by the front door and also let no one out. Then she entered the bar with Tushay. As she was in her field uniform, she was obviously a police officer, and several people started for the doors, only to be turned back. Some of them might have taken their chances with Constance, but not with Constance holding a riot gun. One man signalled to Marieke and introduced himself as Detective Sergeant Mphoeng. He laughed as he told her that he had been disappointed when she walked in the front door, but had to admire the precautions she had taken to make sure no one left without her say so. He pointed out Bwalya and crooked his finger and told him to come and join them.

"*Dumela Rra*," Marieke said.

"*Dumela Mma*," Bwalya replied.

"I was hoping that you would be able to help me," she said. "I understand that you have a Land Rover for hire?"

"I may do," he replied.

"Specifically a blue Land Rover with a full canvas tilt," she added.

"The Inspector seems to know a lot about me," he said.

"That's Assistant Superintendent to you," Sergeant Mphoeng said.

"Then this is not a traffic issue?" Bwalya asked.

"Sergeant Mphoeng may wish to question you about traffic issues," Marieke said. "But, my concern is murder."

"Murder," he said, shrinking back into his seat. "I've committed no murder."

"I did not suppose that you had," she said. "But, the penalties for being part of a conspiracy to commit murder are severe, so your help would be appreciated and your cooperation will be noted."

"I have nothing to do with murder, what do you want to know?" he asked.

"About a month ago, did you hire your Land Rover out to two white men?" she asked.

"I hired it out to a *muzungu*," he said. "I don't know if he was on his own, or if there was someone outside waiting."

"So, you hired it out from here?" she asked.

"He came with the money, I gave him the keys and I heard him drive away, I did not go out to see," he said.

"What day was that?" she asked.

"The 1st of June," he said. "It was like payday!"

"The man who did hire your Land Rover, what did he look like?" she asked.

"A *muzungu*, about your height, an educated man," he said. "Dressed in safari-type clothes, shorts, boots and a safari jacket, khaki coloured."

"Was it this man?" she asked, bringing out her folder with the pictures she had and opening it to the picture of Patrick McBride.

"No," Bwalya said. "That is not him."

"What about any of these?" Marieke said, leafing through some of the others.

"That one," Bwalya said. "That one, he is the man."

"You are sure?" she asked.

"Sure, sure, that is the one," Bwalya said. Marieke was surprised, Bwalya had picked out Harold Swanson. Perhaps there was credence to the idea that the killing, at least of David Turner had been because of the chair at Oxford. She would need to check on the movements of Harold Swanson and if he and David Turner had had any other disputes.

"You said that he was to come in and pay the money and then you would give him the keys," she said. "Who arranged that?"

"About two months ago this man came to the bar and found me here and gave me some money and instructions," Bwalya explained.

"Who was this man?" Marieke asked.

"A Motswana, educated, grey hair, dressed like a businessman," Bwalya replied. "He was not from here, or Kasane, or even Maun, I think from his accent, he was from Gaborone."

"How did he get here?" Marieke asked.

"I did not see," Bwalya said. "I was in the bar here, he came in, the man at the bar pointed him to me and he bought me a beer and gave me 500 Pula and instructions."

"How did you know how to identify the man who would hire the Land Rover?" Marieke asked.

"I was told that he would ask at the bar for me, then ask me if I wanted a beer, then he was to say that he wanted four beers to clear the dust," Bwalya explained. "Then he was going to give me another 5,000 Pula."

"That's a lot of money, you didn't wonder why or what he was doing?" she asked.

"I never ask questions," he said. "For that kind of money, I would have sold him the Land Rover. He didn't give me Pula, he gave me Pounds, £1,700, I had to change it a little at a time at the bank, or they would have asked many questions. Changing small amounts is common, as we often pick up some Pounds or Dollars from tourists."

"When they came back, how did they give the Land Rover to you?" she asked.

"I told them just to park it outside here and leave the keys at the bar," Bwalya said.

"You said the man who set this up was Motswana, can you describe him?" she asked.

"Motswana, grey hair, a little taller than you, filling out his clothes, I would say that he works in an office, maybe a businessman," he explained again.

"Would this be him?' Marieke asked, opening her folder to a picture of the commissioner.

"Not, not him, I'm sure, not him," Bwalya said. "That other picture you had there, let me see?"

"Which one?" Marieke asked.

"The one that is drawn, not the photograph," Bwalya said.

"Which one?" Marieke said, riffling through the pile of pictures until he pointed to one.

"That one, sure, sure," Bwalya said. "He was here, he gave me money, ask Phiri behind the bar." Marieke took the sketch and went to the bar and the barman confirmed that he had seen him and that it was at least two months earlier. She needed time to compose herself and not give too much away. Bwalya and Phiri had both identified Dr Chebani as the man who set up the car hire. She went back to the table, with her face set, and asked Bwalya if he had noted how many miles the Land Rover had been driven when Swanson had hired it.

"Sorry, the speedometer is broken," Bwalya said. "It's been broken for about three months, I'm waiting for spares. There was something about the hire that was unusual, they wanted eight jerry cans of diesel and two jerry cans of petrol when they hired the Land Rover. The *Mdala* asked for that when he set it up."

"How much diesel and petrol was left when the Land Rover was returned?" Marieke asked.

"About half the diesel and half of the petrol, and I did get a new tyre, but it didn't match the others, it was a Michelin radial and I had to change it," Bwalya said.

"Do you still have that rim and tyre?" Marieke asked.

"Sure," Bwalya said. "I'll sell it to you."

"How much?" Marieke asked.

"50 Pula," Bwalya said.

"Fine," Marieke said. "Where is it?"

"It's in the back of the Land Rover that's parked outside, on that side," Bwalya said, pointing in the Kasane direction. Marieke motioned to Sergeant Maphosa and told him to get the wheel and put it in the back of their Land Rover.

"Did the *muzungu* murder someone?" Bwalya asked.

"Do you think he did?" she asked in return.

"I don't know," Bwalya admitted. "He strutted about like a rooster, he was sure of himself, but murder, I don't know."

"I'm going to ask Sergeant Mphoeng to take a statement from you, do not try and run away back to Zambia, stay here in Kazungula where we can find you," Marieke said. She thought about the jerry cans of diesel, eight cans at five gallons each, forty gallons, at least 1,000 miles of driving, even on dirt roads, more than enough to get to Maun and back, even with a detour to the Linyanti area, and the petrol was surely for the other Land Rover. If the identification of Dr Chebani was accurate, then he was in this up to his neck, but why. Marieke needed time to think about what was she going to do next. She had already set things up with the Zambia police to visit with them the next day and see the fisherman who had had his *mokoro* borrowed, and with the

188

witness who saw the two white men crossing the Zambezi. The next most pressing item was a place to sleep that night. Sergeant Mphoeng commented that the cells at the Kazungula police post were empty and that they were welcome to use them. Marieke laughed to herself when she thought of her report to the commissioner and how it would read, spending the night in a cell!

The next morning, bright and early the team found breakfast at a small place that catered to the lorry drivers who were waiting for the ferry to take them across the Zambezi. It was adequate, if a little overpriced. But, then the vendor had a captive market as the lorry drivers had few other choices. Sergeant Mphoeng had made arrangements with the Chobe Lodge to borrow a motor boat to take them across the river so that Marieke and her team would not be constrained by the vagaries of the ferry operations. The lodge guide met them at the ferry ramp and took them across the river to the Zambian side. There they met with Inspector Kangwa, who suggested that he ride with them up the river to the place where the *mokoro* had been taken. It was not far up the river in a small backwater that had probably once been part of the main course of the river. The owner of the *mokoro* was waiting for them and showed them where he normally kept it. Tushay cast around and found old tracks, which he identified as belonging to the same two that had pulled the *mokoro* from the Botswana side of the Chobe. He followed the tracks away from the river and came to a spot where a vehicle had been parked and turned around. Looking at the vehicle tracks Tushay hesitated to name a type, but thought something like a Fiat 125, or about that size. The next stop was back down river a little to see the man who had witnessed that two poling the *mokoro* across the river and up the Chobe. He was voluble with his description of events, he told how the moon had been up since lunchtime and was about half a moon, but still cast plenty of light, more than enough to see by and to tell that the men in the canoe were white, not black. Marieke thanked him and then they took Inspector Kangwa back to the ferry dock and said their goodbyes. Now Marieke wanted to get back to Gaborone and report all this to the commissioner. The Chobe Lodge guide dropped them at the ferry ramp on the Botswana side of the river and left to go back up the Chobe to the Lodge.

"Thank you for your assistance," Marieke said to Tushay and Constance. "I will send in a report to Inspector Moroka. If I need you again I will call him and request your help."

"Of course, Madame," Constance said for the both of them. "*Tsamaya sentlê*"

"*Sala sentlê*," Marieke replied. "Right, Sergeant, it's eleven, how far can we get tonight?"

"We can be back in Gaborone tonight," he said. "It will be late, but we can do it."

"Good," she said. "Let's go."

Marieke did not go into her office until almost nine the next morning. They had made it back to Gaborone by nine the previous night, but she had overslept and not been up at her usual hour. At the office she went to see the commissioner, only to discover that he was in a meeting. She left a message that she was back and had information to report. Back at her own office, she noted a message from the British High Commission. She called the number given and got straight through to the Third Secretary that she had met with before.

"Good morning," he said. "To whom am I speaking?"

"This is Assistant Superintendent Englebrecht returning your call," she said.

"Ah, yes," he said. "Well, it seems that the Home Secretary has taken an interest in your case and we are instructed to provide you with all the assistance we are able."

"Thank you, Sir," she said. "That is certainly very generous of the Home Secretary."

"I think it's because he was at school at Sedbergh with David Turner," the Secretary explained. "The Home Office has suggested that if you were to go to Oxford to see Dr Nicholas Adams then they would send an Assistant Undersecretary with you."

"Do you think that Dr Adams would be forthcoming in answering my questions?" she asked.

"I rather think that he will," the Secretary said. "It will be apparent, even to him, that the Home Secretary is interested and concerned and that would be in his best interests to be as helpful as possible."

"I see," Marieke said. "Thank you for your help, if I do go to England how do I contact the Assistant Undersecretary?"

"When you go," the Secretary said. "Let me know your flight details, and you will be met at Heathrow."

"Thank you," Marieke said. "I will let you know if and when I go."

"Oh, I think you will be going," the Secretary laughed. "The High Commissioner has been talking to your Minister, and it's all arranged. Let me know the flight number as soon as you can."

"Of course," Marieke promised. "Thank you again."

Marieke was surprised by the turn of events and was mulling over what it might mean when the commissioner came to her office.

"*Dumela Mma*," he said.

"*Dumela Rra*," she replied. "Are you well?"

"I am," he confirmed. "So, Matshwane, you are off to Oxford. Your passport is in order, I presume?"

"Yes, Sir," she confirmed. "I am off to Oxford?"

"You are," he confirmed. "Apparently the wheels of government, even in England, occasionally turn quickly, and it probably didn't hurt that the Home Secretary and David Turner were at school together. So, you are booked on Air Botswana tomorrow to Jo'burg and then on the BA flight to Heathrow. Here are your tickets; you have an appointment with Dr Nicholas Adams in Oxford on Monday morning at nine. That seems to me a little early for British academics, but perhaps they do work regular hours over there. Do you have your questions ready for Dr Adams?"

"I do, Sir," she replied. "We have an identification of Harold Swanson as the man who hired the Land Rover in Kazungula. I want to confirm that Swanson was on the shortlist of candidates for the chair. I also want to trace his movements over the past month and also check on those of Patrick McBride."

"Are you sure of Swanson?" the commissioner asked.

"The man, Bwalya, was adamant," she confirmed. "There was one other piece of information that we learned. Two men identified Dr Chebani as the man who set up the hire of the Land Rover and gave a deposit."

"Really?" the commissioner said. "You are sure of this?"

"I tried them with other pictures," she explained. "Including yours, and he dismissed them emphatically, no, he and the barman were sure that it was Chebani."

"Well, well," the commissioner said. "I wonder why? I think while you are in Oxford, I will do a little digging into our Dr Chebani."

"I wonder Sir, while I am in London if you would talk to the Zambians and ask them if Harold Swanson was in Zambia a month ago, here is his picture, perhaps also someone might remember him buying a gun or hiring a car?" Marieke asked.

"Of course," he said.

The commissioner left and Marieke first called the Third Secretary at the British High Commission and gave him her flight number, then started completing her reports on her trip to Kazungula. She was interrupted by a telephone call and the caller surprised her.

"Superintendent, this is Sara Turner. Have you heard the news?"

"No, what news?" Marieke asked.

"Apparently, after Dad, the next in line for the chair at Oxford was Paulo Schirano, and he just died in a tragic car accident in Italy," Sara replied.

"I see," Marieke said. "And you suspect it was not an accident?"

"Not a chance," Sara said. "Patrick is out of the country in Italy, I've just had an early lunch with Diane who told me that Patrick flew over there two days ago and is due back tomorrow."

"Perhaps he had business there?" Marieke suggested. "How would he be involved in any way in the death of Paulo Schirano?"

"That's what we need you to find out," Sara said. "Somehow, he's mixed up in this, I don't know how, but I'm sure of it."

"Where did this accident happen?" Marieke asked.

"Somewhere in Tuscany," Sara said. "Simon is getting details. He's the one who told me, he is quite distressed, talking about the chair being jinxed, he's been onto Adams at Oxford and they're trying to decide what to do now, to wait to name the chair until after the deaths of Dad and Paulo are properly investigated, or to just plough ahead and name the next in line."

"Do you know who that is?" Marieke asked.

"No, Simon didn't tell me that, he's gone off to Oxford to confer with Adams and the rest of the committee," Sara replied.

"When did this accident with Schirano happen?" Marieke asked.

"Apparently, it was in the evening, yesterday," Sara said. "But, I don't have any more details. If I hear, I will let you know."

"Thank you," Marieke said. After Sara had rung off, Marieke went to see the commissioner. She explained what she had heard and suggested that she stop in Italy on the way back from Oxford to see what she might learn.

"Do you know anyone in Italy?" the commissioner asked.

"I may have a contact in Florence," she said. "I will need a day or so to set a meeting."

"Well, talk to BA when you're in London, and if they need any funds to change the ticket, get the High Commission in London to take care of it for you," the commissioner suggested.

"Very good, Sir," she said. She left and went back to her office, and called Inspector Moroka in Maun and asked him to contact Pitse Safari and have them call her. That call did not come in until much later that afternoon. She talked to Bridget and then asked if she could talk to Valeria.

"*Dumela Mma*," Valeria said. "What can I do for you?"

"*Dumela Mma*," Marieke said. "I remember you saying your father was in the Italian police. I wonder if he might be able to help me?"

"I'm sure he would do everything he could for you," Valeria said. "Do you have something specific in mind?"

"Yes," Marieke replied. "There was a traffic accident yesterday evening in Tuscany and a Paulo Schirano was killed. I would like to learn all I can about that accident. I will be in England for a few days soon, and perhaps could stop in Italy on the way back?"

"I'm sure Pappi will help you," Valeria said. "When you're in England, call him and tell him who you are and what you want. I will send a message to him to expect your call. If you're ready, I'll give you the telephone number for his office and our house."

"Thank you," Marieke said, writing down the numbers that Valeria gave her. "That would be most helpful. How is the holiday?"

"Oh, it's wonderful, the tourists you met have all gone and we have a new batch now," Valeria said. "All Brits, all terribly snooty and highbrow, they're all experts in everything, so I don't know why they came."

"What have you been doing?" Marieke asked.

"I've been out shooting with Francesca; she's getting to be competition now, so I'll have to do some more," Valeria said. "When you get back, will you come out and tell us all about the investigation?"

"When it's over," Marieke promised. "Thank you for the help. Go well."

"Stay well," Valeria replied.

Marieke then called in Sergeant Maphosa and told him that she was going to Oxford. She asked him to have all the reports and statements properly typed up and to have the forensic people confirm what Tushay had told them about the tracks. She also asked him to check with Jannie at MJ Motors and see if he had sold the tyre that they had brought back with them from Kazungula. Lastly, she asked him to send one of the sets of copies they had of all the pictures and drawings of people involved in the case to Chief Superintendent Phiri of the Zambia Police. She suggested that he use the courier package system of the airlines and make sure that it got to Lusaka post haste.

Marieke went home and reviewed her wardrobe. She packed as best she could. It was July, so England might be having warm weather. At least she was certain there would be no snow or ice, so there was no need for winter clothes. She packed what she had, hoping that it would be enough. Perhaps if the prices were reasonable, she might buy something extra in England. She reminded herself to go to the bank in the morning and get some cash to take with her. Mbali would take care of getting her Pounds to take. She looked at the ticket and saw that she was seated towards the back of the BA flight to London, no first-class travel for her. She had a window seat, which meant not much as the flight was overnight and there would not be much to see. But, at least when they came into land, she would probably see London as the flights usually landed towards to West. In her briefcase, she put the pictures that she had and her notebook, plus blank paper. She would use some of the time on the flight to London to formulate her questions for Dr Adams.

Mbali was excited for Marieke when she heard that a trip to London was imminent. She had never been, so wanted details, details that Marieke was unable to give yet. All Marieke had, so far, was a flight to London, past that, she would have to see what either had been arranged or what she could arrange for herself. Mbali organised Pounds for the trip and then suggested lunch, after which she would take Marieke to the airport to get the flight to Johannesburg. Over lunch, she asked about progress with the case.

"I am pursuing leads," Marieke said. "But, they may or may not lead anywhere. What did you think of Sara and David Turner?"

"I liked her," Mbali said. "Very organised and I would say, capable, he's a different story, fancies himself, rather arrogant, but just a little stupid, all in all, I would say nowhere near as bright as his sister and has had to live in her shadow his whole life."

"She called me yesterday," Marieke said. "She told me that the next one on the list for the economics chair at Oxford just died in an accident."

"What kind of accident?" Mbali asked.

"Apparently, a bad traffic accident in Italy," Marieke explained.

"Do you think it was just an accident?" Mbali asked.

"That's a good question," Marieke agreed. "Perhaps it's an Idi Amin-style traffic accident; perhaps it was a real one."

"The plot really does thicken," Mbali said. "Who's next on the list?"

"The list of candidates, or the list of suspects?" Marieke asked.

"Suspects," Mbali decided, after a little thought.

"I really don't know," Marieke admitted. "I have ideas, theories, notions, but cannot yet confirm motive, I have means, I suppose I could come up with opportunity, but motive is difficult, unless of course the death in Italy turns out not to be accidental, then a motive becomes clearer and then the list of suspects becomes more apparent."

"Even if you had a suspect, how would you prove they did it?" Mbali asked.

"With difficulty," Marieke admitted. "I would have to place them at the scene of the crime, which is hard because there are, were, no witnesses to the crime, I would have to prove they did it, which again is hard as the physical evidence is all really circumstantial."

"I don't envy you the task, oh, by the way, I received a discreet enquiry from your boss today about someone, is that related?" Mbali asked.

"If it is who I think, then probably," Marieke replied. "But the whys and wherefores are a little murky."

"Well, I will do what I can for your boss, but at some point, the bank is going to need warrants to protect ourselves," Mbali said.

"I'm sure the commissioner knows that and will get one in due course," Marieke promised.

"We should get you to the airport," Mbali said.

The flight to Johannesburg was short, under an hour, and then there was the interminable wait for the flight to London. Marieke wandered around the airport, such as she could; the transfer lounge was by the gates, so there really was not that much to see or do. At some point, it seemed obvious to Marieke that the South Africans were going to have to either build a new airport to accommodate the traffic, or seriously upgrade the existing facility. Her seat on the BA Boeing 747 was towards the back, but unlike many of the window seats, it only had one seat companion as the fuselage of the plane narrowed and the seating configuration was changed from the usual 3-4-3 to 2-4-2. Marieke considered herself very fortunate in that she had no seat companion for the journey and was able to make herself quite comfortable. When they arrived at Heathrow, it was already warm; England was going through a heat wave. Marieke was one of the last off the plane as she had been seated far in the back, but at the end of the jetway, there was a perky BA representative and another lady, dressed in an elegant dark blue suit.

"Assistant Superintendent Englebrecht?" the lady asked.

"I am," Marieke confirmed.

"Welcome to London, I am Assistant Undersecretary Wilson, the Home Secretary has asked me to accompany you to Oxford and assist in any way I am able and can, the Home Secretary is most distressed by the death of his friend and wishes to provide every facility to you to help bring the perpetrators of the crime to justice," Ms Wilson said.

"Thank you," Marieke said. "I am sorry to have kept you here waiting, but I was seated towards the very back of the plane, and it took time for everyone to deplane."

"We understand," Ms Wilson said. "Perhaps we can speed things along a little from here. Ms Edwards of BA has graciously provided transport so we may speed our way to immigration and then the baggage hall."

So, Marieke got to ride in style, passing most of the other passengers who had disembarked before her. At immigration, Ms Wilson took her to the line for diplomats and other officials, flashed a card, and the officer quickly stamped Marieke's passport. In the baggage hall, there was a wait until the bags arrived, and Marieke was amazed that hers was among the first to appear, infiltrating the First Class bags. Once out of the airport, there was a car waiting, a rather official black car with a driver. He stowed Marieke's suitcase in the boot and then looked to Ms Wilson for instructions.

"Oxford, please, George," she said, then she closed the window that was between the driver and the passengers. "Now let me introduce myself again, I'm Courtney Wilson, and I'll be your guide for as long as you need me, please call me Courtney."

"Thank you," Marieke replied. "I'm Marieke."

"Isn't Marieke Englebrecht a very Afrikaans name?" Courtney asked.

"It is," Marieke confirmed. "My father was an Afrikaner, but my mother was a Motswana, so I got the name from him and eventually the home from her."

"I imagine that things were difficult for them under the South African regime?" Courtney said.

"They were, it was basically an illegal marriage, but they lived out in the wilds of Namibia and the government ignored them," Marieke said.

"You say lived, does that suggest that they are no longer living?" Courtney asked.

"They were killed about ten years ago when their car hit a landmine while they were travelling in the north of Namibia," Marieke explained.

"I'm so sorry. I rather think that things are starting to really change in South Africa," Courtney said. "It will be interesting to see how long it is before they hold free elections."

"It will," Marieke agreed.

"Is there anywhere else you might wish to go, apart from Oxford?" Courtney asked.

"Perhaps, I would like to check on some people at Broadway, is that far from Oxford?" Marieke asked.

"Not at all," Courtney said. "It's only about an hour from Oxford; we could be there and back in a morning. Is this your first trip to the UK?"

"No, I came a couple of times when I was a student in France," Marieke replied. "They were just quick jaunts across the Channel, so see the other side; we went to plays in London and saw the sights."

"You studied in France?" Courtney asked.

"I studied law in Lyon," Marieke explained.

"And now you are a senior police officer in Gaborone," Courtney said. "I was in Gaborone some years ago, just after independence. I was just a student then and was trying to see as much of Africa as I could on £1 a day. It was an adventure; I imagine things have changed much since then."

"They have," Marieke agreed. "I only moved there recently from a more remote station in the southwest of the country."

"Tell me, how did David Turner die?" Courtney asked.

"He and Julia Turner were both shot, then beheaded, the heads were then thrown into a *dambo*, a small shallow seasonal lake if you like, and the bodies were transported to a place about 100 miles away and buried there," Marieke explained.

"How on earth did you find them?" Courtney asked.

"We chanced upon the bodies when a safari operator saw an abandoned Land Rover in an unlikely place," Marieke explained. "We investigated and found the bodies, and then we backtracked the transport vehicle and found the heads."

"How on earth did you backtrack them over 100 miles?" Courtney asked.

"I had a San tracker, and we followed the vehicle tracks. Fortunately, there had been little, if any, traffic on the bush road that they had used, so it wasn't as difficult as it sounds," Marieke explained.

"Do you have any suspects for the murders?" Courtney asked.

"Officially, no," Marieke said. "There just doesn't seem to be any motive for the killings. They didn't have that much on them to suggest robbery, and the whole affair was carefully planned out by someone. Putting people at or near the scene of the shooting is difficult."

"But, unofficially?" Courtney asked.

"I'm pursuing the hypothesis that the chair at Oxford that was granted to David Turner was such a prestigious chair that someone else decided that they really wanted it and has started to eliminate the competition," Marieke explained. "Did you hear of the death of Paulo Schirano in Tuscany recently? He was, I believe, the next in line to David Turner on the list of acceptable candidates."

"That death is being advertised as accidental," Courtney said. "But, I am inclined to agree with you that it is either really coincidental or really fortuitous. Who was next after Schirano?"

"That is one of the things I would like to discover on this visit," Marieke said. "I would like the shortlist, I would like to talk to each of the selection committee, and if possible, each of the shortlist."

"Do you know who was on the selection committee?" Courtney asked.

"According to the notes that David Turner made, there was Dr Nicholas Adams, the master of the college, a Professor John Entwhistle, Professor Henry Wilson, Dr Susan Bullock and Dr James Webb, also all with the college, and Simon Bentham, who was actually endowing the chair," Marieke replied.

"Do you have anyone in mind for the murders?" Courtney asked.

"I have two names," Marieke said. "Dr Harold Swanson and Dr Patrick McBride."

"Swanson, he probably was on the list of candidates, I agree," Courtney said. "But who is Patrick McBride?"

"He's an ornithologist who lives in Broadway, it seems that both he and Swanson had visited the area where the bodies were buried, neither have officially been to Botswana in the past month, but certainly Swanson has been identified as entering Botswana, by the back door, so to speak, and McBride was conveniently in Zambia at the right time and his whereabouts in Zambia are unclear," Marieke explained.

"So, what you really need is records of flights taken by both McBride and Swanson in the past month or so, and where they went," Courtney suggested.

"That would be most helpful," Marieke agreed. "The Zambians are now checking their immigration records to see if and when Swanson had been there lately."

"This is going to be delicate," Courtney warned. "Swanson is well known and well respected as an economist, the darling of the Oxford set; I'm a little surprised that Turner was originally selected for the chair."

"I have no intention of showing my hand in any of the interviews," Marieke assured her. "Without being impolite, I'm sure that most of the people we talk to will not expect too much from someone from one of the former protectorates."

"Of that, we may be certain," Courtney agreed. "Why McBride?"

"It seems that Diana McBride, the wife of Patrick McBride, and Julia Turner had had a relationship, and that it had not died when each of them married their respective spouses. My conjecture is that Patrick McBride was disenchanted by the idea and sought to remedy the situation," Marieke explained.

"So, '*Strangers on a Train*', perhaps?" Courtney said.

"That had occurred to me," Marieke admitted. "I learned yesterday that McBride was in Italy at the time of Schirano's accident."

"Interesting," Courtney admitted. "But, the biggest problem you are going to face, even if you manage to put your case together, is extraditing them to Botswana," Courtney said. "There will be challenges in court, particularly because you still have the death penalty. The Home Secretary will not push things that far, even for an old-school friend. Even if you agreed to waive the death penalty, it could still be six to nine months at least before extraditions, by which time they would have their stories straight and would have retained the best legal counsel they could get."

"I am painfully aware of that," Marieke said. "It is possible that this will never go to trial, or will be tried in absentia, and if we get a guilty verdict, the only thing we could do is wait for them to be stupid enough to come to Botswana, which I see as unlikely."

"You have thought about this," Courtney said. "I would advise against any hint of suspecting either Swanson or McBride, no matter who we talk to."

"In the unlikely event that one of them did show up in Botswana, was arrested, tried and convicted, what would your government do?" Marieke asked.

"If the death penalty were involved, we would protest and appeal to your better natures," Courtney said. "It is the official position of Her Majesty's Government that we are opposed to the death penalty."

"And if we carried it out?" Marieke asked.

"I don't know," Courtney said. "There would be questions in the House, your high commissioner would be summoned to the Foreign Office, perhaps even to Number. 10, then the business interests would wish to maintain the flow of diamonds into this country would lean on their favourite MPs, and in the end, possibly nothing would come of it, except newspaper headlines."

Their conversation was interrupted by a buzz; it was George calling on an intercom to ask which hotel they were going to. He was directed to the Old Parsonage Hotel, between Banbury Road and Woodstock Road. Marieke was enthralled by all the old buildings they were passing, the likes of which they simply did not have in Gaborone. Marieke had once heard the poem *The Spires of Oxford*, by Winifred Letts and now better understood it. When they reached the hotel, it was another old building, not a modern edifice; it fit well in the surrounds. She was quite concerned about the hotel and what she imagined the bill might be, and turned to Courtney. "I cannot afford this," she said. "My Government only gave me the minimum of a per diem rate."

"HM's Government regards you as our guest," Courtney assured her. "The hotel is taken care of, as are meals while we are here."

"Are you sure?" Marieke asked. "This seems very elegant."

"It has recently been refurbished," Courtney explained. "I like to stay here when I am in Oxford."

"Do you visit Oxford often, then?" Marieke asked.

"I have had occasion of late to be here more often than in the past; part of my job is to oversee policing, so I get to travel the country a fair bit," Courtney explained.

"Am I not keeping you from something more important than my case?" Marieke asked.

"Not at all," Courtney assured her. "Your case has priority while you are here."

"In that case, I should try and get things done as quickly as possible to let you get back to your other duties," Marieke said.

"Again, do not concern yourself," Courtney assured her. "This is going to be interesting."

Marieke started giggling, and Courtney wanted to know what the joke was. "Three nights ago, I was sleeping in a police cell in our Kazungula police post," Marieke explained. "This is somewhat of a change."

"You were sleeping in a cell?" Courtney asked, exchanging glances with George.

"Kazungula is not blessed with much in the way of hotels or places to stay, the easiest thing for me and my team to do was use the empty cells," Marieke explained. "I did have to double up with my constable early in the morning when some drunkards were brought in."

"I'm presuming your constable was a woman?" Courtney laughed.

"Indeed, Constable Constance Sephoto from our Maun station, my sergeant had to double up with our Police Tracker," Marieke replied. "Constance is very capable, particularly with a rifle or shotgun; she kept the crocodiles away from me while I was hunting for heads."

"I think Oxford will be very tame after that," Courtney laughed. "Look, it's not even lunchtime yet, why don't you get yourself settled, then at eleven we'll take a run up to Broadway and see the McBrides."

"Would that be possible?" Marieke asked.

"Of course," Courtney assured her. "George, we would like to have lunch in Broadway, and then go to the McBride Raptor Centre."

"Very good, Madame," he said.

The shortlist

At eleven, George was waiting outside the hotel. Marieke decided not to bring her briefcase, bringing instead only a notebook. The drive to Broadway was interesting, first to Chipping Norton, then the quaint town of Moreton-in-Marsh, then on the Evesham road to Broadway. Everything was green, unlike the greater part of Botswana, which is brown or sandy coloured, except in the rains and in the Okavango. They had lunch at a pub in Broadway, mingling with the tourists and those out for a Sunday drive. Marieke noted that George did not eat with them, but sat himself close by so that he could always keep them in view. He was obviously not just the driver. Conversation over lunch was about upbringings, educations and careers, which was interesting for both, because their experiences had been so different. After lunch, George drove them to a country manor house, the grounds of which had been turned into the raptor centre. It was open to the public, and tours were in progress. Courtney asked the young lady behind the counter if either Patrick McBride or Diana McBride were there that day, and learned that they had been there earlier and were now back at the house. George took them back down the drive a short way and then up the other drive, with the private sign, that took them to the house. Diana answered the door, and Marieke introduced herself.

"You've come a long way; you'd better come in," Diana said. "I suppose you're still looking into the murders of David and Julia?"

"I am," Marieke confirmed. "I'm trying to learn as much about them as I can, so that I can form a theory as to why anyone would want to kill them."

"Who is it, Dear?" a voice said, and Marieke recognised it as the voice of Patrick McBride.

"It's the Botswana Police, Dear," Diana said. "The superintendent that we talked to before is here."

"I hope you didn't come all this way just to see us?" Patrick said.

"No," Marieke dissembled. "I have an investigation that involves the diamond trade that we have, so was in England anyway. I had time, so my colleague here from the Home Office offered to bring me out here."

"May I get you some tea?" Diana asked.

"That would be most welcome," Marieke said. "I hate to bother you on a Sunday, but it is the only time I had free to do this. I just wanted to learn a little more about David and Julia Turner and why anyone would want to kill them."

"I gather from Sara that you found the bodies?" Patrick asked.

"We did," Marieke confirmed. "I was talking to Ian Ross, and he told me that you had been to Botswana before?"

"Went a couple of times," Patrick said. "You have great raptors there."

"When were you last there, did you see David and Julia?" Marieke asked.

"I suppose about three months ago," Patrick said. "David and I wanted to go out into the Kalahari to look for some kestrels and goshawks. Diana and Julia were less keen, but they came anyway."

"How did they seem at that time?" Marieke asked.

"Fine," Patrick said. "David had just heard about his chair in Oxford, so they were looking forward to coming home."

"I found some lists of birds of David's, I think a life list, a year list and a couple more, is that normal?" Marieke asked.

"It is," Patrick said. "I have a life list, I keep year lists and trip lists, I even added to my lists last month in the Luangwa Valley when I was there, I saw a black-shouldered kite for the first time, I was going to call David and brag about it when he got back from his trip."

"I have been supposing that David Turner was the intended victim and that Julia Turner was also killed, but is it possible that Julia Turner was the intended victim?" Marieke asked.

"I cannot think why anyone would kill Julia," Diana said. "She is, was, a lovely person."

"I am having a real problem," Marieke admitted. "All the friends and neighbours that I talk to in Gaborone all say the same thing, they cannot think why anyone would kill either of them. Do you travel much in the bird world, Sir?"

"I suppose I do," Patrick said. "You never know when some unusual sighting will crop up. I've been to northern Canada to look for snowy owls, Cape Town to chase penguins and just last week, Italy; someone had reported a sighting of a Lammergeier near Florence. They had all but been wiped out on the Italian side of the Alps in about 1913, and the Italians are trying to bring them back. This sighting was really rare; they haven't been seen in that area for aeons."

"How many raptor species do you have here?" Marieke asked.

"We have over 200 species here, a little less than half the species in the world," Patrick said.

"That is incredible," Marieke said. "I suppose I've seen twenty or so. I once saw an Ovambo Sparrowhawk almost to the South Africa border, it was far away from Ovamboland. Have you been to Botswana or Zambia in the rains when all the migratory birds from Europe come for our summer, the European winter?"

"I have," Patrick said. "I went once to the Okavango in January and once to the Luangwa in December, both trips were amazing, but the difficulty was just getting around, the rains do rather slow things up."

"They do," Marieke agreed. "Tell me, have you ever met any of David's colleagues in the field of economic theory?"

"No, I think they live in a different world," Patrick said. "He would sometimes talk about others and their theories, some he agreed with, some he dismissed."

"So, you have no idea who else might have been considered for this chair?" Marieke asked.

"Not really," Patrick said. "About six months ago, David reeled off a whole list of names as those likely to be invited to apply, I think he said that there were something like six Brits, five from the US, a couple of French guys, a couple of Germans and some odds and sods."

"Did he mention anyone by name?" Marieke asked.

"If he did, I don't remember," Patrick said. "You don't think one of them did it?"

"I just want to learn more about him," Marieke said. "I thought that if he talked about someone a lot, then that person might be able to tell me a little about David and his theories and his life."

"Look, I have to go out. Why don't you stay a while and talk to Diana," Patrick suggested. After Patrick had gone, the conversation switched back from David and Julia to birds. Diana made some offhand comments about Patrick's obsession with birds and the fact that she resented the fact that he was using money she had brought into the marriage to indulge his hobby. The centre was not self-sustaining, but was in fact an annual drain. Diana complained about the short-notice travel, the trip to Zambia in late May and early June, and the trip just recently to Italy. On most of those kinds of trips, he did not even offer to take her along, just took off, a couple of times leaving a note to say where he had gone. Marieke gently nudged her until she went off on a tirade about his womanising. Marieke gently steered her back to David and Julia, so that when she reported on her conversation to Patrick later, she would remember questions about the neighbours they had met in Gaborone, about the trip that the Turners had been on and when it had been planned and how many people knew where they were going. All the things that were unlikely to arouse suspicion in the mind of Patrick. She finally thanked Julia for her time and left, saying that she was at sea about why the Turners had been murdered and therefore who would have done it. She left Diana disappointed when she said it was likely the case might never be solved. On the way out to the car, Marieke saw tracks that McBride had left in the soft soil of a flower bed. She took a look and was satisfied.

In the car on the way back to Oxford, Marieke asked Courtney for her impressions.

"McBride lied several times during your interview," she replied. "He and David Turner had talked about people on the list, and he knew very well who they were and had met at least one. He also told enough of the truth so that if we go digging, we can confirm parts of his story. He has to assume that at some point we might check on his travel, so he told us that he was in Zambia and Italy. How far away from your murder site is the Luangwa Valley?"

"I would guess at close to 700 miles as the crow flies," Marieke said. "I can check with the Zambians to see if he did go to the Luangwa, also I can check to see if any plane charters were made to fly from Mfuwe to Livingstone."

"Let's see what George picked up," Courtney said. She pressed the intercom button and asked.

"When he came out of the house, he went straight to a phone," George said. "It was the phone in the foyer of the raptor centre. He only made a short call. I also learned that the place would close down if Diana McBride wasn't paying the bills. Two of the girls who work there are sleeping with him. He has been known to hit on visitors and has been seen going off into one of the outbuildings with a visitor. The girls who are sleeping with him think he's the greatest thing ever, and neither can understand why he doesn't divorce Diana and marry them. The blokes that work here keep their wives, sisters and daughters well away. He went off to Italy last week. He was in Zambia a month ago. He likes medieval warfare and likes to go to re-enactments, dresses the part and all, has an extensive collection of real antique and replica weapons."

"Thank you, George," Courtney said, and then she turned to Marieke and said, "Let's see what he talked about and to whom." She picked up the car phone and called a number, listened for a while, then hung up. "So, it seems that Mr McBride doesn't know any of David Turner's fellow economists, but the first person he called has a number listed to one Harold Swanson."

"How did you get that so quickly?" Marieke asked.

"I made a call when we were at the hotel and authorised taps on the phones of the McBrides and Harold Swanson," Courtney said. "It is within my purview to make such authorisations."

"That was quick work for your technical people. Do we know what was said?" Marieke asked.

"Unfortunately, we weren't able to set that facility up yet," Courtney said. "But, I think we will keep an eye on your Mr McBride. I presume you don't wish to disclose this to him at this time?"

"No, I think just file it away for future reference," Marieke said. "My own records show that Patrick McBride and Harold Swanson were at the same bush camp twice at the same time. It's hard to deny knowing someone when you've met them at one of those bush camps. Typically, there are only eight to ten guests, maybe twenty for one of the bigger camps."

"So, you've established that McBride and Swanson knew each other, even though McBride denies it, you know that McBride, by his own admission, was in Zambia a month ago, that still does not place either of them either in Botswana or at the scene," Courtney pointed out.

"I have an eyewitness who identified Swanson as being in Kazungula a couple of days before we think the murders took place," Marieke said. "But, you are right; I still cannot place either of them at the scene, unless I can get them to walk in front of Tushay, my tracker."

"How would that help?" Courtney asked.

"Evidence of the San trackers is accepted in our court system as being definitive," Marieke explained. "If Tushay says he was there, he was there."

"You looked at tracks when we left," Courtney said. "What did they tell you?"

"That McBride had been at the site where the bodies had been buried," Marieke replied. "But, I am only a small part San, so my evidence might be indicative, but not definitive, it would not be accepted in the courts. It still would only go to prove that McBride had had a hand in burying the bodies, not the actual murders."

"So, your case is likely to be purely circumstantial?" Courtney asked.

"I think so, unless I can get a confession," Marieke confirmed.

When they arrived back in Oxford, dinner arrangements were made, and they went their separate ways for the moment. Marieke got the phone number from her book for Valeria's father and made the call.

"*Pronto*," a woman's voice answered.

"Good afternoon," Marieke said. "I would like to speak to Mr Bernini."

"Who's calling, please?" the voice asked.

"This is Assistant Superintendent Englebrecht of the Botswana Police," Marieke said.

"Oh, you're Marieke, Katrina's cousin, I'm Alex, Vincenzo's wife, I'm the sister-in-law of Katrina," Alex explained. "Valeria said you'd be calling. Where are you?"

"I'm in Oxford," Marieke said.

"Let me get Vincenzo for you," Alex said. Marieke waited a minute or so, and another voice came on the phone.

"*Pronto*," he said.

"Good afternoon, Mr Bernini," Marieke said. "I was hoping that you might be able to help me?"

"Please, call me Vincenzo," he said. "I understand that you have some questions about the traffic accident of Paulo Schirano?"

"That is correct," Marieke said. "A couple of months ago a David Turner was awarded a prestigious chair in economics at one of the Oxford colleges. He has since been murdered. The next in line for the chair was

Paulo Schirano, and now he is dead. I want to be sure that his accident was a true accident and not one staged. I want to be sure that the death in Botswana of David Turner is not related to the death of Schirano."

"Ah, I see," Vincenzo said. "That is certainly worth investigating. Do you have any suspects for your murders in Botswana?"

"Officially, no," she replied. "But, I am working on a theory that those murders were done in connection with the post at Oxford. My theory is that someone else really wanted that position."

"But, you have an idea of whom?" Vincenzo asked.

"I think it might be worth checking carefully into the movements of a Patrick McBride, an Englishman, who runs a raptor centre here in England and says that he was in Italy last week because of a rare bird sighting," Marieke explained. "I think it would also be worth checking to see if a Harold Swanson was also in Italy, my intuition says not, but I would like to be sure."

"You are in Oxford, Alex said?" Vincenzo asked. "Can you come to Italy?"

"I was thinking that when I am finished here, it might be a good idea to stop in Italy," she replied. "That would probably be later this week."

"Good," Vincenzo said. "If you can, get a flight to Pisa and I will meet you there, just let me know the flight number and the day you are arriving. The Schirano accident occurred not far from Pisa on the road from Viareggio to Lucca. I will show you the place and have more details when you arrive."

"Thank you," she said. "I will be in touch."

Over dinner with Courtney, Marieke commented that she would be going to Italy after her business in England was completed. That led to explanations as to how she knew someone in Italy, and then a whole conversation about families. It seemed that Courtney had been married, but that her husband had been killed in Afghanistan while on a diplomatic mission there. Since then, she had turned her attention and energies to police work. The conversation then turned back to the current case.

"Why did you turn your attentions to McBride and Swanson?" Courtney asked.

"Swanson had much to gain by removing Turner," Marieke said. "I also believe that McBride has lately realised that Diana McBride was still in a relationship with Julia Turner, albeit over the miles, but still close."

"Surely, McBride and Swanson would think that you would find out that they had both been in Botswana at the same time and at the same place?" Courtney asked.

"I don't think so," Marieke said. "The safari operator had changed; they had no way of knowing if the past operator kept records. In fact, the way most of these camps are run, they usually don't."

"How do you know the two had met at the safari camp?" Courtney asked.

"The current operator keeps good records, not only of who comes, but also of where they go and what they see," Marieke explained. "The past operator kept some records and notes, not as detailed as Will Martin's, but Piet remembers people, and he identified McBride and Swanson, and I have passenger manifests from the charter company that flew them out there."

"Is this place remote then?" Courtney asked.

"Fairly," Marieke said. "It is not as bad as the Central Kalahari, but it is remote enough and over the past few years has been difficult in that there were incursions from the Caprivi Strip, so some fighting that spilt over our border."

"What if it isn't Swanson at all, but someone you have not even thought of?" Courtney asked.

"Then, I have difficulties," Marieke admitted. "I cannot think of a motive that is not connected to either McBride or the chair in Oxford."

"So, we will have to see what Adams says tomorrow," Courtney said. "I suspect he will wriggle and squirm as he will not want to release his shortlist to us, but I believe I can make him see that it will be in his best interests to cooperate."

"Thank you," Marieke said.

The office of Dr Adams was large, overlooking a grassed quadrangle, everything that Marieke thought an Oxford college office would be: high ceilings, panelled walls, bookcases and a general feel of old-world gentility. Dr Adams was not alone; there were others there, and he introduced them.

"Good morning, this is my selection committee, Dr Susan Bullock, Dr James Webb, Professor John Entwhistle, Professor Henry Wilson and Mr Simon Bentham," he said. "I decided that it would save time if we met as a committee and answered your questions as a group."

"Thank you for gathering everyone," Courtney said. "We will need another room to conduct interviews."

"I thought we could do it here," Adams protested.

"Nevertheless, we will require another room, and we will interview each of you individually," Courtney said.

"These are busy people," Adams said. "I must insist that we conduct the interviews as a group."

"You may insist all you like," Courtney said coldly. "But, either we use another room for individual interviews, or we all go to the Oxford Police Station and use their interview rooms. Do you wish to be seen leaving the college in police cars?"

"Look, Adams," Simon Bentham interrupted. "I for one would be happy to answer whatever questions these people have, and you are making a grave mistake with this approach. It comes across as if you have something to hide and want to keep a story straight. Have I been mistaken about this college? Should I take my endowment elsewhere?"

"No, no, it's just that I thought it would save time," Adams said, all smiles and apologies.

"Fine," Courtney said. "Let me introduce my colleague. This is Assistant Superintendent Englebrecht of the Botswana Police; she is looking into the murders of Drs David and Julia Turner. We have talked about this in the past day we have been together, and Superintendent Englebrecht is seeking background on David and Julia Turner, so that she can try and formulate a theory as to why they were murdered, which may then help to lead to the killer."

"Dr Adams neglected to tell us who we would be meeting with," Susan Bullock said, subtly distancing herself from Adams.

"I am an Assistant Undersecretary of State in the Home Office, and have been directed by the Home Secretary to render all assistance that I can to help resolve this," Courtney said.

"Why the interest of the Home Secretary?" Wilson asked.

"The Home Secretary knew David Turner personally and wonders why anyone would kill him, so is deeply interested in the investigation, be it here or in Botswana," Courtney explained.

"So, how can I help?" Simon asked. "Why don't we use the anteroom that is across the hall?"

"Marieke, let us go with Mr Bentham. George will stay and keep everyone else company," Courtney suggested. Marieke nearly laughed aloud at that. Courtney was going to make sure that the rest of the group did not concoct any or more stories. Simon Bentham led the way to the anteroom and stood aside to let Marieke and Courtney enter.

"Sorry about that," he said. "Adams is paranoid about his secrets and thinks he has stolen a march on the other colleges with this endowed chair. He wants to play everything close to the vest and control what is said, by whom and to whom."

"Thank you for agreeing to help us," Marieke said. "What is your interest in endowing this chair?"

"I run a pretty big fund that has a lot invested in developing economies. I want to get better research into how those economies will behave in the next ten to fifteen years," he explained. "Most analysts look at three, six or twelve months and if you're really lucky, five years, but few take the long view to see where things may go, I also wanted to fund research that was independent of my firm, I wanted to avoid people telling me what they thought I wanted to hear."

"Of the others we just met, are there any economists?" Marieke asked.

"Entwhistle and Bullock," Simon replied. "But Entwhistle is an expert on developed nations; he doesn't have much clue about developing nations. Susan teaches basic economics and is deeply interested in the application of game theory to economic forecasts."

"I have to ask this, but who was on the shortlist of candidates?" asked Marieke.

"Well, there was obviously David Turner, then Paulo Schirano from Pisa, who is now also dead, ostensibly due to a traffic accident, maybe, maybe not, then there was Valerie White from Cambridge, Harold Swanson from here in Oxford, and Camille Frou from Paris," Simon enumerated. "You probably already know that Camille took David's job at your own university."

"Dr Chebani of our university neglected to tell us that when we talked to him," Marieke commented. "It will be the subject of some discussion when I return."

"Why Turner?" Courtney asked.

"He was by far and away the best," Simon said. "He had a good knowledge of developing nations, his work in Botswana has been very insightful and useful, he is well respected in the community, and I just liked the man."

"What will you do now?" Marieke asked.

"I've told Adams that I want to wait until the investigations of the deaths of David and Julia Turner and Paulo Schirano are complete before we name the next person," Simon said. "Did you know that Schirano was dead?"

"Sara called and told me," Marieke admitted.

"I suppose she's convinced that someone is bumping off the competitors and setting up the post for themselves," he remarked.

"I got an impression that she thought that the traffic accident was a little too convenient," Marieke said. "But, who would actually go as far as killing the competition?"

"Any and all of them," Simon said. "Since I've been going through this process, I've learned a lot about the academic world. It's not all tea and crumpets, it's cutthroat and nasty, full of backbiting, plagiarism, theft of work and other nastiness."

"Surely, not all?" Marieke protested.

"No, not all," he agreed. "But the system is structured in that it drives the behaviours of those in it, and that system favours the disreputable, at least in my opinion, obviously most would disagree, and they may be right, it may just be me who is jaundiced by it all."

"When David Turner was selected, was the vote unanimous?" Marieke asked.

"No, it was me, Bullock and Webb for, whereas Adams and Wilson wanted Schirano and Entwhistle wanted Swanson, probably because they're school chums, grammar school and college," Simon replied. "In the end, I played the money card and they caved."

"So, when Turner was killed and you went to the next pick, what was the voting there?" Marieke asked.

"Again, me, Bullock and Webb for Schirano, Adams and Wilson both waffled and sided with Entwhistle for Swanson," he replied. "I think it was the Oxford set working again to make sure that it was one of them who got the post. We had set things up so that in the event of a tie, my vote carried the decision."

"So, why did Adams and Wilson vote for Schirano the first time?" Marieke asked.

"I think they just didn't want Turner, spent too long in the colonies for their liking, but didn't want to be seen putting up their own boy too quickly," he said.

"That suggests that they might have known that Turner would not be able to take up the post?" Marieke asked.

"I don't think they had thought things through that well," he said. "They just didn't want Turner, and were less than thrilled by the overtures that Swanson was making, and I think were sending a message for him to tone it down a little."

"That suggests that someone was keeping Swanson apprised of all that was going on?" Marieke asked.

"I have no evidence, but my view is that Entwhistle gave chapter and verse to Swanson, he's probably going to do so today, he would be now but for your man, you left to keep an eye on them," he said.

"Were there others considered who did not make the shortlist?" Marieke asked.

"We looked at twenty in all," Simon replied. "As I recall, there were six Brits, five from the US, three French, two Italians, two Germans, a Kiwi and an Aussie."

"None of the Americans made the shortlist?" Courtney asked.

"We found that they didn't have what we were looking for in terms of knowledge and experience with developing nations," Simon explained.

"Could any of them be offended enough to seek retribution?" Marieke asked.

"If they did, I would have thought that it would have been against the college and the selection committee," Simon laughed. "But, no, we generally found them all to be very amiable and professional."

"Is there anything else that you think we should know?" Marieke asked.

"I don't think so," Simon replied. "But, if I think of anything, I will get in touch with you. Sara has your contact phone numbers, I believe? Tell me, did you come all this way just to ask about David Turner?"

"I had other business that relates to the diamond trade, that, as you probably know, is a large part of our exports, so I thought I would take the time and find out what I could," Marieke repeated the story she had told the McBrides. "Thank you for your time, as you said, Sara has my contact telephone numbers, should you think of something. Would you be so kind as to ask Dr Adams to join us?"

Dr Adams put Courtney in mind of Sir Humphrey Appleby of *Yes Minister* fame; he had just the right amount of sincere condescension to make one almost believe what he had to say. He apologised for the lack of understanding earlier and managed to put it in such a way as to infer that it was all the fault of Courtney and Marieke. The interview went around and around, with the eventual revelation of the shortlist of candidates. He skipped around the question of who might wish either of the Drs Turner harm and spent most of his time bemoaning the fact that he had to pick yet another candidate. He also danced around the voting for the successful candidate, only admitting that the votes had not been unanimous, but the subject of lively and spirited discussion. Marieke got the impression that he thought that Paulo Schirano must have deliberately crashed his car, just to make Dr Adams's life difficult. Being addressed as Dear Lady, was new to Marieke, but it made Courtney smile a little as she listened to almost verbatim words from Sir Humphrey. Marieke was left with the impression that he thought she was totally out of her depth and unlikely to solve the mystery. Well, that suited her for the moment. There was time enough to bring charges, but she had to get her suspects in the country before she did that. She had no intention, if at all possible, of getting caught up in the quagmire of extradition. Dr Adams was thanked for his time and sent off quite quickly. He had no real relationship with either David or Julia Turner and was able to say little about their lives, professional work or ambitions. He only knew what he had been told by the others.

After Adams left, they went through the rest in quick succession, picking up little titbits as they went. The two who knew David Turner best were John Entwhistle and Susan Bullock. Entwhistle danced around the question of voting for candidates and told Marieke that she just would not understand the culture of Oxford and the need to fit in. He admitted to friendship with Harold Swanson, but claimed that that had had no bearing on his votes. Susan Bullock was fairly forthcoming, discussing the shortlist and the voting quite freely. She also revealed that she was moving soon to the Wharton School in Philadelphia, a move that she saw as a step up for her and a way to get out of the stifling atmosphere of the college and Oxford in general. By lunchtime, Marieke knew a little more about David Turner, but not enough to theorise a motive to kill him, other than the one she already had. She was left with the clear view that the Oxford set, as Courtney called them, was a strong clique who really did not take kindly to outsiders and that they closed ranks and were less than candid and forthcoming. If Simon Bentham had not been there and taken the lead, she doubted whether they would have ever learned the makeup of the shortlist, without resorting to warrants from the Home Office to open files. Marieke thought that she had got as much as she was going to get from this group, so she thanked them for their help and bemoaned her fate of being lumbered with this case that was apparently insoluble.

On the drive back to the hotel, Courtney asked George what had gone on in the office while they were out interviewing individuals.

"They sat and looked at me," George said. "No conversation, no calls, no smiles, if I were a betting man, I would have said that they all had something to hide. There was also tension between Adams and Bentham, but that's not surprising, Bentham is the money man used to taking big risks, and Adams probably never took a risk in his life. All in all, quiet, reserved, all acting as though they were hiding something, but perhaps that's just the nature of who they are."

"Thank you, George," Courtney said. "I suppose that after we left, they all went scurrying to the closest phone to call someone, I wonder who?"

"I imagine that Bentham called his office just to see if he had any calls or messages that need attention," Marieke suggested. "As for the rest, I think it's a fair supposition that Entwhistle called Swanson to let him know we'd been and what we were asking about. I was thinking that the next two interviewees should be Swanson and White. Camille Frou is in Botswana, so I can see her when I return. Swanson is here in Oxford, where is White?"

"I had George check on likely candidates, and he has addresses. I will make an appointment with Swanson tomorrow, then we'll journey up to Cambridge and see White on Wednesday," Courtney replied. "I have also placed a watch on White; I would hate to hear that she also has had an unfortunate accident. You may wish to have someone keep an eye on Frou for a while, until such time as you are satisfied that there is no risk to her."

"I will take care of that this evening," Marieke thought.

"So, we have a free afternoon, what would you like to do?" Courtney asked.

"Perhaps a walk around Oxford?" Marieke suggested. "I've never been before, and this may be my one chance in quite a while."

"We can do that," Courtney agreed. "Give me ten minutes to arrange the interviews for tomorrow and meet me in the foyer."

"So, what do you think of Oxford?" Courtney asked Marieke over dinner.

"It has the feeling of age about it," Marieke replied. "But, for me, it also feels oppressive, the buildings are crammed in together, they are for the most part quite tall when compared to Botswana or Namibia buildings, I grew up on a farm in South West, near a small town called Grünau, which is on the road between Springbok and Keetmanhoop. Our views were desert and mountains."

"What else is different?" Courtney asked.

"Water," Marieke replied. "It is obvious that it rains a lot here, there are green grass areas everywhere, the river must flow all the time, unlike many of ours that are dry unless we get a big rain."

"I would like to go back sometime," Courtney said. "As I said before, the one time I was in Botswana, or for that matter, South Africa or Namibia, I was trying to do Africa on £1 a day. I actually did not get to see too much of any of the countries, only the towns that we went to."

217

"When you come, let me know and I will give you a guided tour," Marieke promised.

"Thank you," Courtney said. "But, back to business, our appointment with Swanson is at nine in the morning, then I thought we would motor up to Cambridge, have dinner with Valerie White and ask her what we need to do then. That will have you back in London Wednesday morning; perhaps you will be able to get a flight to Italy later that day."

"I will call my High Commission first thing in the morning and get them to arrange it," Marieke said. "I'll also get them to rearrange my flights to get me back to Gaborone, which may mean that I come back to London to go to Johannesburg."

"If you need any help with the arrangements, let me know," Courtney said. "We have contacts within BA and can assist."

Harold Swanson had an office in one of the lesser colleges of Oxford. The quadrangle which it faced was not quite as manicured as the one that Dr Adams's office overlooked. But it still had an air of elegance about it. There were bookcases with tomes on economics and personal mementoes, including a large trophy for small-bore pistol shooting, apparently won while Swanson was at LSE, as it was an inter-collegiate competition trophy. Marieke had been surprised by the number of students that seemed to be milling around until she learned that the college had hired out its rooms for the summer to an American college, so what she was seeing were keen young American archaeologists all eager to learn about the history of Oxford and its surrounds, including Stonehenge and the other famous sites to the West. Harold Swanson was all smiles when he greeted them and offered tea or coffee, something that Adams had failed to do. He was effusive in his praise for David Turner, calling him one of the great men in his field, and could not imagine why anyone would want to kill him. He waxed eloquently about his visits to Botswana in the past, apparently taken by the openness of the country and the feeling of unfettered freedom to wander. He said that he had not been back lately, but that he would like to visit again, this time to, perhaps, spend time in the Okavango Delta, something he had heard should be visited at least once in a lifetime.

Marieke got the impression that he was trying a little too hard to keep the conversation where he wanted it, and by rabbiting on about his visits and impressions, he probably felt that he could keep the conversation away from his recent trips. When pressed about the other shortlist candidates, he confessed that he did not like Camille Frou, he quite liked Paulo Schirano and had a great deal of regard for Valerie White, but that was tempered by the fact that she was from Cambridge, so not quite to the levels one expected at Oxford. He also alluded several times to the fact that Marieke would probably never understand the feeling of Oxford; one had to be part of it to truly understand what it meant. She accepted that in good part, she was not sure that she would ever want to be part of this society and its prejudices and insular thinking. One thing that Marieke did find was a brochure about the college with a nice, large picture of Swanson; it was much better than the picture she had.

In the car on the way to Cambridge, Courtney made her opinion of Harold Swanson quite clear. She was not impressed.

"Did you note all the talk about being part of Oxford?" she asked.

"I did," Marieke replied. "I thought it was all rather too much."

"Too much indeed," Courtney agreed. "Swanson went to LSE, both for his undergraduate degree and for his doctorate."

"Tell me," Marieke said. "Would it be possible to find out when he was there and also when a Dr John Chebani was there?"

"I'm sure we can do that," Courtney said. She picked up the car phone and relayed the request to her office, with the adder that she would like any and all information on where the two might have lived and who their associates were. "Were you able to make a booking for Italy?"

"I was," Marieke said. "I have a flight to Pisa tomorrow afternoon. Then I have a flight back to London on Friday, which is in plenty of time for the flight to Johannesburg. That will get me home on Saturday, so a day to recover before I go back to work."

"When we leave here tomorrow, we'll go straight to Heathrow. You may be there a little early, but better to wait there than in a traffic jam on the M-25 wondering if you'll make your flight," Courtney suggested.

"Thank you," Marieke said. "You really have been most kind, and I know that I would not have received the cooperation we got without your help."

"It is the least we could do, remember, if you do need anything else to help with your investigation, please call me," Courtney said. "Well, here we are at Cambridge," she paused and pressed the intercom button, "George, La Margherita please," she instructed, and then she explained to Marieke about the restaurant. "This is a new restaurant, just opened this year, it's a family-run Italian restaurant, I think you'll like it."

The restaurant was just down the road from Magdalene College, where it seemed Courtney had got her degree, and where she had arranged rooms for them for the night. She told Marieke that La Margherita had once been a French restaurant, but the various dips of the economy had not been kind to the owner, and he had sold out, so now it was an Italian restaurant. Marieke was intrigued by Cambridge, in so many ways very similar to Oxford, but yet not. Before dinner, they took a short walk to the college and then the river, where punts and other boats were tied up along the bank, either waiting to be hired or left for their owners. With the students down for the summer, most of the people they saw were tourists, Americans and Japanese being the most evident. Back at the restaurant, they had only just been seated when Valerie White was shown to their table. Courtney introduced herself and Marieke and explained their purpose. Valerie told them that she had received a call from Susan Bullock and had thought long and hard about what Marieke wanted to know and had drawn a blank. She could just not think of anyone who would actually kill David Turner. She was disappointed that she had not won the chair but conceded that both David Turner and Paulo Schirano were excellent choices, with which she had no quibble. She was interested to learn what would happen next, even after Susan had told her that selection was deferred for a while, per the wishes of Simon Bentham. She had few words for Harold Swanson, considering him to be not of the calibre of either David or Paulo. Camille Frou, she knew quite well, but thought that Camille would not be the choice of Simon Bentham, she was a little too much of a socialist for Bentham. She thought that she actually had a good chance of winning the chair, but admitted that the Oxford set were a force to be reckoned with and that Swanson undoubtedly had his allies and cronies on the selection committee. In the end, Marieke thanked her for her time but came away no wiser. Valerie had nothing to tell them that would propel the case one way or another.

Heathrow was crowded with holidaymakers, but Courtney was able to steer Marieke quickly to a special service desk for BA, find her tickets that had been left for her by the High Commission and get her checked in.

"Thank you for all your help," Marieke said to Courtney. "If you ever come to Botswana, please do call and let me know, I would be delighted to show you around."

"I will do that," Courtney said. "Remember, if there is anything else we can do for you, please call, you have my number, it is my private line that bypasses the switchboards and gatekeepers. I will wish you a good journey, what is it that you say, *tsamaya sentlê?*"

"*Sala sentlê,*" Marieke responded, delighted that Courtney had picked up the standard farewell phrase. "Please thank George for me as well."

"I will, bye," Courtney said, handing Marieke off to a BA representative who had been hovering discreetly a little way off. Marieke followed the BA representative to a lounge that was obviously for VIPs. Marieke smiled to herself about that; she in no way considered herself any kind of Very Important Person, but was grateful for the consideration. She did not have to wait long until the flight was called, and the BA agent took her to the gate and handed her over to the gate agent. The gate agent assumed that Marieke must be someone special, so boarded her ahead of the crowd and got her seated and comfortable. This was a life that she could get used to, Marieke thought! The flight to Pisa was only just over two hours, and the plane landed towards the sea, giving Marieke a nice view of the city as they came in. She joined the throng at immigration, and when her turn came, the agent obviously pushed some button or made some sign because she was approached by another agent who asked her to go with him. He took her to an office where she was introduced to Dottore Bernini or Vincenzo.

"Welcome to Italy, Marieke," he said. "Is this your first visit?"

221

"It is," Marieke said. "I studied in France, but never came south."

"We have been talking to Katrina, and she told us all about the issues with your parents and the problems they had with the South African government. Perhaps now those laws will change," he said.

"I would hope so," she agreed. "I know it was difficult for them."

"We should collect your suitcase, and then we can look at the scene of the incident," he suggested. "I have asked the local Polizia who first investigated the crash to meet us there."

"Thank you," she said. "Have the investigations proven that it was an accident?"

"Ah, no," he replied. "At our first look, it had all the appearances of a most unfortunate accident, but when we looked more closely, we found that it had been cleverly created to look like an accident, but Schirano was actually forced off the road."

"You said that it was on the road from Viareggio to Lucca, why there?" she asked.

"The road there is on a long bridge that spans the lower part of the plain by the coast and leads to tunnels through the mountain," he explained. "Where Schirano went off was quite a few metres above the ground, and the fall destroyed his car and killed him."

"How could anyone stage the accident?" she asked. "That suggests that he had a routine that he followed and that someone knew about."

"He did have a daily routine," Vincenzo confirmed. "He would leave the university at Pisa at about seven each evening, drive to Viareggio to his favourite bar for a Campari and soda, then drive home to Lucca. I understand from the local Polizia that one could almost set their watches to the time when he passed."

"Ah, excuse me," she interrupted. "I see my suitcase. You were saying?"

"Our theory now is that someone studied him for a day or two, learned the routine, then staged the accident," Vincenzo continued. "Shall we go and look?"

They walked to Vincenzo's car and he drove out of the airport and joined the Florence to Livorno SuperStrada for a few kilometres before turning sharply north onto the Rome to Genoa highway. After another twenty-five kilometres, he took the exit that led to Lucca. Not far up this road, they saw the police car parked off on the hard shoulder and pulled up behind it. Vincenzo introduced Marieke to the policemen, who shook her hand and went through the normal greetings. Sadly, neither of the local officers spoke English, or even French, that Marieke tried with them, so Vincenzo was left to translate. They pointed out where the car had gone over the edge and then walked up the road a little way and gave voluble explanations as to what they believed had actually happened. It seemed that the person who had caused the incident had been waiting for Schirano to come and then had deliberately reversed towards Schirano causing him to brake sharply and swerve to the right, which put him up against the barrier, but he was going fast enough that he went through the barrier and plunged to his death.

"How did they know that Schirano was coming?" Marieke asked.

"We took a much closer look at the car and found the remains of a tracking device. When we first found the pieces, we could not see where they were from and why they were there, but when we looked at the incident in a different way, it made sense. He knew just where Schirano was and could watch him join the road and come towards him," Vincenzo explained.

"Do you know who set up the incident?" Marieke asked.

"We have no direct evidence," Vincenzo replied. "But the Polizia have reviewed the many traffic cameras that we have, and we believe we can identify the car."

"Would it be possible to see the images?" Marieke asked.

"*Certo,*" Vincenzo said. He had a quick conversation with the Polizia, and they had obviously been expecting this, as they told Vincenzo to meet them at their station, and they left. Vincenzo followed them and quickly came to the imposing edifice on the Via Fratelli Cervi. He obviously knew his way around the station and quickly caught up with the two policemen. They had things set up in an interview room, a map showing the locations of the cameras and a computer monitor on which they could play the traffic footage. With Vincenzo translating, the Vice Superintendent showed the footage from each camera and related it to time. The car they identified as a Renault, registered to someone in Paris. They had contacted the French police and were waiting to hear from them.

"Perhaps I can help?" suggested Marieke. "May I use your telephone to call Lyon?"

"*Certo*," Vincenzo said, handing over the telephone. Marieke called Melisende and was pleased to find her still in Lyon, not yet moved to Paris. "Melisende, *ça va*?" she asked.

"*Ça va*, Marieke, where are you?"

"I'm in Viareggio in Italy," Marieke explained. "I am at a police station and we are trying to find out about a car, or rather the owner of a car in Paris."

"And we are looking into it, *mais trés lentement, oui*?" Melisende said.

"That is the problem," Marieke agreed.

"Do you have the details?" Melisende asked. Marieke said that she did and read off to Melisende all the information that the Italian police had gathered, the make and number of the car and when they had seen it in Italy. What they really needed to know was if the registered owner had driven it to Italy or someone else. She handed the phone back to Vincenzo and then asked him the next obvious question, "Tell me, Vincenzo, is any of the footage good enough to see the face of the driver of the Renault?" That prompted conversations with the two police officers, then one of them left and came back with another man who was apparently a technician. He scrubbed through footage, found images of the face and tried to get the best views he could. Marieke was a little disappointed; the face might have been that of Patrick McBride, but it might not have been, certainly, it would not stand the test of a cross-examination in court. Marieke resigned herself to the fact that that was the best she was going to get and asked for the best copies he could get and for the times that the car was seen at each camera. That all done, Vincenzo thanked the officers for their help and time, and he and Marieke left.

"Do you have enough?" he asked.

"If I could get a copy of the incident report?' she asked.

"*Certo*," he said. "It will be in Italian, do you wish me to get it translated into English?"

"That would be most useful," she said. "And, if I may ask, could that translation be certified by a court authority?"

"Of course, I also have the information you asked for about the man Swanson and the man McBride," he said. "There is no record of

Swanson entering or leaving Italy for the past six months via air, but as you know, the open borders of the EU make it easy to cross country to country without us knowing it. The same is true for McBride; if he entered the country from France, we probably don't have a record. If he did not stay in a hotel, then we also have no record."

"That is a shame," she agreed. "But, we'll see what Melisende can find out."

"*Bueno*," he said. "Shall we go to my house and meet Alex?"

The house was in the hills overlooking Viareggio and also had a view of Pisa. Marieke was sure that with binoculars she would be able to see the famous Leaning Tower and the Duomo of Pisa. The yard was terraced, and on each terrace, there were olive trees, except directly in front of the house, so that the view was not obstructed. Vincenzo showed Marieke into the house where she was met by Alex.

"Marieke," Alex said. "Welcome to Italy. It's so nice to meet you. I've been talking to Katrina, and she tells me that you two have never met?"

"No," Marieke confirmed. "We lived in the wilds of South West, and Katrina lived in Zambia. The families never met for holidays or even just visits, so we never had the chance to meet."

"And now, you've been inundated with family," Alex laughed. "I hope the girls were well-behaved when you met them in Botswana."

"They were delightful," Marieke confirmed. "Valeria was very helpful, taking notes when Will and I went out to investigate the Land Rover that he found."

"So, is your investigation going well? Was Vince able to help?" Alex asked.

"He helped a lot," Marieke said. "But, unfortunately, circumstances make it difficult for me to actually place anyone at the scene of the crime."

"Well, I'm sure that you'll be able to work it out," Alex said. "What can I get you to drink, coffee, tea, beer, wine?"

"Some wine would be very nice," Marieke replied.

"Good," Alex said. "Vince, let's sit out on the terrace. I'll bring wine and some small things to eat. Why don't you help Marieke with her suitcase and show her to her room?"

"It's quiet here," Marieke said when she joined the others on the terrace. "That's because the children are away," Alex laughed. "When all four are here, it's quite a bit different."

"They get on well enough?" Marieke asked.

"They do, fortunately," Alex replied. "Having two at fifteen and two at twelve is convenient. They now all go to the same school, which makes our lives a little easier."

"I feel a little like a fraud," Marieke said. "I came for some information and I have it already, but my flight back to London and then home is not until Friday."

"You must have earned a day off to do nothing," Alex said. "Enjoy the day, where would you like to go?"

"I don't know," Marieke admitted. "Florence, Pisa, Rome, there is so much that I would like to see."

"Well, tomorrow, why don't we quickly visit Pisa in the morning and then take a drive to Florence in the afternoon, perhaps even for lunch?"

"That sounds wonderful, you're sure that won't be too much trouble?" Marieke asked.

"No, not at all," Alex said. "The only issue we'll have is parking in Florence, perhaps Vince, you could arrange something?"

"If you meet Franco outside the city, then he could drive you in and take you to where you want to go," Vincenzo suggested. "Franco is my driver, "he explained to Marieke. "The problem is driving and parking in the city of Florence, one has to have a permit to drive beyond a certain point, and permits are hard to get, but our office is in the city centre, so we have the appropriate permits."

"Please don't put anyone to any inconvenience," Marieke said.

"Don't worry," Alex assured her. "Franco is a dear, and he'll be intrigued by the idea of driving a police officer from somewhere else. What is policing like in Botswana?"

"Probably very much the same as here," Marieke thought. "But, we have fewer people and they are spread out over a much larger area, so we drive a lot, sometimes eight to ten hours just to get somewhere. In my last post, I used to ride camels on patrol before we got Land Rovers."

"Where was that?" Alex asked.

"Towards the West, Tsabong, it is almost on the border with South Africa and not too far from the Namibia border," Marieke explained.

"Who was it that you called in France?" Vincenzo asked.

"Melisende Garnier, she's with the Sûreté in Lyon and is moving to Paris soon, we were friends when I was at university in Lyon," Marieke explained. "She's a Commissaire de Police in Lyon; I'm not sure what she'll be in Paris. I will give you her telephone number. Please call her on Monday to ask if she has information on the car."

"People in high places," Alex said. "Well, now you also know Vince, and he will help you in any way he can."

"Shall we take dinner here or go out?" Vincenzo asked.

"I think we'll eat here," Alex said. "I will start on dinner in a while."

Through the night, Marieke was at first disturbed by the clock of the nearby church that chimed every quarter, but soon enough she became used to it and fell asleep, even though it was busy chiming eleven. In the morning, when she came down for breakfast, Vincenzo was already gone to his office in Florence, Alex explained. They might meet him for lunch if things were not too hectic. So, Marieke and Alex had a leisurely breakfast and then went off to see the sights of Pisa then Florence. Alex obviously knew her way around the streets of Pisa, which seemed to Marieke to be a maze of odd streets meeting in odd places, with no apparent order. The tower was busy with tourists, but Marieke did get a picture, or rather, Alex took a picture of her in front of the tower. Then they went off to Florence for lunch. They met Franco in the car park of a McDonald's, just off the Viale Francesco Valenti, and he then drove them into the city. Marieke had thought that Pisa was bad for traffic, but Florence was even worse. In the centre of the city, the streets were narrow, and Alex tried to explain the permit rules to Marieke. The problem was simply too many cars and too little space to accommodate them all. As it turned out, Vincenzo was unable to join them for lunch, so Alex took Marieke to one of her favourite places. The restaurant was very close to the Ponte Vecchio and overlooked the river. The place was busy, but the owner saw Alex and waved. She was well known, and he made quick work of shooing out some laggards and then gave them a table with a river view. Lunch was excellent, and time passed quickly, so quickly that it was Marieke who first noticed that it was already two in the afternoon. Alex asked Marieke if there was anything particular that she wanted to see, but Marieke could think of nothing that she could see in the time available and still do it justice. So, they meandered through the streets until Marieke finally admitted that she had had enough and would it be inconvenient to go home?

Alex and Marieke were on their own Thursday night, so it was Alex who took Marieke to the airport on Friday in time to catch her flight to London. That flight was on time and put Marieke into Heathrow with about a five-hour wait before her Johannesburg flight departed. But, first, there was the adventure of changing terminals from the BA terminal that handled European flights to Terminal 4, on the other side of the airport. Marieke had checked her suitcase in Pisa, hoping that BA was up to the task of transferring it from flight to flight. In the event that it was delayed or lost, the world would not end, but she would have to go shopping for clothes. By chance, in Terminal 4, she saw Janet Edwards, the BA agent who had been with Courtney when she had arrived on Sunday morning.

"Good afternoon, Superintendent," Janet said. "Have you concluded your business here?"

"I have for the moment," Marieke confirmed. "Now I have to go back to work."

"When is your flight?" Janet asked.

"It's the Jo'burg flight at six-fifteen," Marieke said.

"So, you've a few hours to kill," Janet said. "Let's take you somewhere more comfortable." She turned her cart around and waited for Marieke to be seated, then she motored off to BA's First Class Lounge. There, she introduced Marieke to the staff and made sure that she was in good hands. The lounge was very nice, with windows overlooking part of the airport operations, so Marieke was able to watch the comings and goings of flights to all parts of the globe, a far cry from the simple airport in Gaborone. The staff must have considered her some sort of VIP, because they came and got her ticket and came back later with an upgraded seat to First Class. Marieke thought about that and decided that she would enjoy the experience; it was unlikely to happen again soon, particularly not while on official business. Ministers and other high-ranking officials might travel First or Business Classes, but mere police officers travelled in the back, which is all the budget would stand. The flight was very comfortable, and Marieke was attended to with great solicitation. She wondered what Janet Edwards had said to the staff at the lounge and what they had passed on to the cabin staff. Whatever it was, she was thrilled to be treated to the best service she had ever had on any flight, but that was an easy standard to beat as her previous flights had been the lowest cost fare she could find to get to Lyon from Namibia.

Back to work

When she arrived in Johannesburg, she was among the first off the plane, as the BA staff held back lesser mortals. She had not noticed this on her journey north, but then she had been seated in the very back and had had to wait for almost everyone to deplane before she could get close to the exit. In Johannesburg, she walked over to the transfer desk and found out where her Air Botswana flight was leaving from. There was only a ninety-minute wait, so she spent the time people-watching and trying to guess occupations and their reasons for travel. Soon enough, she was back in Gaborone, pleased to be home, suitcase and all! Before she had left Italy, Marieke had called Mbali to see if she would pick her up at the airport. Mbali was waiting when Marieke came out, suitcase in hand.

"*Dumela Mma*," Mbali said.

"*Dumela Mma*," Marieke replied. "Thank you for coming to collect me. I had thought about getting my Sergeant to meet me, but decided that I needed a day away from police work."

"So, how was the trip? Did you learn anything?" Mbali asked.

"The trip was fine, particularly on the way home when BA put me into First Class, that is a style of travel I like," Marieke said. "Did I learn anything? Yes, I suppose I did, whether or not it really helps me with my investigation remains to be seen. And you, you are well?"

"I am well," Mbali confirmed. "We have lunch ready for you at your house. I get you to buy a new house and you're never there!"

"It seems that way, doesn't it?" Marieke laughed. "First Linyanti, then Kazungula, then England, then Italy, it's been a whirlwind fortnight."

Lunch was a braai, a classic South African braai, with steaks, boerewors, and a few vegetables. Jannie did the cooking with assistance from Khanyo and Nandi, mainly in the form of keeping him supplied with beer, partly for drinking and partly for basting the meat. Mbali wanted to know all about Oxford, so Marieke tried to explain the sense of age of the place and the many, many tall stone buildings and spires. She also talked about the greens of the lawns and the parks, and the recreation grounds of the many colleges and schools there. She talked about the river that had water in it all the time, not just after the rains. She mentioned going out to Broadway and the raptor centre, and the quaintness of Broadway and its sense of timelessness, about to be imposed upon by increasing traffic volumes. Her descriptions were interrupted by two telephone calls; the first was from Courtney, who had information on Harold Swanson and John Chebani. It seemed that they had roomed together for the greater part of three years, in fact, for most of the time they had both been pursuing their doctorates. Courtney gave Marieke dates and addresses and the names of several people who remembered both and had provided most of the information. The next call was from Melisende; her news was less encouraging. The car seen in Italy belonged to a Pascal Giron, but he had loaned it to a friend, Alain Durollet, who had loaned it to an Englishman. Giron did not know who the Englishman was, and Durollet was away from France in Malaysia for another month. Giron had never seen the Englishman, so was unable to identify him, even from a photograph. But, Melisende was able to positively place Patrick McBride in Paris at the time the car was taken, and they had footage from traffic cameras of the car on the autoroute from Paris to Lyon to Marseille and then from Marseille to Genoa, there they had been lucky, the traffic police happened to be looking for someone else, so had been reviewing the footage. Again, sadly, none of the images were good enough to identify the driver, but at least they knew when the car entered Italy. Marieke thanked Melisende and told her that she would be hearing from Vincenzo on Monday. That done, she went back to her description of the trip.

The girls wanted to know about fashions and what people were wearing, both in England and Italy. Marieke told them what she could, but also pointed out that many of the people she had seen were tourists from mainly America and Japan, so her sense of English fashions was only hazy. The people she had met professionally wore suits, both men and women. It was also summertime, so the student population was down to a minimum, except for the Americans she saw, there for the archaeology course. Jannie wanted to know about the car she rode in.

231

That was an easy one; it was a Jaguar XJ6 Sovereign model, black. Jannie wanted more details, but Marieke just did not have them, and she believed it had been modified and was not a standard car from the production line. She told them about the car phone, and how she would really like one for her car, it would be so useful on long trips, or even on short trips around the town. Jannie then wanted to know what car she had used in Italy. Marieke said that there had been two, the first the BMW M5 model, also black, a really fast car that Vincenzo had not really put through its paces, at least while she was in it, and the second being a Fiat Panda, which was handy for getting around in the narrow streets of the old Italian cities and easier to park than the larger BMW. Food was next up for discussion, and Marieke had to admit that all in all, it was very good. The jokes about British cooking did not ring true, at least in her experience. The food in Italy had been really good, but then she had only been there for a couple of nights. Mbali finally brought her back to the reason for her trip; did she learn what she needed to know?

"I found out some things," Marieke said. "But, I also learned a lot about the culture in Oxford. They give you lip service to wanting to help, but are generally very close with information and tell you as little as possible in as many words as possible."

"How do you sort through all that?" Mbali asked.

"You really have to listen," Marieke said. "And as you listen, you realise that they are not telling you anything, just giving you lots and lots of words, many of them long."

"How did you ever manage to get them to answer any questions?" Mbali asked.

"The English lady who was with me would make my commissioner quake," Marieke laughed." She was very polite, but you got the message: mess with me and you will all regret it for a long time."

"Was she a real old dragon?" Jannie asked.

"No," Marieke said. "She was very attractive, about forty, I would say, very sure of herself."

"Did she drive you around?" Khanyo asked.

"No, we had a driver, George, who I think was also the bodyguard," Marieke explained.

"Is she important then?" Khanyo asked.

"Yes, I think she is an important lady in their government," Marieke said. "She would make a telephone call, and things would happen. She told me she'd even been to Botswana once, years ago, probably just after independence, she was trying to see Africa on £1 a day."

"I think we should clean up and let Marieke get some sleep," Mbali suggested. "She's had a busy week."

Sunday was a day for Marieke to do her washing, clean the house and sweep the yard, all things that needed doing. She also met the people who lived next door for the first time. They had seen her coming and going but had never really had the chance to say hello. They were Janice and Joy Kayumba, immigrants from Zambia who had come to work as dentists. They had a practice that focused on children but would take any age group. Janice saw Marieke hanging out her washing and invited her for tea. By that time, Marieke had had enough of housework and was happy to take a break. She went next door, and Janice discreetly asked what she did for a living. Marieke was sure that she already knew that she was a police officer, but played along and supplied the expected answers. Joy wanted to know what kind of cases she worked on, and Marieke just said that it depended on what was needed at the time. She did learn that Janice and Joy had one son, Felix, who was nineteen and currently studying in London to become an engineer. Both Janice and Joy felt that there were great opportunities in Botswana for engineers and were looking forward to his coming home. As the British universities were down for the summer, their son was actually working as a trainee engineer on a bridge project in Cape Town. As Marieke did not yet have a dentist in Gaborone, she asked about being signed up as a new patient, and they were both happy to take her, but suggested that she look around first and make sure that she found a dentist whom she liked and felt comfortable with. They also told her to check with other people to see what they had heard, and with whom they were comfortable. They told her that there was no professional body, yet, that represented dentistry in Botswana, but felt that, in time, such a one would be formed. Marieke finally excused herself as the sun went down and went home to take in her washing and do the ironing, while she still had the inclination.

Monday morning, bright and early, Marieke went for a run, then to the dojo she frequented, and then felt she was able to face the office. Sergeant Maphosa was delighted that she was back and wanted to hear all the details. But, before he did, he had news of his own. The Zambians had made progress and had identified the seller of the gun. He was a known fence by the name of Samson Chikonde, who was also known to trade in illicit firearms. After some pressure had been exerted, he had picked out John Chebani as the purchaser of the gun from the stack of pictures and drawings that had been sent to the Zambians. But Chebani had not taken it with him when he had left Lusaka for Botswana, but had secreted it. The Zambians now wanted to interview John Chebani and find out why he was buying illicit firearms, and where was it. Marieke guessed that it was at the bottom of the Zambezi, with little chance of ever being found and retrieved. The Zambians had made an inspired guess about where the gun had been secreted and had discovered that Chebani had rented a box at the Post Office and had simply left it there in a cardboard box until someone had retrieved it. The postal clerk did remember a distinguished-looking man, dressed in a suit, mailing an envelope to England; he did not remember where in England, and the file copy of the customs declaration was buried in a pile of paperwork that would take some time to sort through. Sergeant Maphosa had checked flight records and had learned that John Chebani had gone to Lusaka on the 21st of May and returned the next day. Marieke thought about that and decided that it was time enough for a small airmail envelope to reach England from Zambia, and who would quibble with the contents, probably just a key. The Zambians had also related a car hire to Patrick McBride. He had not used the name McBride, but the man at the Number One Car Hire of Lusaka had identified him from his picture. He had hired an early model Fiat 124 for ten days.

Marieke then gave the sergeant a quick review of her trip to England and Italy. Her description of her trip to Oxford was interrupted by the commissioner, who came to see her.

"*Dumela* Matshwane," he said. "It is good to have you back."

"*Dumela Rra*," she replied. "It is good to be back, Sir."

"So, England, then Italy," the commissioner said. "Was it worth the price of the tickets?"

"I think so, Sir," she said. "We now know who was on the shortlist of candidates for the chair at Oxford; I made a very useful contact in the Home Office in England and established a link between McBride and Swanson."

"Did the good Sergeant tell you that we have also been busy and that we now know that our Dr Chebani is an acquirer of firearms?" the commissioner asked.

"He did, Sir," she confirmed. "I also learned that our Dr John Chebani and Dr Harold Swanson roomed together in London for almost three years while they were both studying for their doctorates."

"Did they now?" the commissioner mused. "It appears that our good Doctor had been less than candid. Do we arrest him?"

"Not yet, Sir," she said. "Courtney Wilson of the British Home Office pointed out some of the difficulties extraditing people, made even more difficult because we still have a death penalty, so if we arrest Chebani, then he will find a way to let Swanson know and our chances of ever extraditing them drop. So, I would rather see if I can't get Swanson and McBride to visit Botswana, then arrest them here, Courtney said that if we arrest them here, there is little they really can do."

"Ah, I see," the commissioner said. "So, how does this case fit together?"

As I see it, Sir," she said. "Swanson wanted the chair in Oxford; McBride wanted Julia Turner out of his and his wife's lives. Swanson and Turner concocted a plan to fly to Zambia, acquire a gun, drive to Kazungula, cross the Zambezi, hire a car, drive to Khwai, ambush the Turners, then drive back, cross the Zambezi back into Zambia and go home. The quid pro quo for Swanson's help in removing Julia Turner was that he had to stage an accident to remove Paulo Schirano, the next in line for the chair."

"That is a complex plan, any element of which could go wrong," the commissioner pointed out.

"It's not so complicated," she said. "It did need some arranging, but the movements of the Turners were planned and broadcast to the world.

The complex part was acquiring the means to quickly kill the Turners. That could have been done with just the axe, but a gun is more certain."

"Was the death of Schirano an accident?" the commissioner asked.

"After I asked the question and suggested a link to the death of David Turner, the Italians took another look and they believe that they have reconstructed the incident well enough to prove it was staged," she replied. "They even have traffic camera pictures of the car that was used for the incident, which was borrowed from a man in Paris; the French have their picture of it on the road to Marseille. Unfortunately, none of the pictures gives a good enough image of the driver to make an identification."

"A pity," the commissioner said. "So, McBride, was it, borrows a car in Paris, drives to Italy, stages the accident with Schirano, then drives back to Paris?"

"It probably was McBride," Marieke confirmed. "The French placed him in Paris at the right time."

"You realise that all of this is nice, but a good barrister will tear it all apart," the commissioner warned.

"I know, Sir," she agreed. "I do not have definitive evidence that places either of them at the scene of the crime, unless I can get footprints and Tushay, the tracker from Maun, can identify them as the people who were at Khwai and Linyanti."

"So, we really need a confession," the commissioner thought. "Who of the two would most likely break first?"

"Swanson," she replied. "McBride is more composed, but even he was unsettled enough when I visited him to immediately call Swanson."

"How do you know he did that?" the commissioner asked.

"The Home Office lady had had his phone tapped, and she told me that he made a call to Swanson's phone," she explained.

"What was Chebani's part in all this?" the commissioner asked.

"He acquired the gun and left it to be collected by Swanson," she said. "Then he went to Kazungula and arranged for the Land Rover, even paying money down, my sense is that he knew exactly where to go and who to ask for, so he may have a more interesting past than we had thought of," she explained. "At that point, Chebani's part was done, except to be sure that any change in the Turners' schedule was made known to Swanson. That was unlikely to be necessary as Diana McBride was in close contact with Julia Turner and Lillian Mafa."

"McBride's part?" the commissioner asked.

"Fly to Zambia, meet Swanson, between them steal, borrow or hire a boat to take them across the Zambezi and the Chobe and then just help Swanson with the driving from Khwai to Linyanti. His main part was to stage the accident with Schirano," she explained.

"And Swanson?" the commissioner asked.

"Travel to Zambia, collect the gun, hire a car and drive to Kazungula, cross the rivers, collect the Land Rover in Kazungula and pay the rest of the money, kill the Turners, bury the bodies, then go home, after that, his part was done," she said.

"So, a modified '*strangers on a train*'," the commissioner thought.

"Exactly, Sir," she said.

"Put together your case as you have it," the commissioner instructed. "I will take it to the Commissioner and let him know where we stand."

"Very good, Sir," she said.

"This is going to be hard to bring to trial," the commissioner lamented.

"Yes, Sir," she agreed. "That's why we need a confession."

After the commissioner had gone, Marieke turned to Sergeant Maphosa and told him that that was about the gist of her trip to Europe. She gave him the picture of Swanson that she had collected in Oxford and asked him to make copies of all the packets of images that they had. Then she started with the mammoth task of assembling all the information they had, including the forensic reports, witness testimony and statements from all and sundry. That was going to take a while. She detailed off the sergeant to do some of the work and settled down to do the rest. But, before starting, she did owe one telephone call. She called the British High Commission and particularly the Third Secretary.

"Good morning, Sir," she said when he answered her call.

"Good morning, Superintendent," he said. "Was your trip fruitful?"

"It was, thank you," she replied. "I am most grateful for your help and am doubly grateful for the kind assistance given to me by Assistant Undersecretary Wilson of the Home Office. She guided me through the maze of Oxford colleges and the reticence of the people that I met."

"Ah, so they were less than forthcoming?" he asked.

"At first," she confirmed. "But then Secretary Wilson said a few words, and then they were most cooperative, but I feel not altogether candid."

"That is not surprising," he said. "The academic world does not relish scrutiny of any kind, and the Oxford set are known to be very closed-mouthed."

"Well, I did get what I went for," she said. "And I wanted to thank you for your help."

"Any time," he said. "If there is anything else, please call me," he said.

"Thank you," she said. "I have taken up too much of your time, I will wish you goodbye."

"*Sala sentlê*," he said.

Before Marieke could return to the task at hand, there was another call, this time from Koos in Johannesburg.

"*Howzit*, Marieke," he said. "How's the flying?"

"*Howzit* Koos," she said. "I haven't had much chance; I've been away in England."

"Chasing Brit villains," Koos laughed. "Look, I've got those manifests for you; do you want me to post them to you?"

"That would be fine, thank you," she said. "How have you been? Is business still good?"

"Business is too good," he said. "I haven't had a real day off for a while. But, can't complain, it's better than sitting, looking at the wall and waiting for the next charter. Okay, I've got paper and pen ready, if you'll just give me the address." Marieke gave him the address of the Central Police Station, and then they exchanged a few more pleasantries until he said that he had to go as a potential charter had just walked into his office. Trusting that that would be the end of interruptions for the moment, Marieke returned to the task at hand and started by building a timeline of events, starting back when the large group of economists had first gone out to the Pitse Safari Camp. The manifests that Koos was posting would provide the documentary evidence for that. She continued until lunchtime and then needed a break. Lunch she found at a small café in town and she was able to sit and enjoy the sights and sounds of the market as she ate. She thought about her next problem, which was going to be somehow getting McBride and Swanson to Botswana. If they suspected that she was waiting for them, they would never come, so she needed to devise a plan. As she thought about it, she thought that perhaps Sara Turner might be able to help. If Sara could arrange a memorial for her parents in Gaborone and invite all her parents' friends, colleagues and acquaintances, then perhaps her suspects would come and she could take them into custody for questioning. She would call Sara later and put it to her.

After lunch, Marieke returned to her paperwork. She had her timeline now complete and was collecting documents and other evidence to attach to each point on the line. There were going to be boxes of papers, and the prosecution service would either hate her or love her. But that was for the future; she simply did not have a provable case at the moment. By six that evening, she had had enough and packed up and went home. She looked in her pantry and in the refrigerator and realised that she must do some shopping for food. There was enough for breakfast, but dinner was going to be a challenge. So, dinner out it would be. The choices were many and varied, but in the end, she plumped for a small café she had found near the university. It was full of students and was noisy, but there were a few tables still available. Marieke had only been seated a few minutes when she saw Thabo and Violet. They came to her table to say hello, and she asked them if they would like to join her for dinner. They looked at each other briefly and then sat down.

"So, Marieke," Violet said. "Are you well?"

"I am well," Marieke replied. "And you?"

"I am well," Violet reported. I understand from Thabo that you have been in England recently?"

"I was," Marieke confirmed. "I went there to get information on my case; I found out what I wanted to know and confirmed some of my thoughts."

"The commissioner said you'd also gone to Italy?" Thabo asked.

"I did," Marieke said. "I made a quick trip there to see if an accident had been an accident or something staged. The Italians are now of the opinion that it was a staged incident made to look like an accident."

"How was the flight there and back?" Violet asked.

"Long," Marieke replied. "But, on the way back, they took pity on me and gave me a seat in First Class. I have to say it was very comfortable, I could easily get used to flying that way, but doubt that our budget would ever permit me to do so."

"So, are you any closer to solving your mystery?" Violet asked.

"I think I have the mystery solved," Marieke said. "The problem is doing something about it. The normal thing to do would be to arrest someone and then have the prosecution service take them to trial. Sadly, my principal suspects are not in Botswana, and I understand that getting them extradited to stand trial is a long and complicated process."

"So, what will you do?" Violet asked.

"As my father would have said, *maak 'n plan*," Marieke laughed.

"You have a scheme?" Thabo asked.

"I have an idea," Marieke agreed. "But, whether it will work remains to be seen."

"Well, I hope it does," Violet said. "Tell me, Marieke, have you eaten here before?"

"I have," Marieke replied. "The food is quite good, and not expensive."

While they were eating, the conversation varied from the World Cup to Wimbledon, to events in Liberia and the recent nuclear test conducted by the French in the South Pacific. That latter offended Marieke, as she thought that if they wanted to test their weapons, they should do it in their own backyard, not near someone else's home. The territory might belong to the French, but it was still a long way from France, and any fallout or pollution would affect Botswana long before it made its way north to affect France. Violet told Marieke about her new venture in the world of shoes. She had always been fascinated by shoes and was now trying her hand at designing and making, or at least giving her designs to a cobbler she had found, who was quite adept at producing the shoes. Violet was excited about the business and was hoping one day to open a shop where one could buy the shoes, but also where shoes could be taken for repair. That interested Marieke; she had several pairs of boots and shoes that could use some attention, and she wanted to put off buying new pairs as long as possible. Violet suggested that she bring them to her house, and she would get them to the cobbler to see what he could do. Shoes in Botswana were always interesting, so many people went without shoes, or wore slippers, or flip flops as they were known. People got very creative in producing sandals and flip flops from the most amazing things, car tyres being among the most common. Violet said that her shoes were unlikely to be made out of car tyres, but instead, leather that she got from Lobatse. Promising to bring her boots and shoes to Violet one day that week, Marieke paid the bill and then excused herself.

It was time for Marieke to test her idea for a plan to get McBride and Swanson to Botswana. She called Sara Turner in London to float her idea.

"Superintendent, nice to hear from you again," Sara said. "Have you made an arrest?"

"Unfortunately, no," Marieke admitted. "But, I was wondering if you might be willing to try something for me?"

"What do you have in mind?" Sara asked.

"I would like to have all the players in Botswana," Marieke said. "There are many obstacles to progress, caused largely by the fact that most of the people I am interested in don't live in Botswana."

"I knew it," Sara crowed. "You've got the goods on McBride!"

"He is only someone we are interested in," Marieke said. "There are others we would also like to talk to."

"So, what do you have in mind?" Sara asked.

"I was thinking of a memorial to your parents to be held here in Gabs," Marieke said. "If you could persuade all and sundry to come, then I may have the opportunity to make considerable progress."

"When?" Sara asked.

"I don't know that," Marieke said. "How much notice do you think most people would need to arrange a trip to Gaborone?"

"A couple of weeks at least," Sara thought. "A month would be better. Where would we do this?"

"I was thinking of the university," Marieke replied. "That's where they spent most of their time and where they're best known."

"Who do you want there?" Sara asked.

"I have a list Marieke said. "Some are not from England, but I'm sure you can work out how to get hold of them, perhaps Mr Bentham might help?"

"Yes, I was going to ask you about that, you were here in England and you didn't call?" Sara said.

"I'm so sorry," Marieke said. "It was all rather whirlwind, from Oxford to Cambridge and then to Italy."

"Ah, so was Schirano's accident an accident or not?" Sara asked.

"The Italians are taking another look," Marieke said. "They got very interested when they realised that he was the next in line for the job that your Dad got."

"I knew it," Sara said. "Diana told me that Patrick had gone off to Italy, and I put two and two together. It has to be him, I'm sure of it, it is him, isn't it?"

"I'm still investigating," Marieke dissembled. "There are still other leads that I'm following."

"Let me look into getting a memorial set up," Sara said. "I'm sure I can get everyone you want there. Will you fax me the list?"

"It's on its way," Marieke said, watching the paper disappear into the machine.

"I have it," Sara said, after a short delay. "So, you want Simon and others there. I don't know all these people. Who are they?"

"Most of them are economists who were considered for the chair that your father was awarded, some are the selection committee and some I people who may have something to add to the investigation," Marieke explained. "You will note that there are also quite a few people from the university here. It would be better for you to invite them, I don't want to seen to be in any way connected to the memorial."

"That makes sense," Sara agreed. "Otherwise, people might smell a rat and stay away. I'll talk to Simon and we'll see what we can do."

"Thank you," Marieke said. "I look forward to hearing from you."

It was Friday before Sara called Marieke with the news that the all was set for the memorial. Simon had sent out invitations to all on the list, including those in Gaborone. So far, they had had a good response, and to the delight of both Sara and Marieke, McBride had committed to go. Now, to set the stage. Marieke went to see the commissioner about what she thought she should do next.

"*Dumela* Matshwane," he said.

"*Dumela Rra*," she replied. "Are you well?"

"I am, but it would be better if I thought that we could bring this current investigation to a conclusion," he said.

"There may be a chance," she said. "Sara Turner has made arrangements for a memorial to be held for her parents at the university here, and all the players have been invited, and fortunately for us, the people we would like to interview have all committed to be here."

"Ah," he said. "Good, what do we need to convince them that we have all the evidence we need to win a conviction?"

"I think, Sir, that I should retrace the steps of McBride and Swanson, with the Land Rover they used. They must have purchased food for the journey somewhere; they were in Botswana too many days to go without food and water."

"Good," he said. "Take your tracker with you; we weren't able to find much left of the Turners' camping equipment, were we?"

"No, Sir," she confirmed. "As far as we could tell, it had been burned and then the ashes buried."

"Not everything burns the way people expect, so there may be more left than we have found. Ask the BDF if they have some detection gadgets to find metals buried in the ground; they must use some for mines and other things," he suggested.

"Very good, Sir," she agreed.

"How long do we have before the memorial?" he asked.

"A month, Sir," she replied.

"A month," he said. "That's a long time for things to go awry. I'd better put it about at the university that we are stuck for the moment with no real suspects; that way, perhaps Chebani will let Swanson know that it's safe to come. I'm really annoyed with Chebani, fancy getting himself mixed up in this whole affair! So, will you hire the Land Rover from that Bwalya chap?"

"I thought that would be useful," she replied. "Then I can ask people specifically if they had seen that Land Rover, as well as just the driver and the passenger."

"Fine, I'll authorise whatever you need for expenses, just don't pay what Swanson paid!" he said.

"No, Sir," she said. "That was far too much, and Bwalya has every reason to cooperate and will be more inclined to do so if we hire his Land Rover and not just requisition it under a court order."

"Good," he said. "When do you leave?"

"I was thinking of going tomorrow," she said. "Then I can take my time with the canvassing of likely sellers of food, we can re-examine the crime scenes and still have plenty of time to put all the paperwork in order before the memorial."

"Good luck," he said. "I will see you when you return."

Marieke called the company commander of the Botswana Defence Force in Gaborone and explained her problem. He put her onto his engineer, who promised a team with metal detectors. Marieke asked if they could meet her in Khwai on Friday of that week, which would give her plenty of time to travel from Kazungula to Kasane, then down through the Chobe National Park to Maun and back up to Khwai. She explained where the site was in Khwai and suggested that they ask at the Khwai River Lodge where she would be. She then called Inspector Moroka in Maun and begged the assistance of Constance Sephoto and Tushay again. She explained what she was going to do and made the argument that three people canvassing shops, roadside sellers, and others would be more efficient than trying to do it all herself. He was happy to help, and when he heard that BDF was going to lend a metal detection team, said that he would come out to the one crime scene to see how well that worked. He might have use for such skills in the future and wanted to see what could be detected. Marieke then gave the news to Sergeant Maphosa that they were off again, she to Kazungula, and he to Maun and Khwai. She gave him the route map, with locations and dates marked when the Turners would have been there and told him to follow the route, check out each of the stopping places marked, check out petrol stations and make his way to the Khwai campsite. She would meet him there, either on Thursday or Friday. She asked him to contact Sergeant Mphoeng in Kazungula and ask him to ensure that Bwalya was in town and that she would be able to hire his

Land Rover for a week or so. Finally, Marieke called Mbali to have lunch and to make sure that all her bills were being paid, she had spent so much time away lately, that she was sure that she would at some time fall behind with a least one of her bills and then have to run around and correct the problem.

Mbali was waiting when Marieke got to the hotel restaurant; she waved and indicated a chair.

"*Dumela Mma*," she said. "So, you are off again?"

"*Dumela Mma*," Marieke replied. "I am, I want to be sure that I have not missed something, even small things can sometimes lead to good results."

"You said you wanted me to take care of your bills?" Mbali asked.

"If you would be so kind," Marieke said. "I'm afraid that with all the coming and going of the past few weeks that I may have missed one."

"Do you have your current bills?" Mbali asked.

"They are all here," Marieke said, pushing a large envelope across the table.

"I still have a key for your house, so I will go there after the postman has been and pick up your mail. Do you want me to just take money from your account to pay the bills?" Mbali asked.

"Providing there's enough in the account to do that," Marieke laughed. "Fortunately, my salary goes there directly, so I don't have to worry about depositing my paycheque."

"If the balance gets too low, I will run an overdraft, then come knocking on your door to find out what the problem is," Mbali promised. "So, where to on this trip?"

"Back to Kazungula," Marieke said. "I have to find something about my villains; so far, I don't have anything that the prosecution service can use to win a case in court."

"Well, good luck," Mbali said. "Let me know when you get back. I'll have Jannie check on your house while you're away, make sure no one breaks in and makes off with all your belongings."

"Thank you," Marieke said. "You are a good friend."

Trailing suspects

Marieke was in Kazungula by Tuesday evening and had to camp under her Land Rover. The cells at the police post were full, too many drunk drivers on the roads. She had prepared her dinner when Constance and Tushay arrived and set up camp next to her. While they ate dinner Marieke explained her plan to them. She would leave her Land Rover at the Kazungula police post and take Bwalya's Land Rover. There was a chance that people seeing it would recognise it as having been down that road before. She wanted Tushay to ride with her to spot anything that he could see that might help. She guessed that the route that had been taken by McBride and Swanson was the main road to Kasane, then the road that went down through the Chobe National Park to Maun. Along the way they would stop at shops, roadside sellers to see if anyone could identify the two white men. She handed them copies of the photographs she had of McBride and Swanson and Chebani.

At a little after seven the next morning Marieke parked her Land Rover at the Kazungula police post and then went with Constance to the Rhino bar. There they found Sergeant Mphoeng waiting with Bwalya. Marieke asked Bwalya how much to rent the Land Rover for a week and he quoted her 400 Pula, which she was prepared to pay. He handed her the keys and took his money to the bar. Marieke did wonder how much would be left by the end of the day, but that was not her problem. She drove the Land Rover to a petrol station and filled the jerry cans that were in the back. She now had enough diesel to get to Linyanti and back. Then they set off on the road to Kasane, stopping at each and every wayside vendor and shop they could see, asking about the two white men. They struck gold at the thirteenth place they tried, the Elephant General Store. The shopkeeper of the trading emporium remembered the two. They had come in first thing in the morning about six weeks earlier and bought food and drink, but had also bought a couple of blankets and two pans, plates, knives and forks and mugs, and what he thought most unusual, a shovel, a rake and a large yard broom. The shop keeper remembered them because they did not have

Pula with which to pay him, but had used Pounds, which he was happy to take. He checked his records and found the sale for the 2nd of June, 120 Pula, actually paid in Pounds, he even found the note to himself that he had made with the conversion rates of Pounds to Pula. He came outside with them and identified the Land Rover, he had helped them load all their groceries into the back and he remembered all the jerry cans of fuel. The next logical thing to do was try and guess where they might have camped for the night. The times that they entered and left the Chobe National Park would help with that. So, the next stop was the Sidudu Gate of the Chobe Park and a discussion with the rangers there. They dug through old records and found the entries for the 2nd of June. The blue Land Rover had been checked in at 9:10 in the morning. The rangers at the gate identified Swanson as the driver because he did not have enough Pula to pay the entry fee, but had used Pounds and had accepted Pula in change.

After the Sidudu Gate, Marieke had a decision to make, had Swanson and McBride gone via the Nogatsaa area or straight on to the Ngoma Gate. She decided to try the Ngoma Gate first; she could always double back if they had not gone that way. Her guess proved correct, they had left the park via the Ngoma gate at 10:40am. Now onward to the Ghoha Gate and back into the park. McBride and Swanson had made good time for that section of the journey, entering the park at 12:40pm, this time paying the gate fee in Pula. Past the Ghoha Gate on the road to Savute, Tushay called a halt.

"There, Madame," he said, pointing to a small clearing just off the road with a short track leading to it. "They stopped here, we should look."

"Very good, Tushay," Marieke agreed. They stopped and walked towards the clearing, Tushay pointing to old tracks as they went. "These are from the Land Rover, there you see where the tall one got out and made a fire over there. The short one collected sticks for the fire."

Marieke and Constance sifted through the ashes of the fire, but found nothing of note, just the ashes from the wood burned. Tushay looked at the ashes and the remnants of unburned twigs and identified it as mopane, not surprising as they were in the endless mopane woodlands that cover much of northern Botswana.

"Is there anything else?" Marieke asked. Receiving no answer she said that they should go on. She marked on her map where the site was and measured the distance from Kazungula, about 150km, so three hours' drive, give or take, that fit with the entry times at the various gates and would have been time to stop for lunch. They continued south and exited the Mababe Gate at just after three. Just south of the gate the road divided, the fork to the right leading to the Moremi Reserve and Khwai, and the left fork leading to the Mababe Village, then, in time, Maun. Assuming that McBride and Swanson were not going to ride around unnecessarily, Marieke took the right fork to Moremi. They drove past the Khwai River Lodge until they came to the site where the killings had taken place. Marieke looked at the time, just on four, a good time to stop; there was still an hour and a half to sunset, so time to make camp. Their search of the camp site area would have to wait until the morning; the light was going to fade quickly as soon as the sun went down. So, instead they picked a spot that was a little away from the crime scene and which, according to Tushay, had not been used yet this season, and set up camp there.

"So, Constance, have we learned anything new on this trip?" Marieke asked as they ate dinner.

"Yes, Madame," Constance replied. "We had a witness to say that the man Swanson had hired the Land Rover, now we can place that Land Rover as driving through the Chobe. We also have a witness who can identify the man McBride as being with Swanson."

"True," Marieke agreed. "But, perhaps they were just looking for birds; McBride is known to be an avid watcher of birds."

"Perhaps, Madame, we will find something tomorrow that links the two to the deaths," Constance said.

"Perhaps," Marieke agreed. "But, I still have the same problem; a good defence barrister will argue that just because they were close to here does not make them the killers."

"If you confront them with an exact description of their movements, perhaps one of them will panic and confess," Constance suggested.

"Let's hope so, "Marieke agreed. "So, how is the Maun police station?"

"I like it there," Constance said. "We are busy, but our crimes are small compared to this and are more easily solved, mostly because someone in town always knows who did what."

"Tushay, how are you?" Marieke asked.

"I will take a leave soon and go out into the Kalahari to visit with my relatives," he said. "It has been a year since I saw them last."

"When do you leave?" she asked.

"When the rains come," he said. "The beginning of November. Where is your Sergeant Maphosa?"

"He is following the route of the Turners and should be here soon," Marieke explained. "I wanted to see how easy it would be to observe cars coming and going."

"It is easy, Madame," he said. "Since we have been here, there have been three vehicles go south and one north. It would be simple to wait for the Turners' Land Rover, let them set up camp and then strike."

"Well, we'll see what we can find tomorrow, I am interested to see if the metal detectors of the BDF indicated anything," Marieke said. "Did Inspector Moroka tell you he was coming out with them?"

"He did, Madame," Constance confirmed. "I think he is very interested in metal detection and wants to see how it works. Would the metal detection work in water, could it find a gun that had been thrown into the *dambo* or a river?"

"I don't know," Marieke admitted. "We should ask them that when they get here on Friday."

Before the sun came up the next day, Marieke heard Tushay get and go off somewhere. He was back when the sun was up with news.

"Madame," he said. "I have the place where the two in the blue Land Rover camped and waited.

"I will come," Marieke said. "Constance, are you ready?"

"Yes, Madame," Constance said. They followed Tushay a little way and came to another small clearing, this one dominated by some tall trees that Tushay pointed to and announced that they had been climbed and that they offered a perfect view of the road from Maun. Marieke decided to take a look for herself and climbed up the tree to a fork. From there she could watch the road and see just where the traffic went;

it was the perfect vantage point to await the Turners. When she came down, she asked Tushay what else he had discovered.

"They had their fire here," he said pointing to a dark spot. "They filled their Land Rover with diesel and used some to start a fire. I would say that they waited here a whole day, just waiting and watching."

"Constance, bring the shovel and the sieve," Marieke said. "Let's see if we can find anything." Constance was back quickly with the shovel and sieve and started digging in the remnants of the fire. She dug up tins that looked like corned beef tins, then beer bottles, then other scraps of food waste. Marieke told her to collect the beer bottles carefully; they might be able to get fingerprints off them. Or, at least, they could try. This site had not been swept clean, so there were footprints aplenty and Tushay was confident, that despite their age, they belonged to the same two men who had been at the Linyanti site. That for Marieke was good news, she was beginning to see the start of a case against the two, a case that was not just in her mind, but which could be proven.

They worked until lunchtime then took a break. After lunch they went back to work, but with only two of them digging and sifting, Marieke sent Tushay up the tree to watch for the Sergeant Maphosa. At about two he called softly down that the sergeant had arrived. He reported on progress until he saw the sergeant go to the Turners' camp site. Satisfied that she had probably retrieved as much as she could from this location, Marieke suggested that they go and visit the good sergeant. They found him parked a little way from the camp site, waiting.

"*Dumela Rra*," Marieke said. "You had not trouble finding the place?"

"*Dumela Mma*," he replied. "No, Madame, the directions are good, I was able to drive straight here."

"We watched you arrive," Marieke said. "The others were camped over there and one of the trees gives a good view of the road. Did you see the BDF in Maun?"

"I did," he said. "They are coming out now and should be here in short while. Is that them I hear now?"

It was them. Marieke went to greet them and came back with a captain, a sergeant and two privates. She introduced everyone then explained what it was they were trying to do. She suggested that they leave the site until the morning and then go over it thoroughly. The captain, Captain Mogorosi, told them that what they would do first was to grid out the area, then start a sweep on each grid square to see what they could find. Marieke showed them where she was camped and Sergeant Maphosa moved his Land Rover there, as did the BDF. There was enough activity that it was not long before Andries Potgieter came along to investigate.

"*Dumela Mma*," he said, when he saw Marieke. "You're back?"

"*Dumela Rra*," she replied. "I am and have brought reinforcements."

"So I see," he said. "Is there anything we can do for you? Would you all like to come for a *braai*, we're light right now, we've only got two visitors, we're waiting for a new batch to arrive?"

"Captain?" Marieke asked.

"It is up to you Superintendent," the captain said.

"In that case, we accept," Marieke said. "When should we be there?"

"Come around five," Andries suggested. "Then we can watch the sun go down."

The *braai* was good, a treat for the police and the army, and also a treat for the visitors who got to meet so many local people at once. Normally visitors came and went and met very few of the local inhabitants, except for the safari camp staff and immigration and customs officers. While everyone was busy with drinks and conversation Marieke asked Maphosa about his trip north.

"Well, I followed the route you had given me, they made a stop at Palapye for coffee, then they stopped at Orapa for the night," he said. "I gather that Dr Julia Turner had done some statistical work for them, so they stopped for a visit and a tour. They went on to Maun the next day and stopped for petrol and some supplies in Maun, then drove on up here. They left Orapa late in the morning, so after they had been to Maun, they would have arrived here not long before sun set."

"The petrol station people remember them?" she asked.

"They did," he confirmed. "Obviously the Orapa people did because it takes special permission just to get in there. They had heard of the murders and wanted to know who had done it, when I explained that that was what we were following up, they let me in, put me up for the night and fed me very well. Their security chief really wants to know who killed Dr Julia and why, he wants to be sure it has nothing to do with diamonds."

"That makes sense," she agreed. "At the moment I am inclined to think that it was not diamond related, but stranger things have happened. When we get back, write that up as report and we'll add it to the file."

"Yes, Madame," he said. "Did you have any success?"

"We have witnesses that place McBride and Swanson in Kasane and on down through Chobe," she said. "If we build a good enough picture we may be able to bluff one of them into a confession."

"I hope so," he said. "I do not like the idea of them getting away."

"So, *howzit*," Andries said when he came to join them. "Still on the trail of the *skelms*?"

"We are," Marieke confirmed. "We're retracing steps and making sure that we've missed nothing. Tomorrow we'll go north and then be back again here before sunset."

"How many of you will there be tomorrow?" Andries asked.

"I would think just three of us, the same three that were here before," she replied.

"I can accommodate three," Andries said. "So, if you're back here in reasonable time come here, I'm sorry I can't accommodate everyone, but you've got quite an army there, sorry didn't intend the bad pun. Why have you got the army along?"

"I have borrowed their engineers who are used to looking for mines, to see if we can find buried metals," she explained.

"Good idea," he agreed. "You think you'll find anything?"

"I don't know," she confessed. "But, I have to try. You said before that some of the children talked about a blue Land Rover, would they know it again if they saw it?"

"Maybe," he said. "Do you have it here?"

"I do," she confirmed. "When we come back, perhaps you could get the children to take a look and see if any of them do recognise it. I know they're just as likely to say they recognise it because they'll think that's what we want, but I have to try."

"I'll get them here, but won't tell them why, and we'll see if any of them do recognise the *bakkie*," he suggested.

"Thank you," she said.

Before they could all have too many beers, Marieke took her party back to their own camp. She wanted clear heads in the morning. When the morning came it was to the aromas of coffee and breakfast cooking. The army was working its magic and she was delighted with the product. After breakfast, she led them to the site and showed them the old fire pit and places where they had found buried items. The captain strung out lines for a much wider area and set his people to work. They quickly got returns from an area and Constance went to dig up what they had found. It was pots and pans and personal items, two watches, some jewellery and other items. Marieke and Constance were cataloguing the items when Inspector Moroka arrived. Marieke introduced him to Captain Mogorosi who explained the procedure and the technology that they used. His men discovered four more places where items had been buried and then declared the area swept as best they could.

"What next, Superintendent?" the captain asked.

"We drive north to the next site and see if there is anything there," she replied.

"Very good Madame," he said. "We'll just pack up our things, strike camp and we'll be ready to go."

"Are you coming with us, Inspector?" Marieke asked of Inspector Moroka.

"I think I will," he said. "It will be interesting to see just where these people were buried."

"Tell me, Captain, can your detectors find things in water?" she asked.

"Not these," he replied. "But there are VLF detectors that are built for water and land use."

"How deep can they find things?" she asked.

"About two metres," he said. "Why do you think there's something in the *dambo*?"

"I'm looking for a .22LR semi-automatic handgun," she said. "My guess is that it's at the bottom of the Zambezi."

"We couldn't find that, even if we had a waterproof detector," the captain said. "The Zambezi is just a little too deep. You don't think it's here?"

"It may be," she conceded. "But I don't have the equipment to search for it, neither, I suspect, do you."

"True," he agreed. "Our detectors are designed for sand and dry land, put them in water and I think they would fail very quickly."

"Ah well," she said. "It was just a thought that Constable Sephoto had."

"It was a good question," the captain said. "With shallower water we could, with the right detector, find any metallic object."

"So much for that, shall we go?" Marieke suggested.

The convoy of Land Rovers had been on the road for over an hour when they saw another approaching from the West. They stopped and waited until it came and also stopped.

"You're back," a voice called out. Marieke got out of the Land Rover she was driving and walked towards the newcomer.

"You weren't driving when I last saw this *bakkie*," the driver said.

"*Dumela Rra*," Marieke said. "I am with the Botswana Police, and we are investigating two murders. You said that you'd seen this *bakkie* before?"

"*Ja*," he confirmed. "It must have been five or six weeks ago, there were two *bakkies*, that one and a light-coloured station wagon, they were just finishing changing a wheel, it looked like they'd taken the spare from the station wagon and put it on the blue *bakkie*, odd because I could swear that they were mixing radials and cross plies. I asked if they needed help, but they said not and drove off to the North. I had to ask twice because I first asked in Afrikaans and they looked at me with really blank looks, so I switched to English. I suppose I thought that anyone driving a Land Rover with Botswana number plates, especially ones that old had to be *Boerjies*."

"Could you identify the drivers?" she asked.

"Sure, sure," he said. Marieke went back to the Land Rover and got the pictures she had, and gave the whole stack to the driver. He riffled through them and picked out pictures of McBride and Swanson. "These are the *ouks* that were driving them.

"You are sure, Sir? Marieke asked.

"*Ja*, sure sure," he confirmed. "This one driving the blue open *bakkie*, this one driving the station wagon.

"Thank you," Marieke said. "Can I get your name, please?"

"Sure, I'm Piet van Heerden, I'm a PH that Botha hires sometimes to take clients out for him," Piet said.

"Did Mr Botha mention that we were looking for someone?" she asked.

"No," he said. "Should he have done?"

"We asked him to," she said. "But, perhaps he forgot."

"More likely he said *voetsek* to the bloody police," Piet said. "It's not in his nature to help."

"Would you be prepared to give a statement to my constable?" she asked.

"Sure, hey you *ouks*, you don't mind waiting a few minutes while we take care of this?" he asked his clients. Whether they objected or not did not seem to matter as he got out of his Land Rover and went with Marieke to see Constable Sephoto, who took his statement. After he had signed it and given them his address and telephone number, Marieke thanked him, then thanked his clients for their patience, and saw them off on their way. She was elated; she now had a witness who saw Swanson driving the blue Land Rover and McBride driving the Turners' Land Rover. After van Heerden had driven off into the distance, Marieke signalled the convoy to continue, and they went north to the place where the bodies had been buried. There, they went through the same routine, Captain Mogorosi and his team gridded off the area and started looking. They only found one item, and it turned out to be a pendant. The design on the pendant was unusual, and Marieke was certain she had seen it before, but could not remember when and where. Captain Mogorosi asked what had been buried there, and Marieke told him that they had discovered two bodies. He asked how she had first discovered that something was there and immediately grasped the significance of the flies. "Pity flies can't pick out mines," he said. "They can pick up the scent of putrefaction from amazing depths, better than our detection equipment can go."

Marieke then suggested they all go back to Khwai and from there go their separate ways. She needed to go back to Kazungula to collect her Land Rover and also needed to check on the return dates and times for the blue Land Rover through the various Chobe gates. Back at Khwai, the army decided that they would go back to Maun, as did Inspector

Moroka and Sergeant Maphosa. Personally, she would have rather stayed in Khwai, even if her business was concluded; she preferred the bush to the town, even a town as small as Maun. She, Patience and Tushay then went to the Khwai Safari Lodge to beg the indulgence of Andries. He saw them and waved them in.

"*Kom, kom,*" he said. "We've just finished booking in a new batch of visitors, so you've come at a good time. I'll put you where I put you before. Tushay, you want a tent here or do you want to go with the staff again?"

"I will be happy with the staff," Tushay said. "Jackson is my friend; we have known each other for many years."

"Okay," Andries said. "Marieke, Constance, if you'll come with me."

"You said you have new visitors, where are they from?" Marieke asked.

"These are all Americans," Andries replied. "The booking was made for a group of twelve; the two that were here yesterday have left, so the Brits have gone. I understand that this is the first trip to Africa for the new batch, so they're a little uneasy about things. I think they were expecting electric fences, armed guards and patrols."

"How did they get here?" Marieke asked.

"They had chartered a plane in from Jo'burg to Maun, so we went into town with two *bakkies* and picked them up," he explained. "When you're ready, come to the bar and I'll introduce you."

What Marieke enjoyed most about being invited to stay at any of the safari camps, that the facilities were always good. So, a shower was the first order of business. Then she left Constance to shower and went to join the guests in the bar. Katrina saw her come in and introduced her to the guests. "Everyone," she said. "This is Superintendent Englebrecht of the Botswana Police; she's not here to check on us, but is just staying the night before she goes on again tomorrow."

"Good evening," Marieke said to the company, ignoring the promotion that Katrina had just given her. "How do you like our country?"

"It's beautiful," one lady said. "I was a little surprised that there aren't a lot of fences around the lodge. Is that normal?"

"It is," Marieke assured her. "Last night, I slept on the ground under my Land Rover and have done so for many nights in the past. I've never been bothered by anything."

"You carry a gun?" one man asked. "I saw you come in and you didn't have a sidearm?"

"We typically don't carry side arms," she said. "But, I do have a rifle and a shotgun in my Land Rover. We never know when we may need them, and often, sadly, it is not animals but poachers and other miscreants."

"What are you working on now?" another lady asked.

"Oh, it's a complicated case, that sadly I am having difficulty with," Marieke replied. "Tell me, where in America do you come from?"

"We're all from New Mexico, from Los Alamos, "the first lady replied.

"That's towards the north of the state, isn't it?" Marieke asked.

"It is," the lady confirmed. "It's in the mountains, so quite different to here; here is more like eastern New Mexico or down near Roswell and the Texas border."

"Well, I hope you enjoy your stay here," Marieke said. "I'm sure Andries and Katrina will take excellent care of you."

"Dinner is served," the chef announced, and there was a general move towards the dining table. Dinner was excellent, another reason Marieke liked to stay at the safari lodges.

The last thing Marieke wanted to do on this trip was make their way back to Kazungula and see if they could find where the two had stopped on the way back and where the broom, rake and shovel had gone. They might well be in the Zambezi, but she thought it unlikely, two white men carrying a rake and a broom would have been noticed, so she felt that they had probably dumped them somewhere along the way. She, with Constance and Tushay, left the lodge in the morning and went back north through the Chobe park, stopping at the gates as they went to examine the entry logs for the dates they had deduced. Tushay twice pointed to places where the Land Rover had left the road, but they found nothing of interest. Finally, between the Ghoha gate and Kachikau, they found a spot where there had been a fire, and there they found the tines of a rake and the blade of a shovel. The handles of both had been burned, and so presumably, had the brush. So much for that, but they were able to recover the plates and cutlery, or rather the fragments of the plates and the cutlery. They pushed on to Kazungula and arrived there late in the afternoon, too late to turn around and go back south, so they all spent the night in the cells again at the police post. The next morning, Marieke thanked Tushay for his work and said that she would be sure to send a commendation to the inspector. Without him, much of the trip would have yielded little. She also thanked Constance and then set off on her long drive back to Gaborone.

"So, Matshwane," the commissioner said when he saw her in the office. "What did you find?"

"*Dumela Rra,*" she said, observing the formalities. "We found most of the hardware items from the campsite, everything that could not be easily burned. We also found this medallion at the Linyanti site. I know I have seen the like of it before, but cannot for the moment think when and where."

"Does it come from either of our suspects?" he asked. "Most likely, Sir," she replied. "It was in the clearing where the bodies were buried. The most important piece of evidence we collected was a statement from a PH that he had seen McBride driving the Land Rover that the Turners had borrowed."

"Where did you meet this PH?" the commissioner asked.

"On the road from Khwai to Linyanti," she explained, "We were going north and he was coming east on a cross track. He told me that Botha had never passed on our request to be told if anyone had seen anything or anyone."

"There is still one item that you need to clear up," the commissioner said. "How was McBride able to be in Luangwa and Moremi at the same time? I presume he did go to Luangwa?"

"I checked with the Zambians," she said. "And, yes, a man who said he was McBride did indeed go there and stayed for a week, making it impossible for him to be in Botswana at that time."

"So, if this man wasn't McBride, who was it?" the commissioner asked.

"At a guess, I would say John Entwhistle," she replied. "He is a great supporter of Swanson, and who knows, perhaps would go a long way to help his friend, or perhaps Swanson has some hold over Entwhistle."

"Could your Home Office friend help with that?" the commissioner asked.

"I will call and find out," she said. "I will also ask the Zambians to take all the pictures I sent them and send someone out to the Luangwa and see if they can make an identification."

"Good," the commissioner said. "It is good to have you back here; perhaps you will stay here long enough to join Lerato and me for dinner?"

"I would be delighted, Sir," she said. "When?"

"Friday evening," he said. "At about six."

"Very good, Sir," she said. "If you will excuse me, I should call England and Zambia and get my enquiries moving."

Marieke called Courtney and asked her if she could check whether or not John Entwhistle had flown to Lusaka any time recently. She also asked her to contact the post office that serviced the address of Harold Swanson and ask if any of the postmen remembered a package from Zambia. She then called Chief Superintendent Phiri in Zambia and asked him if they could check their immigration records for John Entwhistle and if he could send someone out to the Luangwa Valley and see if someone there could identify McBride or Entwhistle from the pictures she had sent him. Barring this one discrepancy, her case was coming together. She had enough evidence to at least arrest both McBride and Swanson and then see which one of them would panic under questioning. She doubted it would be easy, but she had to try. She might even have enough evidence to ask for an extradition hearing, but that would be complicated, and the British would probably ask Piet van Heerden to go to England to identify the two, something he might or might not be willing to do. She would almost certainly have to go as the officer seeking extradition, or she wondered if that would not fall into the hands of the prosecution service. Either way, she felt she had to prepare for the eventuality, in case McBride and Swanson begged off the memorial. By Thursday, Marieke had her answers from England and

Zambia; Entwhistle had indeed gone to Zambia at the time of the murders. Swanson had received a package from Zambia; the postman remembered it because he was interested in post-colonial postage stamps. The package had been delivered on the 25th of May. Finally, Entwhistle had passed himself off as McBride at the Luangwa safari camp. She relayed that back to Courtney, who was now most interested in Professor John Entwhistle and instituted an investigation into his background and life and his relationship with Harold Swanson. Entwhistle may have broken no English or Botswana laws, or for that matter even Zambian laws, but to provide an alibi for someone smacked of conspiracy, so he was likely to have to answer a lot of questions at some point, just not the present, as Marieke asked Courtney not to move until such time as she was ready. Marieke then called Chief Superintendent Phiri of the Zambia Police and laid out her plan. He said that he thought that either he or his representative would come to Botswana to sit on the Dr Chebani interview. They were looking into a request for extradition to charge him for an illegal firearms purchase. Finally, Marieke called Vincenzo in Italy and told him her plan; he said that he would come to sit in on the interviews with Patrick McBride. He said that they were preparing a case and would seek an extradition order to get McBride to Italy to answer for the death of Paulo Schirano. They had put together enough evidence to have a good case against McBride, so if the Botswana prosecutor was not successful, then they were waiting in the wings.

Dinner on Friday evening, Marieke was relieved to see, was not just her and the commissioner and his wife. Also, there were Thabo and Violet and a Dr Frederick Harding and his companion, Dr Emily Bishop. They were both law professors from the United States and taught at Northwestern University, particularly at the Pritzker Law School, which Marieke was intrigued to learn was founded in 1859. Now, in 1859, what was now Botswana was a series of chiefdoms, and there was dispute between many of them, including Sekgoma, Sechele and Matsheng, and they were all concerned by incursions by the Amandabele, so it was an unsettled time in their history. Harding and Bishop were researching the melding of British-style law with traditional law and how conflicts between the two were resolved. They were guests of the University of Botswana, so Marieke was surprised that no one from the university was there at the dinner. Harding explained that they had asked for contacts in the policing service and had been referred to the commissioner. He had met with them and then invited them to dinner, to meet his best forensic pathologist and his best investigator. That sounded good to Marieke, but she wondered if he was being sincere, or if she was just the most convenient person to get for the dinner. In any event, Harding and Bishop were interesting to talk to, particularly when they talked about policing in Chicago and the challenges that it posed. Marieke was surprised at the sheer number of murders that occurred in Chicago, and she wondered how many went unsolved. They asked her what she was currently working on, and she merely said that it was two murders and that she had yet to formulate a cogent theory as to why they had been killed, and therefore, by whom. She saw the commissioner nodding slightly and knew that she had given the right answer. She thought she now saw one of the motives the commissioner had; he wanted Chebani to hear that the investigation was stalled. Stalled it was until they could get all the people involved to Botswana, and that was almost a month away; it was going to be a long few weeks.

Recalling the dictum, follow the money, Marieke got a warrant to access the back records of Dr Chebani. She went through them and found payments received from England totalling 4,000 Pula, which would more than cover the down payment on the Land Rover and the purchase of the handgun. With this last piece, she felt that she now had as complete a case as she was going to be able to build. She was then thrilled when Melisende called her to tell her that the French Embassy in Malaysia had tracked down Alain Durollet, and he had identified Patrick McBride as the Englishman to whom he had loaned the car of Pascal Giron. They had a statement, in French, that she would fax to her. That was very useful in that it definitely put McBride with the car that was used to stage the accident that killed Paulo Schirano. Melisende then went on to say that she had posted copies of fingerprints lifted from the car of Pascal Giron, with notations as to which was which, the French Embassy in Malaysia had taken the prints of Durollet and the Sûreté in Paris had those of Giron, so the third set belonged to an extra driver, perhaps those of McBride. This was even better news. She would take the fingerprints of McBride while he was there and compare them to those that Melisende was sending, a match would be compelling evidence, not definitive in that a good defence counsel would argue that there could have been another driver who wore gloves and therefore left no prints, but Melisende had said that the prints were very clear and not smudged or blurred in any way. Anyone holding the steering wheel of the car would have smudged prints that were already there, as they had found with those of Giron and Durollet. Their prints they had found on other places in the car, as well as remnants and partial prints on the steering wheel.

The Memorial

Sara Turner called Marieke at home on Saturday, the 11th of August, to let her know that she was taking the overnight flight to Johannesburg. Marieke promised to meet her at the Gaborone airport, but with the caveat that if she felt that there were too many other people associated with the case, then she would beg off, so as not to alert a possible suspect. Sara understood, but said that she thought that most of the people were coming on the Sunday or Monday flight. Her brother, David, was not coming; he was off in the United States selling antiques to the Americans. Simon Bentham was coming, but he was leaving on Sunday and coming with his wife, and he had also booked a few days at the Pitse Safari camp after the memorial. Vincenzo also called to let her know that he and Alex would also be arriving on Sunday. They would be staying in the house of Will and Bridget in Gaborone, and after the interviews were going to go north to see them and the children.

Marieke went to the airport on Sunday and watched passengers arrive. As far as she could tell, the only ones she knew were Sara and the Berninis. She waved as Sara exited the airport with her suitcase, and when Vincenzo and Alex also came, she just introduced them as her friends who were visiting family.

"So, have they got the goods on Patrick?" Sara asked.

"Let's just say that we would like to talk to him again," Marieke said. "Do you know who is coming?"

"Adams, he called me to give me condolences for the deaths of my folks," Sara replied. "I got the impression from Simon that the rest of the selection committee will all be here, along with quite a few friends of Mom and Dad."

"We won't do anything until after the memorial," Marieke promised. "Can I take you to your hotel?"

"Thank you," Sara said. "I'm meeting with Dr Chebani tomorrow to finalise arrangements at the university. It will be at ten in the morning in their main auditorium."

"I will be there," Marieke said.

263

At the office, Marieke collected together the group of officers she was going to use to, as she put it, cut the suspects out of the herd of attendees. She put the four pictures up on a board and assigned three of her people to each of them. She also put others on standby. If there were wives present with the suspects, then they would need to get them back either to their home, in the case of the Chebanis, or to their hotels for the rest. She would take care of Diana McBride, so she needed three others. Tushay and Constance had come down from Maun, and she told Tushay that she would make sure she got tracks from all the suspects that he could then examine. She was concerned that it all be done with as little fuss and show as possible, so she asked, "How many of you have read *Smiley's People*, by John Le Carré?" Three of the group had. She suggested the rest at least take a look at the book, particularly towards the end when they persuaded the Soviet agent to come with them. She was not suggesting high-handed tactics, but there were elements in the description that were worth remembering. The next order of business was to take a look at the university, so she told them that sometime that afternoon or Tuesday they should all take a good look, find out where the auditorium was, where the exits were and where they could park to make a discrete exit without attraction a lot of attention. Once they had their man, they should all take different routes back to the station and coordinate so that they did not all arrive at the same time, and when they did arrive, to put the four suspects in different interview rooms, trying not to let the one see the other. The suspects were to be guarded at all times, treated with respect, but not be permitted contact with the outside until either she or Assistant Commissioner Mochage had seen them. She asked for questions.

"What if they try and run?" an inspector asked.

"Then, just take them down and arrest them," she said. "I don't want them leaving Botswana until we have had a chance to talk to them."

"Why don't we just pick them up at the airport when they arrive?" another inspector asked.

"I promised Sara Turner that I would not interfere in her memorial for her parents," Marieke replied. "I would also like them as complacent as I can for as long as possible. But you make a good point. Watch them from the time they arrive at the airport until you pick them up. If you have to borrow some men from traffic for the overnight watches, find out which hotels they are staying at, and watch the back doors as well as the main entrances. If they look as if they suspect something and try and run before the memorial, just stop them at the border and bring them back to the station."

"How do we know when they will arrive?" Sergeant Maphosa asked.

"Get on to Air Botswana and get passenger manifests," Marieke said.

"Which one will you interview first?" Inspector Bangwata asked.

"At the moment, I'm leaning towards John Chebani," Marieke replied. "He has a lot to lose here in Botswana, and I suspect will not want to be extradited to Zambia on illicit firearms charges. That reminds me, at the interview of Chebani, we will be joined by Chief Superintendent Phiri of the Zambia Police. He wants to hear what he has to say."

"What do we do if they want to use the loo?" Inspector Bangwata asked.

"Escort them, don't lose them and try to avoid meeting any of the others, perhaps set up a watch in the corridors to only go if none of the others are out," Marieke suggested.

"What do we wear to the memorial?" Sergeant Maphosa asked.

"Plain clothes," Marieke said. "The commissioner and I will dress up, but we don't make the police presence too obvious."

"What do we do if we have to keep them overnight?" Inspector Bangwata asked.

"We put them in separate cells," she said. "I would prefer no contact between the four."

"If we have to keep them overnight, why don't we transport at least two to the substations?" Inspector Bangwata suggested.

"I like that idea," Marieke said. "If we have to hold them without formally charging them, then I'll need to come up with some statute that lets me do that. Is there anything else?" There being nothing, she sent them off with their pictures of their respective suspect. She saw that they met again and obviously decided who was going to the university that day, and who would go on Tuesday. Satisfied that she had done all that she could for now, she went and reported to the commissioner. He listened and nodded with approval when he heard her arrangements. Having other teams in place to apprehend the suspects meant that he and Marieke could focus on those left and misdirect speculation and also reassure the wives of those taken away. He asked whether or not they should let the British High Commission know, and Marieke said that she thought not. They had no real idea of what the British might do and certainly did not want them warning their citizens. He told Marieke to find out what aid and services the High Commission might offer after an arrest, but rather thought that it would be informational rather than anything else. The High Commission could not interfere with legal proceedings. The protests might come later if the prosecution service decided to seek the death penalty.

Marieke left for the day and drove to the house of Will and Bridget Martin. Alex and Vincenzo had made themselves at home, but then, they had been before, so were familiar with the house.

"*Allora*, Marieke, you are ready?" Vincenzo asked.

"As ready as I will ever be," she replied. "I have teams of three for each of my four suspects. I have told them to watch them from the time they enter the country."

"How good are your people at surveillance?" Vincenzo asked.

"I think we'll manage," Marieke thought. "The only one who might see my people is John Chebani, so he will need special attention. But, to more mundane matters, I brought some wine with me, would you like to try some?"

"What do you have?" Alex asked.

"My friend Melisende sent me a selection and I brought a Médoc and a Graves with me, which would you like to try?" Marieke asked.

"Let's try the Graves, you open it while I organise some *antipasti*," Alex suggested.

"Have you told your children that you are here?" Marieke asked.

"We have," Vincenzo said. "We'll drive there on Saturday, spend a week and then go back to Italy. You should come to Italy sometime for a holiday. You could stay with us, even if the children are all there, and we could show you more of Tuscany than you saw when you came recently."

"I will try," Marieke promised.

"Drink up," Alex said. "Vince is cooking tonight, so we just have to sit back and enjoy the meal."

Marieke spent Tuesday going over her interview questions. She had her detailed timeline of all that had occurred, at least by day, if not by hour. She had enough witnesses to confirm her timeline; the only thing she did not have was a witness to the actual murder. So, a confession would be most useful. At lunchtime, she went to the university for a look around and saw Sara Turner with Dr Chebani.

"Superintendent," Sara called. "It is good to see you again; I hope you will be joining us tomorrow?"

"I will be there," Marieke promised. "I was just finding out where I needed to go. Good afternoon, Dr Chebani, you are well?"

"I am well, thank you, a little overwhelmed at the moment with all the dignitaries that are coming," he replied.

"Really," Marieke said. "Well, I suppose that both Dr Julia and Dr David Turner were well known, and people will come to pay their respects."

"There are some very important people coming," Chebani said. "Would it be too much trouble to ask for a couple of policemen to be here?"

"Of course," Marieke said. "I will be here, as will the commissioner, but I will detail a couple of inspectors to be here in case you need them."

"Are you any further with your investigation?" Chebani asked.

"Well, I still cannot say for certain what the motive for the deaths may have been," Marieke replied. "Without a motive, I am rather at sea to find the person responsible."

"I'm sure that the superintendent will succeed eventually," Sara said. "I would be distressed if the case goes unsolved."

"I will do my best," Marieke promised. "If you will excuse me, I should get back to work."

The commissioner and Marieke were at the university at nine on the day of the memorial, both in their best uniforms. Sara Turner saw them and came to say good day, then others demanded her attention. The two police officers found seats at the back of the auditorium that had

267

clear views of the hall and allowed them to see almost everyone in the place. People started arriving, and Marieke found herself looking at two men for a few minutes before she realised that they were one of her teams. She found the third deep in conversation with Harold Swanson, and she wondered just what they were talking about. She saw Diana and Patrick McBride arrive and saw Patrick dashing off autographs in books he had written about birds. She had put the books in the hands of her people and asked them to get autographs. When he had done with the autographs, he and Diana came over to say hello to her, and she introduced them to the commissioner. Then Sara saw them and came to get them to sit closer to the front. Marieke saw the McBride team, and they were indistinguishable from the university staff that had come in numbers. She saw Thabang Kanedi with an older white man, and she wondered if that was not Ian Ross, back from his trip to Scotland. John Entwhistle came in with Nicholas Adams and Susan Bullock, so no wife to worry about there. When John Chebani came, he was with his wife, but Marieke noted that the Chebani team had acquired two female officers and concluded that they were there to take care of Mrs Chebani. Vincenzo and Alex came and sat with them, as did Chief Superintendent Phiri and introductions were made. The memorial started at ten and included pictures of the lives of Julia and David Turner and comments about them from not only Sara, but also from others, including Nicholas Adams and John Entwhistle. At eleven, Sara thanked everyone for coming and announced that there was a reception in the university refectory that all were invited to. That led to a general exodus from the hall, not a mad rush to get out, but a general drift towards the doors and promise of food and drink. Marieke never saw her suspects led away, so assumed it had been done very well. She came across the female officers talking to Mrs Chebani and heard them explaining to her that Dr Chebani had gone to help the police with an important development in the Turner case. No one really missed Swanson and Entwhistle, as it was assumed that they had already gone ahead for the food and wine. The last out was Diana McBride, who saw Marieke and asked her if she had seen Patrick.

"Your husband has important information about the Turners that we need to hear," Marieke explained. "If you like, I can have an officer take you back to your hotel when you are finished here."

"No, that's fine," Diana said. "I'd rather Patrick was helping you than running off again after another woman. I saw him this morning making what looked like an assignation with a woman at the hotel. I'll stay and go back with Sara."

Inspector Bangwata came up to her and reported that all four were now at the station awaiting them. Marieke looked to the commissioner, who nodded and said, "Let's see what they all have to say, Simon, shall we go?" Chief Superintendent was sad to miss the food and wine, but duty called. Vincenzo said goodbye to Alex and also came with them; Alex would go back to the house and wait for him, as she had done many times before. As they went to their cars, Marieke remembered where she had seen a pendant similar to the one they had found at the burial site; it matched one worn by Diana McBride. She speculated that it may have belonged to Julia Turner and Patrick McBride had removed it, but had not destroyed it, but kept it and either lost it while they were burying the bodies or left there as a matter of respect. She was more inclined to believe he simply lost it while they were burying the bodies.

At the station, Sergeant Maphosa told Marieke who was in which room and they went first to see Dr John Chebani.

"What is this?" Chebani demanded when they walked into the room, more than a little alarmed at the sight of three men and one woman all arrayed against him.

"This is about being an accessory to murder and being complicit in a conspiracy to commit murder," Marieke said.

"You are mad," Chebani said. "I have taken part in no murder."

"Tell me, Dr Chebani, did you go to Kazungula on the 12th of May of this year, and did you meet there one Isaac Bwalya at the Rhino bar?" Marieke asked.

"What of it?" he asked.

"So, you did go to Kazungula on the 12th of May and meet Isaac Bwalya at the Rhino bar?' she asked again.

"So, what if I did?" he asked.

"Humour me, if you would, Sir, I have paperwork that I have to fill out. Did you go to Kazungula on the 12th of May of this year and meet Isaac Bwalya at the Rhino bar?" she asked again.

"Yes, yes, so what?" he asked.

"I see," she said. "Did you give Isaac Bwalya 500 Pula?"

"I may have done," he said. "Is it a crime to give a man some money?"

"Did you give Bwalya instructions about hiring out his Land Rover?" she asked.

"A friend of mine wanted reliable transport to go to Chobe, so I arranged it for him, what's wrong with that?" he asked.

"Tell me, Dr Chebani, how well do you know Harold Swanson?" she asked.

"Never heard of him until today when he made the speech at David Turner's memorial," he replied.

"I have here information from the British Home Office that tells me that you and Harold Swanson were both doctoral candidates at LSE at the same time and that you shared a flat on Great James Street. How would you not know a man you had roomed with for three years?" she asked.

"I didn't know he was going to kill Turner," Chebani said, pleading, wringing his hands and looking from Marieke to the commissioner.

"Who says that Swanson killed David Turner?" she asked.

"It's obvious, isn't it?" Chebani said. "Swanson came to Botswana via the Kazungula ferry, got the Land Rover from Bwalya, then went and bludgeoned Turner to death."

"How do you know he was bludgeoned to death?' she asked.

"Well, how else would he have killed him?" Chebani asked.

"Perhaps you should tell me all about it?" Marieke suggested. Chebani then talked solidly for fifteen minutes and laid out the story of how Harold Swanson had called him and asked him to arrange for the hire of a Land Rover in Kazungula. Swanson had wanted extra petrol, or if it was a diesel, then diesel, but some petrol besides. Swanson had told him that he was going to the Tsodilo Hills to get some pictures of the rock paintings there and look for artefacts. The plan was for Swanson to go to the Rhino bar, meet Bwalya, pay the money and then he would take the Land Rover.

"How much did Bwalya say he wanted from Swanson?" Marieke asked.

"He said he wanted another 5,000 Pula, that's a lot of money, but Harold didn't want a paper trail, I thought he was going to steal something from the Tsodilo Hills," Chebani said.

"I see, thank you, Dr Chebani, that is most helpful," Marieke said. "Now tell me, you were in Lusaka on the 19th of May?"

"I was, so?" he asked.

"Did you meet a Samson Chikonde there?" she asked.

"I met quite a few people, I don't remember anyone with that name," he said. "Look, I've been very cooperative; I don't know what else I can tell you."

"You can tell me where the Ruger .22LR semi-automatic handgun you bought from Samson Chikonde for 500 Kwacha is?" she asked.

"I don't know," he said.

"You don't know what?" she asked.

"I don't know where the gun is," he said. "All I did was buy it, then I passed it on."

"I have here a statement from the General Post Office in Lusaka that you rented a post office box for six months under the name of John Chebani," Marieke said. "Did you rent the post office box?"

"If it says so in that statement, then I suppose I must have done," he said.

"Did you rent a post office box at the General Post Office in Lusaka?" she asked again.

"Yes, yes, don't you listen?" he demanded. Marieke could see that he was getting rattled, and if she pushed too hard, then he would probably sit quietly and demand a solicitor, so she had to get this finished and quickly.

"I'm sorry, Dr Chebani," she said. "You boxed up the gun and placed it in the post office box, and then posted the key to Harold Swanson, who, by the way, received it on the 23rd of May of this year. Is that what happened?"

"Yes, yes," he said. "I didn't know what Harold was going to do, how was I to know that he'd go after David Turner? Is that all? Can I go now? My wife will be wondering what has happened to me."

"Dr Chebani, this is Chief Superintendent Phiri of the Zambia Police. He would like a few words about Samson Chikonde. He may also start extradition proceedings to have you in Zambia to answer charges of purchasing illicit firearms. I imagine his enthusiasm about extradition will be tempered by how much you tell him about Mr Chikonde," she said. "When Chief Superintendent Phiri has finished, we may release

271

you, or we may not, it depends on whether we see you as a witting or unwitting accomplice in this crime."

"I didn't know what he was going to do, you must believe me," he pleaded. "My career's over, my wife will probably leave me and all because I agreed to help an old friend. How stupid could I have been?"

"You didn't connect the chair that Turner got to Swanson activities?" she asked.

"Only after you came to see me the second time to tell me that you'd identified David and Julia," he said. "I didn't know what to do; I daredn't tell you what I'd done, in case you placed the wrong interpretation on my actions. I was terrified you'd start asking me questions in the office."

"Well, thank you for your help," Marieke said, "You will appreciate that I must check the story of Harold Swanson first."

Outside the interview room, Marieke looked at the commissioner. "So," she asked. "Witting or unwitting accomplice?"

"Idiot," the commissioner replied. "I would say unwitting, he knew Swanson was up to something, but I believe him when he said he only realised what it was when we went to see him. I think after that he sat back and put all the pieces together and was horrified with what he came up with and what his part in it may have been."

"I am inclined to agree," Marieke said. "Do we let him go?"

"I don't see the good Doctor trying to leave the country, but we'll get him to surrender his passport anyway and release him on his own recognisance, to appear here again tomorrow. By that time, Simon should have decided whether or not he wants to go ahead with getting Chebani extradited to Zambia. My guess is not, it's a lot of work for a gun we will never find and which will probably never be used again, if it's at the bottom of the Zambezi as we think it is."

"Very good, Sir, I'll arrange it with Sergeant Maphosa to have him taken home to explain himself to his wife. What will you do about the university?" she asked.

"I think nothing at this time," the commissioner said. "I rather like the idea of having someone in the university that we can call upon if we have to."

Simon Phiri came out of the interview room and joined them.

"I won't be looking for extradition," he said. "The gun is probably at the bottom of the Zambezi, so I've got no physical evidence, and a good barrister would carve up Chikonde. I have what I wanted, which is how one contacts Chikonde and who makes the arrangements. It fits with what we have been thinking about illicit gun sales, and we can now round up the whole lot of them, which will be delightful. Thank you for this, it has been most helpful. Assistant Superintendent, you did a good job in there, just enough pressure to make him squirm, but not enough to cry for a solicitor."

"Thank you for all your help, Sir," she said. "Without the identification of the Land Rover, this would have taken much longer, and the guess about the post office box was inspired."

"So, who's next?" the commissioner asked.

"I think Entwhistle," she said. "I'd like to keep the main suspects until the end. Excuse me, I'll just go and give Chebani the good news." She went back into the interview room, and John Chebani looked at her with such a pathetic look that she almost felt sorry for him.

"Well, Dr Chebani," she said. "Chief Superintendent Phiri is happy with the information you have given him, so he will not be looking for you to appear in Lusaka. We are also of the mind that, whereas your actions may have been ill-advised, you were an unwitting accomplice in this affair. We are releasing you to your home; we would like you to surrender your passport for a while. We will not be communicating any of this to the university. We would ask that, if in the future, any of your old friends come to you with unusual requests, that you let us know."

"Oh, thank you," he said, the tears streaming down his face.

"I will have one of our officers drive you home. What you tell your wife is up to you, but our suggestion is that you've provided us with valuable insight into the deaths of Julia and David Turner."

"Thank you, thank you," he said. "I think I'll just try and forget this whole affair. I had no idea Harold wanted that chair so badly that he'd kill for it."

"Tell me, Dr Chebani, when we came to see you, you already knew that Camille Frou had been given the job that David Turner was vacating, why the secrecy?" she asked.

"I don't know," he admitted. "I suppose I just resented your questions about the university. I realise now that as you uncovered more that you would have found that out and started wondering why I was less than forthcoming. You should come by sometime and meet Camille Frou."

"I already have," Marieke said. "I was in the co-pilot's seat of the plane she flew up from Cape Town in."

"You were?" he asked. "Well, I should not have underestimated you."

"It doesn't matter," Marieke said. "Here is Sergeant Makwala; he will take you home, go well, Doctor."

"*Sala sentlê*," he said.

Marieke watched him go, a chastened man. She wondered what he would tell his wife. She supposed it would all depend on how well she could keep counsel. If she was inclined to tell her friends everything, he would be well advised to tell her nothing, lest it get back to the dean of the university. Now, for the next one, Entwhistle had technically broken no laws, particularly in Botswana, but he had been an accomplice in the affair, providing an alibi for McBride. Marieke wondered why he had provided the alibi for McBride and not his friend Swanson; that might be worth exploring; perhaps it was a question of money, perhaps something else. Before they talked to Entwhistle, Marieke found Constance and told her to take Swanson, then McBride to the dirt yard at the back of the police station and have them walk across it, then get Tushay to examine the tracks to see if he could confirm that they were the two who had been at the site where the Turners and been killed, then at the site where the bodies had been buried, lastly to make plaster casts of the tracks. Constance, delighted to be doing something and not just sitting around, went off to find Tushay, then another constable to be with her when she took Swanson and McBride outside.

Entwhistle looked up when they trooped into the interview room. He looked annoyed, which was to be expected; he had been removed from the gentile setting of the university to the police station with no clear explanation as to why.

"Good afternoon, Professor Entwhistle," Marieke said. "Thank you for coming."

"Superintendent, what was it again, Englebright, I was shanghaied and brought here. I demand to speak to your superior," Entwhistle said.

"Allow me to introduce Assistant Commissioner Mochage; he is my superior," Marieke said.

"I have complaints, Mr Mochage, this woman came and interrogated me in Oxford, and now she apparently means to do the same again here, what is going on?" Entwhistle demanded.

"What is going on, Mr Entwhistle," the commissioner said. "Is that I am trying to decide whether or not to charge you with conspiracy to commit murder."

"What do you mean, conspiracy to commit murder? All I did was do a favour for a friend. I doubt that he murdered anyone." Entwhistle protested.

"Tell me," Marieke said. "Were you in Lusaka on the 31st of May of this year?"

"Yes," Entwhistle said.

"Did you meet Patrick McBride in Lusaka?" she asked.

"Yes," Entwhistle confirmed.

"Did Patrick McBride give you information, instructions and booking details for a charter flight to Mfuwe, Zambia, and a stay at the Leopard Safari Camp in the South Luangwa National Park?"

"Yes," he said.

"Did you take the charter flight on a plane operated by the charter company Sky Link on the 31st of May of this year?" she asked.

"Yes, yes, you see to know all my movements, why do you have to ask?" he demanded.

"I have paperwork that needs completing," Marieke bemoaned. "It is the bane of my life, but my superiors want me to properly document all that I do. To continue, did you stay at the Leopard Safari Camp from the 31st of May of this year until the 7th of June, also of this year?"

"Yes," he said, resigned now to the pedestrian nature of the questions.

"Tell me, how well do you know Patrick McBride?" she asked.

"We belong to the same ornithological society, the Cotswold Birding Group," he explained. "Patrick is going to have a very good year for sightings; he's in big competition with Bill Cook to see who can spot the most. I came to Zambia to help Patrick throw Bill off the scent. If Bill thought that Patrick was going to Luangwa, then we would have as well, so I went instead, letting Patrick go where he wanted."

"I see," Marieke said. "Would you excuse us for a moment?" Outside the interview room, Marieke looked to the commissioner, "Do we believe this story?" she asked.

"I am inclined to," the commissioner said. "Simon, would it be possible to check whether or not a Bill, or William, Cook entered Zambia on or about the 31st of May?"

"Of course," Simon replied. "Do you have a telephone that I can use? If you recall, I had all the immigration records delivered to us for that period, so it should be easy to check. Let me do that, and I will join you in a few minutes."

"I also need to make a telephone call," Marieke said. She called the office of Courtney Wilson, who was not there at that time, but whose aide took the message. Marieke wanted to know about the Cotswolds Birding Group, Bill Cook and whether or not Cook had travelled to Zambia in late May or early June. The aide promised an answer shortly. Back in the interview room, Marieke asked about the ornithological society.

"We are the Cotswolds Birding Group," Entwhistle explained. "We're based in Broadway at Patrick's raptor centre. We're most interested in publishing good guides to birds, both for the UK and other countries. We are currently working on a guide to Central Africa, which will cover Zambia, Malawi, Tanzania, Angola and Zaire. It is quite a monumental task, but we are getting there."

"How long have you belonged to this society?" Marieke asked.

"Ten years now," Entwhistle replied. "The society was founded in 1975 by Patrick and myself, and Bill Cook, they are friends at times and bitter rivals at others, strange relationship."

"How well do you know Harold Swanson?" Marieke asked.

"Known Harold for years, we grew up together and stayed friends through college, even if he did go to LSE," Entwhistle replied. "But, I don't see what this has to do with Patrick and me?"

Marieke's next question was forestalled by the entry of Simon Phiri back into the room. He handed her a note, which she looked at quickly.

"Well," she said. "It appears your ruse may have worked. Bill Cook arrived in Zambia on the 1st of June, hot on the trail of Patrick McBride. He then hired a car and drove out to the Luangwa, you didn't see him there?"

"No, never saw him, any idea where he stayed?" Entwhistle asked.

"He stayed at the Mfuwe Lodge," Marieke said.

"I wonder what he saw?" Entwhistle thought. "Still, no matter, Patrick stole a march on him wherever he went. But, back to Harold, what has this all got to do with Harold?"

"Did you know that Harold Swanson was in Zambia on the 1st of June?" Marieke asked.

"He was?" Entwhistle asked. "Funny, I didn't see him on the plane from London.

"That's because he flew to Johannesburg and took an SAA flight up to Lusaka," Marieke explained.

"Did he now?" Entwhistle wondered. "Why was he in Zambia?"

"He was your friend, Professor, we were hoping you could tell us," Marieke suggested,

"No idea," Entwhistle said. "It wouldn't be birds, he has no interest, I don't know if he had any consulting work in Zambia, no, no idea."

"Would it surprise you then to learn that Harold Swanson was also in Botswana at about the same time, particularly from the 1st of June until the 6th of June?" Marieke asked.

"Botswana, why was he here? Why go through Zambia to get here, why not just fly straight from Jo'burg?" he asked.

"We were hoping that perhaps you could tell us," she suggested.

"Wait a minute," he said in great alarm. "You said early on that you were trying to decide whether or not to stitch me up for conspiracy to commit murder, don't tell me that Harold killed David for the chair in Oxford?"

"Did he?" she asked.

"I have no idea," he protested. "I suppose Harold is ambitious enough to do something stupid, but murder, that's hard for me to fathom."

"Let's go over this again," she suggested. "Patrick McBride asked you to go to Zambia and impersonate him to throw Bill Cook off the trail of wherever he was really going?"

"True," he said, back to monosyllabic answers.

"When did he make this arrangement?" she asked.

"Must have been about the 1st of May," he said.

"You flew to Zambia on the BA flight from London, arriving on the 31st of May, got your instructions from McBride and flew out to the Mfuwe airport in Luangwa?" she asked.

"True," he confirmed.

"You stayed in Luangwa until the 7th of June when you flew back to London?" she asked.

"True," he confirmed again.

"You did not see Harold Swanson at the Lusaka airport on either the 31st of May or the 7th of June," she asked.

"True," he confirmed.

"Who paid for the flight to Lusaka?' she asked.

"Patrick did, cheap bastard only gave me a Club seat, but he did pay," Entwhistle complained.

"So, you got a free holiday in one of Zambia's, probably one of Africa's best national parks, and you did not wonder why?" she asked.

"You have to understand the rivalry between Patrick and Bill, they'd sell their souls to beat the other," Entwhistle explained. "Look, I was happy to help Patrick beat Bill, but I had no idea that Harold was up to something. I think I've been most cooperative, but if this goes on much longer, I'm going to demand to talk to my embassy."

"It's actually the British High Commission here in Botswana," Marieke pointed out. "The staff there have been most helpful, but if you would like to speak to someone from your legation, we would be happy to arrange it."

"So, they're part of the stitch-up job," he said. "I should have known when you came to Oxford with that woman from the Home Office. I looked her up after you'd gone. She's the top official for policing in the country; someone must have dropped a big clanger. It wasn't me, if Harold did something stupid, then it was without my knowledge or help, and if Patrick was involved, then again, it was without my knowledge and any help I may have given him was unwitting."

"Thank you, Professor Entwhistle," Marieke said. "Commissioner?"

"I think we're done for the moment," the commissioner said. "When are you planning to leave Botswana?"

"I have a booking for the flight to London from Jo'burg on Saturday, I aim to be on the flight," Entwhistle said.

"At the moment, I see no reason that you should not be on that flight," the commissioner said. "But, if McBride emphatically denies all this, then you will understand that we may wish to talk to you again."

"Of course," Entwhistle said. "But, it looks to me as if you have chapter and verse on my movements, so I'm betting you've got the same on Patrick and Harold."

"Thank you for your time and cooperation, Professor," Marieke said. "We will have an officer take you to your hotel. We should let you know that we have communicated with the British Home Office about this issue. We do not believe that you knowingly broke any laws, either those of Zambia or those of Botswana, but may have unwittingly aided in the commission of a serious crime," Marieke said.

"Oh crap," Entwhistle said. "I just remembered you people still have the death penalty."

"We do," Marieke confirmed. "But, it is only used in cases of aggravated murder. That is why we are trying to determine what level of involvement you had in this affair."

"I've told you everything," he said. "I honestly didn't know what Harold was up to and that Patrick might also be involved."

"Well, we will of course be talking to both of them," Marieke said. "If you are ready, then one of our officers will take you back to your hotel."

After Entwhistle had gone, the commissioner said that he believed the man, another sad soul duped by his friend into providing a false alibi, but not knowing what for. Marieke looked to Vincenzo and asked for comment.

"You have investigated this very thoroughly," he said.

"We had great help from the Chief Superintendent," she said. "Without the Zambia Police, we would be struggling to piece things together."

"What is your interest in this case?" Simon Phiri asked.

"One Paulo Schirano died in what at first seemed to be a tragic car accident," Vincenzo explained. "But then Marieke raised the question of a staged accident to remove Schirano from the chair at Oxford, as this followed so closely the death of David Turner who had also been awarded the chair, we took another look. We are satisfied that it was a staged accident and have evidence that it was Patrick McBride who staged the accident."

"So, if he is convicted here of the crime of murder for the death of Turner, what will you do?" Simon asked.

"We'll wait," Vincenzo said. "There is no time limit to murder cases, and if he is not hanged, but is released from prison in 25 years or so, we would seek extradition and try him for murder in Italy."

"You are that patient?" Simon asked.

"Not normally," Vincenzo admitted. "But, Marieke has him and I do not, so I must wait. I will listen to his story and if Marieke asks him about the death of Schirano will take special note of his answers."

Further discussion was halted when an inspector brought Marieke a Fax. It was from the office of Courtney, fast work indeed. The Cotswold Birding Group did exist, McBride and Entwhistle were both founding members, William, Bill, Cook was also a founding member. Cook had gone to Zambia on the 31st of May, arriving on the 1st of June. So, it looked on the face of it as if Entwhistle were telling the truth, another poor soul misused by his friend.

"So, who's next?" the commissioner asked.

"I think Swanson," Marieke said. "I think he would collapse quicker than McBride, and I have a plan."

"Fine, Swanson it is, are you still with us Simon?" the commissioner asked.

"Absolutely," Simon replied. "I want to see this to the end."

"Excuse me, Madame," a voice said. Marieke turned and saw Tushay approaching.

"*Dumela Rra*," she said.

"*Dumela Mma*," he replied. "I have looked at the tracks of the two men and they are the same ones that crossed the Zambezi and the Chobe and were at Khwai and Linyanti."

"Thank you, Tushay, good," she said. "This is Assistant Commissioner Mochage from here in Gaborone, this is Chief Superintendent Phiri of the Zambia Police and this is Dottore Bernini of the Italian Polizia, they all have an interest in this case."

"Will there be anything else Madame?" Tushay asked.

"No, thank you, Tushay, *tsamaya sentlê*," she said.

"*Sala sentlê*," he replied.

Prime suspects

Harold Swanson was sitting at the desk in the interview room, nursing a cup of tea that had been brought to him by one of the officers. He looked up at those who came in, but only recognised Marieke.

"What the hell is this?" he demanded. "Why was I hustled into a car like a common criminal and brought here? Who the hell are these people?"

"Good afternoon, Dr Swanson," Marieke said. "I am sorry we kept you waiting so long."

"Why was I taken out into the yard out there and walked around, like an exhibit at a dog show?" he demanded, again.

"All in good time, Sir," she said. "This is Chief Superintendent Phiri of the Zambia Police he has some concerns about a trip you made across the Zambezi at Kazungula on the night of the 1st of June of this year. I think he may be concerned that you are involved in smuggling or poaching, why did you cross the river that night?"

"It was for a bet," Swanson said glibly. "A friend bet me I couldn't slip into Botswana unseen and back out again."

"And your friend paid you on the bet?" she asked.

"He did, it was £20," he said.

"Perhaps you should think about giving that back to him and paying up your £20?" she suggested. "You were seen crossing the Zambezi and the Chobe and entering Botswana. So, Chief Superintendent Phiri should not be concerned about illicit cross-border traffic?"

"No, is that all this is?" Swanson laughed. "A harmless prank and a bet?"

"Well, there is the matter of the gun you brought with you into Botswana without the necessary permit," she said. "That is of concern to both of us."

"I had a gun for protection, but lost it overboard on the way back across the river," he said.

"That is a pity," she said. "It's a shame to lose anything. Did you bring the gun with you to Zambia?"

"No, a friend lent it to me, in case I needed something in the bush," he said.

"So, what was it, a .375, a 9.3, what?" she asked.

"I'm sorry a what?" he asked.

"A .375 rifle or a 9.3mm rifle, for bush protection, that's what I would have taken, anything smaller is too risky," she explained.

"Oh, a .303 rifle," he said.

"That must have been an unpleasant loss for your friend to know that his rifle is at the bottom of the Zambezi," she remarked. "How did you cross the river?"

"We borrowed this dugout canoe," he said. "We almost tipped it over a couple of times and put ourselves in the drink, but we managed. We put the canoe back where we found it."

"The owner complained," Marieke said. "Apparently he had wanted to go out and do some fishing at night and was distressed to see his *mokoro* gone."

"Sorry, his what?" Swanson asked,

"His *mokoro*, what we call the dugout canoes," she explained. "Who was with you when you crossed the river?"

"How did you know there was someone with me?" he asked.

"You said, we borrowed this canoe and we almost tipped it over," she explained. "So, who was with you?"

"Patrick McBride," Swanson said. "He had met me in Lusaka and I explained the bet, so he was game for it."

"How long did you stay in Botswana?" she asked.

"Not long," he said. "Long enough to have a beer at some bar, then go back."

"Ah, I see, that explains the tracks we found leading from the river bank to the Rhino bar and back," she said.

"Is that why I was walked around the yard out there, so you could look at tracks?" he asked.

"Tell me, did you see anyone in the bar?" she asked, ignoring his question.

"There were a few people there," he said. "Very unsavoury characters for the most part."

"Did you see this man there?" Marieke asked, pushing a photograph of Isaac Bwalya across the table. "We are very interested in him relating to illicit diamond trafficking."

"I remember when you came to Oxford, someone said something about you investigating diamond sales," he said. "You know, I did see that chap, he was there in the bar."

"Did you see if he met with anyone?" she asked.

"Really couldn't say," he apologised. "I didn't stay long, long enough for a beer, then back to the boat."

"You didn't buy any groceries from the Elephant General Store?" she asked.

"Oh, I'd forgotten about that," he said. "We needed some groceries so it seemed like a good idea to just buy them at the first reasonable-sized store we saw." Marieke could see that he was beginning to get a little rattled, he had reasonable-sounding explanations for his actions so far, but she wondered how much longer he would be able to keep inventing things. "So, tell me," she said. "How did you carry all that stuff back to the boat?"

"Oh, that wasn't too hard," he explained. "We bought some tools from the store and made a travois, you know, like the American Indians used to use, we put our stuff on it and just dragged it back."

"Very ingenious," she said. "But, if you made a travois, why did you need the store owner's help to load the stuff into the back of a Land Rover?"

"I don't understand," Swanson said.

"What don't you understand?" the commissioner asked. "You bought groceries at the Elephant General Store and loaded them into the back of a Land Rover; I'm not sure how much clearer that could be?"

"I see, I'll have to be a little more candid," Swanson said. "Our bet included borrowing a Land Rover and driving to the Chobe Park and back, it took a little longer than we anticipated."

"Why didn't you tell us this straight away?" Marieke asked.

"Well, I didn't want to admit to borrowing the Land Rover, borrowing a canoe in Zambia is not a Botswana problem, but borrowing a Land Rover in Botswana definitely is. We did take the Land Rover back," he explained.

"And did you make it to the Chobe National Park?" she asked.

"Oh, yes, marvellous place," he said. "Never seen so many elephants in my life."

"How did you pay the entry fee?" she asked.

"We didn't have enough Pula, so we had to use Pounds," he explained. "The Game Ranger at the gate was nice and took Pounds and gave me Pula in change." Marieke was quite impressed by the way he admitted to those things he would be guessing by now that they could check, so entry into the park should not be denied because the game guard would probably remember someone paying in Pounds.

"Where did you after you left the South gate of Chobe?" she asked.

"We had thought about going to Maun, but then I remembered that David and Julia were going to be camping near Khwai, so we thought we'd surprise them," he replied.

"Did you find them?" she asked.

"We did," he confirmed. "I know I should have told you before, but imagine how it would look. I was stunned when I heard that they had been killed."

"Whose idea was it to behead them?" she asked.

"Patrick's," he said, before thinking, then clammed up as he realised what he had said.

"I think you have better start again, and this time try the truth," she suggested.

"It was all Patrick's idea," he said, panicking now. "We were to go to Lusaka, drive to Kazungula, cross the river, pick up a Land Rover he had arranged, drive to Khwai, kill David and Julia, then go back. But, he decided to get creative and chopped their heads off. I threw up when he did it."

"Where did he get the axe from?" she asked.

"There was one on the Land Rover that David and Julia had," he said. "He just used that and then he threw the heads into the pond there."

"Whose idea was it to bury the bodies in the Linyanti area?" she asked.

"Patrick's," he said. "We had both been there in the past and he thought it would be a good place to bury the bodies, he thought that no one would ever find them there."

"How did he kill them?" she asked.

"Whacked them on the head with a shovel," he said.

"The shovel that you purchased at the Elephant General Store?" she asked.

"That's the one," he said.

"We'll take a short break here," Marieke said. "When we come back, we'll take a full statement. It would behove you to remember that we still have the penalty of hanging for aggravated murder. Beheading might fall into that, so your cooperation will go a long way to convincing us that you merely aided and abetted in this and that Patrick McBride was the principal agent."

Outside the room, Marieke looked to the commissioner who nodded his approval. They all knew that they did not yet have the whole story and that it was probably going to be up to a prosecutor to sort out the lies from the truth, but if they could present the prosecutors with statements that implicated each other, then they had done the best they could. Marieke went to find Constance and came back with a file. She showed the others what she had; eight pages of typed words and the last page a simple statement that this was a true and accurate statement and a signature of Patrick McBride.

"This is his signature?" the commissioner asked.

"It is," she confirmed. "He gave it to one of my officers today when he autographed one of his books."

"So, you plan to wave this in front of Swanson and let him examine the signature?" the commissioner asked, all smiles.

"Something like that," she admitted.

"If you ever get tired of Botswana, we would be happy to see you in Zambia," Simon said. "Very sneaky!"

"I knew I had to get a confession," she said. "I still don't know who pulled the trigger, but my guess is Swanson, he was a marksman at college, even winning a trophy for it, which he has on display in his office."

"So, shall we continue?" the commissioner asked.

They trooped back into the room and sat down. Swanson looked at them with resignation, he had held out as long as he could, inventing along the way, with a story that would fit the facts, he was kicking himself for getting complacent and being tripped up with the simple question. Now was the time to put the best face on it he could and try and lay it all off onto Patrick.

"So, Dr Swanson shall we try again?" Marieke asked. "When was this scheme first discussed?"

"Patrick and I were talking about the chair that David Turner had won, it must have been the 2nd or 3rd of April," he said. "He said that he wanted to get rid of Julia Turner, because of her relationship with his wife, and if I would help him, he'd get rid of David at the same time."

"Go on," Marieke encouraged.

"Well, we set things up so that Patrick would travel to Zambia on the 29th of May, arriving on the 30th and renting a car. He also arranged for a gun to be purchased and left in a post office box to be collected when he got to Zambia. I flew in the next day and we met up and drove to Kazungula and parked the car. We borrowed the canoe and crossed the river, beached the canoe in some long grass, then walked to the Rhino bar where a hired Land Rover was waiting for us. We drove towards Kasane, picked up groceries at the Elephant General Store, then drove on through the Chobe Park to Khwai. We waited there until we saw David and Julia, then he killed them, chopped off their heads, threw the heads into the pond, then we loaded the bodies into the Land Rover we had hired and drove north to the place where we buried the bodies. He stripped their Land Rover of the number plates and maker's plate and set it off on its own into the bush. We drove back to Khwai, then Kazungula, took the canoe back across the river and went home," he said.

"Let me get the dates correct," Marieke said. "You crossed the Zambezi on the 1st of June?"

"Correct," he said.

"You drove through Chobe and arrived at Khwai when?" she asked.

"That would have been the 2nd of June," he said.

"When did David and Julia arrive?" she asked.

"Right according to their published itinerary, on the 5th of June, those couple of days waiting seemed forever, we watched the road from a tree, but nothing came until they were supposed to come. We let them set up camp then Patrick killed them," he explained. "We drove north that day and buried them, then on the 6th of June we drove back to

Kazungula and back across the river to Zambia. We drove back to Lusaka on the 7th, I flew out that same day and Patrick the next day."

"Tell me what did you do with the .22LR Ruger pistol that was waiting for you at the post office" she asked.

"I don't know what you mean," he said.

"I'm talking about the pistol that John Chebani purchased for you in Lusaka and left in the post office box, the key of which he posted to you and which you received on the 23rd of May," she explained.

"Oh," he said. "Well, I threw it into the Zambezi."

"Before or after the Turners had been killed?" she asked.

"Oh, before," he said.

"Then how is it that the Turners were both shot with a .22LR gun? Did McBride have one as well?" she asked.

"Patrick shot them, then I threw the gun into the Zambezi on the way back," he said.

"Would you recognise the signature of Patrick McBride?' she asked.

"Of course," he said.

"Well, I have here a document," she said. "I leave you to imagine what it says. It is dated today, about ten minutes ago. Is this the signature of Patrick McBride?"

"The bastard," he said. "I'm telling you he shot them, no matter what he says, and you can't prove otherwise because you've got no gun, so my word against his."

"Tell me," Marieke said. "If Patrick McBride arranged for the gun to be purchased, why does John Chebani say that it was you, and why did he send you some £1,700?"

"He was paying off old debts that he had from college," Swanson said.

"I see," she said. "He waited quite a while before paying his debts. Why did he post the key to the post office box to you?"

"Because he knows me, he doesn't know Patrick," Swanson said.

"But, if he doesn't know Patrick, why and how would he buy a gun for him?" she asked.

"You're getting me all confused," he said. "John agreed to help me, so fixed the Land Rover and the gun, but it was Patrick who used it."

"Even though you're the marksman?" she asked.

"I'm no marksman," he demurred.

"How did you manage to win an inter-collegiate trophy for small bore pistol then?' she asked.

"Christ Almighty, is there anything you don't know? How the hell did you find the bodies and the heads? I would have bet my life that they would never have been found," he said.

"Why don't you start again, I'll have an officer come in and take your statement, she'll type it up and then you can sign it," Marieke said. "You really have been most cooperative. This is Inspector Bangwata. He will go through the customary cautions and take down everything you say and bring it to you for signature."

Out of the room, Marieke sat down and looked at the others. "You're doing fine," the commissioner assured her. "Only one to go."

Sergeant Maphosa saw them and came with his news. They had lifted fingerprints from a glass that McBride had used, and they were a match for those found in the French car that had been used in the Schirano accident. Vincenzo smiled at that news and asked for a copy of the report and the prints. Marieke told Maphosa that it was fine and to provide them to Vincenzo.

"How do you suggest that we approach McBride?" Marieke asked the commissioner.

"I think I would just ask him straight away if he or Swanson shot the two Turners. We can tell him that Swanson has told us all and that what we would like to confirm is who actually killed them," he replied.

"If we have conflicting statements from the two involved, how does the prosecution service sort that out?" she asked.

"Fortunately for us, that is their problem," the commissioner said. "But, I think we should make our best efforts to get the story straight, even if it means going back to Swanson with a promise that the death penalty will not be sought."

They all went to the room where McBride was being held. He looked up as they came in and said, "About time, I want to know what the hell is going on."

"Good afternoon, Mr, McBride," Marieke said. "We're sorry to have kept you waiting, but we had some issues to clear up. I have here a set of documents from various government agencies, both here and in Zambia and from a series of witnesses that sets out the chronology of events from the 30th of May of this year, until the 8th of June. We can place you at the *dambo* in Khwai where David and Julia Turner were shot, then beheaded, and in Linyanti, where bodies were buried. We have an eye witness who saw you driving the Land Rover that David and Julia Turner were using, and by the way, we know that you stopped here to refill fuel tanks and here to change a wheel," she added, pointing to places on a map. "The question we have of you is, was it you or Harold Swanson who used the gun to shoot the Turners with the .22LR pistol, Harold Swanson maintains that it was you, but we are less convinced. Was it you?"

"How can you place me where you say the Turners were shot?" he asked.

"One of our San trackers found your tracks at Khwai and Linyanti and matched them to prints you gave us here," she explained. "He also found where you had borrowed the *mokoro* from the Zambian side of the river and where you had beached it in the long grass on the Botswana side of the Chobe River. We also found where one of you had vomited at the scene of the shooting, and we found and unearthed all the camping gear of the Turners and what was left of their personal items after they had been burned. We recovered the heads from the dambo and the bodies from their place of internment. Dental records were used to confirm the identities."

"You'll accept the word of a bloody Bushman?" he asked.

"Our courts will accept as definitive evidence given by our San," she explained. "Even though you are wearing different shoes today, he says you were at the scene of the shooting and at Linyanti where you buried the bodies. You were not sufficiently thorough with the rake and broom you bought at the Elephant General Store."

"That bastard Swanson," he said. "Anything to save his own bloody skin. No, it was not me that shot them, it was bloody Harold, the whole bloody scheme was Harold. How the hell did you find the bodies, for that matter how did you find the heads?"

"When you say that the scheme was Harold Swanson's, could you tell us a little more about that?" she asked.

"It was about the beginning of April, Harold was pissed that Turner had won the chair that he wanted, so he came to me for help with a scheme that he said was foolproof to get rid of Turner," he explained. "We were to go to Lusaka, rent a car, drive to Kazungula, cross the river, pick up a Land Rover that he had hired, drive to Khwai, rub out the Turners, then go back across the Zambezi, drive to Lusaka and fly home. He said that we should bury the bodies far from where they were killed, so no one would ever find them. He had a gun organised through an old college friend of his and the same chap fixed the Land Rover. It all went well; I had the bright idea of getting rid of the heads and the fingerprints, so that if the bodies were found they couldn't be identified. It seems I was wrong. Look, I know you chaps have the death penalty, but I did not kill them, I just chopped off the heads afterwards and singed off the fingerprints. Harold did the shooting, he's better at it than I am."

"Would you be prepared to give sworn statement that Harold Swanson was the person who shot the Drs Turner?" she asked.

"Absobloodylutely," he said. "That fucking little weasel trying to pin the killings on me. He got the gun, he shot them and he threw it into the Zambezi."

"Let me get an inspector here and we can take care of that now," she said. "Then, I think we'll have another talk with Mr Swanson."

"Fine, then can I go out and kill the little bastard?" he asked.

"We'd rather you didn't do that just yet," she said. "But, I can appreciate your sentiment, you trusted him and he betrayed you."

"Bloody right he betrayed me, the snivelling bloody rat," he said.

"If you will excuse us for a moment, we'll have your statement, then we'll confront your Mr Swanson," she said.

Marieke got one of the other inspectors at the station, to go in and caution Patrick McBride, then take his statement. She was confident that they would get the statement, McBride was passed thinking about solicitors and such, he was irritated with Swanson and wanted his say. Now to go back to Swanson and see what he had to say. They went back

291

to the interview room where Swanson was waiting. He looked up at them and half smiled.

"Good afternoon again, Dr Swanson," Marieke said. "We have a slight discrepancy in the accounts of what transpired when you met up with the Turners. Patrick McBride has sworn that you shot the Turners; he says that you got the gun through Chebani, you shot the Turners and you dropped the gun into the Zambezi. He admits to chopping off the heads and singing off the fingerprints, but insists that you shot them."

"He would," Swanson said. "I suppose it comes down to who do you believe, me or him. My statement says that he shot them and I'm staying with that."

"I see," she said. "Well, it will be up to our prosecution service to decide what they will do; I suppose it may come down to which one of you is more convincing to a jury. Tell me, who did he shoot first?"

"Julia Turner, he wanted to get rid of her, then when she was gone, he did David Turner," he explained.

"Tell me about the death of Paulo Schirano?" she said.

"I thought he died in a traffic accident?" Swanson asked.

"The Italian authorities have determined that the accident was staged," she said. "What was your part in that?"

"I had nothing to do with that," he protested. "I was in college when Schirano died, there must be fifty witnesses that can verify that."

"Oh, I believe you," she said. "Was the death of Schirano quid pro quo for the death of Julia Turner?"

"I've no idea what you're talking about," he said.

"Well, the Italians may take a different view," she said. "This is Dottore Bernini of the Italian Polizia; he is investigating the incident and has been following our investigation into the related deaths of the Turners."

"Well, I wasn't there, you won't find anything that links me to that," he boasted.

"Do not be so sure," she cautioned. "They already know where the car came from that was used to stage the accident, they know how it was done and by whom, so, again, was it a quid pro quo because we can find no possible motive why Patrick McBride would kill Schirano except as a quid pro quo?"

"No comment," he said, finally using some common sense.

"Very well," she said. "You will be formally charged with the murders of David and Julia Turner, you will also be charged with conspiracy to commit murder and there will be a few other administrative charges relating to the importation of a firearm into Botswana and entering Botswana illegally. Then you will be taken to our cells, pending the hearing of the case in front of a judge."

"I would like to see someone from the High Commission," he said.

"I will arrange that," she promised.

Back at the other interview room, there remained just one thing to do and that was ask McBride about the death of Schirano. McBride was surprised when Marieke brought up the subject and even more so when she told him that he had been driving the car that had forced Schirano off the road, also how they had matched his fingerprints on the steering wheel of the car to prints taken from a glass he had used at the station. She detailed his movements from Paris, by the minute, and then explained how the accident was staged. All she really wanted to know was, was it a quid pro quo for the death of Julia Turner?

"Of course it was," McBride said. "I'm not going to let that little bastard hang this all on me; I did his, if he did mine."

"So, you agreed that in exchange for his help in removing Julia Turner that you would help him eliminate David Turner and Paulo Schirano?" she asked.

"That's about the size of it," he admitted. "If, I'm going down for this, then so is he, but why are you interested in what happened in Italy, you have no jurisdiction there."

"I don't," she agreed. "But, Dottore Bernini of the Polizia does and he has been most interested in our case and he, or one of his successors will be waiting for you when you leave Botswana."

"Well, if I'm going down for that, then bloody Swanson's coming with me," McBride said. "Get your inspector back and I'll give you chapter and verse on how Harold wanted it done, when and where."

After they left the room the commissioner congratulated her on the job and asked her how she felt about it.

"Somewhat of an anticlimax," she replied. "I expected to be thrilled that I got what I wanted, but I'm just sad and disappointed that three people died and four people have ruined their lives. I suppose I half expected shouting and screaming from the suspects, or stony silence, I didn't expect them to admit to things as quickly as they did."

"Well, we've done a good job," the commissioner said. "Now it's up to the prosecution service. I've arranged a meeting with them tomorrow, is the evidence file complete and up to date?"

"With statements we got today, then it is complete," she said. "I will add the statements as soon as we finish with them. The prosecution people are going to have fun with Swanson and McBride both pointing the finger at the other, I wonder who they'll believe?"

"I think McBride's story holds together better," the commissioner said. "I believe him before I believe Swanson. In any case, we have them both on conspiracy to commit murder, so it'll be a while before they get out of prison, that is supposing a jury finds them guilty."

"If, Sir?" she asked.

"There is always the chance that the prosecution may mess up the case, no matter how watertight we may think it, add to that a good defence and anything is possible, unlikely I grant you, but possible," he said. "Have you given evidence in the High Court before?"

"No, Sir," she said.

"Go there, after hours, sit in the witness box, look around the place, familiarise yourself with the way it looks and sounds, go there when there is a trial on and sit in the public gallery, get comfortable with the place," he advised.

"Very good, Sir," she said.

"Well, Simon, I think that's it for the day, do you have want you want?" the commissioner asked.

"I do, thank you," Simon replied. "It has been interesting."

"And you Dottore, you have what you want?" the commissioner asked.

"I have the statements, I will have to wait for the suspects until such time as you are finished with them," Vincenzo said. "But we will have an active file and will be here when they are released from your prison."

Marieke went back to her office and called Courtney in London to let her know that they had charged the two with the murders of David and Julia Turner. She then called the British High Commission and told them that an arrestee was asking to see a representative. The Third Secretary promised to come the following morning and see the two who had been charged. Finally, she called Melisende and gave her the news. Then it was just a case of waiting for the typed and signed statements and she was done for the day. Even so, it was six in the evening when she left the station, to go home in the last glimmer of daylight. Her job on this case was almost done, what remained now was the trial and the giving of evidence. Well, she was prepared for that and had extensive notes, diagrams and maps. What she really needed now was a glass of wine and to sit down and let the day unwind. But, before that, she had to go to the hotel where Diana McBride was staying and tell her that her husband had been arrested and charged in connection with the murders of David and Julia Turner. Diana was in the bar with Sara and they waved to Marieke and asked her to join them.

"I'm afraid I have some unpleasant news," she told Diana. "Do you wish me to tell it to you privately?"

"No, it's fine, Sara can hear," Diana said. "You're going to tell me that Patrick has been arrested for the murder of David and Julia?"

"I have indeed arrested and charged your husband, Patrick McBride and Harold Swanson in connection with the murders of David and Julia Turner," Marieke confirmed. "Do you wish to see your husband?"

"I suppose I should, just to let him know that I'm filing for divorce," Diana said. "How could he do that?"

"The two of them made some kind of arrangement," Marieke explained. "Rather like the film, *Strangers on a Train*, only they weren't strangers."

"How long will they get?" Sara asked.

"That is up to the court and the outcome of the trial," Marieke said. "I have done what I can."

"I'd say you've done a bang-up job, sorry, Diana," Sara said.

"No, it's fine," Diana said. "We were headed for divorce anyway; this just propels things a little faster."

"Well, if you need anything while you are here, you know where to find me," Marieke said. "I am sorry that things turned out this way."

"Thank you," Diana said. "I'll be going back to England and shutting down the raptor centre, and then I'll decide what I'm going to do."

Epilogue

"So, the trial is over?" Mbali asked Marieke.

"It is, 40 years each," Marieke replied.

"They will not be hanged?" Mbali asked.

"Neither admitted to the killing, each accusing the other, in the end, the court decided that they were both guilty of conspiracy to commit murder and they both shared culpability in the actual deaths but went with a long-term prison sentence rather than inadvertently hang the wrong man," Marieke explained.

"Will they serve 40 years?" Mbali asked.

"Probably," Marieke thought. "And when they get out, the Italians are waiting with their own murder conspiracy."

"I read the newspaper reports of the trial, you had all the evidence, it must have taken ages to put it all together?" Mbali asked.

"It was a lot of work, with some really valuable help from the Zambians and the Brits," Marieke replied. "I also had really good people here who trailed around with me and found things."

"Is it true that you went off into a dambo, with crocs, to find the heads?" Mbali asked.

"Not the smartest thing I ever did, but yes I did go wading with the crocs, I had a shotgun with me and Constance covered me with a rifle, I got into some small trouble with the commissioner for that," Marieke explained.

"Now what?" Mbali asked.

"I have the personal items of the Turners that I need to send to Sara Turner, and then the case is closed," Marieke said.

"You said your friend from France is coming to visit?" Mbali said. "Are you taking her somewhere nice?"

"We have an invitation to the Pitse Safari Camp, it will be nice to go there and just enjoy the bush," Marieke laughed. "But, before we go I will make sure you meet Melisende."

"I would hope so," Mbali said. "Cheers!"

"Cheers!" Marieke responded. "This is good, what is it?"

"You tell me," Mbali said. "You're the wine expert."

"South African, Pinotage, let me guess the new winery, Beyerskloof?" Marieke asked.

"Full marks," Mbali said. "Jannie brought some back with him when he went to the Cape recently. I have a couple of cases; we should let your friend Melisende taste some and give us her opinion."

"We'll do that," Marieke promised.

"What does your British lady think of the verdict?" Mbali asked.

"I talked to Courtney today and she said that they were satisfied with the verdict and the sentence, particularly because there was no imposition of the death penalty," Marieke said. "She told me that the Home Secretary was pleased that we had been able to bring the case to trial and to get such a good result. I think if we had gone with the death penalty then there would have been protests from their government, for form's sake if nothing else."

"And Sara Turner, what does she think?" Mbali asked.

"Sara says that she would have liked to have seen McBride hang, but I think that is more talk than reality, she seemed delighted with the forty years, commenting that they would both be old men when they got out of prison," Marieke replied. "Personally, I would not fancy forty years in one of our prisons, it won't be easy for them; they could well die before they have served their full sentences."

"So, all in all, lives destroyed all over the place," Mbali said. "And all for ambition, such a waste."

"Such a waste," Marieke agreed.

Glossary

Abbreviations

BA	British Airways
BDF	Botswana Defence Force
FCO	Foreign & Commonwealth Office
LSE	London School of Economics
PH	Professional Hunter
SAA	South African Airways
VLF	Very Low Frequency

Words

Ag	Afrikaans	alas, oh, ah
Allora	Italian	so, and now
Baie	Afrikaans	very
Bakkie	Afrikaans	truck, container
Bien	French	well
Boerevors	Afrikaans	Boer sausage
Boerjies	South African slang	diminutive form of Boer
Bonjour	French	good day
Braai	South African slang	barbecue
Bueno	Italian	good
Bundu	Shona	bush
Chérie	French	dear
Dambo	ChiChewa	semi-arid waterhole
Dankie	Afrikaans	thank you
Déshabillé	French	undressed
Dood	Afrikaans	dead
Doos	Afrikaans	unpleasant person
Dorp(ie)	Afrikaans	small town (smaller town)
Gemors	Afrikaans	mess
Goed	Afrikaans	good
Goffel	South African slang	person of mixed race
Howzit	South African slang	how is it?
Ja	Afrikaans	yes
Kaffir	South African slang	black person
Kom	Afrikaans	come
Lekker	Afrikaans	sweet, nice, pretty
Lightie	South African slang	child, teenager

Lobola	Zulu	marriage price
Magtig	Afrikaans	gracious, heavens
Mdala	Zulu	old man
Meisie	Afrikaans	girl, young woman
Middag	Afrikaans	afternoon
Mokoro	Setswana	dug out canoe
Moor	Afrikaans	kill
Môre	Afrikaans	morning
Muzungu	Swahili	white man
Naand	Afrikaans	evening
Oomie(s)	Afrikaans	uncle, man, ancestor
Ou, ouk(s)	Slang	man(men)
Ou frou	Afrikaans	old lady
Ou maat	Afrikaans	old friend, old mate
Ouma	Afrikaans	grandmother
Pronto	Italian	phone greeting
Regte	Afrikaans	real
Rooinek	South African slang	British
Sacrebleu	French	expression of surprise
Skelm	Afrikaans	villain
Skop	Afrikaans	head
Spoor	Afrikaans	track
Stoop	Afrikaans	deck, porch
Tannie(s)	Afrikaans	Aunt, woman
Toujours	French	Always
Verdomde	Afrikaans	damned
Voetsek	South African slang	go away, fuck off
Wazungu	Swahili	white men
Zim	English slang	Zimbabwe

Phrases

À bientot	French	later
Aangename kennis	Afrikaans	how do you do
Au revoir	French	good bye
Bly te kenne	Afrikaans	pleased to meet you
Bwana ena kona lo munya bantu - Chikabanga		Boss, there are other people
Bwana lo munya banto yena kona lapa futi - Chikabanga		Boss those other people are still there
Ça va	French	how is it going
Dumela Mma	Setswana	good morning Madame
Dumela Rra	Setswana	good morning Sir
Geniet die dag	Afrikaans	have a nice day
Hoe gaan dit	Afrikaans	how goes it
Maak n'plan	Afrikaans	make a plan
Mag ek asseblief met praat?	Afrikaans	can I speak to......?
Mais, trés lentement, oui	French	yes but very slowly
Met jou	Afrikaans	with you
Moenie the twee languages op mix nie - don't mix the two languages		
Sala sentlê	Setswana	stay well
Tot siens	Afrikaans	good bye
Tsamaya sentlê	Setswana	go well